Praise for Lisa Wingate's Accent novels, the "Tending Roses Series," which include *Tending Roses*, *Good Hope Road*, *The Language of Sycamores*, and *Drenched in Light*

Drenched in Light

"Heartfelt and moving, enriched by characters drawn with compassion and warmth."　　—Jennifer Chiaverini, Author of *Circle of Quilters*

"Another winner."　　　　　　　　　　　　　　　　　—*Booklist*

"A deep character study."　　　　　　　　　—The Best Reviews

"A poignant tale of self-discovery."
　　　　　　　　　　—Kendra Young, *Lake Travis View* (TX)

The Language of Sycamores

"Heartfelt, honest, and entirely entertaining . . . this poignant story will touch your heart from the first page to the last."　　—Kristin Hannah

"Wingate's smoothly flowing prose fills the pages with emotional drama."
　　　　　　　　　　　　　　　—*Romantic Times* (Top Pick)

continued . . .

Written by today's freshest new talents and selected by New American Library, NAL Accent novels touch on subjects close to a woman's heart, from friendship to family to finding our place in the world. The Conversation Guides included in each book are intended to enrich the individual reading experience, as well as encourage us to explore these topics together—because books, and life, are meant for sharing.

Visit us online at www.penguin.com.

Good Hope Road

"A novel bursting with joy amidst crisis: small-town life is painted with scope and detail in the capable hands of a writer who understands longing, grief, and the landscape of a woman's heart."
—Adrian Trigiani, author of the *Big Stone Gap* trilogy

"Wingate has written a genuinely heartwarming story about how a sense of possibility can be awakened in the aftermath of a tragedy to bring a community together and demonstrate the true American spirit."
—*Booklist*

Tending Roses

"A story at once gentle and powerful about the very old and the very young, and about the young woman who loves them all. Richly emotional and spiritual, *Tending Roses* affected me from the first page."
—Luanne Rice, author of *Sandcastles*

"You can't put it down without . . . taking a good look at your own life and how misplaced priorities might have led to missed opportunities. *Tending Roses* is an excellent read for any season, a celebration of the power of love."
—*El Paso Times*

Praise for Lisa Wingate's "Texas Hill Country" Series

Over the Moon at the Big Lizard Diner

"A beautifully crafted and insightfully drawn page-turner . . . this is storytelling at its best."
—Julie Cannon, author of the Homegrown series and *Those Pearly Gates*

"A warmhearted tale of love and longing, grits and cowboys, horse psychology and dinosaur tracks."
—Claire Cook, author of *Multiple Choice* and *Must Love Dogs*

"A feisty, flirtatious, homegrown Texas tale."
—Dixie Cash, author of *My Heart May Be Broken,*
But My Hair Still Looks Great

"Wingate lets her magical Texas setting and idiosyncratic supporting characters shine." —*Kirkus Reviews*

Lone Star Café

"A charmingly nostalgic treat. . . . Wingate handles the book's strong spiritual element deftly, creating a novel that is sweetly inspirational but not saccharine." —*Publishers Weekly*

"A beautifully written, heartwarming tale about finding love where you least expect it." —Barbara Freethy

"Leaves you feeling like you've danced the two-step across Texas."
—Jodi Thomas

Texas Cooking

"Lisa Wingate writes with depth and warmth, joy and wit."
—Debbie Macomber, author of *Susannah's Garden*

"*Texas Cooking* . . . will have readers drooling for the next installment . . . [a] beautifully written mix of comedy, drama, cooking, and journalism."
—Joy Dickinson, *The Dallas Morning News*

"Takes the reader on a delightful journey into the most secret places of every woman's heart." —Catherine Anderson

"The story is a treasure. You will be swept along, refreshed and amused. . . . Give yourself a treat and read this tender, unusual story."
—Dorothy Garlock

A
THOUSAND
 VOICES

LISA WINGATE

NAL
ACCENT

NAL Accent
Published by New American Library, a division of
Penguin Group (USA) Inc., 375 Hudson Street,
New York, New York 10014, USA
Penguin Group (Canada), 90 Eglinton Avenue East, Suite 700, Toronto,
Ontario M4P 2Y3, Canada (a division of Pearson Penguin Canada Inc.)
Penguin Books Ltd., 80 Strand, London WC2R 0RL, England
Penguin Ireland, 25 St. Stephen's Green, Dublin 2,
Ireland (a division of Penguin Books Ltd.)
Penguin Group (Australia), 250 Camberwell Road, Camberwell, Victoria 3124,
Australia (a division of Pearson Australia Group Pty. Ltd.)
Penguin Books India Pvt. Ltd., 11 Community Centre, Panchsheel Park,
New Delhi - 110 017, India
Penguin Group (NZ), 67 Apollo Drive, Rosedale, North Shore 0745,
Auckland, New Zealand (a division of Pearson New Zealand Ltd.)
Penguin Books (South Africa) (Pty.) Ltd., 24 Sturdee Avenue,
Rosebank, Johannesburg 2196, South Africa

Penguin Books Ltd., Registered Offices:
80 Strand, London WC2R 0RL, England

First published by NAL Accent, an imprint of New American Library,
a division of Penguin Group (USA) Inc.

First Printing, July 2007
10 9 8 7 6 5 4 3 2 1

REGISTERED TRADEMARK—MARCA REGISTRADA

LIBRARY OF CONGRESS CATALOGING-IN-PUBLICATION DATA:

Wingate, Lisa.
    A thousand voices/Lisa Wingate.
        p. cm.
    ISBN: 978-0-451-22129-2
    1. Adopted children—Fiction. 2. Musicians—Fiction. 3. Choctaw Indians—Fiction. 4. Parents—
Fiction. 5. Self-perception—Fiction. 6. Oklahoma—Fiction. I. Title.
PS3573.I53165T54 2007
813'.6—dc22   2006038598

Set in Adobe Garamond
Designed by Spring Hoteling

Printed in the United States of America

To those who walked,
And those who remember,
To those who carry the soil and the stories,
And those whose voices sing
Among a thousand leaves.

ACKNOWLEDGMENTS

In considering the list of friends and kind strangers who contributed time, encouragement, and expertise during the writing of *A Thousand Voices*, it seemed fitting to invoke a quote from John Donne's famous meditation: "No man is an island, entire of itself; every man is a piece of the continent, a part of the main. . . ." The same holds true for books, I think. No idea travels from the mind of author to the printed page without having been ferried by at least a dozen passing ships. While journeying through this final story in the *Tending Roses* series, I've sailed along with some fantastic and generous people, for whom I am truly grateful.

My heartfelt thanks goes out to members of the Choctaw Nation, specifically personnel of the Capitol Museum and festival organizers, including Willard Polk, who answered questions about the festival and provided valuable information about Choctaw beliefs and traditions. Thank you, also, to staff members and participants at the Choctaw Labor Day Festival and powwow—as gracious, fun-loving, and hospitable a group of people as exists anywhere.

I am especially thankful, as always, to members of my family, including my mother, Sharon, and my mother-in-law, Janice, for proofreading, traveling to book events, and shuttling kids to various activities. My thanks, also, to Mandy Carter for fantastic editing and research help. Thank you to Buck and Cara McAdams (aka Uncle

Buck and Aunt Sut) for helping with research in the Antlers area, and for always having cookies on the counter and a light in the window. Thanks, Aunt Sut, for sitting up with me until all hours, digging through land abstracts and bits of Choctaw history. Thank you to my boys for cooking boxed macaroni and cheese for supper when necessary, and always being willing to trek off on research trips at a moment's notice.

My gratitude goes to the wonderful people at Penguin Group (USA) and NAL, who turn stories into books. To Leslie Gelbman, Kara Welsh, Claire Zion, and to my editor, Ellen Edwards, thank you for being the strong, talented women you are and for believing in me over the years. Thank you also to my wonderful agent, Claudia Cross of Sterling Lord Literistic, and to the many booksellers and media personnel who have given so much support to my books.

Last, my heartfelt thanks to readers, far and near, who have sent letters and e-mails, encouraged me when I needed it, inspired stories to beget more stories, recommended the books to others, and made the dreams of a would-be writer come true.

"... *they are a people that will walk to the last, or I do not know how we could get on.*"

—Major Francis W. Armstrong,
Choctaw Removal Agent, 1832

A
THOUSAND
VOICES

CHAPTER 1

❧

The old Choctaws say that a man who walks away from his past will wander lost forever. If he takes root in a soil that is not his own, the tree of his life will struggle for breath, and water, and nourishment. In dry seasons, the leaves die easily because his roots are shallow. We are meant to be grown in ground that is rich with the bones, and the blood, and the voices of our ancestors. In 1831, the first of the Choctaw were forced from their lands in Mississippi and moved to reservations in Oklahoma. They took with them their language, their customs, their stories of the old times—and they took soil. The women ground the bones of the ancestors and sewed the dust and soil into the hems of their clothing. As they left their homes, they touched the leaves, and the grasses, and the waters of the streams, saying good-bye to the old places. They marched in the bitter cold of an early winter, carrying the young, the old, and the sick, yet they did not pour out the soil and the bones along the trail. In open fields, with only blankets for protection from the snow and the wind, they huddled together. Death, it is said, was hourly among them, claiming nearly one-third of their number, yet those who remained carried the stories and the soil. They spread it in a new place and watered it with their tears, and the tree began to grow again.

The Choctaw are a wise people. They know that ancestor bones nourish all who come after, and so they keep the past alive.

If not for that fact, I might have wandered forever. The summer I found the Choctaw was the summer I found myself. Until that time, I'd never even wondered about my real father and his Choctaw heritage. He was a faceless shadow in my mind, the reason my skin was dark and my eyes were brown, not blue like Mama's. He was the reason folks in town looked at me like I was dirt, and the reason Uncle Bobby called me *little nigger girl* when he started coming around Granny's house after Mama died. Uncle Bobby said I was just darned lucky Granny kept me on at her house, because who else would want a little brown-skinned, knobby-legged butthead like me hanging around?

Old Mrs. Vongortler, the lady who owned the farm across the river from Granny's house, said I shouldn't listen to talk like that. She said every bird in the air came from a thought of God, and so did I. I'd never imagined God thinking about me. It's a powerful thing to realize you were put in this world on purpose. It changes the way you feel about everything afterward. It changed the way I felt about Mrs. Vongortler. After that, she became Grandma Rose to me. She loved me in a way my real granny didn't, in a way nobody else ever had. Grandma Rose and I understood each other. When she died, I wanted to lie down on that bed and die right along with her.

Even after she was gone, Grandma Rose took care of me. Her granddaughter and grandson-in-law, Karen and James Sommerfield, adopted me at twelve years old and gave me the family I'd always wanted. I left the little paper-thin house on the river and moved into a life that was both foreign and frightening, and filled with possibilities. I buried the past in the grave with my real granny, and tried to forget it ever happened.

The old Choctaws would say I had poured out the soil and the bones, and that everything that came afterward—a life in Kansas City with James and Karen, an education at an arts high school where I could pursue my love of music, concert opportunities, and chances to travel—would be shallow-rooted. The past, even if you don't talk about it, still exists, and no matter how hard you try to turn your back, no matter how dangerous it is to look at, part of you cries out to understand it. You move through life like a person balancing on a log fallen over a river, waiting for the moment the wood will crack and you'll sink into all the dark things you can still see below.

I could never tell James and Karen, my new parents who loved me, that somewhere inside there was the scared, silent little girl from the tiny house in the tall grass above Mulberry Creek. That girl was filled with questions, and even years later, she was still wandering the world, in search of answers.

When I graduated from high school, I traveled as far away from her as I could—to Europe for a year in a student musical exchange orchestra, and then to Ukraine for a term of teaching English and music in a mission project for orphaned children. My commission there was over too soon, and it was time to go home. College was waiting, and life was waiting, and my family was waiting.

Barry was waiting, too, even though he wasn't supposed to be. Barry and I had dated since my first year at Harrington Academy, when he befriended me, tutored me, and rescued me from teenage oblivion. When I left for Europe, we'd decided it was time for both of us to move on. Still, Barry kept the cards and e-mails coming, telling me about the music department at Missouri State. He talked about college life and dorm rooms, fraternity houses and apartments, things that seemed a million miles away to me. When I came home, he dropped everything and met me at the airport.

"Hey, D," he said, just like no time had passed. At some point in our history together, Barry had shortened my name to D. He gave nicknames to everyone and everything he cared about. Even his saxophone, Puff.

I turned from the luggage carousel, surprised by the sound of his voice. It was deeper than I remembered, different from on the phone. "Hey, Bear-bear." I paused to study him. He looked older, his chin more square and his baby-faced cheeks slightly hollowed out. He'd let his brown hair grow longer and put brassy highlights in it. "You look different," I said, and he grinned, seeming pleased.

"Got highlights." Grabbing a strand of hair, he held it out for inspection. "Like it?" His eyebrows rose hopefully, and I couldn't help smiling. Same old Barry. He could never be cool about anything.

"I do." I motioned to the hair. "I really do."

Stepping back, he inspected me slowly. "Gosh, Dell, you look great." He blinked like he couldn't quite take in the picture. "I mean, really great. You do." He leaned slightly closer, as if he thought he might kiss me.

"Thanks." It was hard to know how to respond, and I shifted away uncomfortably. The compliment was sincere. Everything about Barry was sincere, which was what had always made our relationship so hard. He sincerely loved me, and I sincerely needed him as a friend, and that isn't the same thing.

Stretching out his arms, he grabbed me in an impulsive bear hug, and as usual, I went stiff. I'd never been good at hugs and things like that—Barry knew that about me, and he didn't mind. He understood that those feelings came from long before I met him. When Mama was messed up, she used to hug me until I felt like I'd smother. All I could smell was weed and sweat and the faint scent of VO5 shampoo as we staggered back and forth in a painful embrace.

Barry let go and reached for something on the luggage carousel. "That yours?" he asked, grabbing the battered wheelie bag that had been through two continents and over a dozen countries.

"Yeah," I answered, bewildered as he hauled it off the luggage carousel with a grunt, then snagged my bedraggled garment bag. "How'd you know?"

"I bought it for you." His mouth hung open in disbelief. "Remember?"

The memory came rushing back, and I laughed. "How could I forget that?" How, indeed? While all the other high school couples

were exchanging promise rings, senior charms, and framed graduation photos with endearments like *Yours 4 Ever* and *True Love Always,*
Barry bought me luggage.

"You didn't speak to me for a week, remember?" He gestured
with his hand, churning up the past.

I hooked my fingers in the belt loops of the Levi's that I could
have sold for a small fortune in Ukraine. "That's not true." There had
never, ever been a time when Barry and I didn't speak for a week.

"All right, maybe it was a day. But it seemed like a week," he
joked, and we laughed together. A woman with a luggage cart bumped
into him from behind, and he stumbled forward, then glanced over
his shoulder and apologized for being in the way. The woman didn't
answer, and Barry shrugged good-naturedly, then started scooping up
my suitcases. "Guess we should get out of here. You hungry? Want to
get something to eat?"

"No, thanks. They gave us a snack on the plane." Leaving the
baggage area, we exited the building near a small flower bed, where
a stunted dogwood tree was wilting in the August heat. Not far
away, a row of redbuds looked dry, and tired, and ready for winter
to come. A maintenance man was mowing grass beside the curb,
lacing the air with a scent so strong it eclipsed the odor of damp
pavement and exhaust fumes. A rush of memories swirled over me,
and for a moment my mind was caught in the illusion that I'd never
left. Standing there on the sidewalk, surrounded by the sights and
scents of Kansas City, I could have been any age from twelve to
eighteen, at the airport to pick up James, who'd just piloted a 747
full of happy travelers home from some faraway locale. If it was
summer or a school holiday, Karen and I might have ridden along
on family passes to enjoy a short vacation or a music festival during
his layover. . . .

I was suddenly aware that I'd stopped on the sidewalk and people
were squeezing by. Beside me, Barry patiently balanced my luggage

and waited. I was filled with a rush of affection for him that wasn't romantic love, but something deeper.

"What?" Quirking a brow, he hiked my garment bag higher onto his shoulder.

"Nothing." Embarrassed, I reached for one of the suitcases. "It's just good to see you. Here, let me carry something."

He shifted the luggage handles possessively and started walking. "I've got it. You sure you don't want to stop off for something to eat?"

"Only if you're hungry," I said, as we headed toward the parking lot.

"No. I mean, not unless you are."

"I'm fine, but if you want to stop, that's good, too."

"It's up to you, really." He shrugged, hefting the heavy garment bag higher onto his shoulder again. "You're the world traveler."

"Tell you what." As usual, between the two of us, Barry and I couldn't come up with a decision. "Surprise me. Let's just head toward Hindsville, and if you see someplace you feel like stopping, then stop. If not, we'll be at Aunt Kate's farm in time for supper." What I really wanted to do was get to the farm. I hadn't seen anyone in my family since James and Karen had flown to London to watch our final concert almost a year ago. Suddenly that seemed like an eternity. I tried to imagine what it would be like, walking into the family gathering at Aunt Kate's place this weekend, surprising them because they thought I wouldn't be home for two months yet.

Barry started up a conversation about college life as we loaded my things and headed south in his new Mustang, a reward for keeping a straight-A average at Missouri State. Sitting behind the wheel of the glossy new convertible, Barry looked almost cool, which was a feat, considering that our senior year he'd cruised in his mom's old hatchback wagon.

Outside the window, the scenery turned from urban to rural, the highway slowly leaving the flatlands and winding upward into the foothills of the Ozarks. It began to look more like Hindsville, more like home. Somewhere during Barry's dissertation about dormitory life, his new fraternity house, and algebra class, the road disappeared altogether. . . .

"Hey, Sleeping Beauty." Barry's voice wound into the blackness, pulling me back into the Mustang from someplace far away. "Hey, Sleeping Beauty, wake up. We're here."

Opening my eyes, I blinked against the bright afternoon sunlight as the car turned into the farm's gravel driveway. One side of my hand was numb against the glass, and the other side was imprinted into my face, complete with the St. Christopher's ring one of the girls at the orphanage had given me when I left.

"I'm sorry," I muttered, pulling myself upright. "I didn't mean to fall asleep on you. That was rude. You should have poked me or something."

"I was enjoying watching you snore."

"Gross," I muttered, reaching into my purse for a hairbrush. My heart fluttered into my throat as we wound slowly past the farm fields, then uphill through the shade of Grandma Rose's old silver maple trees. On the bluff above the river, the big white house loomed imposingly, its dormer windows watching our approach. My entire family would be gathered there, all of them having come to see my cousin, Jenilee's, new baby. The first baby to come into the family since Aunt Kate's youngest, Hanna, who was five now. The birth of Jenilee and Caleb's baby was cause for celebration. They'd waited until Jenilee finished medical school to start a family. Now the baby was a week old, and Jenilee and Caleb still hadn't picked out a name. Aunt Kate figured it was time for a family meeting. Karen and James had filled me in on all the drama by e-mail. Of course, they had no idea that I'd actually be there for the family name-brainstorming session. For just an instant, I had the thought that I should have waited in Kansas City for James and Karen, instead of coming to the farm. My unexpected return would steal the spotlight from Jenilee's new arrival. James and Karen might be upset that, after being away so long, I'd asked Barry to meet me at the airport instead of asking them.

My hands shook as I dragged the brush through my hair.

"You look fine." Barry frowned sideways at me.

I rolled my eyes. I could imagine what I looked like after four transfers and two days of planes, trains, and automobiles. "Maybe I should have called them instead of surprising everyone. They—"

"Why do you do that?" Barry cut me off.

"What?"

"Second-guess yourself." Pulling into a parking space behind the garage building, he braced an elbow on the console and leaned across toward me. "You look great. You're beautiful. They're going to be thrilled to see you." Dropping the keys in the console, he exited the car. I opened my door, swiveled around and watched my feet touch home soil, then stood and stretched, taking in the warm late-summer air. It smelled of leaves and freshly cut grass, the farm fields down below and late-blooming roses in the garden. Familiar things, the same as always. The scents snuggled around me like a blanket as I closed the car door and started toward the house.

The yard gate squealed a high-pitched protest as Barry pushed it open. "C'mon, slowpoke." As usual, Barry was in a hurry to get to the kitchen.

I paused to take one more look at the blackberry patch behind the old hired hand's house out back. Hidden in the tall tangle of brambles was a path I could have walked with my eyes closed. Even now, I knew every inch of the trail that led across the river to the little house I'd lived in with Mama and my real granny. The house was gone now, having caved in under the weather and then been bulldozed, but the trail remained.

"Who's . . . ?" Aunt Kate's voice came from the screen porch, somewhere near the kitchen door. "Barry? Barry, what are . . . ?" There was an audible intake of breath as I rounded the garage building and hurried down the path to the gate. "Dell? Dell?" Yanking open the kitchen door, she hollered into the house, "Dell's here! Karen, Dell's here!" A moment later, Aunt Kate was on the walkway, stretching out her arms, hugging me, then examining me at arm's length. "How in the *world* did you get here?"

"On a plane."

She shook a finger in a way that reminded me of Grandma Rose. Grandma Rose hated surprises, because it meant that somebody had managed to outmanipulate her. "Oh, you!" She pointed at Barry. "And *you*. How much did you have to do with this, huh? How long have you known Dell was coming home?"

"Ummm . . . not *too* long," Barry muttered.

Aunt Kate's gaze shifted back and forth between the two of us. "You two are *so* in trouble. I'm going to . . ."

The threat went unfinished as the rest of the relatives hit the door, and we became a wiggling, squirming, squealing mass of family. Barry retreated to keep from being trampled in the commotion. By the time it was finally over, we'd made such a racket that we'd awakened Jenilee's baby, who was sleeping in the bassinet in the living room. I walked inside with James holding one hand and Karen holding the other, and Barry trailing behind. Both Jenilee and Caleb, followed by Kate's three children, went to the living room to rescue the newest member of our crazy family.

We were standing in the kitchen, talking about how I'd managed to come home early, and why, when Jenilee returned with her baby girl, newly fed and freshly diapered. Hanna, Kate's five-year-old, held the used, rolled-up diaper like it was a time bomb. Her older sister, Rose, fawned over the baby, trying to fasten a loose snap on the fluffy pink terry sleeper. Joshua, Kate's oldest, had disappeared sometime during the baby retrieval mission.

"It's a good thing this is a girl," Jenilee commented, her soft blond hair falling over her shoulder as she shifted the baby so we could get a better view. "Because your daughters have just carefully observed the *entire* diapering process, if you know what I mean. I'm going to let you explain about the umbilical cord, Mom."

"She gots a stem," Hanna reported. "It's icky, but I like her."

Everyone laughed, and the door inched open behind Jenilee. "Of course she does." Aunt Jeane slipped through the opening, peeking in first to make sure the swinging door wasn't going to take anybody out. "All babies come with stems—that's from growing in the pumpkin patch."

"Aunt Jeane!" Kate squealed. "Don't tell them that."

I giggled, and Aunt Jeane noticed me standing there. "Well, what in the world did I miss while I was upstairs having my nap? All of a sudden, Dell's here."

"She came home early," Karen reported. "Sneaked in on us."

"I wanted to see the baby," I said, trying to put the focus back on Jenilee and her new arrival. "Can I hold her?"

Jenilee crossed the room and slipped the bundle into my arms. With Kate's girls arranging the blanket, buttoning the sleeper, and petting the baby, I looked into the wide blue eyes of my new cousin for the first time. "She's beautiful," I whispered, and the baby gurgled and smiled. "Look, she's smiling."

"One-week-old babies don't smile," Caleb corrected, standing over my shoulder and gazing down at his daughter. "Except maybe this one. She's exceptional."

I barely heard the last part of the comment. My mind was racing backward instead, rocketing through the years, until I was seven years old, holding my baby brother, Angelo, in my arms. He had soft blond curls and blue eyes like this baby.

He's smiling at me, I said.

He ain't smiling at you. Little babies can't smile, because they don't know anything, Mama snapped. She was having a hard time, back living with Granny and me, trying to take care of the baby and keep herself off meth so she and Angelo's daddy could get married. He told her if she got herself clean, he'd rent a house for all of us. Granny said it was about as likely for pigs to fly. She said Mama'd be there about long enough to dump another baby on her, and then light out.

I knew that Mama really wanted to try this time. I could see it in her face. She loved Angelo's daddy. He took her out of some dumpy hotel and helped her stay clean. She'd been working at his Handi Stop store off and on, and living in the back room—until she got pregnant, and the back room of a gas station wasn't any place to keep a baby. . . .

"She has Aunt Sadie's eyes," I heard Aunt Jeane say, and my mind snapped back to the present in a way that left me feeling like I was in someone else's body. I didn't answer, just sat staring down at the baby, trying to get my bearings.

"Well, she's got hair like Nate's and Joshua's—look at those blond baby curls," Aunt Kate chimed in.

"Who knows?" Karen added. "I mean, baby Rose was a blonde, and then her hair turned reddish when she was about a year old."

Rose paused in her fawning over the baby. "It did?" She breathed in with eight-year-old amazement. "Really?"

"Yes, ma'am," her father answered. "You used to have hair like this baby, little miss. But you didn't have that tiny little nose. That's a Gray family nose, for sure. Your nose was grea-a-at big."

"Da-ad," Rose complained, and Ben laughed, tussling her hair.

The conversation went on, moving from the baby's face to her toes, and whose feet she might possibly have. Somewhere in the middle, as the baby lay in my arms, her wide eyes moving slowly from one admirer to the next, I looked up.

Everyone was so focused on the baby, no one noticed as I gazed around the circle of faces. Something painful stabbed deep inside me, solidified into a conscious thought where there had been only a vague awareness before.

There wasn't a single face in that circle that looked like mine.

And there never would be.

CHAPTER 2

Karen shooed me out the door so she, Aunt Kate, and Aunt Jeane could make supper. We stood for a long moment in the doorway. "You've grown up," she said, her eyes moist. "You don't look like a teenager anymore. Who's this beautiful young woman on my sister's porch?"

I laughed under my breath, wondering if I'd really changed that much. I didn't feel any different. Inside, I was still a combination of Karen and James's adopted daughter and the little girl from the house on Mulberry Creek. "Same old Dell." I squeezed her hand. My experiences in Ukraine had made me more grateful for her and James, more aware of how lucky I was. Compared to the struggles of the kids in the orphans' home, a drug-addicted mother, an unsupervised childhood, and an adoption into a perfectly wonderful family at twelve was an incredibly good life. "It's great to be home."

That pleased her, I could tell. She never said it, but I knew she'd always wondered whether I loved her the way a daughter should love a mother—as much as she loved me. That feeling was inside me, but I never knew how to show it. Those early years of keeping my distance from people had created barriers that seemed as much a part of me as the way I walked, or talked, or held a pencil—habits formed long before I was conscious of them. Everything that came afterward stayed outside. Karen never complained, but I knew she sensed a part of me that even our family's love couldn't penetrate.

Karen, more than anyone, had been nervous about my wandering these last two years. She'd wanted me to accept one of the music scholarships I'd been offered and go straight to college, maybe even Juilliard. Someplace she could visit during long weekends. She was afraid if I left for Europe, I'd never come back. She was worried that I'd find one excuse after another to hitchhike around the world, never stepping back into real life to figure out who I was supposed to be as an adult.

Now here I was on Aunt Kate's porch with all the old questions still unanswered, and the barricades still in place.

Karen touched the side of my face, combed a few stray strands of dark hair behind my ear. "Is something wrong? You seem a little . . . I don't know . . . down." She'd always had a sense about me, that motherly sixth sense that told her when something was wrong.

"Just a little tired, I think." I couldn't tell her that coming home and seeing Jenilee's baby hadn't felt like I'd thought it would. "Jet lag probably."

She rubbed a hand up and down my arm. "Well, why don't you relax a while—maybe sit on the porch and close your eyes for a few minutes? Barry and the guys are in there looking at pictures of James's latest tractor restoration project. That could take a while."

I hesitated a moment, and Karen gave me a nudge. "Go on. It's okay. You know how it is when your dad gets started talking about his tractor obsession. He'll keep Barry prisoner for an hour, at least."

I chuckled, struck as always by the sense that I liked it when she called James *your dad*. They'd never really pushed the issue of whether I should call them James and Karen or Dad and Mom. Instead, we'd settled for a strange mishmash of whatever seemed right at the moment. "Poor Barry. Maybe he can work the conversation around to his new Mustang. He's really proud of that car."

Karen glanced toward the driveway. "I'll bet. It's a pretty sweet ride." We both chuckled at her imitation of James's car-lover lingo. "But, all the same, Barry's in trouble for picking you up at the airport and sneaking you here without telling us. He just helped me with a

Jumpkids after-school camp a week ago, and he never said a thing. How long has he known you were coming?"

"A couple days. I wasn't going to tell anyone. I thought I'd just catch a cab from the airport and surprise you and James at the house, but then I got the e-mail about all of you getting together at the farm this weekend for the big baby-naming extravaganza. I didn't know if my car was still at the house in Kansas City or not, so I called Barry to pick me up." That wasn't the whole truth. At the last minute, I'd panicked about coming home, and I needed a familiar face. I knew Barry would come for me without saying a word to anyone. He would stay by my side and hold my hand and be the friend he'd always been.

"I guess I'll forgive him, just this once," Karen acquiesced. "Since he did bring you home." Squeezing my arm, she turned back toward the door. "See you in a bit."

When she was gone, I stood for a while on the screen porch, then walked out the door and crossed the yard to the old hired hand's house out back, where Grandma Rose had lived after Kate and Ben moved into the main farmhouse. Sitting in one of the old porch rockers, I laid my head back and curled my feet into the seat with me, picturing Grandma Rose in the other chair, rocking back and forth, her gardening galoshes tapping lightly on the worn wood floor.

Smiling, she lifted her hand and reached out, her fingers weathered from hours of working in the soil. "Be patient," she whispered. "All the answers don't have to come today. There's time."

I thought of Jenilee's baby, the family gathering, the circle of faces, familiar yet foreign. Where was the circle of faces that looked like mine? Did they exist somewhere, or was I the last surviving member of my family? In the mist beyond Grandma Rose's hand, I could almost see them—ancient faces with strong cheekbones and smooth, cinnamon-colored skin. Dark eyes, and broad smiles. . . .

The dog barked somewhere in the yard, and I jerked awake. Barry was coming around the corner of the house, looking for me.

"Over here," I called, still thinking about the baby's soft blue eyes. She had Grandma Rose's eyes.

We'll never sit in Kate's kitchen and talk about who in the family my baby looks like. . . .

Tears prickled in my throat, even though it made no sense. Children, if ever, were years away for me, yet somehow I felt cheated. My babies would never have Joshua's hair or Grandma Rose's nose or Aunt Sadie's long, thin feet.

Barry started up the steps and I rubbed my eyes, pushing away the sting.

"Good nap?" Barry asked, leaning against the porch post.

"Yeah." Standing up, I stretched my neck, getting my head together. "So you managed to escape my dad and the tractor scrapbook?"

"Yeah, no thanks to you," Barry joked. "You left me stranded there."

"Sorry. Karen told me to do it."

He shrugged, amiable as usual. "It's all right. It was pretty interesting, really. I haven't seen your dad since I got out of Harrington. Every time I help your mom with one of her after-school camps, your dad's out of town flying." I nodded, and as was often the case, Barry went right on talking. "Whenever the Jumpkids see me, they ask about you, of course."

"I miss the kids." One of the things I hated about being gone was not being able to help Karen run the Jumpkids after-school arts program. Half of my teenage years were spent teaching kids to sing, dance, play music, and give theater performances. Those skills came in handy in Ukraine.

Barry jabbed me in the shoulder. "Hey, guess who else I saw the other day." He waited until I shrugged helplessly, then answered. "Mrs. Bradford. I was downtown and I went by Harrington and popped into the counselor's office. Mrs. Bradford asked about you, by the way. She wanted to know if you ever worked on those scholarship applications she e-mailed you."

"Some of them," I admitted. "Not the ones with all the Native American stuff on them. I'm really not sure I want to get into all that. I did e-mail the Choctaw tribal . . . headquarters . . . whatever it's called down in Oklahoma. I don't even have a roll number—I think that's what they call it. Anyway, it's a big process to get one, especially since all I know about my biological father is his name. I'd probably have to go to Oklahoma to start on it, and even then it's a long shot. You have to find records tracing your ancestry back to someone on the original tribal lists. It sounds complicated."

Barry looked disappointed. "Mrs. Bradford thinks your father being Choctaw would help you get into Juilliard. You ought to go for it. Why not?"

I shrugged off the question. I couldn't explain why not. "I'll try to go by and see Mrs. Bradford."

"She'd like that. You'd better hurry, though, before she goes out on maternity leave. She's as big as a house, but don't tell her I said so. It's twins, you know."

"She told me that in an e-mail when I asked her for the scholarship stuff. It's great that they're finally having a baby. I think they've wanted one for a long time."

"I think so," Barry muttered, and our conversation fell into a rare lapse as we watched Josh and Rose's dog, Tracker, chase a squirrel up a tree. My mind drifted to the scholarship paperwork. If I went to Oklahoma and found the Choctaw tribal offices, would there be a Thomas Clay listed on the membership rolls? Would I be able to prove he was my father? If I did, what good would that do? Before my adoption by James and Karen became final, child protective services had searched for my father and found no sign of him. They'd concluded that he was probably deceased. End of story. For years, James and Karen and I had skirted the issue of my Choctaw heritage, for fear that delving into it might cause my presumed-dead biological father, or members of his family, to resurface and lay claim to me.

Now that I was of age, that danger was gone. What if I really did have a biological family out there somewhere? If I searched for them, what would James and Karen think? How could they possibly understand? Yet, if I didn't, there would always be the unanswered questions, the hollow place that had ached when I gazed at Jenilee's baby and saw the family resemblances.

Barry was looking at me, watching the wheels turn.

"Barry?" I said slowly.

"Hmm?"

"I know it's a lot to ask, but are you up for a little road trip?" Somehow the unknown seemed easier to face with Barry along. "We could stay here tonight, and then hit the highway in the morning."

He drew back curiously. "Where to?"

"Oklahoma," I blurted, then glanced around, afraid someone might have heard, but the yard was empty. Everyone was still inside with the baby. Barry blinked, taken aback, and I added, "Will you go with me?"

"I . . . I can't." Grimacing, he squeezed one eye shut. "Well . . . there's this . . . girl." His loafer scraped dully against the porch as he rolled a pebble under the sole and shoved his hands deep into his pockets like he wanted to fold himself up and disappear. "Her sorority's having their spring cotillion, and I've . . . we've . . . well, I've been planning to go for a while. With her. To the dance, I mean."

I suddenly clued in to the fact that Barry had a life I knew nothing about. "Bear-bear, did you go and get a girlfriend while I was away?"

Sagging, he nodded with a sigh of resignation.

"A *girlfriend* girlfriend, or just a date-for-the-spring-cotillion girlfriend?"

He winced. "The first kind."

"And you didn't tell me?" I smacked him on the arm, a little harder than I meant to, actually. "Shame on you."

Bracing his hands on the railing, he leaned over. "I didn't want to upset you while you were half a world away."

"I'm not upset. I think it's great." Part of me did, but another part felt surprisingly bleak. For years, Barry had been the one constant in my life. Even with thousands of miles between us, we were sidekicks. Now he was moving on. Leaving me alone. "I'm happy for you, really."

Drumming his fingers on the railing, he gave me a sad, wry, sideways look. "I didn't want you to be happy for me, either."

My heart melted into a star-crossed pool, and I leaned out over the flower bed, shoulder-butting him. "We've come a lot of miles together, huh, Bear-bear?" He nodded, and emotion tightened my throat. The past was fading. Time to move on.

"Yeah," he said softly, and I rested my head on his shoulder. "We have."

We stood that way, quietly watching the late-August sunlight fade into the pale pink of evening. My mind paged through a photo album of Barry, the past, the future, a girlfriend, an engagement, a wedding, kids. He would become a band director at some high school, just like he'd always planned. Strangely, I could picture his future but not my own.

Why was I stuck in this state of arrested development—uncertain of who to be, what to do, where to go next? Karen and James's plan to go forward with the application to Juilliard seemed to make perfect sense. Until I found out whether or not I'd been accepted, I could live at home and take classes in Kansas City, help Karen with the Jumpkids programs, and maybe see about guest performing with the symphonic. The director there had once been my mentor.

He'd be horrified to know that I'd hardly touched a piano or a violin this past year, and I couldn't explain why. It was as if the drive had slowly faded out of me during the year of traveling around Europe with the student exchange orchestra. By the time I went to Ukraine, I was glad to be away from the pressure, away from the noise, the constant crowds of people, the director screaming every time someone botched a note or missed an accidental. Even my fascination with the European cities, their narrow streets and ancient stone buildings, had faded by the time my year in the orchestra was over. I didn't know if I was exhausted from the constant performing or if something had changed inside me, but for the first time in years, I didn't feel the overwhelming desire to play my violin, or the old piano we used to teach music classes at the Internat mission in Ukraine. I didn't go to sleep hearing music, dream about it, and wake up with yet unwritten melodies in my head.

I still had knowledge of music, but I'd lost the feel for it. I'd read about prodigies who suddenly grew out of their talents, and now I wondered if I was one.

Barry was talking about the trip to Oklahoma, offering to go with me next week, after the cotillion was over. "It'd be fun—a little road trip, just like the old days."

"It would probably be a waste of time. I should be picking out some classes at KBJC. I can still do late enrollment for the fall semester, get a few credits in."

Barry gave me an incredulous look. "What are *you* going to do at KBJC? They don't even have a music department there."

"I don't know—take some basics, I guess."

"You should go to Oklahoma."

"I'd probably be better off getting my enrollment taken care of, for now. I can go to Oklahoma some other time . . . maybe."

"You won't." The remark was surprisingly frank for Barry. "You're just making excuses. I thought you'd step right off the plane talking about getting into Juilliard, making plans to put together some pieces for your application CD, and instead you're talking about KBJC. What's going on, Dell?"

Sagging forward, I sighed. "I don't know. I'm just not sure Juilliard is the right thing for me. I'm not sure"—*who I'm supposed to be*—"I have what it takes."

Barry drew back, his eyes flashing the way they always had when he felt the need to defend me, even from myself. "What are you, nuts? Dell, you've got more talent in your little finger than the rest of us will have in a lifetime. If anyone should be in Juilliard, it's you, and if being Native American can help you get in, you have to go for it." He held his hands up, ready to either plead with me or strangle me. Maybe both. "D, you've got talent. You're amazing." He paced away, thinking for a moment, then turning back to me. "We'll go to Oklahoma next week, all right?"

"I don't think your girlfriend would like it much," I pointed out. "If I were your girlfriend, I wouldn't like it. It's a stupid idea, anyway. If I went to Oklahoma, I wouldn't even know where to begin. What am I going to do, show up at some tribal office and say, 'Hi, I'm Dell Sommerfield, used to be Jordan, but my real father's name is Clay. My CPS records say he was a member of the Choctaw Nation, so I was wondering if you have him on your list somewhere?' "

Barry nodded. "Sure. Why not. That probably happens all the time there—people looking for their ancestors and stuff."

I pushed off the rail and slumped into a chair. "Except I'm not looking for my ancestors, Barry. I'm looking for my father. What if . . ." Possibilities swirled through my mind, unanswered questions, altered realities. In my mind, my father was someone like my mother—mixed up, messed up, too irresponsible to care for a child. "What if I find out something really bad? What if my father was . . ." Was a perfectly normal person, and the truth was that he didn't know me because he didn't want to? What if he chose to leave me behind? What if my father was the man I remembered Mama dating just before she died—the stone-faced man with the long dark hair, the one who took Mama away to an apartment in Kansas City and let her pump meth into herself until her heart stopped beating? What if my father was the one who killed my mother?

Barry perched on the arm of the chair, taking my hand. "What if he never knew you existed?" His voice was soft, compassionate, dependably logical and practical. "Did you ever think about that? What if you have family out there you've never even known about? What if you could find them?"

My throat tightened. "I don't know if I'd want to." For years, I'd been struggling to become Dell Sommerfield, daughter of Karen and James, great-granddaughter of Grandma Rose. Having concrete information about my real identity might change that in some way I couldn't predict.

"Let's see what we find out. Then you can make decisions about how far to go with it." Straightening my palm against his, Barry smoothed his free hand over the top of mine and let out a long breath, the kind that told me he was about to level with me. "D, I think you need to do this. These last two years, there's been something going on with you. It's like you're . . . lost. One minute you're a senior at Harrington, on the straight track to Juilliard, and the next thing, you're not applying to Juilliard or anywhere else. You're heading off to Europe for some student music exchange program no one's ever heard of. And then next thing you're off to Ukraine, of all places, to teach orphans in a mission school. What's going on with you?"

"I don't know," I admitted. "I just . . . You know, when CPS did the investigation for my adoption, I really felt like I'd made peace with the fact that they couldn't locate my father, and I'd probably never know any more about my biological family. But then, when we started on all the scholarship applications our senior year, and Mrs. Bradford brought up the whole issue of applying as a Native American and that maybe I could find out about my father through the

Choctaw Nation headquarters . . . I don't know . . . it opened up a lot of doors I thought I'd closed. I couldn't deal with it. The opportunity for the student music exchange program came up, so I took it. I guess I thought that eventually I'd know the right thing to do." There. I'd said it. I'd finally told someone the truth.

Barry didn't answer at first. As usual, he took time to consider the implications. "Have you talked to your folks about this?"

"I don't want them to know." The answer was so emphatic that Barry blinked and drew back. "They'll think our family isn't enough for me, that it's not real. James and Karen have given me everything."

"I think they'd understand that—"

"No, they wouldn't." My voice rose and carried over the yard. Giving the house a cautionary look, I paused and got myself under control. "They wouldn't understand, Barry. They'd be hurt. *I* can't even understand the way I feel. How could they possibly understand it?"

Chewing the side of his lip, Barry finger-combed a few strands of highlighted hair away from his face. "All right then, we'll go next Friday. I have to work Monday through Thursday, but after that I'm off for the weekend. Tell James and Karen you're coming to visit me at MSU the end of next week, and we'll head out on a little road trip, see what we find out."

I squeezed his hand, filled with affection for him. "Thanks for understanding, Bear-bear, but I think this is something I'd better do alone. Besides, I don't want to upset your girlfriend."

"She'll understand." Clearly his feelings were hurt because I was pushing him away. "We can leave early Friday morning and get down there while it's still business hours. If this tribal place is more like a tourist trap it might be open on Saturday, but if it's like real offices, we'd better hit it during a weekday. I've got a"—he paused and glanced away, then finished—"test in my mini-mester class on Tuesday, so I have to be back." I could tell he didn't have a mini-mester test. He had plans of some other kind, probably with his girlfriend. Barry was a terrible liar.

"Let's just see how the week turns out," I said, as James and Karen came across the yard to call us in for supper. "I'm kind of wiped out right now—jet lag, I guess. I might not go anywhere next weekend."

"Where you headed next weekend?" James asked.

"Maybe down to visit me at Missouri State," Barry answered before I could, which should have been a tip-off to James and Karen. Whenever we were up to something, Barry always did the talking.

"Ah, college life," James waxed nostalgic.

Karen narrowed an eye at the words *Missouri State*. She didn't want me thinking about any place but Juilliard. She wasn't going to be pushy because, in her own words, she realized I was an adult now and capable of making my own decisions. But the undercurrent was there just the same. I had a sense that, after all the time and work and love they'd put into me, I wasn't panning out the way they'd planned. By now, I should have been halfway through a BA degree, playing music, performing with the symphonic in their young artist spotlight program. Instead, I was drifting, and that concerned Karen. She knew there was something wrong and it frustrated her that she couldn't figure it out.

Jenilee came out the back door of the main house with the baby and waved for us to hurry up.

I waved back, thinking again of the baby, of how holding her reminded me of my little brother, Angelo. He would be thirteen now, still a minor, still young enough that his records were sealed and no one would give me any information about him—not even his last name or his father's name. If Granny knew either of those things, she'd never revealed them to me. *That baby's daddy don't want no more to do with us,* she said. *That's that. Now, git on outside and find somethin' to do with yourself. Stay off them cliffs by the river. You'll fall in and drown.*

That was that. But I never forgot the way Angelo looked, the way he smiled, the way he liked to lie on my legs in the tall grass and stare up at the sky. Just before his daddy took him away, he had started crying when I left for school. He'd toddle out the screen door, calling *Dee-gee, Dee-gee!* And I'd run back, scoop him up, hug him, and take him inside to Mama or Granny. When he wasn't looking, I'd sneak out, then slide a rock in front of the screen door, so he couldn't get out and hurt himself. I always wanted him to be all right while I was gone, and through the school day I felt like I was holding my breath until I got home and saw that he was fine. I'd had that feeling for twelve years now, every time I thought about him. I needed to know that he was fine.

I wondered, sometimes, if I might have passed him in the mall, or on a street someplace in Kansas City, and never even known it. When James and I went to the Royals games, I scanned the crowd for boys his age, read the backs of their Little League jerseys, listened when their fathers called them by their names, just to see if I might find Angelo there.

It was an impractical fantasy—one I could never surrender, or tell anyone else about. It was our secret, Angelo's and mine, that I would always keep looking until someday I found him.

Chapter 3

My jet lag turned out to be a case of international flu. Back home in Kansas City, I spent three days with Karen bringing homemade gingersnaps and soup I couldn't eat, our next-door neighbor, Dr. Rollings, coming by to bring me Tamiflu and sample bottles of electrolyte solution, Barry calling between classes to make sure I was all right, and my mind drifting between the orphanage and home, while conjuring occasional pink elephants on the ceiling and snakes under the bed. When I awoke on the fourth day, sunlight was pressing, hot and insistent, against my eyes. Dimly, I knew that wasn't right. We were always up before dawn at the mission center so we could dress and attend a short daily devotional with the Spencers before walking next door to begin classes with the orphans at the Internat school. Someone must have forgotten to wake me up. . . .

Rolling over, I pulled open my eyes and blinked at the blur. The room smelled of cedar and freshly washed fabric, but the scents were out of place. There should have been the odors of damp cement, the antiseptic cleaner that was used regularly to mop the dormitory floors, aging wool blankets, and frozen earth outside. Instead of birds chirping, there should have been the slow, rhythmic drip, drip of icicles lengthening outside the window. . . .

My vision slowly cleared, and I lay gazing at the steeply pitched pine ceiling, its lazily whirring ceiling fan slicing through the curtain of sunlight.

I wondered if I was still dreaming—if perhaps I was only home in my mind, and in a few moments I would wake up in the mission in Ukraine. Perhaps even the mission was a dream, and I would wake up back in London.

I turned to look at the clock on the night table—the same alarm clock that had been there since James, Karen, and I moved into the Kansas City house just before I turned thirteen. The numbers were covered with a folded washrag, still slightly damp.

Snuggling into the pillow, I let my eyes drift closed again and fell into empty space, vaguely wondering if, when I awoke, I would still be home.

My dreams took me back to Ukraine, to the Internat mission, but now, rather than being surrounded by the winter-bare remnants of unmowed lots, the faded concrete building sat in a grove of trees along the river. It was summer, and a high, hot sun hung overhead in a cloudless sky. The children were playing in the water, dashing through the shallows with their arms outstretched, their feet so light they skimmed the surface. The air was filled with the sharp, angular sounds of their native tongue.

Grandma Rose was there, sitting on the shore with a baby in her arms. Even before I reached her, I knew it was Angelo. As I came closer, he smiled and babbled, studying my face just the way he used to when he was tiny. Sometimes, when things were too loud at Granny's house, I'd take Angelo and carry him to the woods and sit by my favorite tree with him balanced on my legs. He'd frown and hold a hand up toward me, and study my face like he wanted to know everything about it.

I loved the way Angelo looked at me. I loved the way he smiled. I wanted to sit with him in the quiet of the woods forever. Every time Angelo's daddy saw me taking him off like that, he'd complain and say I might drop Angelo, or fall into the river with him, or set him down in an ant nest or something.

Mama would just shrug and tell him it was fine. I was never sure if she was defending me, or just arguing with Angelo's daddy.

I wondered if she ever sat with Angelo and just looked at him. . . .

I could see her down the river now, my mama, in the bandana halter top and the faded denim jeans that were her favorite, her long auburn hair swirling around her shoulders, her eyes blue like the washed-out jeans.

Grandma Rose stood up, moved along the riverbank, and even though I wanted to, I couldn't follow. My feet were trapped in the thick deposits of a sandbar. I could only watch as Grandma Rose took my baby brother and gave him to Mama, and the two of them walked away together.

"No!" I screamed, but no one seemed to hear me. In the river, the kids from the orphans' home began singing in Russian as Grandma Rose slipped her arm around my mother. Together they walked into the water and disappeared beneath the overhanging branches of a sycamore tree. As they passed, the leaves shuddered, then hushed and folded inward, hiding them away.

"Angelo!" I called. "Angelo! Angelo!"

"Dell?" I felt someone shaking me, pulling me from the sand. "Wake up, honey. You're dreaming again."

With an intake of breath, I jerked awake and was once again in my bedroom.

Karen laid a hand on my forehead. "Hey, sleepyhead," she said, "you must have really been dreaming. Feels like your fever's broken, though. Dr. Rollings thought you were probably over the worst of it when he checked on you last night. He thought you'd be perking up by this morning." Sitting on the edge of the bed with a stack of folded towels in her lap, she smoothed my hair away from my face the way she used to when I was younger. "Did you have a bad dream? You were talking in your sleep just now."

"I don't know." My throat was raspy and raw. The dream was still fresh in my mind. I could see Grandma Rose and my mother disappearing beneath the sycamore leaves with Angelo. Tears seeped into my eyes, and Karen slipped an arm around me, pulling me close.

"Honey," she soothed, "what's wrong?"

I couldn't answer. I just sobbed, filled with emotions I couldn't frame into words. James's footsteps came up the hallway and stopped at the edge of the bedroom carpet. I felt Karen shrug helplessly. Her cheek tightened into a clench, then relaxed against my head. I pictured the silent conversation between them, my dad's face asking, *What's wrong with her?*

And Karen's answering, *I don't know. She just woke up and started crying. She was talking in her sleep.*

Talking in her sleep? She hasn't done that in years. I thought she was over that.

I don't know what's going on with her. . . .

James turned around and walked down the hall without a word. I heard him in the kitchen, putting dishes in the dishwasher, changing the trash bag, frying bacon, doing what he always did—something practical—when he didn't understand the pervasive female emotions in the room.

When I'd finally pulled myself together, Karen handed me a tissue and sat rubbing my arm. "What was that all about?"

"It's just . . ." I didn't have an answer, of course. Not one that I could share. ". . . good to be home. When I woke up, I thought I was still in Ukraine at first. It . . . took me a minute to realize I was really back."

To her credit, Karen didn't say something like, *If Ukraine was that bad, why did you stay so long? Why didn't you come home sooner?* She was thinking it, though. She was wondering if something terrible had happened to me over there.

"It's not that I didn't like it there." Switching to a defensive posture at the slightest sign of parental disapproval was one of those kid habits I had yet to overcome. Mr. Spencer at the orphanage had pointed that out once when he overheard my monthly phone conversation with my parents. He chuckled as I hung up, muttering to myself that this was *my* life and there was plenty of time for college later.

"When you can say those things *before* you hang up the phone, it'll be your life," he joked. Mr. Spencer approached everything with a good sense of humor and an abiding understanding of human nature that made him good at mission work.

"When does that happen?" I asked glumly. As much as I loved James and Karen, I could never be totally real with them.

Mr. Spencer's thick gray mustache curled upward as he laughed. "I'll let you know when I get there. Mama Flo still sends new underwear in my care packages." Walking out the door, he added, "Don't be too easy on 'em, kiddo, or they'll be sending you underwear when you're fifty-four years old. . . ."

I chuckled at the memory, and Karen drew back, surprised at the unexpected emotional rebound.

"I was just remembering something from the mission," I explained. "Mama Flo still puts new underwear in Mr. Spencer's care packages."

Catching the hidden meaning, Karen rolled her eyes. "Pppfff. Some parents don't know how to let go."

The two of us smiled at each other and I wiped my eyes as Karen set the towels in the bathroom. "Sounds like James has some breakfast under way. Do you feel like eating anything?"

Groaning, I rubbed my stomach, which felt like it had been reduced to the size of a pea. "I think I'd better wait a while." Every muscle in my body protested as I climbed from the bed. "I'm sorry for coming home sick. Guess about now you guys are probably wishing I'd stayed in Ukraine, huh?"

"Not a chance." Leaning against the door, she smiled at me. "If you were going to get sick, I'm glad you were home where we could take care of you."

"Me, too," I said, and stumbled off to the bathroom to clean up.

By the time I'd showered and dressed, James and Karen were finished with breakfast. Karen said she'd planned a *lazy day* for us, which in our family was code for popcorn and old movies. I fell asleep on the sofa halfway through *It's a Wonderful Life* and spent the rest of the day fading in and out of movie land, nibbling on soda crackers, sipping chicken noodle soup, and enjoying being home together, just the three of us. "Like the old days," Karen said.

By nighttime, I was wide-awake. I lay for hours in my room as the house grew quiet. The dream about Grandma Rose, Mama, and Angelo wound through my thoughts like fine silver mist. I hadn't dreamed about Mama in years. Why was I dreaming about her now?

Finally, somewhere near morning, I drifted off. I was in a quiet, dreamless place when I heard James and Karen moving around the house, Karen getting ready to go to work downtown at the Jumpkids office, and James heading for the airport. He was already dressed in his pilot's uniform. The sound of his heavy black shoes and rolling overnight bag on the ceramic tile told me he was about to leave.

He poked his head into my bedroom the way he always had when he left at odd hours. When I was younger, he'd kiss me on the forehead and pull the covers up around my shoulders, thinking I was asleep. Sometimes I pretended to be asleep so he would do that. I liked the way it felt.

This time he stopped at the door, and I had a pang of loss. Now that I was grown up, there was a closeness we couldn't share anymore. I wondered if it would be that way if I were really his daughter.

"Be back tomorrow night, Pooh." At least he still called me *Pooh*. Some things hadn't changed.

"Safe trip," I muttered drowsily. That was what I always said to him when he left for work. It was our family phrase, code words for all the things that went unsaid. *I love you. Be careful. We'll miss you while you're gone. Hurry home.*

Safe trip. When I'd left for Europe, we'd parted with only those two words.

This time, he hovered in the doorway, as if something more needed to be said. "Sorry I have to leave so soon after you're back home."

"It's okay."

"I love you."

"I love you too, Dad."

He turned around and left, his travel case clicking down the hall.

I rolled over and stared at the KC Symphonic Spring Duet poster on the wall—a remnant from my high school days. The picture had been taken during Harrington Academy's annual performance with the symphonic. There I was in the string section with my violin tucked under my chin and my eyes closed, lost in the music.

The violin was somewhere in transit between Ukraine and here now, along with other things I'd shipped. It had been sitting in my cubby at the orphans' home, untouched for almost a year now.

Who was that girl in the poster? Where had she gone? Now that I was home, why did I still feel . . . unsettled, restless, as if there were somewhere else I needed to be?

I knew the answer, even though I didn't want to face it. I knew why I was dreaming about Mama again, and talking to Barry about Oklahoma, and why I couldn't look at my cousin's new baby without feeling cheated. No matter how much I wanted to escape them, questions about all that had happened in Granny's little house on Mulberry Creek were still with me. They stood like a wall blocking out everyone, everything else in my life. I'd spent two years wandering the world trying to find myself, and I was still lost.

Tossing off the covers, I sat up, looked hard at the girl in the poster, and made a decision. I was going to Oklahoma. Today.

I was dressing and condensing clothes into a duffel bag when Karen came into the room. Leaning on the doorframe, she gave the duffel bag a questioning frown, then cut her gaze back to me, her eyes narrow with concern. "I was wondering if you felt good enough to go to the Jumpkids office with me this morning, or if you'd rather stay here and rest."

Pretending to be busy putting extra jeans in the closet, I steeled myself and formulated an excuse. I hated lying to James and Karen. I'd never been good at it. But then, in another way, everything about me was a lie. There were so many things I'd never told them, so many leftover emotions I'd never confessed. "I thought I might go by Harrington and visit Mrs. Bradford, then drive on down and see Barry for a couple days."

"Really?" Karen sounded surprised and hurt.

Guilt dropped to my stomach like molten lead, then solidified there. "Since Dad's out of town, I mean. I thought it'd be better than going later, when we could all be home. Plus, you know, Barry's got a girlfriend now, and if I go on the weekend, I might be interfering with, you know, dates and stuff. I don't want to cause problems between Barry and his girl." I knew I was talking too much, the nervous string of words rushing out in a way that wasn't like me. If I didn't stop now, Karen would figure out I was covering up.

"Are you sure you feel well enough?" Her brows knotted doubtfully in the center. "You've been awfully sick, Dell."

"I feel good today," I chirped, adding a toothy grin for effect. "I'm just in the mood for a little . . . road trip, you know? It'll be fun to have Barry show me around the college and everything."

She thought for a few minutes before answering. As a teenager, I'd always hated those *Jeopardy!* minutes—the ones in which she tried to read my mind, figure out what was really happening on the inside.

Her lips twitched upward. "Sure you're not going there to check out the girlfriend? See what old Bear-bear's up to there at Missouri State?" She gave me a knowing smile, one that said she thought she'd figured out my secret.

My face flushed hot. "Of course not, but . . . but I'd kind of like to see . . . for myself." The blush deepened, fanned by an intense wave of conscience. It was wrong to be telling her an outright lie, especially on my first noncomatose day at home. But it was for her own good. For our good. I couldn't tell her I wanted to skip off to Oklahoma, to the Choctaw Indian headquarters, to see if I could find out anything about my birth family. I could never make her understand that. I could never say that to her.

"You're sure this is a good idea?" She twisted her lips to one side.

I'm not sure of anything. "Yeah, it'll be fine. I'll be back Saturday. Sunday at the latest. Some of the girls from Harrington are at Missouri State. I'll just, you know, give them a call when I get there. See if I can bunk on somebody's couch."

Karen made the I-know-you're-a-grown-up-but-I-hate-it sound. Something between a sigh of resignation and a whimper. "Take money for a hotel room in case that doesn't work out. Do you need money?" She glanced toward the kitchen, where her purse was undoubtedly on the counter next to her briefcase.

Opening my desk drawer, I found my checkbook, right where I'd left it two years ago. "Not unless you two have drained my money market while I was away." All through high school, I'd worked part-time and never really had much use for the money, except to save it in my money market account, ostensibly for college expenses.

"Well, there was this one little Caribbean cruise. . . ."

"Yeah, right." Chuckling, I tossed the checkbook into my purse. "But, come to think of it, a Caribbean cruise might be good for you guys." Grabbing a ponytail holder and a brush from the desk,

I smirked at her in the mirror. "How long has it been since you two have done something wild and fun?" For the past few years, it seemed like all they'd done was worry about me.

"I beg your pardon." She grabbed the brush from my hand, combed my hair into a ponytail, and gave it a yank. "What are you insinuating—that your father and I could use a little livening up? Think we've settled into the doldrums of midlife since you've been gone?"

"If the shoe fits . . . ," I teased, and she pulled my hair harder. "Ouch. Okay, okay. You two are the hippest parents on the planet. You're cool, you're boss, you're phat, you're way bad."

"That's more like it." Taking a hair clip from the drawer, she flipped my hair up into a twist and secured it so that dark shoots fanned out the top. It was fancier than the usual ponytail I would have done. My time in Ukraine had cured me of any need to primp in the morning. Straightening my shoulders, Karen smiled at our reflection in the mirror, then kissed me on the cheek. "Okay, kiddo, I've got to head for work. I'm meeting with the owners of Mariposa restaurants this morning to talk to them about providing suppers for our Friday after-school program. We've had to give the kids sandwiches lately because our old Friday vendor changed owners."

"Oh, man, no more Shakey's Barbecue Fridays?" From the seventh grade through high school, I'd had Shakey's Barbecue with the Jumpkids every Friday night. "It won't be Friday without Shakey's."

Karen gave me a last kiss. "Times, they are a-changin'," she said, a little sadly, then turned to leave the room. "Stop by the office later?"

I shook my head, wincing inwardly. Being with her only made me feel that much more guilty for what I was about to do. "I think after I visit Mrs. Bradford, I'm just going to head on, okay?"

"Okay, kiddo. Your car should be all gassed up and ready. James ran out and filled it up, checked the oil and so forth this morning." Glancing back over her shoulder, she smiled. "Safe trip."

I watched her disappear in the mirror, then tossed the last of my things into the bag and zipped it up. Grabbing the duffel, my backpack, and my purse, I took one last look around my room and headed for the garage. In the kitchen, I found my keys in the usual spot, with three hundred dollars underneath.

Tucking the money in my pocket, I shook my head at myself. Grown up, yet not so grown up after all.

CHAPTER 4

❧

The second-period bell was ringing as I pulled into visitor parking at Harrington Arts Academy. Standing at the bottom of the middle school steps, I gazed at the art deco frontispiece, remembering how I'd felt entering that building for the first time, the year I turned thirteen and James and Karen took me in. Walking up those steps the first day between them, I felt at once suffocated and exhilarated. My head was full of music and my heart was full of fear. I wanted to go in, yet I wanted to run back home to Hindsville, to my secret places along the river, where no one would find me. Ever.

Those desires were at war inside me as we neared the front door, and I didn't know which one would win. I only knew that my life was changing and I was powerless to stop it. My hands trembled and my throat felt thick and dry, but I couldn't tell James and Karen that. I didn't want them to rethink taking me into their family.

Karen slipped her hand over mine, and we walked through the door together. I'd never had anyone walk me to school before. Back home, if I went at all, I caught the bus on Mulberry Road and sat in the back, as close to invisible as possible. When I got to the little school in Hindsville, I went in the side door, where the other kids wouldn't bother me. At Harrington Academy, I walked right in the front entry, just like everyone else.

Shaking my head at the memory, I trotted up the steps and slipped into the administration office. Mrs. Jorgenson, who'd been the school secretary since before I could remember, was writing something on a sticky note. Glancing up, she did a double-take, blinked like she'd seen a ghost, then rolled her chair backward off the plastic mat and almost fell over.

"Well, Dell!" she said with her usual huge smile. "Aren't you a sight for sore eyes?" Motioning toward the door to the principal's office, she gave a regretful frown. "Mr. Bradford isn't here, though. He's at the downtown street festival with the jazz band. He'll be gone all day. One of the guitar players has a broken finger, so Mr. Bradford's serving as principal, chaperone, and bass guitarist."

"Actually, I'm looking for Mrs. Bradford," I said. "Is she here?"

Mrs. Jorgenson rolled her eyes. "Unless the labor and delivery wagon has taken her away by now, she's here. She's in her office. I'll buzz her if you want."

"No, that's all right. Can I just go surprise her?"

"Sure." She shook a finger at me. "But not too much of a surprise, all right? I don't want to be delivering twins on the floor of the counselor's office. Don't say boo or anything, okay?"

I turned to leave, remembering back to when I thought being in the principal's office was the end of the world. "I won't. Thanks, Mrs. Jorgenson."

"Sure thing," she said, then tore off the sticky note and pasted it on her computer with several dozen others.

I crossed the hall and peeked around the corner. Mrs. Bradford's door was closed and I could hear her talking to a student inside. I waited in the hall, thinking of all the times I'd come to see her for tutoring or just to talk. Mrs. Bradford had saved me during that lost, lonely first year at Harrington. I could talk to her about anything—even issues I couldn't bring up at home, like my curiosity about my biological father.

The door opened, and I waited as the student walked out, giving my Russian Coca-Cola T-shirt a curious glance as we slipped past each other.

Mrs. Bradford had already turned to her computer. "Yes?" she said, without looking up.

"Ummm . . . excuse me?"

She finished a few keystrokes, then turned around. Her mouth fell open, and she was momentarily dumbstruck. "Dell?" she gasped. "What in the world . . . ? I thought you were overseas for weeks yet."

"I'm . . . uhhh . . . I came . . ." I couldn't stop gaping at the huge belly beneath her flowered maternity top. Mrs. Bradford had always been tall and thin. "I . . . ca-came back early." To my horror, I started to giggle.

"Stop that." Pushing out of the chair with one hand and holding her stomach with the other, she stood, then stretched out her arms, waddling around the desk to me. "You just stop that laughing and come here." She pulled me close in a hug, and I felt something squirm against my ribs.

"Oh, my gosh!" I stepped back. "I think something kicked me."

"Probably Keiler Junior," she joked, motioning me to one of the student chairs by the file cabinet. "Every time they do an ultrasound, he's the active one. The girl is much more sedate."

"Awww," I said as she hobbled back to her chair. "He's a chip off the old block. Mom e-mailed me and said you were having a boy and a girl. That's so great."

"Yes, it is. After trying for so long, we're really excited." Her eyes glittered with an abiding contentment. I wondered if that would ever happen to me—if there would be a point someday when I would feel perfect in my own skin.

Mrs. B. smiled. "So, when did you get back? I want to hear all about your trip. How was Europe? And how in the world did you end up going on to Ukraine? I never did get the full story on that. Your mom just said you met a friend over there who was going to volunteer in an orphans' mission, and you decided to go, too. . . ." She trailed off, leaving an empty space at the end of the sentence, an old trick she'd used on me in my middle school days. She knew I'd feel compelled to fill in the blank.

"I don't know." I felt like the shy, uncertain seventh-grader who'd first come to her office. "I just wanted to do . . . something different, I guess."

Pursing her lips sympathetically, she nodded. "Something other than come home and start college, you mean?"

I glanced away under the weight of her X-ray vision. "I just needed . . . I don't know . . . time."

"Time to . . ."

"I don't know." How could I explain what I didn't understand?

Leaning back in her chair, she waved a hand in the air, swatting away the inquisition like fog. "Sorry. Once a counselor, always a counselor. I forget that you're an adult now. It doesn't seem possible. Just yesterday you were this stringy little transfer student singing 'Jesu' in the spring fling." The two of us laughed together and the tension floated away. Mrs. B. clapped her hands, then rubbed them together lightly. "So, you're back here now and headed off to college?"

"Yes . . . yeah, I guess."

"Juilliard?"

"Maybe."

"Missouri State?"

"I have friends there."

"NYU?" Mrs. B. had pushed me toward NYU my senior year of high school. She thought it would be a good place for me if I didn't go to Juilliard.

"I don't know. . . ."

"Timbuktu?" she teased, and I pressed the pads of my fingers over my eyes, feeling like an absolute loser.

"Is it that obvious?"

Her chair squealed as she leaned across the desk. I knew what she'd be doing—resting her chin in her hand, waiting for me to unburden myself of whatever was bothering me. "Only because every time I start sending you college admissions information, you avoid me."

"I don't. I . . ."

Her frown stopped me. "Come on, kiddo. I've known you forever. This is like when I used to try to get you to talk about your past—the things that happened before you came to live with James and Karen. You'd either shut down or change the subject." Drumming her fingernails on the desk, she raised a brow. "I know avoidance when I see it, especially from you. So what's up?"

"It's not avoidance." I focused on the wall, hoping I could pull this off. "In fact, I came by here to get some information from you . . . about the whole Native American thing. Remember, you said it would be a good idea if I checked into whether I could get a Choctaw roll number and all that stuff? With being out of school a couple years, I figured my chances of getting into Juilliard or another good music program might not be so high. Maybe the Native American angle could help give me an edge, you know? I thought I might . . . do some checking around. See what I can find out." *Play it cool, play it cool,* a voice inside my head warned. *Don't say too much.* "I was hoping you'd give me that information again . . . about the Choctaw tribal headquarters, and all that." Mrs. B. stared at me with her mouth open, shocked either by the rush of words or the request, or both. "If it's not too much trouble."

She blinked rapidly. "Well, of course not. It's not too much trouble, but what happened to the information I e-mailed you a few months ago?"

"I sent it to the recycle bin." I winced guiltily. "I'm sorry. It seemed like a crazy idea at first, but now . . . well, I thought I should check it out, that's all. I probably won't find anything. I mean, just because my CPS records said my dad was Choctaw doesn't mean he's actually listed in their books. There's no telling how many people they have listed. Thomas Clay is a pretty common name. There could be dozens of people with that name."

Mrs. B. swiveled around to her computer. "Well, who knows? It's worth a try." I wished I could see her face, so I'd know whether she believed this was about a scholarship application, not about finding my biological father. "Let me print up a copy of those applications and the online directory of the Choctaw tribal offices. I don't know how much help it will be, though. The Choctaw tribe has offices spread across at least three or four different counties. You'll probably have to do some digging to find out who you need to talk to. I could help you, if you want."

"No, that's all right," I said. "I know you're busy."

I waited while she searched for some documents and printed them out, then laid them in stacks on the desk between us. "Now here is some information about scholarships, programs, and fellowships specifically for those of Native American ancestry." She handed the first stack across the desk. "I know that financially you don't really need a scholarship. Your parents can afford the tuition, but some of these carry quite a bit of prestige. They're worth applying for, just for the recognition. There's also a good deal of interest in the study and recording of traditional Native American music right now." She handed me a second stack of papers. "Here's some information about that subject." In the hall, the lunch bell rang. Mrs. B. grabbed the third stack of papers as the corridor filled with a cacophony of kids jostling, lockers slamming, and sneakers squeaking on the old wooden floors. "That's my cue." As she handed me the third stack of papers, she pushed herself to her feet. "That is information about the Choctaw tribal offices in Oklahoma. The biggest complex seems to be in Durant, but there are other offices and a museum in the old tribal council building in some other town with a long name I can't pronounce. You can look it up on the map. The tribal court system is headquartered there, so it could be that's where birth and membership records are kept. You'll just have to make a few phone calls or do some asking around if you go there." She laid a hand on my arm and gave a squeeze. "Good luck, kiddo. You're off on an adventure."

"Thanks," I said, following her to the doorway, where we stopped just before entering the crush in the hall. "Mrs. B.?"

"Yes?"

"If you see my folks, don't . . . well . . . don't say anything about this, okay?" Her brows drew together, and I added, "They were always a little nervous about me digging into things in Oklahoma, you know?"

She started to cross her arms, then remembered the belly and let her hands drop to her sides. "I'm sure you'll tell them all about it soon, though, right?"

I nodded, but it wasn't true. I'd probably never tell James and Karen I'd been to Oklahoma. "Thanks for helping me, Mrs. B."

"Anytime, kiddo." Leaning over, she gave me a quick hug, and I bounced off the belly again. "Let me know what you find out."

" 'Kay," I said, then we parted ways, Mrs. B. heading for a skirmish in the cafeteria line and me heading out the door and down the stairs.

In my car, I stopped to look at the map before pulling out of the parking lot. My fingertip traced I-75 south. Straight shot south past Tulsa, then beyond into country that held nothing but towns marked with tiny black dots. Flipping through the papers Mrs. B. had given me, I unearthed the information about the Choctaw Nation and studied the list of offices. The main tribal complex was housed in an old Presbyterian college building in Durant, a town just above the Texas border. That was probably as good a place to start as any.

I drove out of the parking lot and headed toward southeastern Oklahoma, an area I'd studied on the map many times in my life, starting with a geography assignment in the second grade, a report about where I was born and what it was like.

"Where was I born?" I'd asked Mama. She was sitting on one of Granny's kitchen chairs on the front porch, waiting for a man to come by—I could tell because she kept looking toward the road. I hated it when she did that.

"Oklahoma. Down in the bottom corner, by Arkansas and Texas," she said absently, peering into the distance. Cutting her gaze my way, she frowned with one side of her mouth and smiled on the other. "Why, Baby?"

I didn't answer her at first, just wrapped my knees against my chest and hugged. I loved it when she called me *Baby*. She didn't do that when she was messed up, so when she called me *Baby*, I knew she was all right.

She shivered even though the day was hot, then wiped beads of sweat from her forehead. I could feel her attention fading off. She'd turned back to the road.

"I gotta do a project for school," I said. "What's it like?"

"What's what like, Baby?" She slumped forward in the chair, then stretched the back of her neck, kneading the muscles with her long, pale fingers, sighing impatiently, her feet fidgeting in and out of her worn leather sandals.

If the man with the long hair didn't show up soon, she'd start to cramp up in her stomach, go in the bathroom and throw up all over the place. She already had the headache and the stiff neck. That was always the first sign she needed him to come with some *stuff*. *Stuff* was like medicine—it took away the things that hurt, Mama said.

"Oklahoma," I pressed, trying to lure her back. "What's it like?" Her brows drew together, her blue eyes again drifting my way. "I gotta know for my report."

"Ohhhh." She nodded, smiling on both sides this time. "Well . . ." She paused to think. "It's a pretty place. The Kiamichi Mountains are there, and lots of rivers and lakes and rocks, kind of like here. You'd like it." She studied me, seeming to think about something, then suddenly she jerked and shivered again, shifted her attention to the road, and absently finished with, "It's pretty there."

In the house, Angelo stirred and started to whimper, dreaming his baby dreams.

Mama slid a hand over my hair, her fingers moist and trembling against my neck. "Go on in there and check on him, okay? Put the thing in his mouth before he wakes Granny."

"Okay." Unfolding my legs, I went inside and slipped Angelo's pacifier into his mouth, holding it in while he rooted around in his bed with his eyes closed. Finally he laid his head down, and I waited to make sure he was asleep. I pulled the sheet back over his milky skin so the mosquitoes wouldn't get him, then went back outside.

Mama was already gone.

I'd wondered about Oklahoma and those Kiamichi Mountains ever since, tried to imagine what happened there, tried to picture the circumstances of my birth.

Granny never talked about it after Mama died. Granny said I was born in Missouri, right in Hindsville, and if anybody asked me, that's what I should say. She said my mama was wrong about Oklahoma, just like she was wrong about everything else.

But deep down, I wanted to be born in the Kiamichi Mountains. A pretty place. A different place. A place that made Mama smile when she thought of it. If there was something good about those mountains, then maybe there was something good about me.

Those long-buried yearnings swirled around me in the car, trailing tangled strings of memory, until I was wrapped so tightly I couldn't breathe. I opened the vent, then turned on the stereo and pushed the CD button. No doubt James had some of his classical guitar tracks in there, since he'd driven my Acura a few times a month to keep it in good condition while I was away.

When the music started, I recognized it immediately. It wasn't my dad's seventies classical guitar jam, but my favorite Blues Traveler CD—the one I'd accidentally left in the stereo the day I boarded the plane to London. James must have kept it for me the whole time I was gone and then made sure it was in the CD player when I came back. It was a little thing, but it meant that he'd never stopped thinking of me while I was away. In a logical sphere of my mind, I knew that already, but in the back of my heart, in the empty space that never quite believed good things could stay good, I felt full again.

A rush of warmth enveloped me, pushing away the sting of memories. I snuggled into the realization that so often pulled me to the surface when I lost myself. If I wasn't worth loving, James and Karen couldn't possibly love me so much.

Tears clouded my eyes as Blues Traveler played on. They were happy tears, the grateful kind that made me feel solid and grounded, complete. Pulling off the highway, I thought about going back home to Kansas City.

What could I possibly hope to find in Oklahoma? What else could I possibly need? I had a family, a home, parents who loved me, college applications to fill out. Yet there was an emptiness swelling inside me, and in the past year it had eclipsed even my music. Where the music had been, there was a thickening mire of old memories, lingering insecurities, and unanswered questions.

Maybe some of the answers lay in Oklahoma.

I didn't know where else to look.

Pulling back onto the highway, I fished my cell phone from my purse and dialed James's number, even though I knew he would probably be flying and wouldn't answer. When his voice mail came on, I turned up Blues Traveler and held the cell phone close to the speaker as the first notes of "The Mountains Win Again" blasted through the car. It was our traveling song, the one we always played on family vacations to the mountains of Colorado and California. Our theme song as a family.

When the intro was over, I put the phone to my ear. "Hey, Dad. I'm headed out of town to visit Barry and I just turned on the radio. Thanks for putting my CD in here. See you later this week and . . ."

I paused, thinking I should say something more, something that encompassed my feelings, that was worthy of the unconditional love the CD represented. I was afraid that if I did, James and Karen would clue in to the fact that I was sounding too emotional for a simple junket to Missouri State. They might start to wonder what was going on, and call Barry.

Finally, I swallowed hard and settled for ending the call with, "Safe trip, okay?" Then I slipped my cell phone back into my purse and focused on the road

CHAPTER 5

In the late afternoon, I pulled off the turnpike into a combination gas station, McDonald's, and convenience store built in the grassy median between the northbound and southbound lanes. Climbing out of the car, I yawned and stretched, bracing my hands on the window frame and taking things in like a dreamer waking from a deep sleep. For hours, my mind had been so far away, I barely remembered the drive.

My stomach rumbled as I surveyed the surrounding folds of tree-clad earth, at first glance similar to the Ozark Mountains back home. But up close, the sights and smells were different. The air was heavy with humidity, scented by thick stands of pine. Back home there would have been mostly hardwoods. At the end of the parking lot a logging truck was pulling in, laden with a towering stack of tree trunks. The hills showed evidence of clear-cutting and reforestation. In the grass next to the convenience store, near a few picnic tables, a patch of small sycamore and redbud trees rustled in the breeze. Nearby, some women in floppy straw hats and gardening gloves were planting petunias in a flower bed beside a sign that read, KIAMICHI GARDEN CLUB WELCOMES YOU!

I didn't feel welcome. I felt out of place, insecure, guilty of something I couldn't put into words. *Calm down,* a voice whispered in my head. *There's nothing to be afraid of here.*

Deep down, I was afraid. I was afraid that this trip would bring my life tumbling down like a house of cards, and when it was all over, I'd be left with nothing.

"You lost?" one of the gardening ladies asked, standing up and stretching her back.

"No, ma'am." The words were thin and uncertain, and the woman cocked her head to one side, taking a step closer, her trowel dangling at her side.

"Everythin' all right?" she asked, and I nodded, clearing my throat.

"Long drive," I told her, and she formed her lips into a silent O. "How far to Durant?"

"Durant's a piece down the road." She mopped her forehead with the back of her arm, her trowel dropping bits of dirt into a nest of teased silver hair. "Which way you comin' from?"

"North." I waved vaguely in the direction of home. "Kansas City."

She clicked her tongue against her teeth sympathetically. "Oh, hon, you should of got off onto sixty-nine at McAlester. It's a lot shorter. But you can go this way. Just keep on the turnpike to Hugo, then take seventy west . . . ummm . . . little over an hour from here, dependin' on exactly where you're going. You headed to college at Durant?"

"No, ma'am." My body, still stiff from the flu, protested at the idea of another hour in the car. "I'm looking for the Choctaw tribal center." Saying it out loud felt like treason. I reminded myself that I was miles from home and nobody here knew me.

"Ohhh!" she exclaimed with a burst of enthusiasm that made me draw back. "Well, now wait a minute. If you're lookin' for the Choctaws, you've got to go back the way you already been. They're all at the tribal council house grounds this weekend. You should of exited back at Daisy, but from here, you just take the Antlers exit and go up two-seventy-one through Finley and Snow to Clayton, then cut off on highway two just a few miles to the council house grounds. It's a pretty drive up through the mountains. My husband and I used to go out that way every spring and fall, just to look at the colors. There's something special about the change in seasons."

"How far is it? To the council house, I mean."

Shifting her hips to one side, she squinted toward the east as if she were getting a visual on my destination. "Not too far. Less than an hour." She glanced over her shoulder at the rest of the gardeners. "Nita, how many miles to the Choctaw Council House grounds?"

Nita, a heavyset woman in a denim broom skirt and tennis shoes, stood up and squinted eastward. "I don't know for sure, Cecil. Never clocked it, but I'd say it's likely forty-five miles or so, probably. Bit of a slow trip this way, up and down the mountains and all. Take ya . . . maybe an hour. It's a pretty drive, though. Not much traffic on that road, ever. More than usual this weekend, of course, what with all the Labor Day festivities." Wandering a few steps closer, she pursed her lips and puffed away a fallen strand of curly, artificially-red hair. "You here for the powwow?"

Cecil slowly rolled her chin sideways. "Nosy."

"I was just makin' conversation."

"We don't have time for conversation. We got eighteen flats of pansies to plant." She waved toward the rest of the women, who were still busily planting flowers.

One of them sat back on her heels and eyed us from beneath her sun hat. "Nineteen, now," she corrected. "They're growing faster than you two are putting 'em in the ground." Around her, the other ladies chortled.

"They're multiplyin' all over the place, you better git over here," a dark-skinned woman added, bracing her hand on the ground and lifting her chin so that her strong Native American features were visible beneath the hat. I had an odd sense of being Native American, too. "It's a full-scale pansy invasion, and we're gettin' trapped in it, 'cause Cecil and Nita cain't stop talkin' to the folks on the sidewalk. First it was that family with the twins, then the lady in the motor home, and now they're harassin' the customers again. We're gonna git swallered up by a full-scale pansy invasion, and Cecil and Nita ain't even gonna notice."

Cecil glanced at Nita, her lips twitching. "Guess we better get back to work."

"Guess so." Both of them burst into laughter.

"Pansy invasion." Nita hip-butted Cecil, knocking her sideways.

Cecil wrapped her arms around her stomach. "Oh-oh-o, stop that. You're givin' me bladder control issues."

"I know a good doctor for that," someone else interjected, and the rest of them laughed harder.

Cecil turned back to me. "You need me to write down those directions, hon?"

I thumbed over my shoulder toward my car. "No. I have a map. Guess I should have gotten it out and looked at it sooner. Thanks, though. Is there a good place to stay over there? Something not too expensive?"

Pinching her bottom lip between her thumb and forefinger, she blew air through her teeth. "There's a couple little hotels in Clayton, but things'll be booked up for the Choctaw Labor Day Festival, especially bein' as it's Thursday night, and the events start tomorrow. There's no hotel right there by the tribal grounds at Tuskahoma."

I blinked, blood draining from my face at the mention of *Tuskahoma*, a word so far back in my memory it was like an archaeological clue buried deep below the surface. My mother had said that word to me once. She told me I was born there. "Oh. . . ."

"Honey." Cecil's eyes met mine, and beside her, Nita's face narrowed with concern. "Is somethin' wrong? You're white as a Sunday shirt. Are you all right?"

"No . . . no, I'm fine," I said, trying to regain my senses. *Tuskahoma.* The word whispered in my mind. "I didn't think about all the hotels being full, that's all. I can stay in the nearest big town if I have to. It's no big deal."

Nita's lips pursed skeptically. "Try the Four Winds, out by Sardis Lake on two-seventy-one north of Clayton. They might have a place, being as it's kind of out of the way." Taking a step closer, she leaned in and lowered her voice, so that only Cecil and I could hear. "Child, are you sure you're not in some kind of trouble?"

"I'm fine. Thanks." With a wave, I headed toward my car, feeling like a teenage runaway.

"Safe trip," she said. At least I thought I heard it, but when I glanced back, she'd already returned to the pansies.

A chill ran through me, and I wrapped my arms around myself, hurried into the McDonald's for a hamburger and a soda, then back to my car. After checking my map, I headed out of the parking lot, past the garden club ladies. Nita and Cecil stopped to watch as I drove away, headed for Tuskahoma, the place where I was born.

The trip was pleasant, scenic, as the garden club ladies had promised. The road wound lazily through thickly wooded hills and rolling valleys of pastureland, where horses and cattle grazed among the bright green lush grass. I thought again about how Mama had described the Kiamichi Mountains. *It's a pretty place,* she'd said. Had she traveled down this very road? How did she feel about this place? What was she thinking? Why had she come? Why did she leave and go back to Granny's without my father?

I wished she were in the car with me—not because I missed her. Mama was a fading memory in my mind, an aging picture, the colors muted. I couldn't remember her voice anymore. When she spoke in my dreams, she sounded like an actress from some recent movie. I didn't yearn for her like I used to, but still I wished she could come back just for five minutes. Just long enough to answer the questions about my father, about where I had come from, and the one question that mattered most of all.

Did she ever love me at all? And if she did, why did she leave me behind?

The questions slid into the shadows of my mind as I pulled into Clayton, passing a gas station, a mini-mart, and a couple of old-fashioned motor court motels. Signs with removable plastic letters proclaimed "No Vacancy" while ironically welcoming visitors to the Choctaw Labor Day celebration and music festival.

I pulled into the parking lot of a mom-and-pop pizza place and sat trying to figure out my next move—search for the Choctaw tribal building or drive toward Sardis Lake to find the Four Winds motel the garden club ladies had mentioned? It was already four forty-five. Even if I could quickly find the Choctaw offices, I had no idea what I was going to do when I got there. I hadn't planned anything beyond arriving and checking into a hotel. What came after that? Did I just walk into some office and say, *I was born here. My CPS forms say my father was part Choctaw. All I know about him is his name, Thomas Clay, and that CPS couldn't find any sign of him when I was adopted into a real family. Can you help me find the truth?*

It was like a line from a bad made-for-TV movie, the sappy, overly dramatic kind in which the woman at the counter would magically recognize the name. She would know all about my father, tell me what a fine person he was, and how it was a shame that he'd died young, the father of a baby girl just a few months old. A daughter he dearly loved and would have raised, if he'd been able to.

I would know then why my mama came back to Granny's house, and why she stayed so messed up afterward. She loved my father the way she loved Angelo's daddy, and she could never quite get over the loss of him. She couldn't stay and raise me, because I looked like him, and it broke her heart.

The woman at the counter would tell me there were relatives, and they'd searched for me all these years. . . .

The story sounded ridiculous, even in my mind, but my hopes clung to it like a leaf hanging on to the last threads of summer, fighting to keep from being swept into a cold wind.

Closing my eyes, I forced the fantasy away. It was too painful to dwell on, because it was so completely unrealistic.

Behind me a car honked, telling me I was blocking the gas pumps. I pulled the car back onto the highway and turned toward Sardis Lake, in search of the Four Winds.

The road continued past a small main street with brownstone storefronts and another hotel with no vacancies. Outside of town, a sign read SARDIS LAKE 5. I punched the odometer button to clock the mileage, a habit that came from James. As soon as James passed a mileage sign on a trip, he automatically rolled the odometer back, so that he could track the distance to the destination. Karen always laughed at him for it, said he should quit worrying about the destination and enjoy the journey.

Now, here I was, fulfilling James's role, and in my mind Karen was saying, *Just enjoy the journey.* Traveling the road out of town, I had an intense sense of missing my parents. I'd never been on a road trip without them in charge. I wanted to be safe in the backseat, with someone else measuring the mileage, and mapping the route, and finding a place to stay when all the hotels were full. In Europe, and even in Ukraine, the schedules, the meals, the lodging had all been handled for me. It was a chance to be grown up, yet not really responsible for myself. Now I was on my own for the first time with no safety net.

I wished I could call my parents for advice, but I knew if I did I'd probably give myself away. When I was settled in at a motel and had my head together a bit, I'd check in at home, tell Karen I'd made it safely to Missouri State and found some friends to room with. They didn't have a phone, so if she needed me, she should call my cell. . . .

I'd be able to pull it off once I was registered for the night and there wasn't so much raw emotion boiling over inside me. I also needed to call Barry and tell him I was over the flu and not to call our house to check on me this weekend. Knowing Barry, he'd pursue it until I had to admit that I'd gone to Oklahoma without him.

Blowing out a long breath, I rolled down the window and let the miles pass, hoping the gently curving road and the breeze filled with the late-summer scents would soothe away the pointless insecurities. I'd spent the first twelve years of my life taking care of myself. I could handle this.

When I'd come nearly eight miles, passed several boat ramp signs and crossed over the lake, yet still hadn't seen any sign of the Four Winds motel, my confidence faded again. Maybe I was on the wrong road. Maybe I should have asked the garden club ladies to write down the directions. They'd said to take 271 toward Sardis Lake, hadn't they?

I crested the hill, and the Four Winds materialized out of the distance ahead, a faded neon sign shaped like a tepee marking its location. The word *Four* blinked rapidly as I pulled into the parking lot. So did the word *Vacancy.* Breathing a sigh of relief, I surveyed the semicircle of tiny log cabins nestled among overhanging pecan trees on the shores of a small pond. The place was old, but not run-down—the kind of spot families might come to for summer vacations, or groups of guys might rent for hunting or fishing trips, a down-home destination that felt welcoming and safe, and friendly. On the pond, a grandfather and a young boy were drifting lazily around in a johnboat, trolling for fish in the late-afternoon shadows. They waved at me as I got out of my car and climbed the steps to the manager's office.

A bell on the door announced my entry as I walked up to the tall wooden counter, where a sign offered everything from bait and fishing tackle to inner tubes and cabin rentals. If I had time later, maybe I'd rent a pole and try the lake. Having grown up on the river, I could spot a good catfish hole from fifty feet away. Grandma Rose had always said that fishing worked out the knots in the soul, especially a troubled soul.

"Be there in a minute," a voice called from the back room.

"No rush," I answered, and occupied myself by looking at the rental spinner rigs while I waited. Cheap rods—James would never have approved—but they would probably do for the pond out back.

A heavyset woman with ridiculously blond hair came around the corner, and I stepped away from the fishing poles.

"Need to rent some equipment?" Looking me up and down in a quick, critical way, she added, "Gotta have a deposit and a copy of your driver's license."

"Well, actually, I was—"

"Can't rent anything without a deposit and a driver's license," she interrupted, leaning to one side, her quick gray eyes peering past me toward the parking lot—to see what I was driving, I assumed.

I wondered if the four-year-old Acura, a hand-me-down from Karen, met with the woman's approval. "Actually, I wanted to rent a room . . . cabin. Whatever. I need a place to stay. Do you have any cabins open?" I motioned toward the neon tepee out front, the one directly behind my respectably nice car. "I saw your vacancy sign."

Swinging her hips to one side, she tossed a frizzy blond lump of hair over her shoulder. "Only got one cabin empty. Just till Saturday mornin', then it's booked. Seventy-five dollars a night. And that's for just you. No parties. You can't have none of your *people* stay over."

"I don't have any people." Suddenly, I was catching her drift, and I didn't like it. I felt like I was eight years old again, the kids at elementary school circling around me, chanting *smelly Delly, smelly Delly* and making Indian whoops because of the way I looked. If the Four Winds hadn't been potentially the last hotel in town, I would have turned around and left. "I'm here by myself."

She reached under the counter and pulled out a receipt book, seeming satisfied that my *people* and I wouldn't tear up her cabin. "All right. One night or two?"

"One for now. Then we'll see." Stepping up to the counter, I fumbled with the zipper on my purse. "Do you take checks?"

"Ukhhh," she huffed, still writing on the pad. "No. Cash in advance, or credit card. Visa. MasterCard. No American Express."

That hardly mattered, since I didn't have a credit card—another one of those grown-up rites of passage that had been on hold these past two years. Thank goodness for the three hundred dollars Karen had left on the counter. "No problem. I'll just pay cash. Then if I stay another night, I'll come back and . . ." My pocket was empty. My throat went dry as I reached into the other one. Nothing. "I don't . . . I had . . ." Frantically, I checked my back pockets, then my purse. Nothing but the change from the twenty-dollar bill I'd broken at the convenience store. Fifteen dollars and twenty-one cents. Where was the three hundred? "I must have dropped . . ." Vaguely, I remembered pulling my keys in and out of my pocket at the store. "Oh, no." I looked up at the woman behind the counter, pleading. "Are you sure you can't take a check? It's from out of state, but it's good, I promise. I have eight thousand dollars in my money market. You can call the bank and check."

Wagging her chin, the clerk threw the hair wad over the opposite shoulder, pointing at the fish-shaped clock on the wall. "It's after five. How'm I gonna call the bank? They're all closed. Anyway, we don't take checks."

"Shoot," I muttered, trying to decide what to do. What next? Go back to town, try every hotel, hope to find a vacancy someplace that would take a check? Try to find somewhere that would cash an out-of-state check after five o'clock?

"Good luck finding someone that'll take an out-of-state check," the clerk barked, probably anticipating my next question. "Too many *people* bouncin' checks around the lake these days. Hotels are all full anyhow."

"I know." I stood staring into my purse, still trying to come up with a plan. Any plan. "Do the grocery stores around here let you write checks for over the amount?" A favorite teenage after-business-hours trick, one I'd learned from Barry. Buy something at the grocery store and write the check for ten or twenty dollars over to get cash back.

She tore the partially used ticket off her receipt book, then wadded it up and took a free throw at the trash can. "Some. Ten bucks, max. Too many . . . *people* around here write bad checks."

I did a quick mental calculation. At ten dollars each, I'd have to visit seven or eight grocery stores, depending on whether I wanted to eat tonight in addition to paying for the room.

The clerk was in a hurry to have me out of her lobby. In the back room, *Inside Edition* was coming on, and she was trying to watch it over her shoulder. "There's a state campground down on Clayton Lake, two-seventy-one, back on the other side of Clayton. Might try there. Better hurry. Later it gets, more the campsites fill up." Tapping the ends of her fingers together, she backed toward the other room, pasting on a customer-friendly smile. "Anything else?"

"No," I said glumly, then walked out the door, got in the car, and headed for the campground. I didn't have a better idea. There were worse things than sleeping in my car overnight. At least a campground would have bathrooms, showers, other people. If I was going to sleep in my car, I didn't want to be in some rest stop or deserted parking lot. Tomorrow I could go by the bank, cash a check, and find someplace to stay—hopefully other than the Four Winds.

Checking the hotel signs wistfully, I drove back through Clayton, then stopped on the edge of town to call home. No telling whether my cell phone would work at the campgrounds. The last thing I wanted was for Karen to get worried because she hadn't heard from me.

I dialed our home number rather than Karen's cell, so that I could leave a message instead of having to talk to her. The fewer questions, the better.

"Hey. It's me. I made it. The girls here don't have a phone, so if you need me, just call my cell. It might not pick up down in some of

the buildings, so don't worry if I don't answer, okay? Love you guys."
My voice cracked at the end, and I stopped to clear my throat before
adding, "Bye."

I hung up, then called and quickly left a message on Barry's voice
mail. "Hey, Bear-bear. Listen, I decided to go ahead and make a road
trip to Oklahoma today. Don't mention it to James and Karen, all
right? I love you for wanting to go with me, but I just . . . needed to
do this myself, all right? I'll call you in a day or two. Bye."

Setting the phone in the passenger seat, I pulled out of the parking lot and followed two-seventy-one back the way I'd come until I
found the campground on a wooded hillside next to a sparkling lake.
The good news was that, according to the sign, overnight camping
was only seven dollars, which I could afford even if they didn't take
checks. The bad news was that, as I drove in, every space in the campground was full, jammed with groups of tents, RVs, pickup trucks
with campers on the back. People sitting at picnic tables and in lawn
chairs around barbecue pits paused to watch me as I idled past, finding one site after another full, full, full.

After circling once, I made the turn and started around again,
hoping I could find someplace to pull in. The sign at the campground
entrance clearly warned that parking was allowed in campsites only.
Even so, as I drifted through a second time, I looked for places to
pull off the side of the road, by the restrooms, behind the Dumpsters,
anywhere. Maybe nobody would notice me. . . .

At the end of the horseshoe, I spied an empty picnic table with a
broken bench, hidden between a huge RV on one side and a campsite
crammed with tents and a couple of small campers on the other. The
parking spot in front of the table was empty, so I pulled in, uttering
a silent prayer before I rolled down the window to talk to the owner
of the RV—a short, bald man in coveralls who was trying to light the
charcoal in a portable grill.

"Is this space empty?" I sounded as desperate as I was.

"Far as I know," he answered with a noncommittal shrug that wasn't exactly unfriendly, just pointedly disinterested. "Those people have the other three spaces on the row. Their danged dogs bark all night and they got their tents further over than they're supposed to." Glancing up from his hibachi, he gave the tents a disdainful glance, then turned his attention back to his charcoal.

"Thanks," I said, and the man only lifted the spatula in a gesture that might or might not have been a wave.

Looking in the back of my car, I assessed the possibilities for the night. I hadn't planned on camping. I had plenty of shampoo and clean clothes, even a swimsuit I'd thought I might use in the hotel pool, but no sleeping bag, no towels for the restroom, and worst of all, no food except for a half cup of melted ice in my McDonald's cup, some cold leftover fries, and in my backpack, a few airplane snacks, a Snickers bar, and a bottle of water that had been there since the plane trip. It would have to do. If I went to town and bought supplies, someone might take my campsite.

I climbed out of the car, walked over to the stone picnic table with my McDonald's cup and bag, sat down with my head in my hands, and tried to think.

What now?

Chapter 6

I sat there for a long time, my mind flipping through random images from the past two years like a PowerPoint presentation gone haywire. *This is Dell's life. Two years of finding herself, and she's still lost.*

I thought of the girls from the Internat mission in Ukraine—lost in every way a child can be lost, abandoned, discarded, faced with a crippling cultural stigma, yet filled with hope, with determination. At fifteen, they were sent out into the world, confronted with all the adult realities of life—getting jobs, finding places to live. Most had no one to turn to once they left the orphanage. In the mission, we tried to arm them with functional knowledge of the English language, in hopes that it would help them find jobs that didn't include prostitution or the drug trade. I read them *Tom Sawyer*—I didn't know how much they understood, but they laughed when one of the Ukrainian helpers translated. They understood Tom's need to find a place to belong, to know he was wanted and loved. Watching them take in the story, I saw myself all those years ago, sitting under the windowsill in Granny's little house, looking up at the stars and wondering if life was really any different anywhere else, or if this was the way it was supposed to be. . . .

Somewhere among the tents in the next campsite, music started playing. The melody wound into my thoughts, a diaphanous ribbon of sound from a simple wooden flute. A missed note testified to the fact that it wasn't a CD, but someone playing live. Right now, the melody was "Bridge over Troubled Water," one of James's favorite songs.

I missed my dad.

In my mind, I could hear him playing one of his guitars on Grandma Rose's porch. Karen came out the door with a plate of brownies and nudged him. "Got any Neil Diamond in there, big guy?" she asked.

James grinned, wiggling an eyebrow flirtatiously. "You'd be surprised what I've got in here."

"All right, you guys, no PDA," I joked, laughing. "Child on board. You two have to act like grown-ups now."

"This is grown-up." James winked at me. "You ought to see us when you're not around."

"Eeewww," I moaned. "Too much information." I'd forgotten how much I loved his lame jokes, how easy and comfortable it was when the three of us were together as a family, how good I felt inside when the two of them teased and flirted in ways they thought I wouldn't notice. I'd always noticed, and it had always fascinated me. Until I'd become part of Grandma Rose's family, I'd never known that men and women could be that way with each other. All I knew of men and women was Mama in the next room arguing with Angelo's daddy, or the man with the long dark hair coming to pick her up, snaking his arm around her neck and holding her in a chokehold when he kissed her, the two of them staggering and laughing, finally falling down in the weeds on the front lawn and doing things I wasn't supposed to see.

If it hadn't been for James and Karen, Aunt Kate and Uncle Ben, that's all I would ever have known. I wondered, sometimes, if I'd ever be able to feel about somebody the way Karen felt about James—open, comfortable, passionate yet at ease. I wondered if I'd ever be anything but guarded and stiff. There was a boy in Ukraine—a student on sabbatical from Berkeley. He had beautiful blue eyes, and an easy smile. He liked to sit outside the door at night and talk about becoming a journalist and traveling the world, doing work that mattered.

He reached across the space between us once, cupped my hand between both of his, and rubbed off the chill of the night. "What about you, Dell? What do you dream about? Where do you go from here?"

I told him I had a boyfriend back home. I wasn't sure why I said it, but he kissed my fingers and let go. I felt like I'd failed at something, but at the same time, I felt relief. He tried another time or two before he went back home to California. He even sent a Valentine's card to my home address, because he'd lost the one for the mission. Karen forwarded it on. She wanted to know if something was up. I told her Tyler was just a friend. She was probably disappointed.

Over the lake, the sky faded from evening blue to the watercolor pink of dusk. I thought about my parents, and what they were probably doing—James landing a plane somewhere and heading for a hotel, Karen finishing a long day of Jumpkids camp at one of the downtown schools. She and her volunteer helpers from Harrington Academy would pack up the instruments, the leftover snack food, the bin of old beach towels we used for yoga mats, and haul everything to the car. A few Jumpkids whose parents were late would be straggling around, waiting for their ride. Karen would put them to work so they wouldn't be worried. . . .

My mind was there for a moment—back home where I should have been, sharing a hug with some kid who needed it, promising we wouldn't leave anyone stranded at the school building, watching some tiny dancer in gym shorts and a T-shirt practice steps in the fading window light. . . .

Next door, the flute was playing "Tiny Dancer" by Elton John, another of James's favorites.

In the motor coach on the other side of me, the retired couple was talking by the kitchen window, snatches of their conversation drifting through the screen.

". . . wish they'd stop with that danged music."

". . . imagine they've started up for the night again."

"We ought to complain to the park ranger. They got too many people over there, anyway."

"What's that girl doing?"

"Dunno. Just sitting there on the picnic table, far as I can see. Came in about an hour or so ago and asked was there anyone in that campsite. I figured she was one of their people, but she hasn't gone over there. Just sat down on the picnic table and hasn't moved since."

". . . sure looks like one of them . . . should of told her that campsite was taken. Now she's probably holding the spot for a whole other batch to come in, and we'll have a racket right outside our window all night. It's like their danged powwow's here, instead of Tuskahoma. Folks ought to have a right to some peace and privacy without a danged powwow right outside their door."

"You'd think that girl'd do something beside just sit there. Suppose there's something wrong with her, or . . ."

". . . oughta go find the park ranger. Bet she didn't pay for a campsite when she came in."

I turned slowly toward the motor home, and the voices hushed. A moment later, the window slid shut, and the rooftop air conditioner kicked on.

Over in the tent village, the flute music had stopped.

In the motor home, Elvis began crooning gospel songs loudly on the stereo. I thought of my dad, who was known for the dubious Elvis impersonation he performed for the Jumpkids occasionally, and more frequently in our living room at home.

Glory, glory haaa-layyy-luuuu-yaahhh,
His truth is ma-a-a-arching ah-ah-ah-ahn. . . .

I could hear James giving the big finish at my graduation party two years ago. The memory made laughter bubble into my throat, and I felt myself smiling at no one in particular, just into the distance toward the lake.

As quickly as it had come, the joy was gone beneath a wave of guilt. Pressing my hands over my ears, I closed my eyes, shut out the Elvis music, and thought instead about the clear, sweet notes of the wooden flute. I could see the melody, eighth notes, quarter notes, key signatures, ritards, rests, and fermatas floating by like sheet music on an invisible page, pulling me deeper and deeper into myself, toward a place I hadn't touched in so long. When I was young, every emotion took me there—happiness, sadness, fear, uncertainty, despair, confusion, hope. Every door led to the room where all the music was.

Lately, I couldn't find the way in.

A dog barked somewhere in the tent camp. The sharp sound pulled me away, sent me speeding like a roller coaster in reverse until I was back in the campground, staring at the lake as dusk fell around me.

The campground had darkened, the insects chirring overhead. My stomach rumbled, and I opened the McDonald's bag with the leftover fries. Not much of a supper, but between that and the airline snacks in my duffel bag, I could make it. Before tomorrow night, I would find somewhere else to stay. If there was any reason to stay. Going to Tuskahoma might just as easily be a dead end.

A cloud of smoke blew over from the tent camp, carrying the scent of charbroiled meat. My mouth started watering. Pulling out a soggy French fry, I started dinner. This wasn't how I'd pictured my first night in the mountains where I was born.

But things could have been worse. Grandma Rose always said, *When you're down, think about how things could be worse.* At least I had a place to stay, something to eat, and I had found my way to the Kiamichi Mountains, my mother's pretty place.

By the time I'd finished my leftover fries, the tent village barbecue was in full swing. The air smelled like one giant, juicy steak. I could hear the low rumble of men talking, the rhythmic sounds of female voices, the high-pitched jingle of children laughing, run-

ning and screaming as they played tag among the tents. Through
the colored nylon, their images created a shadow-puppet play in the
firelight. Occasionally, one of them ventured outside the camp to
hide. As quickly as they came, they squealed and dashed back into the
circle, so that they were little more than darting shadows themselves.
One little girl with long blue-black hair and soft, dark skin put her
finger to her lips when she saw me.

"Sssshhhh," she breathed, and I nodded. Her eyes narrowed as
she crouched behind a tent, hiding as a shadow hunter towered over
her, then passed by behind the thin screen of nylon.

"Autumn, you better not be hidin' outside them tents," a boy's
voice called. Pressing her finger to her lips again, Autumn shook her
head, and for a moment our gazes held in the dim light. A memory
rushed over me, and I was the dark-haired girl, eight years old, crouch-
ing in the dark outside Granny's house, hiding in the shadows beneath the stream of window light, as Uncle Bobby passed overhead.

"Girl, you better not be hidin' out there," he said, his words
slurred and uneven.

I waited until his footsteps moved to the other side of the house,
then I bolted into the night, running down the path by memory, not
stopping until I reached the river, where no one would find me. Off
in the distance, a mountain lion screamed, and even though it was a
bad sound, I didn't head home. I knew I was safer at the river.

Tipping her head to one side, Autumn squinted at me, opening
and closing her fingers in a timid wave.

I waved back, and she smiled, her eyes twinkling in a frame of
long black lashes. I wondered if she was Choctaw. She looked like
she was. Hers was the round, dark face I saw in the mirror when I
was eight or nine years old—the face I hated, because it wasn't like all
the other faces at school in Hindsville. There were no Choctaw faces
there. I didn't fit in, and everyone knew it.

But here, Autumn smiled at me, and I knew it was because I had a Choctaw face. For the first time in my life, I had a sense of belonging *because* of the way I looked, rather than in spite of it.

"Bye," I whispered, and Autumn turned to scamper off.

A smaller boy stopped her before she rounded the tent. "Ummmm," he said, slapping a hand over his mouth, and pointing.

Shrugging, she hissed, "Hush up, Willie." Then she snatched his hand away from his mouth and turned to leave with him in tow.

Pulling against her grip, Willie gaped over his shoulder in my direction. "Who'zat?"

Autumn rolled her eyes like the mother of a badly behaved child, her look saying, *Kids! What are you gonna do with 'em?* "A lady," she whispered, sounding surprisingly parental considering her age. "It isn't nice to stare at people, Willie. Come on." With a yank, she dragged him forward, stumbling.

"Is she one of our aunts?" Willie surveyed my campsite as Autumn pulled him along.

"I don't think so. . . ." Autumn's voice trailed off uncertainly, and they disappeared behind a red tent, their shadows purple against the crimson screen.

"She looks like one of our aunts." Willie's shadow glanced back again.

"Hush. She's just camping there, that's all."

"How come she don't got any camping stuff or a tent?"

"Shut up, all right. You're gonna get us in trouble, stupid."

"Ummm. You said a bad word, I'm gonna tell Dad, and he'll . . ."

The shadows melted away until finally they disappeared. In the tent camp, the noise died down, and the children quieted as supper was served. In the RV on the other side, a rerun of *Gunsmoke* was blaring on the television.

The light from the motor home windows cast a pale glow over my campsite as I walked back to the car and retrieved my backpack.

Setting it on the table, I dug out my leftover airline snacks and laid them out in a line. Two bags of peanuts, a Milky Way bar, a bottle of water, a pack of gum, and a few chocolate-covered almonds I'd bought at the gourmet candy store in the airport.

"Almonds and Milky Way for breakfast," I muttered, tucking them into my backpack. "And peanuts." Adding one bag of peanuts, I opened the other package, then took out the water bottle, which I could refill later at the restroom. Never let it be said that I didn't have survival skills.

A park ranger's truck cruised by, and I stiffened as it stopped at my campsite. Standing up, I prepared to explain that I hadn't yet made it up to the ranger station to pay the camping fee.

The ranger waved, then glanced toward the tent camp and waved again before driving on.

"Doesn't look like much of a supper."

The sound of a man's voice surprised me, and I stumbled backward, turning clumsily to find a stranger standing outside the tent circle. His face was silhouetted by the firelight, so that I couldn't tell much, except that his hair was shoulder-length, kind of blunt cut, and he was tall and slim, dressed in jeans and some sort of button-up shirt that let the light show through.

"I'm sorry?" I muttered, not sure what else to say, or why he was there, or if I should be nervous.

"That isn't much of a supper," he repeated, motioning to my collection of snack food. "We've got plenty next door."

"Oh, no . . . no, thank you," I stammered, blood rushing into my face, because, even in the dark, I could tell by the tilt of his head, the slight rounding of his shoulders, that he felt sorry for me and thought I needed help. In the back of my mind, I could hear Uncle Bobby saying, *We don't need nothin' from nobody. You stay away from people, y'hear?* "I'm fine." I thumbed over my shoulder toward the park office and restrooms up the road. "I . . . ummm . . . ate before

I came, and actually I'd better head up to the ranger station and pay for the campsite, and . . ." *And what? Set up my tent? Pull out my sleeping bag?* I didn't even have a flashlight. If I drove to the office, I might come back and find my campsite gone; then I wouldn't have anyplace to stay.

My visitor came closer, slipping his hands into his pockets, perhaps to let me know he didn't mean any harm. "The campsite's already paid for." He leaned toward me as if we were sharing a secret. "You're welcome to use it, though. It's fine."

"Oh, no, I . . ." Where was I going to go? Now? In the dark? "If it's yours, I can leave. . . ."

"Really. It's fine." He filled the gap in my sentence, and in the dim light I caught a reassuring smile. "Just don't tell anybody you didn't book this one." He chuckled under his breath in a warm, natural way that was nice. "Long story, but when Nana Jo lays out that big seven bucks for a campsite, she wants to be darned sure she gets her money's worth. She won't admit the Reid family's big enough now that we need four campsites, so we secretly book a fourth site for overspill. Saves a lot of family discord that way."

I felt my body sag forward, the tension flowing out of me. "I'll never tell." The words conveyed much more relief than I'd meant them to.

He chuckled again, and I felt more comfortable. If he knew I was desperate, he was kind enough not to point it out.

"So you're having a family reunion over there?" I nodded toward the tents, watching the shadow people move in and out of the firelight near their picnic table.

"Every year." His hand disappeared into the darkness as he combed stray strands of hair away from his face, then tucked his hand back in his pocket. "We always hold a Reid family campout during the Choctaw Labor Day Festival. Usually there are a few more of us. We'll probably get some late arrivals in Camp Reid, yet."

Leaning against the picnic table, I peered past him toward Camp Reid. "I don't know where you're going to put them. Are you sure I'm not in the way here?"

He shook his head. "Not a bit. Just go ahead and make yourselves at home."

"There's just me." *That wasn't such a brilliant thing to let on.*

His shoulders raised and lowered in a silent *go figure*. "Well, anyway, don't feel like you have to just sit here on the picnic table. Feel free to set up your tent, drag out your cooler, whatever. If you need some help, I could probably get a couple of kids on loan for you. Just don't tell them you didn't actually rent the campsite. If it gets back to Nana Jo, it'll be a Reid family meltdown. Not pretty."

I chuckled, fully able to relate to the concept of family meltdown. We'd been known to have a few of those ourselves. "I wouldn't want to be the cause of that. My lips are sealed, I promise."

"Great . . . good." His silhouette hesitated, seeming unsure of what to do next. He glanced over his shoulder toward the camp, and I caught the profile of a strong nose and wide, full lips. "You need any help over here or anything?"

"No. But thanks. I don't have a tent or gear to unload." His head tipped to one side, and I added, "I hadn't planned on camping, but when I got here, all the hotels were full. I didn't know there was a big festival this weekend." For a second, I hoped he would ask why I was here. I wanted to tell someone the whole story, to see how crazy it sounded when I said it out loud. *Of course it'll sound crazy*, another voice whispered inside me. *You've already told him too much.*

He surveyed my car. "Well, then, you're in for a treat. You haven't been anywhere until you've been to the Choctaw Labor Day Festival." The words held a mild note of sarcasm. "Big doin's in Pushmataha County."

A soft breeze wandered through the campground, carrying the scent of barbecue. My stomach gave an embarrassingly loud growl.

"Sure you don't need anything?" he asked, turning an ear toward the tents again, so that I caught another glimpse of his face. He was nice-looking, with Native American features, like an actor in some old western movie. Probably a few years older than me.

"Yeah, I'm sure." Rubbing my palms together, I pressed my hands to my lips and blew hot breath over my fingers. The evening was turning surprisingly cool, and there was a faint scent of rain in the air. It would be a long night in the car. "I'm going to turn in pretty soon, then get up in the morning and"— *and do what?*—"get busy." Next door in the camper, the *Gunsmoke* music rose to a crescendo, complete with blazing guns and whooping Indians. I winced, feeling vaguely embarrassed. "I might wait until things quiet down in Dodge City, first."

He gave the joke an appreciative nod. "Watch out for the neighbors. They don't like Indians."

I drew back, surprised by the frankness of the comment.

"Hey, Jace, you coming?" A woman's voice called from beyond the tents. "K-bobs are on."

"Right there," he answered, then turned to me before he left. "Come on over, if you get bored. Got shrimp on the barbie." His imitation Australian accent made me laugh.

"Thanks. But I don't want to bother you all." Once again, I was tempted. Food and companionship sounded better than sitting by myself in the dark, waiting to see if a storm would blow in. Someone in the camp was clumsily trying to tune a guitar, and even that was alluring. I wanted to go over there and put the instrument in tune the way James had taught me.

Jace turned to leave. "No bother. Come over if you change your mind. There'll probably be something on the grill all night long." He headed back to Camp Reid, his strides long and unhurried.

I watched first his body, then his shadow disappear behind the tents, until once again I was alone. The park ranger cruised by, slow-ing but not stopping as he passed. On the lake, a boat rumbled past, its lamps reflecting red, yellow, and white streaks on the water. Across the park, someone hollered a string of obscenities, then a campsite burst into raucous laughter.

The closing theme to *Gunsmoke* played in the motor home. First the television went off, then the lights, leaving me in darkness.

In Camp Reid, a woman was helping children put on pajamas in the red tent. The silhouette of a toddler jittered up and down with raised arms as the woman slipped a nightgown over her head, then fished her long hair from the neckline, twisted it into a ponytail, and kissed the top of her head.

The flute began playing a soft tribal melody I'd never heard before.

I stood up and walked through the darkness, toward the music.

CHAPTER 7

I stopped at the edge of the fire's glow, stood there in the murky light outside the circle and took in the grouping of people sitting in lawn chairs, atop ice chests, on overturned buckets. An elderly man was perched on what looked like a boat seat, and near the fire kids sat on blankets and sleeping bags, cradling plates of food. The scene was peaceful, the campsite filled with a soft hum of chatter and laughter intermingled with the crackling flames and the sweet, clear notes of the flute.

Searching for the flutist among the crowd, I found myself entranced by the faces. Young faces, old faces. Dark hair, brown eyes, round cheeks and sienna skin, like mine. Not all of them, of course. Some of the young people had blond hair, red hair, fair skin, blue eyes. But in the crowd of perhaps thirty people, most of the faces looked like mine. It was the first time in my life I'd ever been in the majority.

I felt a sense of belonging, as if I'd hungered for this but never realized it. A sharp blade of shame quickly rooted out that idea, cut it away like a rotten spot in an apple. James and Karen didn't look like these people. Aunt Kate, Uncle Ben, the rest of my family didn't look like these people. No one who loved me looked like this. It was wrong to think that the dark hair and brown skin had anything to do with our capacity to be a family. It was like wishing James and Karen weren't my parents.

The conflicting emotions were too hard to understand, so I concentrated on the flute music instead. The flutist was sitting cross-legged on a stone picnic table, bent over his simple wooden flute in the soft white light of a hanging Coleman lantern. He was young, probably still in high school. As he swayed with his instrument, his hair fell around him, long and thick, a gleaming blue-black curtain in the lantern glow. Closing his eyes, he tipped back his head and allowed the melody to sift into the night. A puff of breeze caught his hair, spinning it around him in a web, laying dark ribbons against his white cotton shirt, then whisking them away. He seemed otherworldly, as if he might open his wings to the music and take flight, like an angelic being in some southwestern work of art.

I saw myself at fifteen, in a photograph Karen took. I was standing on a rock ledge above the river, my eyes closed and my hair sailing on the breeze. My violin was tucked beneath my chin, my fingers curled over the bow as I played the bridal march for my cousin Jenilee's wedding in a grassy clearing on the riverbank. The music joined with the earthy sounds of water stroking rocks, leaves whispering, breeze combing the spring grass. Somewhere in the distance, a dove called to its mate. All around me, inside every part of me, there was music, and I was lost in it.

I never saw my cousin walk up the aisle between her brothers, Drew and Nate. I didn't see the audience rise, or Jenilee's grandmother, Sadie, begin to weep in the front row. I was in the music, taking flight, disappearing among the sycamore leaves, echoing from the rock bluffs across the river. When I finally opened my eyes, I realized I'd played too long. Brother Baker and the wedding party were all in place, waiting to get on with the ceremony. Beside Jenilee, Nate was grinning at me. I'd always had a crush on Nate, but nothing ever came of it. He was a college boy, and I was just a kid in high school. Nate always had too many girls around him to be interested in me. But that day at the wedding, he looked at me like he saw something different, something more. When I was into my music, I was larger than myself, transcendent in a way that couldn't be explained in words but only understood by the spirit. I felt as if I could hear God breathing all around me.

Watching the flute player, I relived that feeling, that sense of being filled with spirit, beyond the physical, pure and at peace. These days, my mind was cluttered with so many other things, I was never at peace. Grandma Rose used to say that a cluttered mind was a sign of an untidy life, and she was right. My life was untidy—a closet hastily stacked with unwanted emotions, unexamined memories, unanswered questions. To put things in order, I would have to pull everything out, examine all of it, and decide what was worth keeping. It was easier to leave the mess behind the door.

Autumn noticed me standing at the edge of the firelight as she walked back from the pickup camper that served as a camp kitchen. Tipping her head to one side, she regarded me with her lips pursed, then tossed her hair over the shoulder of her pink Barbie nightgown, lifted a hand with a cookie in it, and waved tentatively.

I waved back, and she popped part of the cookie into her mouth, then circled the fire and climbed into the lap of a man sitting in a lawn chair with his back toward me. After handing him a canned soda, she curled her legs underneath herself, and eyed me over his shoulder.

The flutist played on, though the crowd around the fire hardly seemed to notice. They went about the normal business of finishing supper, throwing away paper plates, opening and closing ice chests.

"Come eat something, Dillon," an elderly woman called to the flute player. "The food's getting cold."

"Be there in a minute, Nana Jo," he answered, then caught his breath and brought the flute to his lips again.

Nana Jo shook her head, the turquoise clip on her gray bun glittering in the light from a string of colored camp lanterns strung between one of the tents and a nearby tree limb. "Dillon Albert Reid, you better listen to your Nana Jo. You're going to starve to death."

A young woman sitting beside Nana Jo shoulder-butted her. "Nana, you think everyone's gonna starve to death."

The family members laughed, and Nana Jo sat back in her chair, crossing her arms so that her thick turquoise-and-silver necklaces jingled against her flowered cotton shirt. "When all of you starve to death, Shasta, don't come crying to me, that's all."

Autumn's brows knotted, and she lifted her head from the man's shoulder. "Nana Jo, if we starve to death, we won't be able to." Everyone chuckled and then Autumn added, "Because we'll be dead. When you're dead, you don't cry anymore."

The crowd grew suddenly somber, and Nana Jo's lips trembled in a pleated line.

Autumn rested her head on the man's shoulder, and he patted her back. "No, you don't, sugar."

Autumn's gaze focused on me again as the circle fell into a meaningful silence. I could only guess at the undercurrent. Her eyes were contemplative and sad, filled with some deep emotion that was mysterious and compelling. I turned to leave, and she cupped her hands around her mouth, whispering something in the man's ear. He stretched, half turned in the chair and looked over his shoulder at me. I recognized his profile. Jace, the man who'd stopped by my camp before.

"Come on in and grab a bite." Standing up with Autumn in his arms, he waved me closer, and everyone turned to look. Across the circle, Dillon stopped playing and watched me with a mixture of curiosity and reserve.

A hot flush prickled into my face. "Oh . . . ummm . . . I was just . . . I was just listening to the music. The flute, I mean. I hadn't heard the song before. It's beautiful. I didn't mean to bother you, though. I'm sorry." Waving vaguely over my shoulder, I backed up a step.

Pushing against the arms of her chair, Nana Jo pulled herself forward in her seat, her eyes like polished black stones, moving down, then up, taking me in. "You're no bother. Come on and join us, Little Sister. Are you camping nearby?" Her words held a strange rhythm, an accent I couldn't place.

"Next door," I answered, glancing at Jace, who gave me a covert wink. He set Autumn on her feet.

Nana Jo grabbed a carved walking stick from the ground beside her, and scooted to the edge of her chair, causing it to rock sideways precariously. I stepped forward with my arms outstretched, to do what, I wasn't sure. I was too far away to catch her if the chair collapsed.

"Careful, Nana Jo." The young woman next to her, Shasta, grabbed the chair arm. "You'll get folded up in this thing again."

Nana Jo turned a shoulder to the comment, then quickly offered me Jace's empty seat, on the other side of hers. "Come sit," she said. It was more of a command than a request. Slipping through the crowd of onlookers, I slid into the lawn chair, tucking my hands between my legs, and thinking, *Now what?*

Shasta leaned forward and shrugged at me apologetically, then readjusted the blanket wrapped around her shoulders.

Nana Jo gave a royal wave toward the flute player, who'd abandoned the empty picnic table and headed for the food with his flute tucked carelessly in his back pocket. "Play something for us, Dillon."

Dillon, his hand suspended above a plate of hamburgers, quirked a brow.

"Oh, no, it's all right," I said quickly, thinking that just a minute ago Nana Jo had been worried that Dillon would starve to death. "I don't want to interrupt anyone's dinner." The scent of charcoal-grilled meat wafted by, and my stomach gurgled and rumbled.

Smoothing her hands over her long broomstick skirt, Nana Jo relaxed in her chair, bracing an elbow on the armrest and assessing me with a narrow eye. I could imagine what she was thinking. "Have you had supper?" she asked.

I was embarrassed to admit that I hadn't.

"I told her to come over when she got hungry," Jace interjected, then turned from Nana Jo to me. "So I guess you got hungry?" In the firelight, his eyes were large and dark, his features distinctly Native American, though, unlike the flute player, he had his hair cut in an ordinary, if slightly long, style.

My stomach rumbled again. "Yeah, I guess I am."

Nana Jo went into action. She grabbed her walking stick again and rose to her feet, her joints crackling like logs in the fire. She was only slightly taller than she had been in the lawn chair. Her long green broom skirt whisked the tops of well-worn leather sandals as she headed toward the kitchen area, her steps slow, her toes twisted and curled like the roots of a very old tree.

Nana Jo was a small woman, but she commanded respect. At the food table, Dillon grabbed a handful of chips and backed out of the way. A thirty-something woman in tight denim shorts and a camisole top stood up from one of the chairs and came over to take charge. "I'll get it, Nana Jo." Laying her hand on Nana Jo's arm, she patted gently. "You relax. You're not supposed to be up and down so much." There was a lilt in her voice that mirrored Nana Jo's, making the words flow together like lines of poetry. "Come, sit back down." Leading Nana Jo toward the chair, she cut a feline glance my way, her exotic, upward-tilted eyes starting at my tennis shoes and raking upward as she tossed a length of silky black hair over her shoulder. "What would you like, sweetie?" The sentence held an intonation that might have been used on a six-year-old who was just a little too much trouble. "You look hungry." The words ended in an unspoken, *Poor little thing.*

"I've got it, Lana." Jace started toward the kitchen as the woman in the Daisy Duke shorts put Nana Jo back in her chair.

"No, it's fine." I stood up, mortified by all the fuss, the fact that everyone was looking at me, and the fact that I was receiving less-than-welcome vibes from the cat lady, Lana. "I'll get—"

"I can do it." Sidestepping Jace, Autumn slid her hand into mine. "I found her first. She's *my* friend."

"I found her, too," Willie protested, suddenly switching his interest from Matchbox cars on a blanket to me. "She was right over there." Pointing to my campsite, he trotted around the fire and took my other hand.

"Hush up, Willie," Autumn scolded.

"Well . . . I . . . did." Willie's head wagged back and forth with each word, his chin jutting out like he was facing off a school-yard bully. "When we was out behind the tents."

Jace took a step closer. "You two aren't supposed to be out behind the tents."

Autumn threw her free hand up, then let it fall to her thigh with a slap. "Geez, Willie. You stupid."

Catching her eyes, Jace put a finger to her lips. "Watch your language, young lady."

"Yes, sir," she muttered, ducking her head. "Sorry, Daddy."

Resting a hand on her hair, he tipped her face back so that he was looking at her very directly. "No going outside the tents. You know better."

"Okay," she replied, fidgeting, obviously ready to be removed from attention central. "Can I go and help the lady get some food now?"

"She probably has a name."

"Dell," I answered, greeting the crowd with a self-conscious wave. "Dell Sommerfield."

Nana Jo squinted. "Sommerfield . . . Sommerfield . . . I don't believe I know that name. Are you from around here?"

I shook my head. "Kansas City." *You shouldn't have told them*

that. What if they call James and Karen? The minute the thought ran
through my head, I realized how idiotic it was. "I was . . ." Was what?
On a mission to trace the long-lost family roots of a man who allowed his name to be put on my birth certificate, then disappeared,
leaving me with only Thomas Clay and a potential Choctaw heritage?
"I was . . . traveling, but all the hotels are full, so I ended up here. I
have some genealogical research to do at the Choctaw Nation offices." That sounded plausible, reasonable. No doubt people came
here to research family roots all the time.

Nana Jo's lips parted in a wise expression. "Ah, I see. You'll find
that most of the genealogical information is at the tribal complex in
Durant. Those offices will be closed until after Labor Day weekend,
but while you are here, you shouldn't miss the Labor Day celebration
and the museum at the Choctaw Capitol Building in Tuskahoma, if
you've never seen it. On the second floor, there is a copy of the original muster rolls listing Choctaw families in Indian Territory as early
as 1832. You may see the names of some of your ancestors there. It's
important that we know where we've come from. *Chahta imanumpa
ish anumpola hinla ho?*"

I stood staring at her, wondering if my ears had gone haywire, or
if she'd just asked me a question in some other language. Around the
fire, everyone watched me expectantly. "Excuse me?"

Willie let go of my hand, bored with the conversation and ready
to return to his Matchbox cars. Autumn squeezed my fingers. "She's
asking if you speak Choctaw."

"Oh," I said, feeling out of body. "No, I don't."

Nana Jo grunted, and Autumn tugged my hand, pulling me toward the camp kitchen. "Nana Jo thinks all the young people in the
tribe ought to know how to speak Choctaw. She doesn't like it if they
don't."

"Oh," I replied, sensing that I'd failed some test for which I could
not possibly have prepared. I wondered if my father spoke Choctaw—

if he talked to my mother in that odd, rhythmic language. I would probably never know for sure, but it was a nice thing to imagine—my father, my mother, gathered with a family like this one, spending a peaceful night around a campfire. Unlikely, but nice.

"The food's over here," Autumn said as she handed me a plate and began offering everything from steak kabobs to hamburgers, a dozen different kinds of chips, homemade salsa and several varieties of desserts.

"Food's part of our celebration." Autumn's explanation was carefully worded, as if she were taking her position as official Reid family tour guide very seriously. "It's a tradition."

Jace came to check on us after I'd filled my plate. "Now you know why we have to drag people over from other campsites," he joked. "Where the Reids gather, there's guaranteed to be three times too much food. They cook for a week ahead of time, then empty out every fruit stand and Wal-Mart bakery on the way to the campground. Most of us live within an hour or two of here, but every year it looks like we're moving in for the duration."

"I can see that," I agreed, laughing as I finished arranging my plate and walked back to my seat. Autumn held my soda while I settled in, then handed it to me and went to sit on the blanket beside Willie.

Lana passed by with a trash bag, picking up empty soda cans. She stopped next to Autumn and Willie. "You two should be in bed. Come on, you can brush your teeth in my camper, and then your dad can tuck you in. If ya'll are tired of that old tent, I might even make you up a bed in the camper tonight." When the kids didn't move, she fluttered her long, slim fingers in their direction. "Come on. Bedtime."

"A-a-awww," Willie groaned, "Aunt Lana, it's not late."

Swiveling toward her father, Autumn made a pouty face. "Da-a-aaad."

Jace turned over a five-gallon bucket and perched in the space between Nana Jo and me. "They're all right. I told them they could stay up late tonight." Lana frowned over her shoulder, her gaze sweeping past me to Jace, and he added, "Thanks, Lana."

Shrugging, she continued on around the circle, picking up cans and used paper plates. I was glad when she disappeared into the shadows behind the kitchen area. Everyone else might have been jovial and welcoming, but Aunt Lana was clearly ready to wrap up the evening festivities and get rid of me.

The fireside conversation fell into an easy rhythm again, and I was relieved to no longer be the focus of attention. Taking my time with my hamburger and chips, I listened absently to the conversations— Nana Jo and Shasta comparing lawn chairs and deciding which type was best; a heavyset young girl, probably about my age, talking about playing on the college softball team somewhere in Texas; a middle-aged woman giving child-rearing advice to her daughter; Jace and another man discussing the Little-League T-ball season; Autumn and Willie creating a pretend city on their blanket, and enjoying staying up late. The sounds made me think of home, of weekends on the farm when all of us were together. Except for the rhythmic lilt in some of the voices, this could have been one of our gatherings, filled with people sharing food and common experience, the universal sounds of family.

On the empty picnic table, Dillon started playing his flute again, and I lost track of the conversation. I wondered what the song was called, then finally even that question left my thoughts as I sailed away on the music. When I came back, the leftover food on my plate was cold and Dillon had set the flute aside. He was trying to tune his guitar by ear, and not having much luck at it. I stood up, and took my plate to the trash, then waited there watching him. He was tuning the A string on the wrong fret.

"Up a fret," I said, then stepped closer and touched the string in the right place. "Right here. Tune it to the E string on the fifth fret."

Cocking his head to one side, he gave my advice an appraising look, then finally moved his finger up a fret and tried to tune the string. "I still can't hear it," he complained, setting the guitar aside and reaching for his flute again. "I've got an electronic tuner at home."

"Electronic tuners will ruin you." Those were James's words. My dad firmly believed in tuning his guitars by hand. He said it kept his ear sharp. Karen complained that he spent more time tuning than playing music.

Tossing his long hair over his shoulder, Dillon arranged his fingers on the flute, then shrugged toward the guitar. "D'you play?"

"Used to." I couldn't remember the last time I'd picked up a guitar. At some point during my years at Harrington Academy, I'd become so intent on piano, violin, and voice that everything else had gone by the wayside. Between school and private lessons, competitions and performances, it had seemed as if there was never time to sit around learning guitar licks from James. Now I wished I'd spent more time on the back porch, watching my dad play.

Dillon grabbed the neck of the guitar and handed it to me, raising an eyebrow. "Think you can tune it?"

"Maybe. I'll give it a try."

"Go for it." Bracing his elbows on the ragged knees of his jeans, he watched as I climbed onto the table and took the guitar.

It felt strange in my hands, heavy and foreign, a cheap beginner instrument with the action too high and the strings too stiff. Nothing like James's collection of classic guitars, which played silky smooth and practically fell into tune on their own. "Where did you get this thing?" I asked, laughing when I tightened the string and it fell out of tune again.

"In Mexico on a youth trip. Twenty bucks." Brushing a moth off his jeans, where a knobby knee showed through the tear, he added, "Why?"

With my cheek on the guitar, I listened to the strings, picking E and A over and over until finally they were in tune and I could move on to D. "Well, it's not your ear. This thing's just hard to tune." I stopped to listen again. "The action is really high, and the strings are shot. You might try a new set of strings. That may improve the action some and then it'll stay in tune a little better."

"Cool." Dillon seemed properly impressed with my long-lost guitar tuning skills. "There's a Wal-Mart in Hugo. I can pick some up tomorrow."

Pausing over the D string, I frowned at him. "Go to a music shop. Real guitar players wouldn't be caught dead buying strings in a place that sells milk and bread."

"Cool." He held up his palm like a notepad, then made an invisible scribble with the end of his finger. "No Wal-Mart strings."

"Right. Wal-Mart for milk and bread. Guitar shop for strings." That was another direct quote from James. Once when we were down in Hindsville, he drove all the way to a guitar shop in Springfield because he wouldn't buy discount store strings. *Some things in life you just can't skimp on,* he'd said. Karen thought he was nuts.

"So play something," Dillon urged when I strummed all the strings together. It still wasn't perfect, but about as good as could be expected. "See if it sounds all right."

"I'm not sure I remember anything."

"You remembered how to tune it."

"That's the easy part," I said, then bent over the instrument and closed my eyes, wishing music would come the way it used to. These days, I couldn't seem to play from the inside out.

I heard Dillon take a breath and push air into the flute. He was playing "Tears in Heaven," an old Eric Clapton song that still came on the music video channel from time to time, a tribute to Clapton's son, who died in an accident when he was just a preschooler. It always made me think of my mama and Grandma Rose. When

I was younger, I'd wondered if my mama, with all the things she'd done wrong, all the ways she'd failed Angelo and me, went to heaven. Brother Baker at Grandma Rose's church said that God's grace was sufficient for any sin, if only we would ask for it. I'd always wanted to know for sure: Before my mother died, did she ask?

As "Tears in Heaven" drifted into the night, the question whispered through my soul again.

Is my mama in heaven?

The thought slipped away, and I felt the music. It swelled in every part of me as I curled my body over the guitar and began to play.

Chapter 8

I drifted away on the music, random images from my life floating by in a swirl of color, and light, and emotion—James playing "Tears in Heaven" at Grandma Rose's funeral, when I was just ten. The same tune coming on the old clock radio at my real granny's house later that night when I felt alone and lost. The sound was crackly and rough, but it wrapped around me like a blanket. I knew Grandma Rose was right there with me, only I couldn't see her because she was on heaven's side of the door and I was on mine. Later, when James taught me to play that song on the guitar, I told him about Grandma Rose being just on the other side of the door. He patted my hand and said that was a good way to look at it. . . .

When I played the last chord, Dillon tipped his head back and coaxed a long, wavering note from the flute. As it trailed away into silence, I looked around the circle. The voices had gone quiet, and everyone was watching us. Jace rested his chin on Autumn's head, and she looped her arms drowsily around his shoulders. His gaze met mine, his face filled with emotions. I wondered what he was thinking.

Around us, everything was impossibly quiet. Finally Nana Jo raised her hands and clapped, breaking the silence. "Wonderful!" Her voice crackled like the clock radio at Granny's house. "Just beautiful! Play something else for us. Something happy."

Dillon rolled his eyes. Wetting his lips, he raised the flute again and rattled off the beginning of "Yankee Doodle," with a distinct lack of enthusiasm.

Nana Jo clapped again. "Oh, that's a good one. It's one of my favorites. Play that one." She turned to me. "Do you know it?"

"I think I can follow along."

"All right, then." Moving her hands like a drum major, Nana Jo struck up the band.

With an exaggerated sigh, Dillon raised his flute and began to play. I settled my fingers on the guitar, and we skipped off on a happier note.

Tapping both feet on the ground, Nana Jo clapped in rhythm, the loose sleeves of her shirt billowing in the breeze. "And e-e-everybody sing," she commanded, as we finished the first verse and started over again. "Yankee Doodle went to town, a-riding on a pony . . ."

"That's on my movie!" Willie cheered, then stood up and started dancing on his blanket as Nana Jo coerced the others into singing along. Autumn climbed down from Jace's lap and joined in the dance, hopping on one foot and twirling in the firelight, her short, sturdy legs silhouetted against the pink nightgown.

Beside me, Dillon paused to catch his breath between verses, muttering, "I hope there's nobody I know here."

I threw my head back and started singing at the top of my lungs. I felt free, light, filled with music. Here in the moonlight, among this odd family band, my normal existence seemed light-years away.

When we'd finished "Yankee Doodle," someone called out, "Play 'You Are My Sunshine,'" so we did. We stumbled through that and a dozen other campfire songs. The notes were less than perfect, and the old guitar sounded bad, but the lack of quality was eclipsed by the enthusiasm of the crowd. As we played, people from neighboring campsites wandered over, and Nana Jo invited them in. Among the visitors were four members of a family gospel band, who were to perform tomorrow at the Labor Day festival. They joined in with a Texas fiddle, a harmonica, a mandolin, and another guitar, and we filled the night with music.

We'd played every song we could think of, and most of the campground was gathered at the Reids' fireside when the park ranger came by and apologetically told us we'd have to quiet down, because the people in the motor home were complaining about the noise. "If it was just up to us, it'd be fine," he said. "But we have to try to keep everybody happy." He slanted a glance toward the RV, where, in the dim glow of a nightlight, faces hovered near the window.

Nana Jo checked her watch. "Why, it's not even ten thirty yet. I don't see . . ." Beside her, Uncle Rube, the largest member of the Reid clan, stood up, crossing his thick arms over his ample stomach and towering above the park ranger.

Jace preempted whatever Uncle Rube was about to say. "We'll tone it down." He shook the park ranger's hand pleasantly. "Sorry you had to come over here. It's probably time the kids headed for bed, anyway."

Lana rose from her chair, the one I'd vacated beside Jace and Nana Jo, and started toward Jace's kids, clapping her hands rapidly. "Come on, you two. Not that it hasn't been *fun* having *visitors* in camp." She spat out *fun* and *visitors* like they were dirty words, flashing a plastic smile toward our impromptu band. The message was clear. We'd worn out our welcome. "But it's way past bedtime. Come on in the camper and wash up."

Autumn and Willie groaned, and one of their cousins scowled resentfully at Lana, then tugged his mother's T-shirt. "Mom, do we have to go to bed, too?"

The park ranger chuckled. "Hate to be the bearer of bad news." Tipping his hat, he turned to leave. "Y'all have a good night."

I handed Dillon his guitar as the campfire gathering began to break up.

The members of the bluegrass band packed their instruments and said good night. "It was a pleasure." The fiddle player pointed at me as he turned away. "You're good, young lady. You put this old fiddler to shame. You performing at the festival tomorrow?"

"No, I'm just here visiting." In spite of the bum's rush from Lana,

I wished the evening didn't have to end. I couldn't remember the last time I'd experienced such complete joy while playing music. Tonight it was effortless, as natural as breathing.

"Everybody come again in the morning! We'll have breakfast!" Nana Jo called out.

Lana glanced over her shoulder, widening her eyes. "Nana Jo," she protested, pausing in her quest to hustle Willie and Autumn off to her camper, "we've got enough people to cook for already."

Nana Jo stabbed her walking cane into the ground, and pulled herself to her feet. "You can never have too many mouths to feed." With a definitive nod, she hobbled off toward the camp kitchen to check supplies. "Dillon, John, you two boys come get this trash and take it up to the Dumpster, y'hear?"

Dillon sulked off to do his grandmother's bidding.

In the camp kitchen, Nana Jo started giving orders, directing the storage of the food and deciding what could be saved for the next night's supper.

"Lord," Shasta muttered to the woman beside her, who, judging from the resemblance, might have been her mother. "Next thing, she'll invite the whole campground to supper." Standing up, Shasta unwrapped herself from her blanket, and I realized she was pregnant. I caught myself staring, thinking that she couldn't be much older than me.

The woman next to her nodded ruefully. "By the time she spends a few hours at the festival tomorrow, she'll have found fifty-seven lost relatives and invited everyone who stops by the booth to look at her quilts. Nana Jo loves a party."

Rubbing the pads of her fingers across her cheeks, Shasta cupped her face in her hands. "We'd better have someone make a run to Wal-Mart."

The older woman hugged her around the shoulders, then headed off to the camp kitchen to help. Shasta stood gazing into the fire, her eyes reflecting the dancing flames. Her lips were full and wide, her face slightly heart-shaped with high cheekbones. She had beautiful skin, a rich cinnamon color that was smooth and slightly iridescent in the amber light. I'd always hated that skin color on me, but on Shasta, it seemed glorious. She was beautiful, her features exotic and earthy. It was hard to imagine anyone at school ever making fun of her because of the way she looked.

A toddler bolted from one of the nearby tents and wrapped himself around her legs, whining about going to bed. She picked him up and braced him on the side of her swollen stomach. He laid his head on her shoulder as she smoothed a hand over his hair.

"Where's Daddy, Benjamin?" she asked, and he pointed toward one of the tents. "Did he fall asleep?"

Benjamin nodded.

"And you came back out here?"

"Uh-huh. I not tire-red, Mommy."

Groaning, Shasta laid her head wearily atop his. "Oh, Benji, I am."

"I not." Benji yawned.

Closing her eyes, Shasta rocked back and forth with him, as if she might fall asleep on her feet.

I stood watching her, contemplating the way her long hair fell around Benjamin like a blanket, the way her beaded earrings swayed against her cheek as her son snuggled contentedly under her chin. Together they looked like an artist's rendering, a Native American Madonna and child—young, innocent, weary, yet at peace. I tried to imagine myself in her place. Shasta couldn't have been much over twenty, yet she was married, with a toddler in her arms and a baby coming. The rest of her life was planned, decided in some sense that mine was not. How would that feel?

I was envious in a way I couldn't explain.

If Shasta could construct a future for herself, if Barry could, if everyone else I knew could move on into adulthood, why couldn't I? What was wrong with me? Was I so damaged that I would never be normal? Uncle Bobby had told me over and over that I was making a fool of myself, hanging around Grandma Rose's family, pretending I could be like them—everyone could see that I was a screwup, just like my mama, and I always would be.

The memory opened up an old wound, so I pushed it back into the closet and shut the door. Nearby, an elderly man and Uncle Rube were engrossed in a small fold-up tackle box, making plans to go fishing in the morning. Dillon had sneaked away from trash duty to join their conversation as they laughed and joked about past Reid family fishing expeditions.

"We're headed up to the bathroom." Shasta touched my arm as she passed by, carrying her son. "Want to walk with us? Nana Jo doesn't let any of us go up there alone. We've camped here every year for, like, forever, and she's still paranoid about us going to the restroom building by ourselves."

I nodded. Come to think of it, walking up to the bathrooms by myself, and without a flashlight, wasn't the best idea. "Sure. Let me grab my duffel bag, and I'll catch up." I hurried to my campsite and took a few unneeded items out of my bag to lighten the load, then tossed the strap over my shoulder and jogged up the road after Shasta and the others. Ahead of us, one of Shasta's aunts was giving the kids the usual admonishment about going into public restrooms alone. The speech reminded me of Karen's. She always followed her parental warnings with a few carefully edited snippets from news stories about young women in perilous situations, then finished by smoothing a hand over my hair and saying she didn't want to scare me, she just wanted me to be careful.

I know, Mom, I'd say, but in reality I was aware that she was only doing what mothers were supposed to do. The knowledge was always bittersweet because my real mother and my granny hadn't protected me like that. The older I became, the more I knew how close I'd come to disaster. If my granny hadn't died when she did, if Karen and James hadn't fought for foster custody of me, I probably would have been given to Uncle Bobby, who was messed up like my mama had always been, only worse. He'd started hanging around me before Granny died—taking me places in his truck and telling me to sit in the middle next to him, accidentally walking in the bathroom door when I was getting dressed, watching me when he thought I wasn't looking, asking me to rub the knots out of his shoulders when he sat on the sofa. He'd smooth his hands up and down my arms, brush against my chest.

He was nice to me sometimes, buying me things he said a pretty little lady ought to have. He told me that for a kid who was born butt-ugly, I was sure coming up to be fine. Now that I was grown up and knew what that interest meant, I realized those covert touches weren't accidental. He was just trying things out, seeing how I'd react, finding out whether I'd tell Granny. Now I knew that those touches, that attention, was headed someplace sinister and dark, but back then I took it for love. I fell into the trap bit by bit, and if James and Karen hadn't taken me out of that house when they did, things would have gone on until the doors slammed shut for good. Uncle Bobby said he loved me, and, for all I knew, that was the way love was supposed to be. I would have done almost anything to get someone to love me.

I'd never told anyone the truth about Uncle Bobby. Even now, I was ashamed that, at twelve years old, I didn't have more sense. I should have known that someone who's never been nice to you doesn't turn nice overnight without a reason.

"Did you have enough to eat at supper?" Shasta interrupted my thoughts as she fell into step with me, leading Benjamin by the hand.

"I did. Thanks." I blushed, thinking of myself starting the evening with airplane peanuts and cold McDonald's fries. I must have looked like an idiot, sitting over there on the picnic table with no tent and no supplies. No wonder the Reids felt sorry for me. "I wasn't planning on camping, so I didn't have any food along. Every hotel in town is full, and I just ended up here."

Shasta's mouth formed a silent O.

"You poor thing." Gwendolyn, the woman I'd surmised was Shasta's mother, gave me an empathetic look.

I waved away her sympathy. "No. It's okay, really. I'm glad I ended up here. Tonight was fun."

Shasta laughed under her breath. "Girl, you're starved for entertainment."

Gwendolyn swatted her arm. "Behave yourself, Shasta Marie." Leaning closer to me, she shielded her mouth with one hand. "Excuse her. She's snippy lately. Too many pregnancies in too short a time."

"Mother!" Shasta gasped, glaring in a pointed way that told me I'd stepped into an ongoing argument. "Geez."

"Leave the girl alone, Gwendolyn," one of the women ahead of us reprimanded. "You had two kids by the time you were twenty-one."

"And it didn't do me any good," Shasta's mother shot back. "Old, fat, and a grandmother at forty."

"Forty-one," a heavyset woman corrected. "I know. I was there when you were born."

"Hush up, Raylene."

Someone behind us snickered, then another woman followed suit, and giggles rippled through the group. Gwendolyn cleared her throat, trying to maintain a straight face, then finally let out a snort of laughter, clamped her hand over her nose, and continued to half snort, half laugh uncontrollably behind her fingers.

"Tha's how da piggies go," Shasta's little boy reported, pulling away from Shasta and reaching for his grandmother's hand. "Oink, g-oink, g-oink."

The group descended into gales of merriment, tossing around

insults about the snort-laugh and its genetic origins in the Reid family. Shaking her head, Shasta inched to the back as Benjamin and his grandmother carried on.

"You must think we're nuts," she said as we fell behind the others.

"Not a bit. It sounds just like my family." I was thinking of the raucous gal-pal conversations that often went on when Karen, Aunt Kate, Jenilee, and Aunt Jeane got together. The men sometimes surrendered the house and didn't come back for hours. James said the estrogen level was too high. "Your Nana Jo reminds me of my grandma Rose."

Shasta gave me a kindred look. "I'm glad you're used to it. I thought maybe Nana Jo embarrassed you, dragging you in and force-feeding you like that. She had bone cancer about a year ago and since then, she pretty much can say whatever's on her mind and do whatever she wants. She can get away with anything, and she knows it. If we fuss at her, she goes to bed for a week and acts like she's having a relapse until we feel guilty."

"That sounds like my grandma Rose, too."

Shasta chuckled. "Your grandma Rose didn't happen to be Choctaw, did she, because I think stubbornness is in the genes."

"No," I said, angling a glance around Shasta as we reached the restroom building. The doorway was filled with laughing, jostling Reids of all sizes. "My father was," I added, uncertain what else to say. It was always hard to know when to tell people I was adopted. "Choctaw, I mean."

"How much?" Shasta leaned against the restroom wall, waiting for the crowd in the doorway to thin out.

"How much what?" Sliding my duffel bag off my shoulder, I let it drop to the cement.

"Percentage, I mean. How much? Most people in the tribe know what percentage Choctaw they are." She wrapped her arms around her distended stomach and let her head fall back.

"Really?" The question had never occurred to me. In my mind, I was always Choctaw enough that I looked it, which, for Granny and Uncle Bobby, was too much.

Shasta's lips quirked on one side. "Sure. Don't you have a CDIB card?"

"A what?"

"CDIB card." Her brows rose, then knotted in the center. "Certificate of Degree of Indian Blood. Your card. You have to have one to get your tribal membership, and you need that to, like, get anything."

"Get anything?" We'd entered a completely foreign world, filled with terminology I knew nothing about.

Shasta lifted her hands like it was elementary. "Well, yeah, you know, like meat, cheese, groceries and stuff like that, Indian doctor, Indian dentist. I had Benjamin at the Indian hospital, and it didn't cost us anything—that kind of stuff, you know? You have to have your CDIB to get it, and—" Snapping her lips shut abruptly, she drew back. "You don't have a clue what I'm talking about, do you?"

"None," I admitted. "I'm not from here. I was born in Tuskahoma, but I've never lived here."

Finger-combing her hair into a ponytail, she absently braided it on one side. The strands glowed blue-black in the dim light as they slid over her fingers. "Well, do you know your dad's CDIB number? If you do, you could take in your birth certificate and get your CDIB, I think."

The restroom line shifted so that we could have gone inside, but Shasta didn't move, and neither did I. I suspected she was as curious about me as I was about CDIB cards and membership numbers. "I don't know if he had one. How would I find out?"

"Oh, gosh, my brother's the one you need to talk to about that. Jace teaches at one of the Choctaw schools, and he always has his history students researching their family roots and stuff. He could probably tell you a lot about it. With kids and everything, I don't have time for all that junk." She glanced into the restroom, checking for her son, as if it had suddenly occurred to her to wonder where he was. After combing out the braid, she anchored her hands under her stomach again. "How come you don't just ask your family? If you want to know about the Indian stuff, I mean."

I shifted away uncomfortably. We'd reached the point in the discussion at which I had to either bow out or reveal my strange and murky family history. A handful of Reids came out the restroom door, and I considered excusing myself from the conversation. It was so much easier than taking a chance on other people's reactions.

Gwendolyn exited the restroom carrying Benjamin, who was sagging on her shoulder. "I think we've got a tired little guy here."

"Awww." Shasta ruffled his hair and kissed his forehead. "Will you take him down with you? We'll be back to camp in a minute."

Gwendolyn frowned. "Don't be too long."

"I won't." Shasta pushed off the restroom wall. "I'm going to wash my face and wait for Dell, so she doesn't have to walk back by herself. I'll be there in a minute."

"All right." Gwendolyn sighed, then headed down the hill after the other women.

When Gwendolyn was a safe distance away, Shasta resumed her position on the wall, propping one foot against the brick and glaring after her mother. "I swear. She drives me nuts sometimes. She's so worried that just because I didn't go right to college after high school and get a degree and *then* get married and *then* have kids, I'm going to be, like, some teenage mother and make her raise my kids. I don't want her to raise my kids. I want to raise my own kids."

"That must be hard." I didn't know what else to say.

Shasta returned to the subject at hand. "So why don't you just ask your family about roll numbers? I mean, it'd be a lot easier. Getting one from scratch can take months, sometimes longer, and there's all kinds of documentation you have to find and stuff. You have to trace your family history all the way back to somebody on the original Dawes Commission Rolls, and that can be tough to do. Even when you know your family's Choctaw, sometimes it's hard to prove it." She watched me curiously.

Taking a deep breath, I stepped over the invisible line into the truth. "I'm adopted." I watched for her reaction. "I never knew my father. All I've ever really known is what was on my CPS paperwork— his name was Thomas Clay and he was at least part Choctaw. My mother told me once that I was born in Tuskahoma."

"Oh." Her interest perked at the high drama. "So you're here, like, looking for information about your birth family and stuff?"

"Kind of," I admitted. "It's a long story. I know you need to get back to camp."

"No, really, I want to hear." She glanced toward the road, where her mother and her son were disappearing beyond the glow of the streetlight with the other women. "Tell you what. Let's finish up here, and then we can walk back together. We can sit up for a little while, and then I'll find you a blanket and a pillow, and whatever else you need for overnight. I had Cody put some extra stuff in our car, just in case anybody wanted it. Some of the family camps over at the Choctaw capitol grounds in Tuskahoma, and everyone's back and forth. There's never any telling who might end up spending the night here."

I had the overwhelming urge to reach out and grab her in a bear hug. A blanket and pillow sounded wonderful right now. "Thanks," I said. "Are you sure you want to sit up, though? You look really tired." After all the evening festivities, I was tired myself. I could only imagine how Shasta must be feeling, heavily pregnant, camping out, and caring for a toddler.

"Are you kidding?" Threading her arm through mine, she flashed her buoyant smile and started into the restroom. "You're the most exciting thing to happen on this whole trip."

Uncertain how to feel about that, I followed her through the door. We stood side by side at the sinks, washing up and brushing our teeth, then I slipped into a bathroom stall to put on my sweats. Shasta had changed into shorts and an oversized sleep shirt when I came out, and we walked back to the camp together. She seemed to be waiting for me to start up the conversation about my family again, and I wasn't sure I wanted to. My eyes were dry, and it felt like the end of a very long day. The backseat of the car was starting to sound very, very good.

Beside me, Shasta walked slowly, her hand braced on her back. "Ohhhh," she said and sighed. "My feet are killing me."

I glanced down at her cheap flip-flops, not exactly sensible pregnancy shoes. Her feet and ankles looked swollen. "You should get some Nikes or something. Good shoes."

She wagged her chin in my direction, her face backlit by the streetlamp, so that she was a silhouette with a misty halo. "Geez. Now you sound like Lana. She was all over my butt about the flip-flops today—like she really cares whether I trip over something. She's such a witch." Huffing an irritated breath, she peered toward camp. "She's probably down there right now telling everybody what an idiot I am for coming on the campout when I'm pregnant. Like she'd know anything about it. *She's* never been pregnant—I mean, my gosh, if she got pregnant she wouldn't be able to prance around camp in those tacky shorts, trying to get everyone to look at her. She doesn't even belong at the family reunion. She *used* to be married to my cousin, that's all."

It ran through my mind that I wasn't family. By that standard, I didn't belong in the group, either.

The comparison didn't seem to occur to Shasta. She continued her rant, lowering her voice as we walked past the motor home and came closer to Camp Reid. "She couldn't care less about seeing any of us. She's just here trolling for Jace. He thinks she's being all motherly to Autumn and Willie, trying to get them to sleep in her camper with her and stuff, just to be nice. Pfff. Please. She doesn't even like kids, but if there's an available guy around, Lana's gonna try to get her hooks in, and she's had it bad for Jace since high school. Shoot, she probably chucked my cousin just so she could go after Jace again. I tried to tell him that, but he doesn't see it. By the way, did you notice her looking at *you* tonight?" She curled her fingers and raked a claw in my direction as we passed my car. "You better check your back for scratch marks, girlfriend. She figured out that Jace invited you over, you know?"

Embarrassment crept into my cheeks again. "He was just trying to be nice. I was kind of stranded."

Shasta shrugged. "My brother's always nice. I got all the nosy, snotty genes in the family." In the dim light, she grinned mischievously, turning into Camp Reid. "So, how come you've never tried to find your father before? Why now?"

I contemplated potential answers as we entered the circle of tents. If we talked here, anyone in the tents would be able to hear us. "It's a long sto—"

Benjamin dashed from the camp kitchen, where his grandmother was putting away the last of the food. "Mommy! Mommy! Mommy!" His voice rang through the campground, shattering the silence. "I go bed you!"

"Ssshhhh," Shasta whispered, laughing as she lifted him onto her hip. "You'll wake everybody up. Why don't you go on in with Daddy? I'll be there in a few minutes."

Benjamin threaded his arms around her neck and squeezed. "I go bed you."

Frowning, Shasta looked toward the tents, then me, then back and forth again. "I guess I'm on night-night duty." She sounded disappointed. "Sorry."

"It's all right. I'll see you guys in the morning." I ruffled Benjamin's hair and he turned his face away, burrowing bashfully into his mother's shoulder.

"Benji, you cut that out," she scolded, turning him to face me. "You're not shy. Blow Dell a kiss good night. Come on, show her how you can blow the best kisses."

Popping his head up, Benjamin complied with a loud smack and a big grin. I caught the kiss in midair, brought it to my heart, said good night, and headed off to bed.

CHAPTER 9

❧

Morning light pressed my eyes, and I rolled over, snuggling into the quilt and letting out a long, slow sigh. I wanted to sleep in, but something was pulling me from my dreams, tearing the fabric haphazardly, so that the dreams went one way and I went the other.

There was a tapping sound over my head. Pushing my hair out of my eyes, I blinked upward, slowly becoming aware that my neck was sore because I was crunched in the backseat of my car. I was sleeping in my car. . . . The air smelled of wood smoke. . . . Folding back the quilt, I traced a finger along the neatly appliquéd patchwork of maple leaves, trying to remember where it had come from. It wasn't one of Karen's quilts.

Outside, the light was the cool pink of early morning, a new sunrise breaking through the lacy poplar trees and towering pines. From where I was lying in the seat, I could see only branches and sky, nothing to tell me where I was.

The tapping came again, on the window over my head this time. I sat up and swiveled around, the blanket clutched to my chest even though I had on sweats. Faces peered back at me from the other side of the glass, and my heart bounded into my throat before I could register the fact that they were only children. They'd squeezed themselves against the window, flattening their noses.

Autumn and Willie. Their names came back in a rush of memories from the night before. I took in Camp Reid, still clothed in the morning hush, only a thin stream of smoke drifting upward, testifying to the fact that no one had risen and started the fire yet.

Pulling away from the window, Autumn pointed toward my

picnic table, her eyes wide and white-rimmed. Beside her, Willie raised a double-barreled wooden rubber-band gun and sighted it in. Following his line of vision, I gasped. On the picnic table, a skunk was busy going through my backpack. From the looks of things, he'd already found the bag of airline peanuts and was searching for more.

Willie let go his ammo with surprising accuracy, and the rubber bands hit the metal barbecue grill with a resounding *ping ping*. The skunk stood at attention, sniffing the air in our direction.

"Willie!" Autumn squealed, and the skunk cocked its tail.

Hitting the lock button, I opened the door. "You two get in here!" I pulled them inside, and we landed in a jumble in the backseat as the door fell closed.

"Willie!" Autumn hollered, stepping on her brother and poking a knobby knee into my ribs as she peered over the driver's seat headrest. "You stupid. You made it mad."

"I was chasing it away," Willie protested. "Why'd you bump my arm? I could of hit it."

Her chin jutting out, Autumn glared at him. "And then it would of sprayed for sure." She pointed out the window, where the skunk stood arched like a cat. "If it sprays now, it's your fault, and I'm gonna tell Dad *and* Uncle Rube *and* Nana Jo."

Throwing himself into the corner, Willie crossed his arms over his chest. "I don't care. I'll tell 'em you got up and went outta camp without telling nobody."

"You *woke* me up," Autumn shot back. "You should of left me alone."

Willie's bottom lip rolled outward and began to tremble. "It was tryin' to get in the—"

"Time out," I said, putting a halt to the melee and untangling myself from the jumble of quilt and little bodies. "What are you two doing over here?"

Both Autumn and Willie turned to me as if they'd completely forgotten they weren't alone.

"So, your parents don't know you left camp?" My question invoked instant looks of panic.

Autumn hooded her eyes and offered a quick explanation. "Willie heard something digging outside the tent. He thought maybe it was a bear."

"A bear?" I repeated.

Autumn nodded vigorously, fanning her long lashes. "There's bears around here. My uncle killed one once."

"Uncle *who?*" Willie interjected.

Autumn flashed a threatening glance in his direction. "Hush up, Willie." Painting on a bright, cheerful smile, she turned back to me.

Willie's interest had been piqued by the bear-killing story. "Who kilt a bear? Uncle *who?*"

"Hush up, I said." Autumn tucked her hair behind her ears, then straightened her nightgown. "You got us in enough trouble already. If Dad sees us over here, we're dead. He said not to bother the lady anymore." By *the lady,* she obviously meant me.

"She don't mind," Willie insisted. Holding his rubber-band shooter against his chest with one hand, he reached for the door handle with the other. "I'm goin' back to the tent before everyone wakes up."

As the door clicked open, the skunk, which had finally relaxed and become interested in my Milky Way bar, raised its tail and stood ready again.

"Hold it, hold it." I grabbed the door and gingerly pulled it shut, wincing as the latch clicked into place again. On the picnic table, the skunk fluffed its tail, then went back to the candy bar. "Nobody's getting out right now. We're all just going to sit here until that thing goes away or the park patrol comes by."

In the corner of the seat, Willie sniffled, then started to cry, more frightened little boy than fearless hunter now. "Dad's gonna kill us! I wanna go home."

"Hush up, Willie. You sound like a baby. It'll leave pretty soon." Autumn chewed a fingernail. "It can't stay there all day." She glanced at me for assurance.

"I think if we just leave it alone, it'll wander off when it runs out of food." I spread out the quilt, covering Willie's bare legs, and slid back in the seat, letting my head sag against the headrest. "It's getting light outside. Skunks are nocturnal. They don't stay out in the daytime, unless . . ." *they're rabid, which skunks often are, especially the ones wandering around in the daylight, showing little fear of humans.* Autumn and Willie probably didn't need to hear that bit of information, nor was now a good time to share the famous Sommerfield graduation party rabid skunk story, but I couldn't help thinking about it.

Even two years later, that smell was enmeshed somewhere deep in my sinuses. I could still see James on the deck of our weekend cabin in Hindsville, boldly fending off the staggering skunk with a high-powered garden hose, which seemed to work until the hose kinked up and the sprayer went dry. Dazed and confused, the skunk regained its footing. James, rendered defenseless, ran backward, tripped over the hose and landed in the bushes. The skunk stumbled a few steps in his direction, Karen ran out the door with a broom, intent on rescuing James, and the skunk, still disoriented, staggered to the edge of the pool, fell in, and promptly sank to the bottom. Before Karen could get James out of the bushes, an oil slick of massive proportions rose to the surface of the water. The smell permeated everything, including friends and family, and my graduation party was over before it began. The event was still a running joke around Hindsville. It was weeks before we could use the cabin again.

Autumn eyed me, as if she knew I had more skunk experience than I was letting on.

Willie burrowed under my arm. "What's oc-turn-ul?" He rearranged the blanket so that it covered both his legs and my sweats, and we were snuggled in together. A shiver ran through his body, and I slipped my arm around him.

"Nocturnal. That means to come out at night. Nocturnal animals sleep during the day, and at night they go out looking for food."

"Like peanuts?" Willie observed, peering at the packages on the table.

I gave him a squeeze. "Yes, like peanuts. Skunks are scavengers, mostly." Willie reminded me of Aunt Kate's son, Joshua. Josh was too grown up for cuddling now, but even at ten years old he was still full of boy questions. I wondered, if Angelo were still around, if he'd be like that—curious about everything from grasshoppers to jet propulsion. Sometimes, when Josh and I spent time together over the years, I imagined that I was with my own baby brother. It was hard to picture Angelo growing up, a teenager now. In my mind, he was a little boy, no older than Willie, and we still had time to snuggle together under a quilt and talk about all the mysteries of the world. It was painful to consider the fact that those years had already passed us by, and, if I ever found Angelo, he would be almost a man by then, someone I didn't even know. We would never have the memories of a shared childhood.

"What's a scav-a-ger?" Willie's large dark eyes blinked upward with interest and admiration. He was impressed with my sophisticated command of skunkology.

Autumn wiggled in on the other side of me, covering herself with the quilt. "Don't pester with so many questions, Willie." Huffing air through her nose, she frowned apologetically, and added, "He just wears me out sometimes."

I fought the urge to chuckle at Autumn. Between her and Aunt Lana, Willie was getting about as much mothering as one little boy could stand. I wondered where Autumn and Willie's real mother was—if she didn't come to the campout because she and Jace were divorced, or if she was out of the picture completely.

"It's okay," I said, laying a hand over Willie's thick, burr-cut hair. "A scavenger is an animal that doesn't usually hunt for its food. Mostly it eats whatever it can find that's already dead."

"Like peanuts," Willie observed.

Autumn yawned. "Peanuts were never alive, Willie."

"Technically peanuts were alive at one time," I corrected, and Willie stuck his tongue out at his sister. "Now none of that." Slipping a finger under his chin, I frowned into his face. "If you hang that thing out there, someone might grab it and hold on." My second-grade teacher used to say that to Preston, the snotty little redheaded boy whose dad ran the bank in Hindsville. Mostly he stuck his tongue out at me, because he thought he was so much better than I was. "And then where would you be?"

"Quiet," Autumn quipped.

The joke went over Willie's head. Tapping his fingers together in his lap, he thought for a moment, then proceeded with his next question. "Where do peanuts come from?"

Groaning, Autumn flounced back against the seat.

"Peanuts come from peanut plants," I answered, keeping everyone pleasantly distracted from the fact that the skunk had finished its snack and was looking for a way off the picnic table. It had apparently climbed up the broken picnic bench to reach the tabletop. Unable to navigate its way back down, it was now marooned. Around us, morning cut through the trees, bringing the campground to life, increasing the skunk's desperation.

Desperate skunks are not a good thing. It scampered back and forth across the cement tabletop, peering over the edges, assessing the drop-off and looking agitated. Eventually, this was going to end badly. Lanterns were coming on in some of the Reid tents, and the thin trickle of smoke from the campfire had thickened, indicating someone was stoking up the morning fire. Turning its tail toward the smoke and the sounds of human activity, the skunk rushed to the opposite side of the picnic table, considered bailing off, then spread its feet and arched its tail instead.

Sooner or later, Camp Reid would go into panic mode because Autumn and Willie were missing, someone would rush around the corner, and the skunk would let loose. Poof. Everything within a half mile would smell like skunk, and the campout would be over.

I continued talking to Willie about peanuts because I didn't know what else to do. "Peanuts are a seed. The plant makes them so it can grow more peanut plants." *Think. Think of something. Do something before this turns into a disaster.*

"Like pecans?" Willie asked. On my right side, Autumn had gone quiet. Burrowing into my shoulder, she yawned again.

"Well, more like a seed pod. Like a pea pod, or a bean pod, I think. I'm not exactly sure." The skunk had frozen in place, and even with the windows closed I could hear voices from Camp Reid. What was I going to do?

My cell phone. I could call the park ranger. Except that I didn't have the park's phone number. Information. I could call information and try to get the number for the campground, or maybe the Department of Parks and Wildlife. It seemed ridiculous, considering that I could see the ranger station from here, but I didn't have a better idea.

"Okay, guys—" I pushed the quilt aside and slipped out from between the kids. "I want you two to sit very still. Don't be worried, and no one try to open the door, all right? I'm just going to climb over to the front seat and see if I can use my cell phone to call the park rangers. Maybe they can think of a way to make the skunk go home."

"I can shoot it," Willie offered, fishing his rubber-band gun from the seat.

Autumn yanked it from his hands. "Your gun is what got us in this mess. Sit still, for heaven's sake."

"I can't."

"That's the truth." Autumn's arms were crossed sternly over her chest, and her voice was the voice of experience. "But you better learn. Next year, when you start kindergarten, them teachers aren't gonna let you just hop around all the time. Then in first grade you don't get to act like a baby anymore at all. You have to sit in your chair and do what you're supposed to do. And then in second grade, if you get Mrs. Bender like I got, she doesn't let *anybody* talk *at all*. Then in third grade, Ryan Mitchell told me you don't even get two recesses anymore. Just one recess. That's all you get." The words rose in pitch, implying, *Can you believe that?*

As I climbed into the front seat, Willie folded his legs under himself, so that he could see the picnic table. "It looks mad."

Unplugging my cell phone from the cigarette lighter, I pushed the power button and waited for reception.

"Of course it's mad. I'd be mad, too, if someone shot me with a rubber-band gun."

"I was chasin' it away."

"You don't chase skunks away, Willie. Don't you remember when old Tank got hisself messed up with a skunk, and then got up under Nana Jo's house? That stink went in everything, and after they got Tank out, Nana Jo had to keep her windows open, and that stink wouldn't go away *one little bit*." Autumn dramatized *one little bit* by pinching her thumb and forefinger in the air. It was obvious that they spent a lot of time this way, Autumn leading and Willie soaking up her valuable life advice, reveling in her attention, even if it wasn't entirely positive.

The phone lazily came to life and began searching in vain for a signal as Autumn went on with her story. "Mom went and helped wash every bit of the stuff in Nana Jo's house, and—"

"Mom did?" Willie interrupted. "How come?"

His sister followed with a thoughtful pause. "Just because, I guess. Mom always did things for people. Besides, Tank was *our* dog, and—"

Outside, a woman's scream split the morning quiet, a cacophony of anxious voices rose in response, and the woman screamed again. The cell phone slipped from my hand, and I scrambled to pick it up again, then stopped with my fingers halfway to the floor. No need to call the Department of Parks and Wildlife. The intruder had just been discovered. On one side of my campsite, the lady from the motor home stood frozen with her hands in the air, fingers outstretched, eyes wide beneath neat rows of pink plastic curlers. On the other side, the men of Camp Reid collided like cars in a traffic pileup. In the middle, the skunk raced from one side of the tabletop to the other, alternately fluffing its tail and looking over the edge for a means of escape.

"Hey, there's Dad!" Before I could stop him, Willie popped the door open, jumped out, and waved. "Hi, Dad!"

The skunk whirled in our direction, and I held my breath. A dog barked in Camp Reid, the motor home lady screamed again, and Willie began explaining, long-distance. "Dad, we heard a bear by the tent, and—"

"Willie, don't—" As I turned to silence Willie, my rear end hit the steering wheel, and the car horn blared through the campground.

Faced with insanity in all directions, the skunk made a break for it. Leaping from the table like a flying squirrel, it circled the barbecue grill, darted past the screaming motor home owner, and promptly disappeared into a large plastic pipe connected to the underside of her RV.

The park ranger's truck skidded into my campsite with lights flashing as the woman stumbled away from her RV, screaming and pointing. Hooking her slipper toe on a twig, she stumbled forward toppled like a falling log.

Uncle Rube snaked out a meaty arm and caught her on the way down. "Whoa, there. Don't hurt yerself. It's just a little varmint." He helped her to the picnic bench beside the table vacated by the skunk. The snaps on her housecoat, already strained to the breaking point, burst free as she sank, and Rube stood with his big hands suspended in midair, his eyes politely averted.

The park ranger rushed in, holding his belt holster. Stopping next to the picnic table, he took in the crowd from Camp Reid, the heavyset woman sitting dazed on the bench with her housecoat flopping open over a Cross Your Heart bra, Rube standing over her with his hands dangling in the air, and my car, where Willie had launched into a rapid-fire defense testimony involving bears outside the tent, his rubber-band gun, and a skunk chasing him and his sister into my campsite.

I could only imagine what the ranger was thinking.

Autumn bolted from my car like a victim escaping a hostage situation, dashed across the camp, and threw herself into her father's arms, sobbing about how scared she was, and how she thought they would be trapped forever, and it was all caused by Willie and his stupid rubber-band gun. Stiff-armed, Willie marched after her, contradicting her story, while Jace looked from one child to the other, thoroughly confused.

The woman in the housecoat turned ashen-faced toward the motor home, wagging a finger. "S-skunk . . . dr-dryer v-vent, my . . . my hus-hus-husb-b-band."

"What in the devil is going on out here?" Nana Jo waded through the crowd into the clearing, wearing a filmy cotton muumuu that allowed the morning light to outline her stooped frame. "Lord o' mercy, you bunch could wake the dead in January." Waving her walking stick authoritatively toward the park ranger, she demanded, "What's the problem, Officer?"

The park ranger pulled off his hat and rubbed his eyes with the back of his hand, then blinked, hoping, no doubt, this was all a mirage. "Ma'am, I wish I knew."

"S-skunk, d-dryer vent," the woman on the picnic bench stammered.

I opened my car door, then climbed out and walked to Nana Jo and the park ranger, all the while carefully watching the accordion-shaped plastic pipe into which the skunk had made its exit. "This is going to sound a little strange," I began.

The park ranger rolled his gaze toward me, setting his hat loosely on the back of his head. He crossed his arms over his chest and rocked onto his heels. "Ma'am, I can't wait to hear."

CHAPTER 10

By the time I'd finished relating the saga of Autumn, Willie, and the stranded skunk, the Reids looked like an audience at a comedy club, except for Jace, who stood over his children wearing an expression of parental reproach.

The park ranger surveyed the scene once more, then turned back to me, struggling to keep his composure. "Sounds like your morning's stunk so far, but just . . ." A puff of laughter convulsed from his mouth, and he pretended to cough behind his hand. "Just for future reference, it's not wise to leave food around the campsite, especially at night. Unattended food is a major attraction for indigenous animals—skunks, raccoons, even the occasional coyote."

"And bears," Autumn whispered as an aside to her father. "Willie heard a bear outside the tent, but I guess the skunk scared it away."

Willie tugged at Jace's belt loop. "Daddy, Uncle-who kilt a bear?"

Jace pressed a finger to his lips. "Ssshhh. We'll talk about it later."

The park ranger went on with his lecture about proper wildlife relations. "Chances are, if there's no food available, the animal will just sniff around the campsite and move on. It would be a good idea to keep edibles in the car from now on."

"I will," I said, too chagrined to admit that I'd spent years in the woods and knew better than to leave food lying around. "Sorry about the disturbance."

The ranger gave a backward wave of his hand. "No problem, ma'am. You shouldn't have any more trouble."

"No more trouble? No more trouble?" The lady in the housecoat suddenly regained her senses and came to life. Standing up, she flailed a hand toward the motor home, then realized her robe was hanging open, and snatched the loose ends in a furious gasp. "She honked her *horn* and chased that *creature* up my *dryer vent*." Her shriek sent a flock of starlings into a cackling frenzy overhead. "Raymond's asleep in there, and without his hearing aid, he won't know a thing." She kneaded the front of her robe with one hand and braced the other on her hip. "What am I supposed to do now?"

Pulling his flashlight from his belt, the park ranger moved toward the vent hose and carefully squatted down to peer inside. "I don't see anything in there, ma'am."

"Oh, it's in there, all right." Positioned safely behind the ranger, the woman bent over, trying to see into the pipe. "She chased it right up my hose, I'm telling you. You better get it out before it goes after poor Raymond."

Behind her, Uncle Rube braced one hand on his hip, clutched his T-shirt with the other, and bent down, wiggling his rear end and mouthing, "You better get that thing out'a there."

The onlookers from Camp Reid chuckled, and Autumn squealed, "Uncle Rube!" then started giggling.

Nana Jo cleared her throat sternly, and Uncle Rube straightened up as the park ranger rose and scratched his head. Clearly, a skunk up a dryer vent was not the usual everyday problem. He surveyed the pajama-clad crowd, looking for suggestions.

Uncle Rube moved closer to the pipe and squatted down to have a peek inside. He looked like a Native American sumo wrestler, feet spread for balance, hands braced on his meaty thighs, long dark hair falling around his shoulders. "Yup. It's in there, sure enough. I can hear it scratchin' its way up the tube."

The woman gasped. "Lord have mercy! What if Raymond wakes up and goes looking for clean undershorts?"

Uncle Rube glanced back at the ranger. "I think you're gonna have to leave it be, till it decides to crawl back out." His suggestion drew a disdainful hiss from the motor home owner, and Rube shrugged helplessly.

"If I wanted advice from *you people,* I'd ask for it." Turning a shoulder to Rube, she faced the ranger. "I want that *creature* out of my dryer vent. *Now.*"

The ranger lifted his hat, scratched his hair, then set his hat back in place. "Well, ma'am, you're going to have to talk to the skunk about that, I'm afraid. My best advice is to leave him be. When it turns hot later in the day, he'll probably get a little warmish in there and decide to crawl out. For sure by this evenin' after dark, he'll be getting hungry and thirsty and ready to get out and move around. As long as nobody leaves any food around tonight, he'll wander off."

"And *what* am I supposed to *do* in the meantime?" The woman's voice rang through the campground, shattering the morning quiet.

A muscle twitched in the ranger's cheek. "My suggestion would be that everyone pack up for the day, go get breakfast somewhere else, head for the Labor Day festivities in town, and don't come back until well after dark. When that little fella does head out of there, he's gonna be confused, and probably in a pretty poor mood. Y'all don't want to be around for that. The less noise there is, the more likely he'll relax and decide to—"

"I don't want that thing relaxing in my dryer vent!" The woman shrieked.

Uncle Rube's hands jerked toward his ears, and he popped to attention with surprising agility.

The park ranger momentarily squeezed his eyes shut. Hooking his thumbs on his belt and holster, he took on an air of decisive authority. "Ma'am, you don't want him mad in there, either. I wouldn't make too much racket in the trailer as you're getting your things together."

"It's a *motor coach*," she corrected, glaring at the pipe as if she might tear it off with her bare hands.

"Yes, ma'am. In the future, it'd be a good idea not to put a vent pipe out like that. It's against camp regulations to have open ventilation or drain pipes lying on the ground."

"The dryer going makes the *motor coach* hot." She bit out each word separately and crisply, the emphasis on *motor coach*. "We have to ventilate it away from the floor."

"I understand how that could be a problem, ma'am, but snakes love warm, enclosed places, too." Straightening his hat, the ranger turned and headed for his truck. "Have a good day, y'all."

The woman gaped at her vent pipe. Her face went pale as she took one last look around our circle, then tiptoed toward the motor home, calling her husband's name in a strained whisper. "Ray-mond . . . Raaa-monnnd . . ."

Grasping her walking stick in the middle, Nana Jo turned back to her circle of bystanders. "All Reids up and dressed. We're going to see Aunt Maemae at the café." She swept her arm through the air like a drum major lining up a band. Willie and two other boys snapped to attention and saluted, and Nana Jo winked at them. "I see my boys are remembering last night's bedtime story about our grandfathers, and how they used the Choctaw language to fool the enemy in the World Wars. It wasn't only the Navaho who relayed secret messages for the army. The very first to carry secret messages in their native language during World War One were young Choctaw men. Can anyone tell me what we call those honored soldiers?"

"Code talkers," Autumn answered.

Nana Jo nodded proudly. "Very good. And can you tell me the Choctaw word for a brave red warrior, which gives our Choctaw capitol grounds its name?"

Three children replied in unison, as if Nana Jo quizzed them often. "*Tushka homma.*"

Tapping her walking stick on the ground, Nana Jo bent forward, and the children fell silent, anticipating the next question. "That is very good. Now, tell me, if you can, how might a code talker begin his message? Remember, no English words now, because the enemy is near. Only Choctaw. They do not know our secret language."

"Halito," Willie answered, his wide eyes sliding upward, waiting for approval.

Nana Jo nodded. *"Hello.* Yes, that is good. He might begin with *hello,* and what next?"

An older boy of perhaps ten or eleven answered next. *"Chim achukma?"* He brightened under Nana Jo's silent approval.

"Oh, yes. Your great-grandfather may have asked, *Are you well?* All of those men who left from here were brothers and cousins and friends. They were all part of the tribe, and they loved each other very much. Their jobs were very dangerous, and each man knew that he must sacrifice his life rather than allow himself to fall into the hands of the enemy. They were sworn to protect our secret language, and they did. Never was the enemy able to break the Choctaw code." Her voice trailed off mysteriously, and she breathed deep, gazing upward into the trees. The lake's fog-laden morning breath rippled her cotton nightgown, outlining her form and lifting her fine gray hair, so that she looked unreal, a picture-book illustration of an ancient woodland spirit. Overhead, the pecan leaves scratched and rattled like static on a field radio.

Nana Jo looked closely at each child. "This is why you must not believe people who say those Choctaw words are old things that don't matter, that learning them is too much work. When the code talkers were young boys in the missionary schools, they were forbidden to speak their Choctaw language. When they used Choctaw words, they were beaten and punished for cursing, yet they would not surrender the language of their ancestors. Those words are your history—the soil in which your lives are rooted. They were so valuable that your grandfathers fought to protect them." Her eyes were clear and wise as she leaned close to the children again, singling out Autumn in particular.

"Remember this when other children make fun of you and say that you spend too much time learning old things. Those friends are like the blossoms on a tree. They come with their pretty colors and their sweet scents. They turn our heads, but when the seasons change, they blow away to somewhere else. Only the soil remains to nourish the tree. A tree can live for months without blossoms, but without roots, it dies quickly." Tapping a finger to Autumn's forehead, she leaned down to catch her gaze. "You remember that, my girl, when that Kaylee Peterson makes fun of you at school."

Autumn nodded.

Overhead, the trees fell into a hush. A slice of cool air crept under my T-shirt, raising prickles on my skin. The talk about history, ancestors, and roots brought back an old pain, a nagging presence that sometimes sat on my chest when my own family was gathered together and the air was filled with stories about the past. There were no stories about me, no roots that drove deep into the soil of family memories and shared experience. Only part of me belonged there—a recent part that began when I was adopted. Another part of me belonged somewhere else, yearned for some other soil I could only guess at. That yearning always came wrapped in a misty layer of guilt that said families are about love, not about bloodlines.

Nana Jo's gaze caught mine for just an instant, and everything stood still. I wondered if she could see what I was thinking. What did she think of me, this strange girl, camping next to them alone in a car, with a borrowed quilt and no food?

Nana Jo broke the connection between us, turned to the children, and clapped her hands. "Now why are all of you still standing around? Let's get ready to go to the café for breakfast. While we're getting dressed, we will pretend we are soldiers, like Great-grandfather.

Remember, the enemy is outside listening, so no English. Only Choctaw. Everyone get ready. We'll leave for breakfast in"—she checked
her wristwatch—"thirty minutes."

Uncle Rube stepped close to Dillon, making the motion of syn-
chronizing wristwatches. Stuffing his hands in his pockets, Dillon
rolled his eyes as they turned around and headed for camp.

Jace offered his arm to Nana Jo, to help her across the uneven
ground. Patting his hand, she swiveled momentarily in my direction.
"You, too. Thirty minutes."

Jace shrugged over his shoulder, then gave me a quick wink and
a smile. I liked the way his eyes glittered when he did that. Watching
him walk back to Camp Reid, taking short, slow steps so that his
grandmother could keep up, I had the sense that the walk fit him,
that he was steady, unhurried, careful.

When they were gone, I grabbed my duffel bag from the car and
jogged up to the restroom to shower and dress. Back in high school,
when the emphasis was on looking perfect, and acting perfect, and
being perfect, I might have been worried about getting ready in thirty
minutes. The months in Ukraine, sharing dormitory-style bathrooms
and bathing in lukewarm or cold water only at designated times, had
taught me that very little preparation is required to get through the
day. Surrounded by girls who owned almost nothing and didn't expect things to improve much, I'd come to understand that so many of
the things I'd always focused on—fitting in at Harrington Academy,
earning accolades for my music, driving the right kind of car, wearing clothes that made me acceptable to everyone else—didn't really
matter at all.

In Ukraine, the burning need to answer the larger questions, to
find out who I really was and where I'd come from, was eclipsed by
the small challenges of everyday life—getting enough food and water,
living in a building with an aging electrical system that seemed to

have a mind of its own, the difficulty of teaching important lessons from ragged textbooks, and from the heart.

When the obstacles are that basic, you realize how much of life is only window dressing. Climbing into the shower at the campground, I was aware of that fact again. Even this facility was more than what was needed, more than the girls at the orphanage could expect, more than I'd expected as a child. At Granny's house, water came through the faucet in a rust-colored trickle, when it came at all. If the turkey farms farther up the rural water line were washing chick barns that day, you had to wait, or go clean up at the river.

When I was like those girls in the orphanage, I'd learned to accept life as it was, to seek contentment in small things—the cool river currents swirling around my legs, leaves whispering overhead, sunlight so warm it enveloped my body and soaked down deep inside me during long afternoons lying on sandbars, or exploring far down the riverbank because I had nothing better to do. I dreamed of running away down the river, of becoming someone else. I started that journey a thousand times, but I never had the courage to go beyond what I knew.

I didn't want this trip to Oklahoma to end that way, with me standing at the edge of the known world, afraid to take a step into whatever might be waiting outside. Closing my eyes, I let the water wash over me and promised myself, *This time I'll have the courage to follow the river. . . .*

When I stepped out of the shower, the bathroom was full of Reid women getting dressed, washing, and putting clothes on squirming kids. The air was alive with voices and laughter. Lana brushed by me, muttering about the water being out in her camper, and everybody taking *way* too long in the park showers. With a pointed glance at me, she disappeared into one of the showers.

If the rest of them thought I was in the way, they didn't show it. As I stood at the mirror, the conversation continued pleasantly around me. Eventually I was called upon to tell the tale of the early-morning skunk encounter.

When I reached the part about the skunk running up the dryer hose, Shasta's mom laughed so hard she doubled over. "Lord o' mercy. I wish I'd gotten out of my tent in time to see that."

"Well, if you wouldn't sleep buck-naked, you'd get out quicker," one of the other women hollered.

"I'd of gone out there buck-naked if I knew a skunk was gonna run up her vent pipe. God bless Brother Skunk."

"Maybe she'll pack up her stuff and leave," Shasta snapped as she pulled a shirt over Benjamin's head, then tucked it into his shorts. "I'm so sick of her giving us dirty looks and calling the dadgum park ranger. She's such a witch."

"Stupid white lady," one of the younger girls muttered.

"Hush, now," her mother murmured. A blond woman and a little girl had just come in the door. The room fell into an uncomfortable silence. The woman hustled her daughter toward the restroom stall and waited by the door, her arms threaded uncomfortably over her stomach.

I knew exactly how she felt. In my mind, I saw myself standing in a room full of people who were different from me, feeling conspicuously unlike them, unwelcome.

"Here, you can have my sink. I'm done," I said as her little girl came out of the stall. For just an instant, her face and mine were in the mirror, our gazes connecting momentarily. She had pretty eyes. Blue eyes. The kind I'd always wanted.

"Thanks," she said as I turned away.

Lana, exiting the shower area, huffed and leaned against the wall, waiting for a spot at the mirror. The woman with the blue eyes hurried her little girl through washing her hands and left the restroom without even stopping to grab a paper towel.

I threaded my way past the crowd of Reid women, then grabbed my duffel bag and went to sit on the bench outside to brush my hair. Shasta came out and sat beside me. "You have to ignore them sometimes. Some of the family can be a little redneck about things, but they don't mean any harm. They just get used to being around their own people, you know? That's why Cody and I are gonna move over to McAlester, as soon as I get done having this baby. Cody's got a friend who can get him on with the sheriff's department over there. Mama will have a fit, but she'll just have to live with it. I don't want my kids growing up thinking there's not a whole other world out there. In our family, everyone's born here, and they die here, and in between they teach at the Indian school, or work at Arrowhead Resort, or at the Choctaw Casino."

Rubbing her stomach, she squinted toward the lake as a speedboat roared by. "I want my kids to get out in the world." Her eyes were far away, filled with the yearning I felt when I looked down the river. I was struck by what a paradox we were—me trying to find my way into this world, and her trying to find her way out.

Drumming her palms on the bench, she turned back to me. "So, I guess your family—your adopted family, I mean—are white? I figured they were last night when we were talking, but you didn't exactly say."

The question made me shift away uncomfortably. I sat cleaning long, dark strands from the hairbrush, pretending to be occupied. "Yeah," I said.

"I'm sorry. I guess I'm being too nosy." Grimacing, she rubbed her stomach, then changed positions, sitting on the bench with her legs crisscrossed and her belly protruding. "Ouch. Gosh, this baby kicks sometimes. I hate being pregnant."

"Oh." I wasn't sure what else to say. *I'm sorry? That's too bad? It'll all be worth it in the end?* I considered telling her about Mrs. Bradford, and how she'd gone through years of infertility treatments, trying to get pregnant. It wasn't something to be taken for granted. Some people yearned, and hoped, and wanted for years, and were never able to have a baby.

And some people had a baby, and left it behind, and never thought about it again. Life was full of painful realities, for which there seemed to be no explanation.

"This one wasn't planned." Bowing her head, Shasta slid her hands under her stomach, her hair falling forward so that she was cupped protectively around the baby. "But I'm not sorry about it. Benjamin's such a doll, and he's so much fun at this age. I'd take five more if I didn't have to be pregnant with them." There was a defensiveness in the comment, as if she were trying to convince not only me but also herself.

"He's really cute." I looked around for Benjamin, then realized he must still be inside the building. "Your little boy, I mean."

She smiled tenderly. "He looks like his daddy."

We sat silent for a few moments, having run out of things to say. Finally, Shasta swung her legs around the end of the bench. "Guess we could start back. Nana Jo will be on the warpath if we're not ready on time." Leaning toward the restroom, she hollered, "Mama, we're going to walk back down. Is Benji staying with you?"

"He's fine," Gwendolyn replied from somewhere within. "Y'all go on."

Shasta braced her hands on the bench, preparing to push herself to her feet.

"Here." I stood up and held out my arm to pull her up. She grabbed my hand, and I stumbled forward, unprepared for her weight against mine.

"I know. I'm like a Mack truck," she muttered as we started down the park road.

"You look good."

"Ffff," she spat. "Hardly."

We laughed together, then continued along in silence until, as usual, Shasta restarted the conversation. "I didn't mean to scare you off, asking about your family again and stuff. I just think it's interesting—you know, you coming here looking for your biological relations. You're like one of those people on *Oprah,* in search of lost loves."

"It's not quite that dramatic." I tried to imagine myself at the center of some fantastic story about a long-lost baby girl, a birth family, who had been searching for years, counting every birthday, mourning an empty space at the table every holiday, stacking unopened Christmas presents in a corner somewhere, in hopes that one day the family would be complete again, and every gift would be opened. "I probably won't find anything."

"You might." I felt Shasta's hand warm on my shoulder. "You never know. Nana Jo says there are lots of Clays around here. There's even some in our family. We might be long-lost cousins."

I flushed at the idea that she'd mentioned my search to Nana Jo. "We might be." But it was about as unlikely as snowflakes in June. Odds were pretty slim that, by pure luck or happenstance, I'd ended up camped next to members of my father's family. Still, it was nice to imagine myself as one of the Reid clan.

"Jace said he'd help you look for information later today, if you want," Shasta went on. "He's tied up giving tours at the Choctaw Museum this morning, but he could help you after that. He has his students do family genealogy all the time. They've even started a library at the school, and—" Arresting the sentence, she grimaced. "Was I supposed to keep that stuff you told me last night a secret?" Clearly, I looked as embarrassed as I felt.

"No," I said, trying to put on an impassive mask, to hide the feelings of shame and guilt, the sense of forbidden territory that had always surrounded any mention of my biological family.

"Oh, good." Shasta blew out a quick sigh. "For a minute there

I thought I'd messed up. Mama says I'm bad about being in other people's business. Of course, she's a fine one to talk, considering I learned it from her and Nana Jo."

"It's fine," I said.

For better or worse, the Reid clan now knew my secrets.

CHAPTER 11

꩜

Lana caught up with us on the road and made some snippy comment about Benjamin throwing a fit in the restroom because he wanted to walk back to camp with his mom, rather than waiting for his grandmother. "I offered to bring him down here to you, but he wouldn't go with me," she said, giving Shasta a narrow sideways look. "He threw himself in the corner and had a fit. He certainly has a *mind* of his *own*." Her body language added, *What a brat*.

"He doesn't know you, Lana." Shasta barely even attempted to sound pleasant. "We've taught him not to go with *strangers*."

Lana straightened upward like a viper sizing up a mouse. "You're such a good little mother, Shasta, I'm sure you have." As Lana worked up the rest of her retort, it looked like we might be headed for what Grandma Rose always called a spit-and-claw hair-snatchin' session. I planned to jump in on Shasta's side, given that she was pregnant, and I already couldn't stand Lana.

Pursing her lips, Lana glanced back toward the restroom. "I just thought you might want to go back and take care of it, since you *are* his mother. I'm sure your *friend* can find her way back to her car on her own." Blinking in my direction, Lana forced a smile. "Did you make it all right last night, sweetie? I heard you had a little adventure this morning. Guess I slept right through it."

"Oh," I muttered, an old sensation clenching the bottom of my stomach, making it seem like I was shrinking. I felt like the little fourth-grade nothing getting on the school bus, watching kids whisper and giggle because my jeans were too short and smelled like musty house, dog hair, and river dirt. *Come on, Dell, think of something smart to say*, a part of me whispered now. *That's what Shasta would do.* The other part of me, like always, wanted to get to the back of the bus and hide.

"Yeah," Shasta piped up. "It's a good thing Dell was there. She probably saved Autumn and Willie from getting sprayed and, man, that would have ruined the campout. Dell put the kids in her car with her and they had a little party in there until help came." Waving her hands in the air, Shasta feigned amazement. "Jace was so grateful, and the kids think Dell's just about the coolest person they've ever met, isn't that great?"

Lana didn't answer immediately, but paused to clear her throat, the side of her jaw clenching as she checked her watch. "I'm going to be late for work," she muttered to no one in particular, then quickened her step and moved ahead of us.

" 'Kay," Shasta called after her. "See ya. Sorry you can't go to breakfast with us." Convulsing in a withheld giggle, Shasta slapped the air in front of herself, then patted her chest, trying to catch her breath. "Oh, that was great. That was great. She's been trying to get Jace's kids to like her forever, and they know she's a witch. I can't figure out why Jace doesn't see that they can't stand her." She watched Lana disappear into the campsite. "Good thing she's working again, or we'd have to put up with her all day. The school finally got rid of her because she was, like, using the school phone and e-mail to harass her ex. How stupid is that? I can't even believe anybody else would give her a job. I hope she's working for city sanitation or something." Shasta hooked her arm in mine like she'd known me all her life, and we moved on down the road, partners in crime.

Shasta's good mood didn't last long after we reached camp. Her husband, Cody, a stocky, good-looking guy with burr-cut black hair and a round face that made him seem younger than twenty-one, had decided to take their truck and go fishing with some other men, which left Shasta without a vehicle and in charge of their son for the morning. She wasn't happy about it.

"It was your turn to watch him last night, Cody," she complained as she wrestled a baby seat from the truck. "When you went fishing with Uncle Rube and Danny-Tom yesterday, you said as soon as you were done, you'd watch Benjamin. But when you got back, you went in the tent and crashed."

"I took him in the tent with me," Cody argued, loading fishing poles into the back of the truck.

Shasta snorted. "He wasn't tired. He got back up, and it was almost midnight before I got him down. I can't do *everything*, Cody." Yanking the child seat out with the seat belt still attached, she sent the buckle snapping back against the doorframe with a resounding clang.

"Hey, Babe, easy on the truck." Licking a finger, Cody attempted to rub away the impact mark, then kissed Shasta's cheek. "I'll meet you at the festival by eleven o'clock, and I'll take Benji around and do the rides and stuff. Promise."

"Don't even speak to me," she shot back, waddling away with baby equipment on her hip.

Cody shrugged, then gave a high sign toward Camp Reid. Dillon and Uncle Rube quickly emerged from behind the tents and jogged toward the truck. As they climbed in, they gave Cody atta-boy shoulder punches.

"Man, she's postal." Dillon tossed a crumpled Coke can in the back.

"She's always postal," Cody complained. "It's a pain in the butt, being around a pregnant woman."

"Well, you know what causes that . . ." The rest of the comment was drowned out by the engine as Cody backed out of his parking space, and the truck rumbled past a crowd of Reid women, returning from the bathroom. Shasta's mother braced her hands on her hips and gave the departure a dirty look, while Benjamin waved cheerfully at his daddy.

Halfway between my camp and hers, Shasta stopped, spun on her heel, and came back. "Can I ride with you?" She glanced toward the road, where her mother was still glaring after the truck. "I don't even want to hear what Mama has to say."

"Oh . . . ummm . . . sure." I had the unwelcome sense of being a foxhole in an ongoing firefight. Gwendolyn looked mad enough to chase down the truck and drag Cody out with her bare hands. I opened my car door and took the baby seat. "Here, I know how to do this. I have nieces and nephews back in Kansas City."

"That's cool." Stretching her shoulders, Shasta rubbed the small of her back, then cupped a hand beside her mouth and called for Benjamin to come on. Pulling away from his grandmother, he started toward us in a stubby-legged run.

Next door, the owners of the motor home were loading suitcases into their minivan.

"I'm not stayin' in this camper with that *thing* in the vent pipe, Raymond." The woman threw a pink patent-leather makeup case into the van. "All this *camper* foolishness was *your* idea. I told you I didn't want to go *tramping* all over the country, staying in *tacky* trailer parks with *wild* animals, white trash, and other *minorities*. We should have bought the time-share in Florida. At least there, you know who your neighbors are."

Scratching his rear end through droopy zip-up coveralls, Raymond yawned and glanced at the vent hose with a lack of concern. "Oh, Irene, for heaven's sake. That thing's probably crawled out already."

Irene faced him with venom in her eyes. She'd exchanged the housecoat for a Hawaiian-print nylon jacket and parachute pants that made her look like a magnolia tree with two sturdy blue trunks. "I doubt *that,* with all the *racket* going on over there in that camp." She fired a visual cannon shot at Camp Reid, where Jace and two teenage boys were securing coolers and plastic bins of food in the pickup camper. "Did you hear that *gibberish* they were talking earlier? *Span-*

ish, or something. Like they think they're too good for all the rest of us. Somebody ought to tell them this is America—speak *American.*"

Raymond gave his motor home a weary look, then closed the minivan tailgate as Irene flounced into the passenger seat. Coming around the van, he shrugged apologetically as I got into my car.

Shasta, waddling up with her son in tow, gave the van a sneer. "Up you go," she cooed as Benjamin climbed into the baby seat. "You're such a big boy."

"Where Gammy?" he asked, trying to see around his mother to the group of women approaching on the road.

"Gammy'll be along in a minute with Nana Jo and everybody else." Shasta ducked her head like a teenager trying to sneak out before her parents could stop her. "We're gonna ride to the café with Dell, so we can show her the way, all right?"

"Okay," Benjamin chirped, scanning my car with his bright polished-agate eyes, looking for something interesting to do. Frowning at the lack of available kid-entertainment, he rubbed the short dark hair that matched his dad's, then tried holding a piece out between his thumb and forefinger, so he could see it. "Mama, what hair I got?"

"Purple hair with pink polka dots," Shasta answered, then closed his door and climbed into the passenger seat, groaning as she swung her legs onto the floorboard. She tucked her purse and a diaper bag beside the console before buckling the seat belt around her stomach. "I feel like a tank."

"This car's just hard to get into," I said, wondering again what it would be like to be her—wife, mother, participant in the yearly Reid family reunion, member of the tribe. I wanted to be her, and then I didn't. I suspected she felt the same way about me.

Benjamin finished trying to examine his hair and was bored by the time I started the engine. "I no got poke-dots!" he squealed. "What hair I got?"

"Black, like your daddy," his mother answered, then checked over her shoulder as I backed out of the parking space. "Sorry," she said to me. "In our family, you get used to looking for kids behind the car."

"Ours, too." Aunt Kate's kids were spread just far enough apart in age that we'd had a preschooler around the house for years. Now that the last one was school-aged, we were starting over with Jenilee's baby.

"I wan' toy," Benjamin whined from the backseat. Since we weren't even out of the campground yet, that didn't bode well for the trip.

"Oh, Benji, your toy bag is in the back of the truck." Shasta's tone was a mirror of Benjamin's—whiney and latently miserable. She reached into the diaper bag and dug around with one hand. "Nope. Nothing in there but diapers, wipes, clothes, and a hairbrush. Dad took off with all your toys." *Dad* took on the aura of a dirty word, and Shasta zipped up the diaper bag with a vengeance. "You'd think he might have checked before he left with everything."

Opening the console, I looked for something Benjamin might like and came up with an extra set of keys and an old cell phone. "Here you go." I stretched into the backseat before we pulled out of the park entrance. "Want to play with my phone?"

"Woooo!" Benjamin's hands clapped in rapid succession, and his eyes widened as I set the phone and the keys in his lap. He picked up the phone and started pressing buttons. "Mommy, I got cep-ha-wone!"

"Don't push anything." Shasta cast a worried glance. "You might not want to let him play with that. He's likely to call China or some-place. He's pretty good with electronics and things. Mama already has him using baby computer games at her office."

In the mirror, I watched Benjamin clutch the cell phone to his chest and frown at his mother. "S'mine." Grabbing the keys, he tried to give them back, instead. "You keys."

"It's okay," I assured Shasta. "It's an old phone. I had the service turned off and got prepaid wireless because I was out of the country for a couple years."

Shasta drew back, her face brightening with obvious fascination. I could imagine what she was thinking—adopted spoiled rich kid, bumming around the globe on Mom and Dad's money while searching for herself and answers to long-buried genetic questions. "Really? Where at?"

"Europe for a year, and then Ukraine." It seemed like fiction, sitting here in a car, driving a county road miles from the nearest airport or city. "Europe was a student exchange orchestra. Not as big of a deal as it sounds. We played concert halls, political events, graduations, things like that. We got to see a lot. One of the girls I met there was headed on to Ukraine for a year with an orphans' mission, and I just . . . I don't know . . . went along."

"That must have been kind of sad—at the orphanage, I mean," Shasta mused. Her face was soft and contemplative, sympathetic. "I saw a report about those orphanages on *60 Minutes* once. Is it really like they show on TV, all those cribs lined up, with babies that just lie there all day long, and never get out? When they showed that on TV, I cried for two days, and Cody thought I was nuts. I kept thinking about Benji, and what if that were him? If I didn't have a baby to take care of and one on the way, I would have hopped on a plane and gone to that orphanage and just sat there all day, hugging kids. I got our Sunday-school class to start raising money and collecting shoes to send over."

"They'll be needed," I said. "It's incredibly cold in the winter. Many of the orphanages can't take the kids outside, because they don't have warm clothes and shoes. Where we were, in Sumy, the kids in the Internat—that's what they call an orphanage for older kids—know almost nothing about the outside world, and then when they graduate ninth grade, they have to leave and try to go find a way to make a living. Our missionary program tried to teach them some arts, computer skills, and proficiency in English, which hopefully will help them have some chance of finding work. But they're still so young. . . ." The sentence trailed off, probably better left unfinished. Shasta's eyes were welling up. It wouldn't help to tell her where a lot of the kids raised in orphanages ended up. When kids left the Spencers' program, Mr. Spencer sent them off with an invitation to return for Sunday services and a promise that if they were ever desperate, they had only to knock on the door, and he would find some way to feed and shelter them. He gave them the one thing they needed most. A family.

Shasta sniffed and wiped her eyes. "The funny thing was that when I went to Sunday school after I saw the show about the orphanages, everybody in the class had seen the same show. Every single person. They all wanted to do something to help. Choctaws have a big heart for kids. It's a cultural thing for us—kind of like it takes a village to raise a child, but for us, it takes a tribe." She laughed softly, and I laughed with her. "If Nana Jo hadn't kept me involved with the tribe and the church, I think I would have been a seriously messed-up teenager. My dad left when I was eleven. I didn't take it as well as Jace did, maybe because he was already eighteen and headed off to college, but I'd always been Daddy's little girl, or at least I thought I was." Her face held a wounded look that spoke of a pain undimmed by the passage of time.

"It hurts to be left behind." I felt a sudden sense of kinship. "You just . . . do the best you can." It seemed strange for me to be talking about things so close to the core, feelings I'd never discussed with anyone. Yet with Shasta it felt comfortable. We were more similar than I'd realized. "Do you ever hear from your dad?"

She shrugged and began picking at her fingernail polish. "Not much. He left us and started a whole other family. I guess that keeps him occupied." Dark, silky strands fell across her cheek as she stared at her hands. "I don't mind it so much for me. I'm a big girl, but I feel bad that Benjamin doesn't have a grandpa on my side. You'd think my dad would want to know Benji." Resting her head against the window, she gazed outward, looking like the wounded eleven-year-old whose father had packed his bags and left her behind. I knew that feeling, what it was like to wonder why someone who should have loved you didn't want to know you at all.

"It's hard to figure people out sometimes," I admitted.

"Yeah, it is." She pointed as we came to a crossroads near Clayton. "Turn here. We'll go the back way."

I turned onto a potholed street, part pavement and part gravel, and we wound through a neighborhood of decaying turn-of-the-century houses, then came to an intersection a block off Main. Shasta pointed out the café and we pulled into the parking lot from the back, then sat for a minute, neither of us knowing what to say. I read the pole sign by the road. The bottom half advertised Labor Day weekend specials and Indian tacos, while the top part simply read CAFÉ in peeling red paint and flickering pink neon.

"C'mon, wet's go, Aunt Maemae," Benjamin broke the silence. He pretended to dial the phone, then pressed it to his ear, upside down. "He-wow, Aunt Maemae? We come bwek-fast." Pausing, he rolled his eyes upward, as if he were listening to someone on the other end, then nodded and answered, " 'Kay . . . 'Kay . . . I waff-wles 'n Twinkie 'n Pop-Tawt. 'Kay?"

Shasta giggled and checked the parking lot. "Looks like we're here first. We might as well go on in and get a table."

"Okay." My fingers hesitated on the keys, which were still in the ignition. "Are you sure I'm not horning in on your family breakfast? I've got some things I need to do this morning—go to the bank, pick up some supplies at a grocery store, maybe see if I can get lucky and find a hotel room for tonight. I could just drop you and Benjamin here and go on."

Shasta stopped halfway out the door. "Are you kidding? You got rid of the people in the motor home. You're our hero. You'll probably have to tell the skunk story two or three more times at breakfast." She pushed to her feet and opened the back door, then leaned through to unbuckle Benji, who was still talking on the phone, this time to "Anta Clause." "Besides, you're family. If you do all the genealogy, you'll probably find us crisscrossed somewhere way back. Less than ten thousand Choctaw people actually made it here on the Trail of Tears, and they all married each other way back when, so there you go. We're all family somehow or other. You'll see more about that at the museum, if you take the tour. Choctaw history's pretty interesting, if you're into that kind of thing." Her bland expression added, *Which I'm not.* "Nana Jo makes a big deal about having all the kids go to classes and stuff. Jace took to it, I guess, and that's why he teaches history. He's into all the tribal stuff. Nana Jo's got it in mind he ought to run for chief one of these days."

"Wow," I said, following her and Benjamin around the side of the café to what looked like a back door. "I didn't know there were chiefs anymore. I mean, one time when I was in school, I got on the Choctaw Web site and saw something about a chief and tribal council representatives, but I thought that was historical stuff."

Shasta blinked at me in a way that said, *Where have you been?* "Oh, no. The Choctaw Nation has elections and campaigns, and all the political rigmarole that goes along with that. I don't know why Jace would want to get involved in it, but I guess he does. That's his deal." Opening the kitchen door and stepping into the dim interior, she called out, "Hey, Aunt Maemae. We're all coming in for breakfast. Where do you want us to sit?"

"Take the back room, and move the chain from the doorway in there. Front's crowded. Lots of tourists in town today." A woman emerged from the freezer lugging a box of breakfast sausage under her heavy, overhanging breasts. She was wearing a cotton dress adorned with brightly colored fabric ruffles and line after line of carefully applied strip quilting. She looked like a dancer at a Mexican Hat Dance, her long hair in a ponytail swinging back and forth in a beaded holder. "Uncle Bart called and said y'all had a skunk in camp. Typical Reid reunion." She paused to look at me, the sausage still in her hands.

Shasta quickly made the introductions. "This is Dell . . . Sommerfield . . . but I guess it's really Clay." She glanced my way, her brows knotted in the center. "Right?"

Before I could answer, Benjamin launched himself at Aunt Maemae, wrapping his arms around her leg with a roar and a gorilla grip. "Aunt Maemae! I got phone!" Wiggling loose, he held up the phone, then pulled it away when his aunt tried to examine it. "Mine mine mine."

Tweaking him on the nose, Aunt Maemae shook her head. "Well, don't call China."

"I not," he chirped, turning loose and looking speculatively toward the stove. "Me got pancakes?"

Maemae extended an arm protectively between him and the cooking area. "Hot," she warned, then turned back to us. "Clay . . . Clay . . . so are you Lawton's girl, or Bonita's?"

The bell rang at the front window, and a teenaged waitress stuck two tickets on the rack, calling, "Order up."

"Excuse me," Maemae said and hurried off.

"You have to pardon us. We're a little ADD around here but, see, there are lots of Clays in our family. I asked Nana Jo if she knew about anybody who had a daughter about my age that moved away to someplace else. She couldn't think of anything like that or anybody with your dad's name, but there's lots of relatives scattered around we don't ever see, so we could still be cousins. It'll help more if you can find out who your dad's parents were and stuff. Nana Jo might know some of those names." She captured Benjamin and guided me through a side door into a small dining room. "Just sit anywhere," she said, then went to take down the chain that had barred customers from entering through the rear of the building. I sat at a table in the back, and Benjamin crawled into the chair across from me, then smiled upward, resting his chin on the tabletop.

"Want a booster seat?" I asked.

"Yup." He grinned, and I got a booster seat from the corner. He stood up so I could slide it underneath him. Shasta finished setting the tables with silverware rolled in white paper napkins as Jace came in with his kids.

"Hey, Jace, come sit with us." Shasta nodded toward our table. "That way the table will be full and Mama can't park here and chew on me because Cody bailed again."

Jace surveyed the empty room as Willie and Autumn scrambled into the chairs beside me, leaving empty the space next to Benjamin and across from me. "Where's Cody?"

"Fishing. Again." Shasta growled under her breath as she squeezed into a chair between Benjamin and the wall.

Smiling sympathetically, Jace slid into the empty seat. "Don't be too hard on him, kiddo. It's a guy thing. He's a guy."

"I know," Shasta grumbled. "That's what I hate about him."

CHAPTER 12

❧

As the room filled with members of the Reid family, Shasta moved
to the end of our table and entertained the kids by drawing
cartoon characters on the backs of the paper place mats. Within minutes, several children were gathered around, watching Shasta dash
off drawings like a Disney animator and hand them out to her fans.
She was amazingly good, creating her pictures with quick, confident
strokes, and had a perfect eye for perspective and detail.

Eventually, the kids began challenging her to draw everything
from Bugs Bunny to the Statue of Liberty. Autumn stretched across
the tabletop in front of me, trying to see, and finally I traded places
with her. The switch left Jace and me on the end beside a wall decorated with a long mural of a river running through a pine forest.
The colors were slightly dulled by a film of grease and dust from
the air-conditioning vent, but it was a beautiful scene, and very
well done.

"Shasta painted it when she was sixteen," Jace offered without
glancing up from his menu. "Art runs in our family, and Shasta got
the gene. Unfortunately, it skips some of us."

"I take it you're not an artist," I said, and he answered with a
rueful twist of his lips.

"Just a history teacher." He went back to looking at the menu.

"Without teachers, there wouldn't be any artists," I pointed out,
and he laughed, a wide, white smile spreading across his face and
making his eyes sparkle. He had nice eyes, the warm color of coffee,
framed with thick lashes. Willie looked like him. I supposed that
Autumn looked like her mother.

"You should go into politics," he joked, and a puff of laughter flew past my lips.

Shasta glanced at us from the end of the table, then went back to drawing.

"I'd be terrible at politics. I hate getting up in front of people." I couldn't count the number of times I'd rushed to the bathroom before a performance to throw up. In the moments before the opening, I waited with my heart pounding in my chest like a bird frantically trying to escape a cage. Air solidified in my throat, and my skin went cold and damp. It was only after the music began that I could breathe again.

"Really?" Jace appeared genuinely surprised. "Last night, you seemed pretty much at home in front of an audience."

Shuddering, I took a sip of my Coke. "Oh, gosh, no. I haven't done anything like that in a while."

"I can't imagine why not." Our gazes tangled and held, and for an instant I wanted to tell him how music carried me so far inside myself there was no place for fear, and how lately that wasn't happening anymore, and I was worried. I wanted to admit that I felt like a woman in mourning, because something I loved was lost, and I couldn't find it.

The intensity of his gaze stirred something that pushed away those thoughts. I couldn't quantify the feeling, couldn't label it and tuck it neatly into the file cabinet of past reference points, but it was a powerful sensation. My stomach tightened, and I heard my heart beating slow and soft in my ears, felt my fingers rise to touch the pulse in my neck.

Breaking the link between us, he leaned back in his chair and focused on his menu. He seemed nervous, slightly embarrassed and surprised, as if he'd stepped over some invisible line he hadn't meant to cross.

Nearby, Nana Jo pushed open the kitchen door, leaned in, and hollered for Maemae to bring some big platters of pancakes, scrambled eggs, and sausage so we could have breakfast family-style. "It'll be easier that way," she said, then announced to the whole room that she intended to pay the bill and no one was to argue with her about it. I touched my purse with a mixture of guilt and relief. Nana Jo shouldn't have been buying my breakfast, but right now I had less than twenty dollars to my name. As soon as we were done here, I needed to find the nearest branch of First Federal Bank so I could get some cash.

"Guess that settles that." Jace shrugged and dropped his menu into the stack behind the stainless steel napkin holder.

"Guess so," I agreed, and we fell into an awkward silence. Jace cocked an ear toward a table on the far side of the room, where a short, heavyset man the others called Uncle A.T. was halfway out of his chair, reenacting the story of Uncle Rube and the skunk. From my vantage point, I could both hear and see the story.

"Now you gotta picture this," A.T. said, cupping his hands in front of his chest like he was carrying a couple of two-liter soda bottles. "The robe thing is hangin' wide open, and she don't even realize it, and ole Rube's just standin' there, face-to-face with it. He don't know whether to cover 'em up or just pretend like he can't see 'em. They're just hangin' there like two dried-up pumpkins in a silk toe sack. . . ."

Jace turned back, shaking his head. I blushed and tried to focus on the place mat.

"There's children in the room!" Shasta hollered without looking up. She was in the middle of sketching The Cat in the Hat, complete with two kids and a goldfish in a bowl.

"Sorry. Got a little carried away," A.T. called back, then returned to his performance. "So the . . . unmentionables are hangin' out, and ole Rube's standing there with his hands in the air, like this, and then here comes the park ranger. . . ."

Jace drummed his palms on the tabletop, then leaned back and relaxed against his chair. "So . . ." He drew the word out, clearly looking for some way to move the subject away from Rube and the pumpkins in the toe sack. "Shasta says you're here to do research on some family members, your father in particular."

The heat deepened in my cheeks. I wished Shasta hadn't told him about me. "It's a long story. I didn't grow up with my father, so I don't know much about him, except that he was Choctaw or part Choctaw, and his name was Thomas Clay."

Jace nodded, cataloging information and waiting for more. I couldn't help feeling that if he knew my whole, convoluted history, his look of interest would turn to one of sympathy.

"It's really kind of a long, boring story."

"I doubt that." Running a finger slowly along the side of his place mat, he studied me with interest. "But I wasn't trying to pry. My sister thought maybe I could help you find the information you're looking for. My history students do genealogy research projects as course requirements. Over the past few years, we've been cataloging the projects and building a genealogy research center as part of our school library."

"Shasta told me. She said you know quite a bit about using the Choctaw records to do research."

He blinked, seeming surprised that his sister and I had been talking about him. "It doesn't work the way most people think. Tracing information through the Choctaw records is a complicated process. Proving a direct Choctaw bloodline, which is what most people are trying to do, in order to become eligible for a CDIB card and tribal membership, is better done by starting with your own birth records, then moving backward through census reports, more birth records, CDIB numbers, and so forth, to someone who is actually listed on the original Dawes Commission Rolls."

Sinking back in my chair, I focused on my hands and absently picked at the rolled-up napkin with my silverware in it. "I don't have any of those things," I admitted. "I mean, somewhere at my parents' house—my *adopted* parents' house—we do have my original birth certificate, and it says that I was born in Tuskahoma, Oklahoma. My father's name was Thomas Clay. There isn't any middle name on the papers. Just Thomas Clay."

"There are a lot of Clays around here." It was meant to be an encouraging statement, but the reality was that having a common family name would probably make things more difficult.

"Shasta told me that."

"We even have a branch of Clays in our family."

"Shasta told me that, too." The voice of reason had started whispering in my head again, telling me this search was crazy and immature. Plenty of adopted kids lived perfectly normal, happy lives knowing less about their birth families than I knew about mine.

Jace leaned forward and rested his elbows on the table. "Come on, it's not *such* bad news. I know the gene pool looks a little shallow from here"—he shrugged over his shoulder, to where his uncle was imitating the RV lady straw-bossing her husband during the loading of the minivan—"but we're not such a bad bunch. We can cook, for one thing. No member of the Reid family has ever gone hungry at a family gathering. If you don't believe me, just look at Rube."

I chuckled, focusing again on the rolled-up napkin. What I really wanted to do was tell him that, for as long as I could remember, I'd dreamed of finding a birth family like this one.

"So, Cousin"—he flicked a packet of sugar across the table at me like a paper football—"I'm giving museum tours at the old Choctaw capitol building this morning, but I'll be finished around one o'clock. Why don't you meet up with us for my last tour at twelve thirty— most people who come here researching their heritage like to take the tour and learn a little more about the history of the tribe—then we'll head on over to the genealogy library at the school, punch some names into the database, and see if we can find anything?"

"I don't want to take you away from the festival. . . ." I hesitated, unsure whether I was ready to share this process, whatever it turned out to be, with someone I barely knew.

He smiled, his face taking on a warm, welcoming look that drew me in. I realized I was leaning across the table, closer to him. "You're not taking me away from anything."

Autumn wandered over and climbed into his lap, lacing her arms around his shoulders. "What's the matter?" he asked quietly, rubbing her back.

"Nothing," she sighed. "I just missed you, kind of."

Smoothing her hair, he rested his chin on her head. "That's all right. We all miss people sometimes."

"Yeah." The word was little more than a breath exhaled. She clung there a moment longer, then wiggled away and returned to Shasta and the other kids.

Her father watched her go, his face clouded with concern that was quickly masked, as if it were something he didn't want anyone else to see. "She checks in a lot," he explained. "Their mom passed away from a heart abnormality almost a year ago, and she's had a hard time dealing with it." Something beyond the words told me that Autumn wasn't the only one still dealing with it. The picture of Jace Reid shifted in my mind, the details quickly changing to accommodate a new reality. He wasn't a divorced, shared-custody dad spending a weekend with his kids, but the survivor of a tragic loss, left alone to raise two young children.

I wondered if he, like I, struggled with how and when to reveal that information to new people. On the other side of the table, he looked stiff and uncomfortable, braced for the expression of sympathy I uttered out of reflex.

"I'm sorry."

He nodded, still watching Autumn. "We were divorced," he added, as if that changed the parameters in a way that mattered. I recognized the tactic. It was the kind of thing I would have said, trying to minimize my past, so that people wouldn't feel the need to comfort me, to rescue or fix me.

"My mother died when I was about Autumn's age." The admission came out of the blue. Normally, I didn't bring up Mama unless I had to.

Jace's face registered momentary surprise. Even people who knew I was adopted assumed it had happened when I was a baby. Resting an arm on the table, he turned a shoulder to Shasta and the kids, closing off our conversation from everyone else. "How did you deal with losing your mother—I mean, if you don't mind my asking. It seems like Autumn's not getting what she needs to move on. She's had some counseling services through the tribe, but she's not the same kid she was. I don't know if she needs more counseling, better counseling, different counseling, or just to be left alone. This weekend is the first time I've seen her come to life a little bit. At home, she mostly spends her time sitting in her room, trying to be Willie's mother, or wandering in the woods by herself. She's lost interest in most of the things she used to love, the things a little girl should be doing, you know?" The questions came rushing out as if he'd been storing them up in a box; suddenly the lid burst open, and everything was crashing out in a disorganized pile.

Shaking his head, he drummed the tabletop with his index finger. "I'm sorry. I didn't mean to dump all that. It's just been kind of a tough weekend. The Choctaw festival a year ago was the last good day they had with their mother. A week later, she collapsed at work, and by the time the ambulance got her to the hospital, she was gone. I wasn't sure whether to even bring them to the family campout and the festival this year, but I guess I was hoping it might break Autumn out of her shell, help her focus on some good memories. I think she's not just mourning her mother, but she's mad about the way things are—that her everyday life has changed and there's nothing she can do about it." Straightening in his chair, he winced apologetically. "Sorry. I just did it again. Let's talk about something else."

"It's okay, really. I don't mind."

"So tell me about your music," he suggested. "Where did you learn to play the guitar like that?"

"From my dad—my adopted dad—but you asked about how things were when my mom—my real mom—died."

"I shouldn't have."

"It's all right." Surprisingly, that was true. I'd never thought there was any use in talking about Mama's death, but now it seemed as if some good could come of it. I sat silent for a moment, watching Autumn interact with the other kids, and thinking about the months after Granny told me Mama was gone. "I can't tell you what it's like for her, what she's thinking, or what she's feeling, but I do know that when my mama died, I spent a lot of time by myself. Some of that might have been because there wasn't really anyone for me to talk to. But later on, when Grandma Rose, my adopted grandmother, died, there were people I could have talked to, and I still chose not to." My mind raced to the moment Granny told me Mama had been found dead in an apartment in Kansas City. She wouldn't be coming home, and that was that. I shouldn't ask about her anymore. I should put her out of my mind. The problem was that I couldn't. I couldn't let it go, as Granny wanted, so I went out into the woods to be by myself. When Grandma Rose died, I couldn't grieve the way Aunt Kate thought I should, either, so I spent time alone by the river, again, where I could grieve for myself and not everyone else.

Jace was studying me, as if he could see the wheels turning.

"Do you try to get her to talk about it?" I asked.

He nodded wearily. "All the time."

"Maybe that's part of the problem." He seemed momentarily

stung, and I rushed in an attempt to explain an experience I'd never tried to put into words. "I'm not saying that you're doing anything wrong—please don't misunderstand. But when you're a kid, your grief is so different. Adults have parameters for the bereavement process—they've seen it on TV, in movies, read about it in magazines, watched other people go through it. But when you're young, you don't have all that. You're just experiencing it moment by moment, not as part of a cycle that's going to get better or worse over time. For kids, it's better one minute, then worse the next, then better again. You keep thinking if you wish hard enough, pray hard enough, things will go back to the way they were. For years, I felt that Grandma Rose was still with me after she died. I dreamed about her at night, and talked to her. All the adults told me it wasn't possible, that she was gone, that I needed to let go. They wanted me to grieve in a way that worked for them. I knew they were disappointed because I couldn't. I knew I was adding to their worries, making their grief more painful, so it just became easier to stay inside myself, where I could feel any way I wanted to. I wish I could explain it better. I'm sorry."

Looking at Autumn, I knew she would never be the same child she was before, but that didn't mean she wouldn't be happy. She would move through childhood as I had, knowing that happiness is fragile, that people go away and you can't wish them back. Sometimes at night or in the morning, just as she was drifting into sleep or coming out of it, she would feel herself near the door to heaven, and she'd know she'd just been with someone on the other side.

"Give it time," I said softly, and the pull of shared emotion reached into me, compelling and powerful. I had the sense that, of all the places in the world, I was supposed to be right here, right now, with him. Whether or not this trip produced the results I wanted, it did have a purpose. "She needs you to anchor her, to hold her hand when she's lonely, but some of the journey she has to take on her own."

Jace nodded, his eyes rounding upward in a wise, tender curve. "You're awfully young to know so much." It felt strange to hear him call me young. It shouldn't have, because just guessing from the age difference between him and Shasta, he was probably eight or ten years older than me.

"I'm not so young," I answered, and he leaned closer, smiling slightly, as if he were trying to figure me out. His eyes caught a tiny sliver of window light, and I found myself falling into his gaze, moving closer, caught in a magnetic connection I couldn't explain.

In the kitchen, someone dropped a plate, and the clatter of shattering ceramic rang through the restaurant. Both Jace and I jerked upright, blinked like sleepwalkers awakening, surprised to find ourselves surrounded by people.

From the table in the opposite corner, Nana Jo was watching with a deepening frown.

CHAPTER 13

Shasta rejoined our conversation after breakfast was served, and we made pleasant chitchat about the weather, the Labor Day festival, and the annual Choctaw princess pageant, which had been held at the festival grounds yesterday. I learned that Shasta was a former princess, and that some of the younger Reid girls had participated this year. Shasta had wanted Autumn to be involved, but Jace didn't think it was a good idea. She and her mother had always helped with the pageant together, and Jace feared there would be too many memories there for her. He planned to distract her from some of their usual events by letting her help at the Reid family craft booth, which sold screen-printed Choctaw homecoming shirts and Native American handicrafts, including some of Shasta's hand-painted trivets and coffee mugs.

"Mrs. Burleson fires them for me over at the high school art room," Shasta told me. "But one of these days, I want to get a kiln of my own—just the small kind, where you can fire a few pieces at a time." Her wistful tone said the purchase of a kiln was probably years away, if ever. Absently, she smoothed her hands over her swollen stomach and watched Benjamin wander off to his grandmother's table to finish eating. It was easy to forget, just talking to her, that her life was filled with responsibilities. "Anyway, I've been looking at art supply catalogs and stuff, to get an idea of what's out there. I think I could make a kiln pay for itself. Cody doesn't believe me, but I could, if I put my stuff in some shops in town." Taking a drink of her soda, she sat watching bubbles dissipate from the surface. "But there's no point getting something like that until after we move and get settled, get some money saved up, you know?" She glanced up, like she needed reinforcement.

"That makes sense. Kilns are pretty heavy. It would probably be hard to move one," was all I could think to say. I knew from experience with Angelo and Kate's kids that Shasta wouldn't get much potting and painting done with a toddler and a new baby in the house. Even as organized as Aunt Kate was, having two kids under four drove her crazy when Josh and Rose were little. My mama gave Angelo to his daddy because she couldn't watch him and do the things she wanted to do.

Staring at Shasta, I realized that when my mama made that decision, she wasn't much older than Shasta. She was sixteen when she had me, and then seven years later she had Angelo. At twenty-three, she should have been just starting out on her own life, but she was already watching the world through a face that looked old. Her movements were slow and listless, as if she knew she wasn't headed anywhere good, so there was no reason to hurry. Once in a while, she tried for something better, and when it didn't work out, she surrendered to life the way it was.

I wondered if Shasta would eventually do that, if there would come a point at which she looked down the road and didn't see a kiln and a ceramic shop anymore. Would she be happy without those dreams?

Shasta broke into my thoughts. "Jace carves Indian flutes." She glanced at her brother, who was frowning at her and had been about to comment on the kiln issue before she preempted him. Whatever he had been about to say, she obviously didn't want to hear it. "He made the one Dillon was playing last night, with the wolf head on it and all. He's an excellent carver. Our grandpa taught him."

"Really?" I asked, and Shasta nodded eagerly, answering before Jace could. "Seriously. It's a tradition in our family—flute making, I mean. Nana Jo says that's where the name Reid comes from. If you look for our family on the Dawes Commission Rolls back in the eighteen hundreds, some of them spelled it Reed, and some spelled it Reid. Nana Jo says probably it depended on who wrote it on the rolls and the census. Back then that happened all the time, because a lot of people couldn't read and write. They didn't really know how to spell their name. I'm not sure if there's another way to spell Clay, but you might find that same thing in your family records." She smiled encouragingly, as if the same effervescent faith that caused her to talk about buying a kiln when she was seven months pregnant also led her to believe I would delve into the tribal records today and discover a long lineage of ancestors.

"I guess we'll see," I said. "I'll be happy to find anything."

"Oh, you will." Shasta seemed sure of it. Her son started whimpering and calling her name from across the room, and she heaved herself from her chair to go see what was wrong.

Jace and I sat in silence, finishing the last of our pancakes. "I didn't know you made Dillon's flute," I said finally, pushing my plate aside. "Do you play?"

Jace was focused on Shasta's mural, his thoughts too far away for him to hear me at first. "Nah," he said finally. "No time for it. I don't carve many flutes anymore, either. Too much else to do these days." He glanced down the table at his kids, who had started arguing over the last pancake on our platter. Each of them had forks in it, and the dispute was rising in volume. "Split it in half, Autumn," Jace ordered. "You cut it and then Willie gets to pick which half he wants." Autumn huffed, and Jace winked at me, leaning closer. "She'll spend the next five minutes taking measurements and making sure she comes up with perfect halves so he can't pick the bigger one. I used to do that to Shasta."

"You did all kinds of mean things to me," Shasta corrected, returning to our table. "When I was in elementary school, my friends thought it was the coolest thing that my brother was a teenager. They all had these huge crushes on him, but he wouldn't give us the time of day. At school, he'd walk right past us with the other football players, and he wouldn't even talk to us." She sneered at Jace. "You were such a turd."

Grinning, he shrugged. "I had a reputation to protect."

"Fart." Shasta's nose wrinkled like she'd caught a bad scent.

"Baby," he shot back.

"Daddy, no calling names," Willie scolded, and all three of us laughed. Around the room, the Reids began getting up from their places, stacking dirty plates and unused napkins and preparing to leave.

Gathering our things, we rose and started toward the door with everyone else. Shasta stopped halfway and reminded me that we had parked out back, and her baby seat was in my car. "Let me tell Mama to wait on me a minute, and then I'll go get my stuff out of your car." She turned away, then turned back. "Or, if you want, I could show you around town real quick, then you can drop me at the festival grounds and I'll point out where our booth is so you can find us later. You are going to come by, aren't you?"

I hadn't even thought about how to spend the rest of the day. "I think so."

To Shasta, that was a definite yes. "Cool. You'll like the festival. There's the shopping, of course, but also the carnival, the Choctaw village where they tan hides and make arrowheads and stuff, the terrapin races, Indian dancers, the powwow, Choctaw stickball tournaments, horseshoes, softball, basketball, and then at night they have really big-time singers give concerts in the amphitheater." Checking over her shoulder, she noticed that her mother was about to walk out the door, and Benjamin was headed back toward us. "Hang on a minute," she said, then threaded her way through the lingering Reids, catching Benjamin's hand and stopping to talk to her mother.

Jace checked his watch as Willie and Autumn stacked up the place mats with Shasta's impromptu artwork. "Guess I'd better head to the museum." Grabbing a pencil and a paper coaster from the table, he jotted down a phone number and handed it to me. "Here's my cell number, in case you get lost and need directions or anything. Cell service is a little inconsistent at the festival grounds, but it'll probably pick up."

He handed me the paper, and I tucked it into my purse, then patted it, trying to look confident. "Thanks."

He leaned in, smiling. "See you at the museum at twelve thirty?"

I felt warm in the pit of my stomach. "Sure. See you then." We hesitated for a moment, bound by some invisible thread.

Autumn broke the connection by handing her dad the jumble of artistic place mats. "Dad, Willie and me don't have to go to the museum this morning, do we?"

Tucking the papers under his arm, Jace shook his head. "No, you don't. You two are with Neenee this morning. Nana Jo's going to drop you by her house. Neenee and Pappy wanted to keep you two for the morning, and then we'll do the festival this afternoon. We'll go to the carnival a while, and then you can help Aunt Shasta and Nana Jo at the booth." He checked his watch again, then looked at me, as if he hadn't factored me into his plans. "But not right after lunch, because I have to help Dell with some things. Neenee can bring you guys over to the booth when Willie and Pappy get up from their afternoon naps."

Autumn threaded her arms around her father's waist and sighed, studying the floor as if she were calculating the hours they would be apart. "Okay," she muttered miserably.

He ruffled her hair. "You'll have fun with Neenee and Pappy. They'll probably take you guys down to the creek to fish."

Willie brightened, clapping his hands and bouncing in place.

"Okay," Autumn muttered again. "But what if Pappy gets to feeling bad, and Neenee can't bring us over to the festival?"

"Then I'll come to Neenee's house and get you."

Autumn tightened her arms around him, her face turned downward. "What if you come to Neenee's to get us and we're down at the creek, and you don't know where we are?"

Jace frowned, his fingers absently smoothing his daughter's silky hair. "Then I'll come down to the creek and find you. Don't worry, all right?"

She nodded again. "Daddy, what time is it?"

"About nine."

Dark strands of hair fell forward, hiding her face. "It's a long way until after Willie's nap."

Jace glanced at me, his expression filled with meaning. "Not so long. You'll have a good time at Neenee's. Come on, now. We'd better head out. Neenee's probably waiting on the porch, wondering where we are."

Untangling herself obediently, Autumn retrieved Shasta's pictures and clutched them against her chest. "I don't like Neenee's house."

"You like Neenee's house." Jace sat down on the edge of a chair so that he was face-to-face with her. "You guys always have a good time there."

"I don't like some of the pictures."

Willie, who had been following the conversation back and forth like a volley at a Ping-Pong match, felt the need to interject, "I like Neenee's pictures."

Taking his daughter's hand, Jace smoothed her small fingers like knotted pieces of twine. "Sweetheart, Neenee loves those pictures because she loved your mommy."

"I know." Autumn nodded glumly. "But it's a long time till after Willie's nap. I forgot my watch, and Neenee's clock has hands. I can't read it and I won't know what time you're gonna get us from Neenee."

"Here, take mine," I said, unstrapping my wristwatch, a black plastic digital I'd bought in Ukraine. "You can borrow it for the day."

Autumn's face lit up. "I can keep it all day? Really?"

"Sure. Here, hold out your arm, and I'll put it on."

" 'Kay."

I buckled the watch into place, then stood over Autumn's shoulder while she looked at it.

"Thanks," she said, touching the readout in awe, then pushing the button to turn on the backlight. "It's so cool. It's even got a light in it."

"And a stopwatch, and lots of other things I have no idea how to use," I pointed out. "But the coolest thing is that all the little words are written in Russian."

Latching onto her arm, Willie stood on his tiptoes to look. Autumn pulled away petulantly. "Just a minute, Willie. You're interrupting." She sounded like a little girl playing the part of Mommy in a game of house. "It's not for little kids."

Taking her hand, I lowered her arm so Willie could see. "Here. Let's let Willie have a look. I'm sure he'll be careful."

Behind us, Jace craned to see the watch as well.

"Ooohhhh," Willie muttered in amazement, his eyes wide around the dark centers. "I like it." He tipped his chin upward with a meaningful look. "A lot."

Autumn pulled away, tracing a finger around the edge of the crystal, squinting at the tiny Russian characters. "Where'd you get it from?"

"I bought it in Ukraine." Autumn frowned at my explanation, her brows knotting. "That's a country near Russia, way on the other side of the world. I worked in an orphans' mission there last year, and sometimes we'd go into town and buy things from people who sell stuff on the street corners. They carry their merchandise in funny little wooden cases, and when they flip the latch, they have a little store, right there on the street."

"Wow," Autumn breathed, regarding both the timepiece and me with equal amazement.

Willie climbed onto a chair so he could see the watch again.

"No, sir," Jace said, guiding him back to the floor.

"I wanna wear it," Willie whined.

Clamping her arm against her chest, Autumn covered the watch with her hand. "Uh-uh. It's not for little kids, Willie. You'll break it." Her voice rose in volume, causing Nana Jo, Shasta, and some of the aunts to turn our way.

"I will not." Willie stretched onto his tiptoes, his chin jutting up and out. "I'm not a baby."

Autumn leaned down, so that her face was close to his. "You are too."

Jace gave a tired sigh. "All right, you two. That's enough." Taking one child in each hand, he separated them, and I had a feeling he was about to use the parental tactic that Aunt Kate often deployed on her kids. Because they were fighting over the item, he was going to take it away, and then Autumn would once again be upset about spending the day at her grandmother's house.

"Tell you what," I said, bracing my hands on my knees and leaning down, so that I was eye to eye with Willie and Autumn. "Let's let Autumn wear the watch for today, but only if she uses the stopwatch to time some things for you—like, how fast you can run across the yard, or how long it takes you to catch a fish. Maybe you two can even keep a chart, and then later today, we can look at how fast you were."

Willie considered the idea, then nodded reluctantly. "I'm real fast." Squinting one eye shut, he took on the look of a boy faced with a double-dog dare.

"I'll bet you are," I said.

"Not as fast as me." Autumn gave me an impulsive hug. "Thanks, Aunt Dell."

"Yeah, thanks, Aunt Dell." Willie joined in the hug, and the force of it knocked me into a chair.

"All right, you two." Jace chuckled, catching me and the chair in one hand. "Now that you've mugged her for her watch, let's leave her in one piece. Time to go."

" 'Kay." Autumn wiggled out of the embrace and trotted happily across the room, holding up her new treasure. "Nana Jo, look what Aunt Dell let me borrow. It's got Russian on it. Over there, they got guys on the street with boxes that they open the latch, and . . ."

Willie remained sitting on my knees, toying with the choker the Spencers had given me before I left the orphanage—an old Soviet coin with a hole drilled in the middle and a leather thong passed through it. The sensation of Willie's tiny fingers against my neck felt nice. It reminded me of my kids in Ukraine, lonely—sad, desperate to touch and be touched, to give and receive love. Despite his usual boundless energy, Willie seemed content to sit on my lap and investigate the coin.

"You remind me of my kids in Ukraine," I said, and he raised his eyes curiously. "I bet they would love to go fishing with you today. They live in a city, so there isn't any place to fish. One time, we made fishing poles from dead branches, and we played a game where they got to fish for candy. It's not as much fun as real fishing, but they liked it."

Willie blinked, surprised. Bracing his hands on my knees, he leaned back, so that he almost slid off, and I had to circle my arms around him to keep him from falling. "You like fishin'?"

"I love fishing."

"Did the 'Crane kids catch any candy?"

His pronunciation of the word made me chuckle. "The kids in Ukraine? Yes, they did."

He studied the ceiling. "How'd they get candy to bite the hook?"

I chuckled. "The teachers have to put it on for them and tug their lines, so it feels like they caught a fish. It takes a little pretending. Sometimes I'd hang on for a minute, so they could fight the line like they had a great big daddy bass on there."

Willie nodded thoughtfully, imagining the game. "Maybe you can come fishin' at my Neenee and Pappy's."

"We'll see," I answered, uncomfortable with the assumption that I would be around long enough for that.

"Autumn don't like to fish anymore."

"That's okay. Not everybody likes to fish."

"My mama liked to fish. I got a picture." Stretching far against the circle of my arms, he arched backward like an acrobat attempting a walkover. "She looked like you look."

A hot flush burned into my cheeks, and I fumbled for something appropriate to say. In the silence, Willie dragged himself upright to look at me.

Jace cleared his throat self-consciously. "We'd better get going, big guy."

"Okie doke," Willie answered, unfettered by the invisible swell of adult emotion around him. Lingering a moment on my lap, he touched the coin necklace, met my gaze, and said, "That's pretty," then slipped away.

Jace rubbed his thumb and forefinger across his dark brows, then held his hand there a moment. "Sorry about that. They have a hard time knowing what's all right to say and what's not." He lowered his hand, his eyes meeting mine with a look of grief and concern that was like a tide, pulling me into an ocean of thoughts he kept to himself.

"It's all right. Really," I said quietly. Shasta was headed our way, and from across the room Nana Jo watched the exchange between

Jace and me with an expression somewhere between concern and dis-approval. She eased a few steps closer, her walking stick making a hollow, almost impatient tap on the linoleum tile.

Jace reconnoitered over his shoulder, as if the walking cane were an unspoken signal, and he knew what it meant. "Sounds like Nana Jo's about to pound a hole in the floor." He turned away, then back, regarding me from the corner of his eye. "See you in a little while."

"Sure," I answered, and he smiled just before he turned away. I smiled back.

Shasta watched Jace go, then turned to me, crossing her arms with a deliberateness that surprised me. Normally, she flitted around like a little girl trapped in a woman's body. "He's too old for you, you know." Her words were astonishingly blunt. "That's why Nana Jo's giving you two the hawk eye."

My mouth dropped open, and I snapped to my feet, a rapid pulse racing in my neck. Last night's biting commentary about Lana flashed through my mind. Did Shasta think I was being nice to Autumn and Willie because I was scheming after her brother? I barely knew Jace, and besides, I'd seen Shasta's bad side, and I definitely didn't want to be on it. "I . . . I didn't . . . I'm not . . ."

Shasta giggled like a teenage girl passing dirty notes in class. "Relax, will you? I'm just telling you what the old folks are saying." We moved to the back door, and she pulled it open, then blinked against the light. "Just watch out. They're kind of protective about Jace and his kids since Deanne died. Personally, I think it's kind of cool to see him act, like, interested in someone again. Believe me, Lana's been trying for months, and he doesn't look at her the way he was just looking at you. I mean, it's sad about Deanne, but it's not like they were still married. They got married straight out of high school, and they just shouldn't of, that's all."

In my mind, Grandma Rose was grousing, *Well, that's the pot calling the kettle black, now isn't it?* I didn't say it, of course. Instead,

I checked the rapidly emptying room behind us and tried to change the subject. "Where's Benjamin?"

"Oh, he's with Mama. She's got an extra baby seat in her car, so they went on and left." With a vague wave over her shoulder, she ushered me through the kitchen door. Aunt Maemae had disappeared into the freezer again. "Mama's about to have a conniption because I'm not headed *right* over to the booth to help *immediately* this morning. I told her I had to show you around town, and it'd be easier if she took Benji with her. She wasn't too happy, but she'll get over it."

We slipped through the rear exit together, and Shasta turned to push the door shut with both hands, then swung around, flinging her hair over her shoulder. The movement caused her to lose her balance, and she wobbled sideways like an off-center Weeble, bumped into me, and caught my arm.

"Geez." Slapping a hand to her chest, she caught her breath, then circled her stomach with the other arm. "I forget sometimes. Sorry."

I hovered beside her as we started toward the car. How could anyone forget the weight of a nearly full-term pregnancy? "It's the flip-flops," I joked.

"You sound like Lana." Shasta sneered sideways, unconcerned by her near fall. She circled the car and waited for the doors to unlock. "I'll show you all the places you need to know, and if you've got a map, I can tell you how to get to the county courthouse. A girl where I worked was looking for her birth parents once, and the first place she started was the courthouse. I never did find out what happened. I got pregnant and had to quit the job." She paused long enough to open the passenger side. "I wish I didn't have to work the booth today. I'd go with you."

"It probably won't be all that exciting." I wasn't sure if I was trying to console her or prepare myself.

Bouncing into the passenger seat, Shasta tossed her hair cheerfully. "Oh, I don't know. I'm sure the ladies at the courthouse can help you at least get your birth records, and that's the first step—anyway that's what the girl at my work told me. Who knows? When I was down at the courthouse paying Cody's speeding ticket, those girls in the office nearly talked my ear off. My stepcousin works there, and Lord knows, she could talk the hair off a horse. If she's there, you might get lucky and find out all kinds of stuff."

CHAPTER 14

Touring the small town of Clayton with Shasta turned out to be an exercise in patience. Shasta wanted to show me the local landmarks, everything from the drive-in to the grocery store. Everywhere she went, she knew people, and people knew her, and we stopped to talk. Half of the people in town were related to Shasta, and the other half had either taught her in school, coached her in softball, had her in Sunday school years ago, gone to high school with her, or knew her because of the murals she'd painted on several buildings in the area.

"We did those back in high school as a community service project," she said with a backhanded wave toward a mural on an old brick building downtown. "They so totally stink. One of these days I'm going to come down here with a sandblaster and blow them away."

"You shouldn't." I was only halfway focused on the painted scene of a stream winding through a village of traditional Choctaw round houses with cone-shaped thatch roofs. "It's beautiful. It's really good." Studying the painting, I tried not to dwell on the fact that my tour with Shasta had blown two huge holes in my plans. I'd learned that there was no branch of my bank in tiny Clayton, or anywhere around that Shasta knew of, and that the county courthouse was forty-five miles away. "The courthouse is a lot farther away than I thought," I admitted, raising my wrist to check my watch, then realizing I didn't have a watch. "I thought it was nearby."

"Guess I should have explained that earlier," Shasta said apologetically. "We don't think anything of making that drive. Around here, you drive to do pretty much anything. We're just used to it."

Leaning in the car window, I glanced at the clock. It was already nine thirty. "I guess I have time to make it down there and back," I said, thinking that I was supposed to meet Jace at twelve thirty. But there was still the problem of money. Getting birth records copied at the courthouse would undoubtedly cost a few dollars, and I had almost no money left. What if they wouldn't take an out-of-state check? "I really need to cash a check somewhere before I go."

"Oh." Shasta chewed her bottom lip. "I'd do it for you, but Cody and I never have any money in our account. Hmmm . . . My friend Kristin works down at the dollar store. She'll cash a check for us." Giving the mural one last disgusted sneer, she started down the street with her hair swinging from side to side like a length of silky black cloth.

I jogged after her, catching up as she pulled open a door and walked into an old-fashioned five-and-dime like she owned the place. I waited a discreet distance away while she cornered the girl behind the counter, a stocky redhead with braces and curly hair. It quickly became clear that the clerk was concerned about cashing a check. Shasta gave her a sales pitch. "Come on, Kristin. It's not that big a deal."

Kristin's pert nose wrinkled like a rabbit's, her eyes darting nervously my way. Shoving her hands into her store apron pockets, she jingled something, then finally pulled out her keys and opened the antique cash register. Shasta waved me over, slipping her arm around me when I got there. "They're not really supposed to give cash anymore, but she said she'll do it, since you're my cousin." Laying her head on my shoulder, she pasted on a huge smile for Kristin's benefit.

Kristin studied us. "Y'all do look a lot alike."

"We all look alike to white folks," Shasta quipped, and I blinked in surprise.

Kristin smirked and rolled her eyes. "Shasta, you're so bad."

"I know." Snatching a pack of gum from the rack on the counter,

Shasta tossed it toward the cash register. "Kristin can only do it for thirty over, and you have to buy something." She stepped back and motioned to the counter. "You can buy me some gum."

"Sure." Pulling out my checkbook, I started writing the check while Kristin punched numbers into the cash register and gave me a total. She frowned at the check when I handed it to her.

Shasta scooped up our purchase and ripped the top off the package. "Don't worry. The check's good." She popped a piece of gum in her mouth, then wadded up the foil wrapper and tossed it into the trash. "It's not one of mine."

Kristin's nose scrunched up so that her eyes slanted upward. "If it was *your* check, I wouldn't of cashed it." After taking the money from the drawer, she counted it slowly into my hand.

Shasta clicked her teeth petulantly. "I haven't bounced a check in, like, six months."

"Uh-huh." Kristin closed the cash register door and braced her hands on the counter, tilting her head skeptically.

"Well, if Cody would write down when he goes to the ATM, it would help. In fact, if he'd stay away from that thing, we wouldn't be so broke."

A puff of air whistled past Kristin's braces. "Huh! If I got all the stuff you guys get from the tribe, I'd never be broke."

"Yeah, yeah, whatever." Shasta headed for the door with an exaggerated swagger. "You poor lily-white thing. You just wish you had my kinda tan."

"Brat," Kristin called after her.

"Paleface." Yanking open the door, Shasta grinned over her shoulder, then stuck her nose in the air and disappeared onto the sidewalk.

I stood at the counter with my cash still in my hand, unable to put my embarrassment into words. "Thanks," I said. "The check really is good."

"You're welcome." Her lips squeezed shut over the braces. "You're way too nice to be hanging out with Shas."

I just smiled, thanked her again, and headed for the door.

Shasta was waiting out on the street. "Mission accomplished," she said, glancing at her watch. "Guess you'd better take me over to the festival grounds before Mama has a coronary."

"Sure." I finally had some money in my pocket, but so far today, I was a long way from *mission accomplished*. The courthouse was forty-five miles away, and my nearest potential bank or check-cashing store was probably farther than that. I would definitely be camping out with bottled water and a mooched blanket again tonight, but the possibility didn't seem so bad. Camp Reid was starting to feel like home, and the Reids like family. "Thanks for helping me get some cash," I said as Shasta and I climbed into my car. "The check really is good. She won't have any problem with it."

"Oh, I know." Shrugging casually, Shasta twisted a long strand of hair around her finger. "You're one of those serious, got-it-together girls who balances her checkbook. I can tell by looking." It was hard to say whether that was a complaint or a compliment.

Putting the car in gear, I pulled onto the street, then rounded the block, passing another of Shasta's murals, a painting of a riderless war pony standing atop a hill, gazing forlornly into the distance. The eyes were so lifelike that I wondered what the horse was thinking.

"So what's Europe like?" Shasta asked, the words dreamy and far away.

I considered the question for a moment. *Not so different from here,* I thought. *Older.* Europe had an ancientness that nothing in the States could match, but beyond the architecture, people went about all the normal patterns of life—work, school, home, love, hate, politics. In some ways, Europe was very much like home. "It's beautiful, especially Switzerland. You can't imagine the Alps until you've been there."

I spent the next few minutes giving Shasta a verbal tour of Europe as we crossed the street and then drove a few miles to the Choctaw capitol grounds at Tuskahoma. She listened to my description of a castle in Germany where the youth symphony had given a performance in the garden. A blond-haired tour guide had flirted with me in broken English, but I left out that part of the story.

"It sounds incredible." Breathing deeply, Shasta closed her eyes and rubbed a hand over her stomach. Through the T-shirt fabric, I saw the baby move. "I'd like to go there someday."

"Maybe you will," I said as we rounded a corner and the festival grounds came into view ahead. The place was alive with activity. Lines of vehicles waited to pull into fields that served as parking areas. Tourists clambered from their cars, pulling wagons and pushing baby strollers toward rows of vendors' booths housed in long open-air metal buildings. Near the craft area, a banner advertised gospel and country-music concerts in a huge hillside amphitheater. Twangy rhythms floated among the din of voices, the electronic whirl and whiz of carnival rides, and the metallic ping of bats and balls from the softball fields near the parking lot. In the center of the grounds, the old Choctaw Capitol Building towered like Gulliver among the Lilliputians, its classic sandstone archways and three-story red-brick walls out of keeping with the tiny village of traditional Choctaw round houses across the road. Rhythmic bits of Choctaw language drifted in the window as we passed the village, where tribe members in historic dress reenacted scenes from an ancient way of life. On the fringes of the grounds, RVs, tents, and modern-day tepees were crowded into camping areas, so that the whole event took on the aura of a giant family reunion, like the Reids' campout, but larger.

"I had no idea there was so much here," I admitted as we stopped behind a line of cars entering the parking lot.

Sighing, Shasta opened her eyes. "Choctaw Labor Day Festival's a big deal," she said, then motioned out the front window. "Pull into the vendor parking. It'll be easier to let me out there. When you come back, you'll have to park out in the big parking area, but later on in the day, you can usually find some spaces up front. Things won't get crowded again until evening when the powwow and the big concerts start." Shasta pulled a vendor pass from her purse and held it up for the parking attendant, who waved us around the line of cars and into a vendor lot.

"This place is amazing," I said as I pulled into a parking space.

"Not compared to castles in Europe, I bet." Shasta sounded unusually melancholy. She opened the door and she pulled herself out of the seat, then leaned back in, pointing toward the festival grounds. "Our booth is down that way, on the row by the stage. It's the one with the striped red flag on top. You can just barely see it from here."

I put the car in park and unbuckled my seat belt, then stood on the doorframe and tried to spot Shasta's flag in the village of metal roofing and plastic tarps.

"Right next to the tepee with the horses on it." Shasta pointed. "That's my uncle Randal's. He sells belts and stuff made from braided horsehair."

"Oh, I see it." The miniature tepee secured atop one of the craft buildings was hard to miss, even in such a crowded setting.

"Okay, then, see you later." A group of guys approached, headed toward the softball fields, and Shasta checked them out covertly, tucking a few stray strands behind her ear. "We'll be here all day."

"See you later." Sliding back into the car, I noticed Benjamin's baby seat in the back. "Do you want me to carry the baby seat over to the booth for you?"

Shasta flashed the softball players a flirty look, then shook her head and turned away, as if she'd caught herself in an old habit. "No, that's all right. You're coming back. I'll get it then. Oh, hey, I'll call my stepcousin at the courthouse and tell her to look out for you.

She's kind of . . . uhhh . . . chubby, with blond hair. Real sweet. You'll know her if you meet her."

"Thanks," I said, wondering how I'd gotten so lucky as to have Shasta on my side. Between her faith, her knowledge of the area, and her connections, the day was looking pretty promising.

I watched her walk away, then sat for a moment taking in the festival. Gazing up at the capitol, its imposing shadow falling from three stories overhead, I had the sense of being part of something large and powerful, with a long history that reached back hundreds of years, like the lineages in Europe. There was so much more to my father's heritage, to my heritage, than I'd ever considered.

I pondered the idea as I left town and headed toward the courthouse in Antlers, winding my way through the Kiamichi Mountains on the thin ribbon of highway. Oak and sweet gum trees arched over the road, the sunlight dappling their leaves. I had a sense of being far from all my normal reference points. The peaceful day outside and the earthy stillness of the hills ran in stark contrast to the turmoil in my head. Questions rushed through my mind like race cars on a track, zipping past in a blur of noise and emotion, only to come around again and again.

Who was my father? How did he feel about being part of the tribe? Did he grow up in these hills, a little boy with dark hair and sienna skin, darting through the carpet of last year's leaves on quick, silent feet, climbing nests of enormous boulders searching for hidden treasure, or shinnying up the gnarled oak trees to see into the distance? Did he grow up here, go to school, play football, do all the normal things? Did he drive this very road, travel it so many times that he knew each curve, each rise and fall of ground, the time of day the shadow of the hills blanketed the highway and how they changed with the seasons?

Did he speak Choctaw like Nana Jo's children and grandchildren? Was there a grandmother who taught him about the code talkers and the Trail of Tears? Did he know his history? Was he rooted here like one of these ancient trees?

Did he bring my mother here? Did they drive along this very road together, her body round and swollen like Shasta's? She would have been younger than Shasta, just a teenager, a pregnant high school dropout, running away from home.

Was she afraid when she felt me move and stretch inside her? Did she wonder who I would be, or was she indifferent, so deep in a haze of drugs that she didn't think about me at all?

Did my father see flutters of movement beneath her shirt the way I saw Shasta's baby move? Did he lay his hand on her stomach and say, *Don't worry, Jesse, I'll take care of you. I'll take care of you both. . . .*

Did they ever talk about me at all?

How had I come to be?

What if the answers were worse than the questions?

The whirling stopped in my mind, and that single thought flashed again, words against a blank screen in a theater with the house lights turned low to block out everything else. All my life, people had been trying to keep the truth from me—Mama, Granny, my CPS caseworker, James and Karen, even Grandma Rose. I'd asked her once if she knew who my father was. She'd always lived across the river from Granny's house, and in a small town, people talk. But when I brought up the question, Grandma Rose only paused momentarily in weeding her flower bed. She patted my hand, leaving little crystals of fresh earth, and said, *Oh, honey, sometimes the past is best left where it is. You're God's child. That's what matters. . . .*

Combing a hand through my hair, I sat with my elbow braced on the window frame, thinking. Outside, a road sign with bullet dings in it zipped by: EED ZONE AHEAD. Someone had shot out the SP. Probably kids, drunk and wild on a Saturday night, desperate to manufacture fun in a place where the entertainment was limited to shooting at road signs, bashing mailboxes, and toilet papering the principal's yard.

I pictured my father doing those things.

Only a few more miles to the county seat. When I got there, I would be near the interstate. I could pull onto the entrance ramp, head north, and just keep driving. Go home to my bedroom, with the antique four-poster bed and the fan overhead making its lazy effort to push air from the vaulted ceiling. I could sleep in my own room tonight, with James and Karen down the hall. Sometime in the wee hours, Roxie and Felix, our overweight tabby cats, would slink in and curl up on either side of my face.

I could leave Shasta's baby seat with someone at the courthouse in Antlers, maybe even find a local who was headed to the festival and would take it to her. I could go home, and no one would ever have to know where I'd been, how close I'd come to screwing up everything . . .

And then what?

Then. What.

I couldn't answer that one simple question. The answer was somewhere on the other side of a lake so big, and black, and thick that there was no way across. The only path around, the only path I could see, led through the past. *You can wish all day long that you felt differently,* Grandma Rose used to say, *but the heart doesn't turn on wishes. Generally, a change of heart requires action.*

There was nothing to do but continue on the path I'd started when I left Kansas City. Was that only yesterday? It seemed like a week. Now here I was, headed for the courthouse, where Shasta was sure I would find clues to my father's identity and the circumstances of my birth. Could it really be that easy? Was it possible that all these years the answers had been here, just waiting for me to have the courage to ask the questions?

I wound through the county seat, a town slightly larger than

Clayton, but still small. Signs directed me to the county courthouse. I turned the corner, and suddenly there it was, a two-story white building with stark art deco architecture. Out front, the Kiamichi Garden Club members were planting a flower bed. I recognized them from my encounter at the mini-mart the day before. Today, they were putting in pansies by the courthouse entrance. Cecil, the one who'd given me directions at the convenience store, set down a flat of plants, braced her hands on her back, and stretched. "Well, hi there!" She squinted at me and waved a soiled green-and-pink garden glove as I climbed out of my car. "Did ya find your way yesterday?"

I was surprised she remembered. "I did, thanks."

"They have any cabins open at the Four Winds?"

I wanted to tell her that I apparently wasn't the right kind of customer for the Four Winds. "No, but she sent me on out to the campgrounds at the lake, so it's all right."

Wringing her gloved hands, Cecil took a step closer. "Oh, you poor thing. I'm sorry. I guess I sent you on a wild-goose chase."

"It's all right, really."

"You shouldn't be out there all alone at that campground, a young little gal like you. That's not a bit safe. Why, just a few years ago, a teenager was attacked and killed right there at that campground. It happens, even here. How many years ago has that been?" Glancing over her shoulder, she waited for input from the garden club ladies, who had tuned into the conversation.

"About fifteen," a dark-haired woman answered, mopping her brow with the back of her sleeve, then returning to her work.

Someone chuckled, then pretended to cough. Cecil frowned, returning her attention to me. "I've got an extra bedroom in my house. It's nothing fancy, but it's open for guests."

One of the garden club ladies muttered, "Cecil, for heaven's sake."

Cecil was unfazed. "It'd be better than a young girl staying all alone in a campground. It'd be safer."

"I'm fine, really. But thanks." I took a step toward the entrance, and her brows tightened into a worry knot. I felt compelled to explain further. "I'm camping out with some cousins who have a booth at the Choctaw Labor Day Festival."

Cecil brightened at my mention of the festival. "We'll be at the garden club booth over there this evenin'. You decide you need a place, you just come find me there. My house is right here in town. B Street, number fifty-two."

"Thanks. That's really nice of you." I wondered if everyone here was so friendly. "Do you know where they have birth certificates and stuff? Which office, I mean?"

Scratching her ear with one knuckle of her glove, she left a little trail of dirt next to a line of melting orange makeup. "Down the . . . well, I'm not sure. Used to be they didn't have those at the county courthouse and you had to write off for them, but I think maybe that's changed. BB, do you know where she needs to go?"

"Here, I'll take her." A heavyset woman with graying hair and Choctaw features stood up. "I need to go get the dead leaves off those ficus trees inside. Can't stand to see a plant in such bad shape. I'm done with my flat out here anyhow." She glanced pointedly toward Cecil's flat. "More than I can say for *some* people."

"Oh, for heaven's sake." Cecil glanced at the waiting pansies. "It ain't a race, BB."

"It ain't social hour, either," BB countered, pulling off her gloves and tucking them in her apron pocket as she started around the railing. "If *some people* don't hurry up, the lunch crowd is gonna beat us to the café."

"There's no lunch crowd at the café today. Everyone's at the festival," Cecil pointed out.

"Even so . . ."

My cell phone rang, and I fished it from my purse while pulling open the courthouse door.

Karen was on the other end. "Hey, kiddo, how's your trip?"

"Good." My throat went dry and prickly, like a puff of cotton with a cocklebur in it, needling me with little stabs of guilt.

"You haven't checked in today." Karen's voice was pleasant, but there was an undercurrent of suspicion. "I just wondered how you were doing."

"Fine. Sorry I forgot to call. It's such a pretty day, I was just out"—*looking for my birth family, because for reasons I can't explain, the one I have isn't enough for me*—"goofing around a little this morning."

Karen hesitated, and I had a feeling I'd tipped her off. "It's not raining there? It's pouring buckets here."

Glancing up at the clear blue sky, I was conscious of the garden club ladies listening, trying to piece together my story like one of their flower plots. I slipped through the door, and let it close behind me, then cradled the phone close to my shoulder. "I've . . . been inside a while," I hedged. The door swished open as BB came in.

"Oh." Karen wasn't ready to let me off that easily. "Are you having a nice visit?"

"Yes." The answer sounded false. I'd never flat-out lied to my parents about where I was. I'd never had to. "I'm meeting some new people."

BB started down the hall and motioned for me to follow. "This way, honey."

"That's good." Karen hesitated again. She wanted me to offer more information. I couldn't, of course.

"Mom, I'd better go. I'm trying to get directions to one of the offices." As soon as the words came out, I knew it was the wrong thing to say. Now Karen would be sure I was considering enrolling at Missouri State. "I'm meeting up with Barry there," I added lamely.

BB quirked a brow at me and looked up and down the hall. "Whoever you're meetin', he ain't here." She waited with her arms crossed over her chest as Karen and I finished our conversation and

I hung up. "They ought to be able to help you in there," she said, pointing through a doorway toward a counter which at the moment appeared to be unmanned. "They'll fix you right up, I'm sure." Patting my shoulder, she gave me a speculative look, then turned her attention to a sickly-looking ficus tree near the office door. "Good luck, sugar. I hope you find what you're lookin' for."

CHAPTER 15

BB had sent me to the right place, but nobody was eager to fix me right up. There seemed to be only one clerk in the office. She was busy doing something behind a row of file cabinets and wasn't in a hurry to acknowledge my presence or find out what I wanted. I could only see the top of her head, but her hair was dark, not blond, so she wasn't Shasta's stepcousin.

"Excuse me," I said, still feeling guilty and nervous about Karen's phone call. Whatever information was here, I wanted to get it and be gone.

The top of the clerk's head hesitated behind the cabinet, then disappeared again. "Be there in a minute. Someone's coffee just got spilled back here." Her voice seemed familiar, but I couldn't place it. I heard the sound of paper towels ripping, then an exasperated sigh. High heels clicked rapidly on the linoleum floor as she headed into a back room. A door swished open in the hallway, then another, and I had a feeling she'd left the office altogether.

Bracing my hands on my hips, I stretched upward and tried to take a deep breath. My chest squeezed tighter, as if my lungs were caught in a vise that was slowly being closed. The scent of plaster, a musty air-conditioning system, and decaying paper transported me to the courthouse back home in Missouri, to the weeks after Granny died, when James and Karen stood with me in front of a weary-looking family court judge and told him that they wanted to raise me.

The judge glanced toward the wall clock, squinting at the numbers through cloudy gray eyes, the edges of the irises faded into the whites. I tried to imagine eyes like that on a young person, but I couldn't. Those eyes looked like they'd seen it all before. He explained that it would have to be foster care, and possibly adoption later, if no biological relative could be found. He pointed out that this was a big decision, not one to be made in a moment of emotion.

James said we didn't need a trial period. Our minds were already made up. Karen slipped her hand over mine, her fingers a warm, trembling circle.

For the first time in my life, I knew how it felt to be wanted.

"That so, young lady?" the judge asked.

Something cold and invisible squeezed my chest.

Karen's fingers tightened reassuringly around mine.

Don't mess this up, Dell, I thought. *You always mess things up.* "Yes." The word was quiet, considering the effort it took to produce. I was afraid anything I said would be wrong. I was afraid the judge would look up, see who I was, and say I couldn't go home with James and Karen, that I'd have to go back to the emergency shelter, De-buke House, where CPS had sent me when the ambulance came for Granny.

The judge never looked my way at all. He only signed something on my paperwork and said he was approving foster placement with James and Karen, pending a search for blood relatives. I didn't know what he meant. There was only Uncle Bobby, and by then he was in jail for DUI, on his way to prison for what would probably be a long time. I tried not to think about how mad he probably was about that, about everything. No doubt, he was cussing a blue streak and throw-ing things around his jail cell.

Someone had to clean up all that mess. In county, maybe they'd make him do it for himself.

Even though I didn't want to, I felt sorry for him, sitting in jail. He'd hate it there, locked up in a cell, with so many people nearby, so much noise. He didn't like to be around a lot of people.

If he got out of jail, he would come looking for me. . . .

The judge was going through a long list of details I didn't under-stand—something about foster care forms, and in-home visits, and when I'd have to come back to Hindsville to see my social worker, Twana Stevens, and how long she would search for my father or members of his family.

Before the judge mentioned my father, it had never occurred to me that was what *biological relative* meant. What if they found him, whoever he was, and he wanted to take me away from James and Karen? What if I had to go away with someone who was like Uncle Bobby? The thought made my head spin. Suddenly the room seemed impossibly hot, and a black tunnel narrowed around my eyes. James caught me and kept me on my feet. "Hang in there, kiddo," he said. "Just a few minutes more and we'll be done." My legs were tired. It felt like we were standing on Jell-O. The air from the vent smelled like the underneath of Granny's house, where a stray cat had just hid-den a new litter of kittens.

If we went back by Granny's house to get the rest of my stuff, I would crawl underneath and get those kittens out. They'd need someone to take care of them. For weeks, I'd been sneaking food under there for the mama, so she'd stay and care for her babies. If she got hungry, she'd wander off, and the kittens would starve. If they crawled out from under the house, my dog, Rowdy, would get them. But by now, Rowdy was probably at Grandma Rose's farm. He liked it better there, anyway . . .

"Can I help you?"

My mind snapped back to the present as a girl in her twenties came in from the hallway and slipped around behind the counter, carrying a stack of foam food containers. She was blond and heavyset, possibly Shasta's cousin.

I paused a moment to get my thoughts together. "I'm here about requesting a birth certificate."

She set the containers on the desk, then glanced up and smiled. "Oh, hey, you must be Shasta's friend. She called and said you were coming."

I nodded. "She told me she had a cousin working here." Thank goodness for Shasta. Was there anyplace in the county she didn't know people?

"Well, we're stepcousins really." Pulling her bottom lip between her teeth, she frowned apologetically. "I told her to call you and tell you we don't give official birth certificates here. You have to write off to the state capital for those. I guess she didn't have your cell phone number to get ahold of you before you drove all the way over here."

I must have looked as shattered as I felt, because she bit her lip again, then went on talking. "I'm really sorry. This happens all the time. We do have a new test program where we can access the records online and print them for you, but it's not the official state-issued long form with the seal on it. Some places will accept a copy, and some won't."

Relief spiraled through me. "That would be great. A copy is all I need."

"All righty, then." She grabbed a pen from the desktop and began searching under the counter. "Where in the world are those forms? Hey," she hollered toward the back room, "where are those forms for the new computer thingy?"

No one answered.

"I think she went across the hall," I said.

"She's always across the hall. That's where the mirror is." Shasta's cousin snorted irritably, glaring toward the door. "Nothing like doing all of your boss's work. Ever since she started here, it's Jamie do this, Jamie do that." Searching the countertop, she came up with a pad of sticky notes. "I've lost ten pounds, though, so I guess stress does have its upside. Go ahead and write your information on here—full name, exact date of birth, place of origin, parents' full names. That'll be enough. The computer brings it up in, like, two and a half seconds. This thing is lightning fast. It's a test link with the Department of Vital Statistics, but I hope they let us keep it. As soon as my *boss* gets back, she can get you the official authorization form to fill out. She probably has them locked away somewhere."

After printing my information carefully on the pad, I slid it over to Jamie. "Thank you so much," I said.

She turned the pad around and read the words, then tore off the top sheet and she stuck it to her finger. "Hey, I'm just glad we can help. Shasta says you're here looking for your family—like on TV. That's so awesome." Waving the sticky note like a tiny flag, she headed toward the back room. "I feel like that private investigator guy on *Unsolved Mysteries.* This is too exciting."

She disappeared behind the file cabinets, and I stood wondering what she would find, if this would be the moment that changed my life. It bothered me that Shasta had told someone, here in this official place, about my background. The more people who knew, the more likely it was that Karen and James would somehow find out what I was doing.

The vent clicked on overhead again, and the combination of food smell from the foam containers and moldy air made my stomach gurgle into my throat.

High heels crossed the hallway in a rapid *taptaptap*, probably Jamie's boss coming back. Hinges squealed, then something crashed in the back room. "Sor-ry," Jamie called. "Go around, all right? I had to move some of those boxes to get to the computer. We need to make some space for this thing."

The footsteps changed direction, and Jamie's boss entered through the doorway behind me. "May I help you with something?" Clearly, she was irritated to find me still standing there, waiting for service. "Jamie, you've got a customer out—" Rounding the counter, she stopped in midsentence as I looked up, and both of us experienced an instant of recognition.

Something heavy formed in my chest and sank downward, pressing on my lungs and stomach. When I saw Shasta, I'd be able to tell her where Lana was working now. She'd changed clothes since leaving the campground—put on a tight-fitting red suit and pumps, pulled her hair back into a bun, and added a thick stroke of eyeliner around her eyes. Her gaze swept down to my feet, then raked coolly upward, her full lips curving into a smile that fluttered like a butterfly about to be eaten.

"She needs one of those request forms for birth records," Jamie hollered from the back room.

I had a sudden urge to turn and run. Lana was the last person I wanted knowing my secrets.

Moving to the counter across from me, Lana blinked in malicious fascination, inclining her head to one side. "Well, sure. Of course. Anything we can do to help." Her long, slim fingers stroked the edges of the counter, slid to the pad of sticky notes between us, moved them aside and tucked them under a stapler. "I knew you weren't from around here. You don't have the accent." Her voice was smooth, red silk wrapping around me. "But we don't issue birth certificates here, sweetie. You have to write to the Department of Vital Statistics for that. I'm sorry. I guess you came all this way for nothing." Her gaze locked onto mine, silently delivering the rest of the message. *Now go home.*

"She just needs a copy." Jamie poked her head through the backroom doorway, stretching to see over the file cabinets. "I told her we can do that here. I've got the database link running, but I couldn't find the form for her to fill out."

Lana cut an irritated glare over her shoulder before she turned back to me. "It's five dollars per copy for the service. Of course birth records are confidential." Her tone made me think of my second-grade teacher, when everyone else was zipping through storybooks and I was still sounding out letters, too stupid to get it. "I assume you've got ID . . . and five dollars."

"Yes," I bit out, determined not to let her know she'd gotten to me.

"Good." Finishing the word on a falsely congenial high note, she pulled a form from under the counter and slid it across. "Then let's get this done and get you out of here. Fill in the top of the paper, and I'll need *two* forms of ID." She held out her hand, and I fished through my purse, wishing I hadn't left my passport at home. I settled for a driver's license and an ID card from the orchestra in Europe.

Her long red fingernails wrapped around my plastic proof of identity. "I'll go make copies." It occurred to me that, for better or worse, Lana now knew where I was from. After I left, it probably wouldn't matter anymore. I'd just be someone who came for the Labor Day festival and then departed, of little importance in her quest to snag Jace Reid.

I turned my attention to the form while she went to the back room. I could hear her talking to Jamie. Apparently something was wrong with the copy machine.

Overhead, the air conditioner, mercifully, clicked off as I filled out the form—my name, my address, my phone number, all the usual information.

Another customer came in with a little boy trailing behind her. They walked to the counter window beside mine. As she tucked her sunglasses into her purse, she rang the bell marked FOR SERVICE.

Lana appeared from the back room, dusting off her hands. "Well hi, April, how are things over at the school?" Suddenly, Lana was sticky-sweet. "Everybody settling into the new year okay?" Leaning over the counter, she smiled at the boy. "Well, how are you, little guy?"

He moved bashfully behind his mother and tried to wrap himself in her skirt. His mother pulled the fabric back into place and continued with the conversation. "I'm only at the school half-time this year. I decided to stay home with the baby, but Micah here needs a birth certificate, and they told me I can get a copy over here now. We can't figure out where we put the one we had."

"Sure." Lana rested comfortably against the counter, taking time to talk about the new school year, and how she surely did miss being with the kids, but she loved working at the courthouse, and the benefits were *so* much more comprehensive than anything the school could offer. "I'll tell you, April, you ought to look into it. It's a much better deal than working half-time at the school," she finished.

"It sounds great," April said with a distinct lack of interest. "I'd love to find out more sometime, but right now Micah and I are on the way to a dentist appointment."

Lana finally got back to business. "I'll have that birth certificate for you in two shakes of a lamb's tail," she promised. As an afterthought, she grabbed a form and slid it across the counter before heading for the back room. "Go ahead and fill that out, April."

"Okay." Whispering something to her son, April pointed to the chairs by the wall. He went over and sat down, curling his legs into the seat, looking around the room, and then at me. I raised a hand and waved. He smiled, then waved back and giggled. Glancing over her shoulder, his mother put a finger to her lips, and he threaded his arms through his legs, tying himself up like a pretzel. He waited for me to notice.

I made a silent "Oh!" and he grinned again, his eyes twinkling. Angelo might have looked like that at four or five years old—blue eyes, curly blond hair, big smile with just a little mischief.

I wondered if Angelo had ever stood in a courthouse waiting for some stranger to give him information about himself, or if his daddy told him everything he needed to know about Mama and me, or if he even knew I existed.

The phone rang, and Lana came out of the back room. She

grabbed the receiver and answered, then said, "Could you hang on a minute?" Still cradling the phone on her shoulder, she stretched the cord as far as it would go and slid my driver's license and orchestra ID card back to me. "These are both expired." The words were punctuated with an irritated sneer.

"I'm sorry." Turning the driver's license around, I looked at the renewal date—my birthday, two months ago. I'd never even thought about it, since I had no car to drive in Ukraine. "I've been out of the country. It didn't occur to me that my license might be out of date."

Lana's expression said, *Yeah, sure. Go tell someone else your sad story.* "I can't take out-of-date IDs. Have a nice day."

She turned her attention back to the phone. "Sorry about that. Yes, sir. I'll be happy to get that file. I'll walk it up there myself. You know I'd do just about anything for you, Mr. Riker, I just . . ."

She continued buttering up the caller, talking about how much she loved her new job and how hard she was working to get the office back in order. The words seemed to drift farther and farther away as all the expectation drained out of me, and a pulse pounded in the empty shell.

You should have come prepared. This isn't something you do on the spur of the moment, part of me said. *Take Shasta's baby seat back to her and go home. This trip was a mistake.*

Don't just lie down and take it, another voice insisted. *Tell her this is ridiculous. The driver's license is obviously yours, even if it is expired.*

I leaned over the counter as she finished her phone call. My hand caught her arm, seeming to have a will of its own. "I'm sorry the license is expired, but I need my birth information. I drove a long way to get here."

Lana gaped at my hand, a tight, determined circle around her wrist, just above her turquoise-and-silver watch. Blinking slowly, she glared at me, her eyes cool and lifeless, as if they'd been put there by an artist who ran out of warm colors.

Overhead, the vent clicked on, puffing out mildewed air.

April halted what she was doing and glanced sideways, her pen frozen in midair. Even the little boy in the chair stopped moving.

The moment seemed to slow down, to freeze us there in a tiny diorama.

"Birth records are *confidential,*" Lana bit out each word individually. "We're not the genealogy society here. We do not help people find lost loves, lost parents, lost siblings, lost ancestors, get CDIB cards or apply for benefits from the tribe, or whatever else it is you're looking for. So why don't you pick up your little issues and go back wherever it is you came from? I can't give you *anything* without a *valid ID*. Period." The phone rang again, and she yanked her arm away, grabbing the receiver. "County Courthouse . . ." She turned her shoulder and moved to the other side of the desk.

April leaned close to me. "You might try the library. They have a local-interest area with genealogy information and family histories in it. Or the Bureau of Indian Affairs in Muskogee, or the tribe building in Durant, or the Indian schools. I did research in all of those places when I was trying to get Micah a roll number." She nodded toward her little boy.

I tried to imagine Micah being part Choctaw, with his blue eyes and blond hair.

"It's easier if you start with yourself and work backward," his mother added.

I can't start with myself and work backward, I thought. *The only copy of my birth certificate is somewhere back home, buried among James's private papers in his safe-deposit box.*

"Oh, hon, it's okay." April reached across the counter, snatched a tissue from the Kleenex box, and held it out to me, muttering, "Ignore Lana. She's just hateful."

Suddenly, all of it was too much—the sympathy, the moldy air, the fact that my birth records were a few feet away, yet I couldn't have them.

I spun around and ran from the room, then dashed across the hall to the restroom. I turned on the faucet, and stood with my hands braced on the counter, watching water go down the drain.

This isn't the end of the world, I told myself. *Let it go for now. Go home. Be glad you have a family who loves you.*

A grateful heart makes a happy life, Grandma Rose whispered in my head.

Closing my eyes, I pictured her there with me. I could feel her stroking my hair, patting my back, protecting me the way she had after she moved from this world into the next. I was never afraid, because I always knew she was there watching over me. She wanted me to be happy. She wanted me to be whole. Why couldn't I be? Why couldn't I find the place where I felt okay, where I felt normal?

Listening as the water ran down the drain, I pleaded silently, *Take away this empty space. Make me stronger. Take away this need. Please . . .*

Grandma Rose's hand was warm on my shoulder, rubbing a slow circle. I opened my eyes, and, in the mirror, Jamie was standing beside me. I hadn't heard her come in.

"Here." Handing me a manila envelope, she pressed a finger to her lips, winked, and added, "Ssshhh. You never saw me here. Tell Shasta she owes me." Then she turned and disappeared out the door.

I wiped my face on my sleeve, tore open the envelope, and slipped my fingers inside with a mixture of fear and anticipation. My hand trembled as I pulled out a printed copy of my birth certificate. Stapled to the back was another piece of paper—a form my mother had filled out when I was born. There at the bottom, I saw for the first time my father's signature.

Thomas Clay. I traced the letters with my finger, and suddenly he became real to me. A man who was there the day I came into the world. He'd signed this paper. I tried to picture the scene, tried to feel him through the reproduced ink, to sense who he was through the curvature of the writing, the shapes of the letters, the forward slant of the words.

The handwriting on the space marked INFANT'S NAME was his. *Dell Jordan Clay.* Was he the one who had chosen my name? Was he the one who'd decided to include my mother's last name as my middle name? All my life, I'd been Dell Jordan. Sometime before enrolling me in school, Mama and Granny had dropped *Clay*. I'd never even known the name was on my birth certificate until social services got involved with my adoption.

Now, here it was in my father's handwriting. *Dell Jordan Clay.*

My father had beautiful handwriting, the letters large and curved, as if he'd written the name carefully, so it would be beautiful in the future.

Did he think I was beautiful? Was he looking at me when he wrote those words? Was I lying nearby, cuddled in a fuzzy pink blanket, blinking against the bright hospital lights, taking my first glimpses of the world, trying to understand, to bring things into focus? Was Mama leaning over me like a Mary on a Christmas card, her eyes filled with rapture, with love and amazement?

In spite of everything, I wanted to know. I needed to know. I wanted some proof that, even for just a few moments at my birth, there had existed the scene I'd dreamed of all my life, the one every child's heart yearns for—my mother, my father, and me, nestled in a moment of tender embrace.

Tracing the writing with my fingertip, his writing, I could almost make the dream become concrete—a moment that existed briefly, then flew away. A memory from a time I was too young to remember.

CHAPTER 16

I stood for a long while reading the form, imagining the day it was created, the day I was born. On the top corner of the printout, Jamie had written in red ink, *Thomas Clay, born 9-17-61, son of Nora and Audie Clay, town of residence Antlers, OK.* The words were in a careful, blocky print, with circles over the *i*'s. A period with a little smiley face punctuated the end of the sentence.

I wanted to run across the hall, grab Jamie and give her a hug, but instead I peeked carefully out the door before leaving the restroom. Across the hall, Jamie was at the counter, enjoying whatever was in the foam take-out container. She waved covertly as I exited the restroom. I waved back, mouthing *Thank you,* then hurried to the door like a thief committing grand larceny. Bursting onto the front sidewalk, I caught a breath of fresh air, finally free of the courthouse smells and the memories attached to them.

The garden club ladies had abandoned their flower bed in progress, probably in favor of having lunch at the café. Micah and his mother were squatted down next to one of the remaining flats of pansies, examining a caterpillar. She was explaining that it would spin a cocoon and stay inside for a long time, becoming a butterfly. I asked her how to get to the library, and she directed me a few blocks down the road.

"Good luck," she said as I headed to my car.

"Thanks." I could feel her watching me as I drove away. Checking the car clock, I realized it was later than I'd thought, already almost eleven. I'd have to hurry to be back in Tuskahoma in time to meet Jace. Unfortunately, I didn't know where to begin, or what exactly to look for at the library. When I walked in, the room was empty, and the librarian was busy eating a baked potato at her desk. "Sorry," she mumbled, shielding her mouth with her hand as she finished a bite. "Let me know if I can help you with anything."

"I'm doing some genealogy research." I held up the envelope from the courthouse, then realized that it might not be wise to show her the unofficial copies of the birth records with Jamie's handwriting on them. "Could you point me in the right direction?"

"Sure." She dabbed her lips with a napkin and took a drink of her tea, then motioned toward the corner of the room. "Our genealogy section is over there. Our materials go way back into the eighteen hundreds. We even have the Dawes Commission Index to the Final Rolls on CD." Her brows lifted. "You from the Indian school? I get a lot of kids from the Indian schools, doing senior research papers."

"No, ma'am." I shook my head, reminded again that in this part of the world my looks put me in a certain category. Member of the tribe. "What if you're looking for more recent people?"

She paused to consider the question, a new interest dawning in her face. "Let me help you, and we'll see what we can turn up." She pushed lunch aside and grabbed a pad and pen. "Who all are you trying to find and when were they born?"

"Thomas Clay."

She jotted it on her notepad. "Middle name?"

"None, I guess."

"And when was he born?"

Peeking into the envelope, I read aloud the birth date from the corner of the form. The librarian leaned over to see, and I closed the envelope again. "His parents were Nora and Audie Clay." *My grandparents.* It seemed strange to be sharing information so personal, so new and fragile. "I'd like to find them, too, if it's possible." The librarian gave me a perceptive look, and I quickly added, "To find out about them, I mean. I'd like to find out about them."

She nodded slowly, as if she were putting together the puzzle pieces in her mind. "Let's see if they're in the phone book." Pulling a local directory from under her desk, she licked her fingers and thumbed through the pages. "Hmmm. There's nothing listed. Those names don't ring a bell, but I've only lived here five years. I came to take care of my sister, Sarah, and I stayed after she died. If Sarah were here, she could have told you right off if those people ever lived in Antlers. She taught Sunday school at the Methodist church and kindergarten at Antlers Elementary, and her husband owned the feed store, so anybody who ever came through this town, she knew." After glancing at her notes, she slipped from behind the desk and walked to the corner of the room, motioning for me to follow. "Let's see . . . take the birth date and add eighteen years, you get high school graduation, more or less." Leading me to a dusty archival area filled with shelves of newspaper catalogs, she stopped and ran her finger along the spines of an enormous collection of high school yearbooks. "Seventy-eight, seventy-nine, eighty maybe." She pulled several books off the shelf and set them on the table, sending a fine coating of dust drifting into the window light. "Look through these. See if you can find anything. Sometimes they put address lists in the back, so if he's in there, you might even find out where he lived. That could be helpful. A lot of these old Choctaw families don't move much. Many of them still own the land that was given to them in allotments back in the eighteen hundreds when they came here. There's some rigmarole involved in selling Indian-owned parcels, so oftentimes it stays in the families."

I sat down at a table with the yearbooks and began leafing through the pages, surveying pictures of football players, FFA kids with show animals, student council members smiling for the camera, kids showing off at school dances and parties. I wondered if one of them could be my father, his image frozen in time.

"Try the indexes in the back," the librarian suggested. "It'll be faster."

She didn't know that I was stalling, looking at each face, think-ing, *Could this be my father? Could this be my father?* I imagined each possibility—my father, football captain. My father, FFA president. My father, a boy dressed up as Pocahontas's dad for the school play. My father, funny kid sticking his tongue out at the camera. . . .

The librarian glanced over her shoulder, and I flipped to the index. It was faster, but also more quickly devastating. After several indexes, it was clear that Thomas Clay had not graduated from high school in Antlers, which probably meant that my grandparents had moved away at some point.

"Here, I have a few books for Rattan and Soper and Hugo, plus some of the Indian schools." The librarian set another stack in front of me. "Try these."

She continued at the shelf, while I checked the yearbooks, one by one. As Shasta had told me, there were plenty of Clays, but no Thomas Clay.

Thirty minutes later, the librarian was out of ideas, and I needed to leave.

"I'm sorry," she said as we returned to the desk. "You could come back and look through old newspapers. Sometimes a kid's name will be mentioned in a parade photo, because they got an award in Cub Scouts, or something like that." Drumming her fingernails on the desk, she took a drink of tea, then set the glass next to her now-cold potato. "Are you sure he lived around here?"

"He was born in Antlers." If this area wasn't his home, why would he have brought my mother here?

"Huh . . . ," the librarian muttered, slipping into her chair and stirring up the potato.

"Sorry your lunch got cold."

"Oh, no problem." She smiled at me. "I love a good mystery. I just wish we could have found some answers for you."

"It's all right," I said glumly, but it wasn't *all right.*

My hopes plummeted as I left town and headed toward Tuskahoma. The scenery no longer seemed interesting. My mind had
stopped painting pictures of my father's childhood.

I didn't see the police car in my rearview mirror until the siren
blared.

My pulse fluttered and I glanced down at the speedometer.
Seventy-six. Way over the speed limit. I pulled over and I rolled down
the window, then let my head fall into my hand, waiting for the officer to come to my car. By the time he finally did, tears were prickling
in the bridge of my nose, and I was squeezing it hard, like the Dutch
boy trying to hold up the dam.

Now, on top of having a secret trip to explain away, I was going
to have a secret speeding ticket to pay. The lies just kept getting bigger and bigger, and it was all for nothing. I wanted to forget this
place existed, to form a reality in which I was born the day James and
Karen adopted me. Dell Sommerfield. Period. End of story.

"License and proof of insurance, please."

My face reflected in the officer's sunglasses as I handed him my
license. He was young, red-haired and freckle-faced, his mouth set in
a stern line. He didn't look much older than me.

Just as the license was leaving my hand, I remembered that it was
expired.

Please don't let him notice. Please, please, please.

"Kansas," he observed, jotting information on his ticket pad.
"On vacation?"

"Sort of," I replied, afraid to move. *Please, oh please, don't let him
notice the date.*

"Here for the Choctaw festival?" The attempt at chitchat made
me feel better, despite the fact that he was writing me a ticket.

"Yes."

"Staying somewhere nearby?"

Maybe if I kept him talking, he wouldn't notice the date on the

license. "Out at the lake . . . with family. Family reunion. The Reids."
Maybe he knew the Reids and would take pity on me.

"Don't know them. I haven't lived here too long."

"Oh." I gripped and ungripped the steering wheel, my hands
sweating and a trail of perspiration dripping, hot and itchy, down
the small of my back. I wanted to wipe it away, but I was afraid to
move.

"You know you were doing seventy-six in a sixty-five?"

Now we were getting down to business. No point denying the
fact that I was speeding. Best to be contrite and cooperative. James
got stopped for speeding all the time, and usually, because he was
such a nice guy, he only got a warning. It didn't hurt, either, that he
was a pilot. For some reason that seemed a passable excuse for speeding. Unfortunately, I didn't have a good excuse. "No. I'm sorry. I
just . . . my mind was on other things. I wasn't paying attention. I'm
really sorry."

"Ma'am, this license is way out of date."

My stomach crashed through the floorboard. What if I ended up
with a ticket that would necessitate coming back here to court? What
if I ended up in jail, in Oklahoma, where I wasn't supposed to be?

"I'm sorry. I . . . I've been out of the country for two years, and
I just got back last weekend. . . . I . . . I didn't . . . think about . . . I
just came here to . . ." Tears sprang into my eyes. The events of the
past few days welled up inside me and flowed forth like blood from
a mortal wound. The next thing I knew, I was sobbing uncontrollably, blurting out my whole story to a police officer on the side of
the road.

By the time I'd come back to my senses, I'd soaked his handkerchief, and he was leaning on the car, listening and nodding, probably
wondering if he should haul me off to a crisis intervention center.
Finally, I stopped babbling and sat with my fingers pressed to my
eyes, feeling like an idiot.

"Ma'am, I didn't need to know all that," he said finally, seeming as embarrassed as I was. Being new on the job, he'd probably never encountered anything quite like this. "I'm going to give you a warning. Let someone else do the driving until you can get back home and have that license renewed. Don't get stopped around here again, all right?"

Nodding, I wiped my eyes one more time, then handed the bandana handkerchief back to him. "I'm sorry. I didn't mean to go into all that . . . stuff. I guess I've just been a little stressed."

He tore a sheet off his ticket pad and handed me my license and the warning, smiling slightly behind the mirrored sunglasses. "Well, I hope that skunk's gone when you get back to the campground. That'd help cut down the stress level a little, huh?"

"Yeah." *Did I tell him about the skunk?* "I'm sorry," I said again.

"It's all right." He closed his pad and he looked down the road in the direction we'd come, his glasses reflecting a miniature mountainscape and a thin ribbon of highway that seemed to go on forever. "Take a minute to settle down before you pull onto the road, all right?"

I nodded, and he patted the window frame, then stepped away. "I hope you find what you're looking for here. My sister and I are adopted. She's been through a lot of the same stuff." He strode off toward his patrol car, and I sat watching him go, feeling an unexpected sense of kinship. In any given place, there were others experiencing the same things I was experiencing. You couldn't tell who was who, just by looking.

In the rearview mirror, I saw the police car make a U-turn and drive off.

Leaving the window down, I pulled away from the shoulder. The breeze lifted my hair, drying the nervous perspiration on my neck. The music of Dillon's reed flute floated through my mind as if it were coming from the rocks, and the hills, and the trees themselves. The melody was an earthy, tribal one I couldn't name, the song that had drawn me to the Reids' camp last night.

In my mind, I was back in that place again, the quiet sanctuary where all the music was.

I heard music in everything—the whir of the breeze, the hum of the tires, the whistle of air through the hubcaps, the rhythmic tapping of a seat belt against the doorframe, in Dillon's flute music playing in my head. A symphony. Everywhere. Just the way it used to be.

I was filled with a peace that was beyond understanding, a contentment that made no other thoughts necessary. I wanted to drive, and drive, and drive.

By the time I reached the festival grounds and parked among what was now a sea of cars in the back lot behind the baseball fields, my sense of peace was starting to fade. Other things were crowding in. I was late for the tour. Would it be best to interrupt or wait until Jace was done? Should I show him the birth certificate and the form with my father's signature on it? Was it too private to share?

I considered my options as I walked toward the council house, passing the baseball fields, where a sign read:

TRADITIONS TO HONOR
- NO ALCOHOL OR DRUGS
- NO SOLICITING
- NO POLITICKING
- NO HARD FEELINGS, AS WE ARE ENTERING NEUTRAL GROUNDS

Beyond the ball fields, a row of horseshoe pits buzzed with activity, kids tried their luck on a man-made rock climbing wall, and a carnival offered games and rides to families wandering by with cotton candy and snowcones. Bright banners and hand-lettered signs advertised everything from Indian tacos and arrowhead jewelry to glowsticks and flashlights that came with a tiny generator inside and never needed replacement batteries. There was even a fortune-teller sitting in front of a makeshift tepee, wearing a fringed leather dress and a Middle Eastern turban. She wanted to tell my fortune, but I passed on by.

"Big changes are coming," she said. "How can you prepare, if you don't know what they are?"

We're not to know, only to go on faith, Grandma Rose answered in my head. Grandma Rose didn't believe in fortune-tellers. She made sure to tell me that often, because my real granny was into horoscopes. Granny would send me three miles to town on my bike just to pick up a paper if it was horoscope day.

The capitol building loomed ahead, and when I finally cleared the carnival and food booths, I could see a tour group on the lawn, the tour already in progress. Shading their eyes with their hands, they were looking up at the old building. Jace stood in front of them, pointing at something on the mansard roof, the style of which I wouldn't have recognized had I not just been to Europe. The building, with its three-story brick walls, arched windows, and rounded dormers in the roof, looked as if it belonged in France rather than in the mountains of Oklahoma. It had the feel of something very old and grand, a structure conceived to make a statement about its creators, to survive the trials of time and the elements.

Walking up the hill, I heard Jace answer a question, then laugh at a response from someone in the group. I instantly felt a sense of lightness. When he saw me, he smiled and waved me in. He caught my eye and winked as we continued around the building, and my pulse quickened.

"The capitol building, as you see it today, was completed in 1884, as a permanent capitol for the Choctaw Nation. Prior to that time, various locations, including a frame structure a few miles from this site, had served as the capitol. This site was named *Tushka Homma,* meaning red warrior. At the time of its construction, a building of this size so far from any large city represented a monumental engineering challenge. Lumber was both milled on-site and hauled in via oxcart. The rounded attic windows"—he paused to point at the attic windows, and the tour group gazed upward again—"were hand-carved, while others were hauled in from nearby towns. The red brick was molded on the capitol grounds using clay hauled from the Potato Hills, and the sandstone window and doorway trims were also derived from the area. The structure housed the tribal Senate, House of Representatives, Supreme Court, Executive Office, and various other national offices. The Choctaw Light Horsemen occupied an office in the building and served as law enforcement for the nation, sometimes using the third floor as a jail. Following statehood in 1907, the tribal government was dissolved and the building lapsed into disuse. After being saved from the wrecking ball, the capitol has undergone several renovations and today houses a museum, art gallery, education center, the tribal court, various staff offices, and, of course, a well-appointed gift shop, where each and every one of you are invited to purchase high-quality souvenirs of your visit to Tuskahoma." Jace grinned, and members of the tour chuckled at the shameless sales pitch.

I stayed in the back of the group, enjoying the chance to watch him work. He was patient and friendly, willing to answer the most trivial questions and take time to explain details. The questions ranged from further architectural inquiries about the capitol and modern-day tribal government to inquiries about the social programs and business interests operated by the tribe, including the new Choctaw casinos and resorts, designed to lure tourists off the highway and bring money into the tribe.

"Today, the Choctaw tribe provides many services for its members," Jace said as we entered the front of the building through large double doors, "including community health programs, housing programs, job training, educational opportunities, food, nursing homes for the elderly, and economic development programs designed to aid small businesses as well as to promote larger factories owned by the tribe and employing its members. The tribe also operates several schools for Indian youth, which provide residential care for children, as well as education, character-building activities, and cultural events throughout the year.

"There are, of course, many difficulties in promoting the well-being of a tribe, now numbering nearly one hundred thousand. The Choctaw as a people have long struggled to balance modern advancement with traditional values. We remain determined to insure that as the tribe grows and changes, we remember our roots and the legacy of our grandfathers."

Jace caught my eye and grinned. I had a feeling he knew what I was thinking—those words were almost a direct quote from Nana Jo. Did she ever come along on his tours? She'd be proud. He was perfect for the job, articulate, charismatic, with a quick sense of humor that made the tourists laugh and put them at ease. As we passed a photo collage of Choctaw chiefs in the front hall, the tourists chuckled at Jace's story about a tribal election scandal fifty years ago. Moments later, the group members were silent and somber as we moved to the second-floor museum and stood before the exhibit detailing the horrors of the removal of the Choctaw tribe from Mississippi to Indian Territory in Oklahoma.

Jace stood by the wall, allowing the group to view the exhibit of clothing and materials used by Choctaws on the forced journey west. "The years of removal, lasting from 1831 to 1833, remain the darkest chapter in tribal history," he said. "The Choctaw were the first tribe removed to Indian Territory, the theory being that if a tribe as large and successful as the Choctaw could be relocated, other eastern tribes could be coerced into moving as well. The Choctaw were forced to leave behind livestock, land, and nearly all personal belongings. The first migration began in mid-October, and was plagued by mismanagement, lack of food and supplies, floods, and an unusually harsh and early winter. Diphtheria, dysentery, typhoid, and pneumonia raged among the people, and along the trail literally thousands succumbed to starvation, disease, and exposure. Having come from a mild climate in Mississippi, the Choctaw possessed little in the way of warm clothing, and young children were often not clothed at all until the age of seven or eight."

Pausing, Jace took a wool blanket from the exhibit barrier and held it up. "Imagine yourself as a young parent, camping in open fields with your children, confronting subzero temperatures, with nothing for shelter except a single hand-woven wool blanket. Imagine it's snowing. Your children are cold and hungry—no clothes, no food, no shoes. Imagine how quickly the snow soaks through the blanket, how the wind forces its way through the cracks to bare skin underneath."

Members of the tour group wrapped their arms around themselves, feeling the chill. Beside me, a woman picked up her little boy and cuddled him against her chest. "Imagine that your child is limp in your arms, yet you're forced to travel. Picture your parents or grandparents walking beside you, old, lame, fording icy rivers on foot and wading for days through rain-swollen swamps. Imagine having to leave the bodies of your family members along the trail. No marker, no funeral ritual, little chance you'll ever come back to see those final resting places again.

"Imagine all of these things in the context of your own family, paint the faces of your loved ones into these pictures, and you can understand the brutality of the march westward. In the first year of removal, one-third of the party, nearly two thousand men, women, and children, died along the trail. Removal in 1832 was equally devastating, owing to a cholera outbreak. Upon reaching Little Rock, one of the Choctaw chiefs was quoted as saying that the removal had been a 'trail of death and tears.' The phrase became synonymous with the forced removals of tribes to Indian Territory. While this museum was created to celebrate the lives of a people who persevered in a new and hostile land, it also memorializes those whose voices were forever silenced along the trail. Their lesson is one we must remember. The darkest hours of history have always been born of the efforts of one people to dehumanize another."

Backing away from the exhibit, Jace allowed the tour group to flow through. I moved along with the crowd, my eyes traveling among the small signs and hand-lettered quotes scattered throughout the exhibit.

. . . Many of these children . . . had nothing under heaven to protect their naked bodies from the pitiless storm . . . Major Francis W. Armstrong, Removal Agent

. . . Etotahoma's people had stopped . . . they said . . . he was old and lame and they were unwilling to go on and leave him behind . . . Lieutenant Jefferson Van Horne

. . . Few moccasins were seen among them. The snow has been on the ground here without diminution . . . If I could have done it with propriety, I would have given them all shoes . . . William S. Colquhoun

. . . I gave the party leave to enter a small field in which pumpkins were. They would not enter without leave, though starving. These they ate raw with the greatest avidity . . . Joseph Kerr, farmer near removal route

. . . The Indians had been six days without food . . . New York Observer

. . . Two large deep streams must be crossed . . . in the worst time of weather I have seen in any country—a heavy sleet having broken and bowed down . . . timber. And this . . . under the pressure of hunger, by old women and young children without any covering for their feet, legs, or body except a cotton underdress . . . Joseph Kerr, farmer

Death was hourly among us . . . Major Francis W. Armstrong

Amid the gloom and horrors of the present . . . we are cheered with a hope that ere long we shall reach our destined home . . . Chief George Harkins

Sadness and awe spread through me as we moved from the Trail of Tears exhibit and passed displays depicting early Choctaw schools, towns, and farms, forged in a raw land as members of the tribe sought to rebuild their lives. At the far end of the museum, I stood face-to-face with an enlarged photograph of the World War I code talkers from Nana Jo's story—proud soldiers who used the language of their ancestors in yet another struggle of good against evil.

In the center hallway, I stood for a long time taking in a collection of sepia images celebrating the slow rebirth of the tribe in Indian Territory—classes of children in mission schools, a dark-haired bride dressed for her wedding, a Choctaw stickball team, a mother with a little boy and a round-faced baby girl, the proprietors of a general store in a Choctaw town, a soldier dressed in uniform, two young girls posing in a freshly tilled garden.

So many faces with brown eyes and prominent cheekbones, cinnamon-colored skin and raven hair like mine. Proud, determined people, forging new lives from the ashes of the past.

Chahta Sia Hoke, the sign read in the middle. *I am Choctaw.*

The idea settled fully into my mind, into my sense of being for the first time in my life. *I am Choctaw. Chahta Sia Hoke.*

I was not an accident, dropped on earth by two people who may or may not have cared about me when I was born. I was the product of a long and proud history, of a people who fought to survive, to persevere, to move forward when adversity stole everything they had, everyone they loved. I was not a flash on the screen of history, an independent entity connected to nothing but an adopted family. I was a member of the tribe.

CHAPTER 17

❧

I waited in the entryway as the tour group dispersed. Jace patiently answered a few final questions from a California couple, retired stockbrokers who'd bought motorcycles and taken to the open road. The husband was writing a book about their experiences. He'd been monopolizing the question-and-answer sessions throughout the tour and scribbling frantically on a notepad. I couldn't blame him. Jace had a way of making the past vibrant and real, of making it live and breathe with the souls of the individuals who had lived it. I could tell he was a good teacher.

"Thanks . . . uhhh . . . Jace," the stockbroker said, glancing at Jace's name tag as they turned to leave.

"My pleasure," Jace replied. "Hope I make the book."

The broker was pleased. "I'll let you know when it's published. Is there an address I can send the information to?" Walking backward, he pulled a pencil from his Harley-Davidson headband and prepared to write down the information.

"Just send it to me, care of the museum," Jace answered, lifting his hand in a casual wave. "They'll pass it along."

"Will do." The stockbroker tucked his pencil back in place. "We're headed to the harvests of the Great Plains next, so it'll be a while before I have the book all together. Indian Territory will probably get a chapter all its own. We'll be stopping by the Five Civilized Tribes Museum in Muskogee on our way north tomorrow, then visiting the Will Rogers Museum in Claremore, then moving on up the Jim Thorpe Highway, since he was the first person of Native bloodline to win an Olympic medal. Thanks for the research material on the Choctaws and the tribal government issue."

"No problem." Jace gave me a quick sideways smirk as the couple walked away. I knew what he was thinking. If the book was as obnoxious and long-winded as the writer, it wouldn't be very good. "I'll give it to Shasta. She's always wanted to tour the country." Jace motioned me in the door, and we stood alone in the center hall, surrounded by art show entries that were placed on easels to advertise the show upstairs in the gallery.

"She should," I said, glancing absently through the open door at a group of Choctaw dancers gathering to perform on the lawn. "Shasta should travel. She'd love it." Unfortunately, the truth was that Shasta was about as far from touring the world as I was from eating lunch on the international space station.

"Not very likely, with two kids and Cody." Jace's pleasant tour-guide mask cracked, revealing a powerful layer of emotion beneath. Obviously, Gwendolyn wasn't the only one who thought Shasta was headed down the wrong path. "Seems like all Shas does is wrap more rope around her neck, and nothing anybody says can talk her out of it. The minute our family fell apart growing up, she started making plans to have one of her own. Before my dad left, she was into sports, and art, and horses, and someday she wanted to be either a veterinarian or a wildlife biologist. It was like she had all the time in the world. After Dad left, all she could think about was finding some guy to be with. With her SAT scores, she could have gotten into any college around here, but she didn't even want to talk about it. She knew Mama and Nana Jo would go ballistic if she got pregnant in high school, so she waited until the day after graduation to run off with Cody, marry him, and get pregnant."

"She seems happy." I moved toward a painting of Hopi women climbing a canyon trail to a pueblo. Some small, self-conscious part of me wondered if Jace could see that I envied Shasta's life. I envied the way Benjamin looked at her as if she were the most amazing person in the world, the way he wrapped his tiny arms around her neck and snuggled his head under her chin and seemed perfectly at peace. He didn't care if his mother had a college degree. Every time I watched Shasta and her little boy together, I felt an instinctive yearning. "There's nothing wrong with having a family."

Jace's sigh was long and slow. "Depends if it's an excuse to avoid life. A lot of girls around here come from low-income families, broken homes, economically depressed areas, whatever. They don't see much opportunity here, but then they look at the outside world, and they can't imagine what they'd do out there, so they get pregnant and answer the question. I don't know what it's like in Kansas City, but that's the way it is here. I never thought my sister would end up like that. There's a long tradition in our family of the women going to college. My mother's a nurse, Nana Jo was a teacher, her mother was a teacher. In the Choctaw tradition, women are the leaders of the family." I heard him cross the hall slowly, until he stood behind me, studying the watercolor wash of canyon and pueblo, the Hopi women so small they were almost nonexistent, their climb seemingly made steeper by the fact that the easel was leaning slightly to the right.

"Shasta could still go to college." I felt obliged to defend her, perhaps because for years now I'd been on the receiving end of the don't-have-children-young speech. Even Grandma Rose, before I was ever part of the family, made sure to point out that she had left her parents' house and supported herself independently, working as a mother's helper, and later inching her way up the chain of command in a department store, before she married. *A woman,* she said, *must always know she can stand on her own two feet, if need be.* "UMKC advertises programs for married students and parents all the time. They have day care on campus and everything. I'm sure some of the colleges around here have that, too." I sounded like one of those Pollyanna university commercials about how it's never too late to get a degree.

"You should talk to her about it." I was suddenly aware of Jace's nearness, and an electric sensation went through me as he leaned around my shoulder to rebalance the easel. "She doesn't want to hear it from us, but I can tell she admires you. She says you're quite the world traveler."

I shook my head, surprisingly pleased that he had been talking to Shasta about me. My stomach fluttered unexpectedly. "I just had a couple of lucky opportunities."

"I doubt that." There was a smile in his voice. "Luck usually has a lot to do with preparation and skill. The older you get the more you'll realize that."

"I guess." His age-related comment let the air out of my balloon, quashing the giddy flutter inside me.

"I tell my students that all the time," he added, and I turned away from the painting. I didn't want to be one of his students.

He glanced out the door as a group of Choctaw girls in brightly colored tribal dress gathered on the front walkway for a picture-taking session. The wind caught their multitiered cotton skirts, and some of the younger ones twirled on the sidewalk, creating swirls of color and fabric. A girl in a blue dress lost the tall, crown-shaped beaded headdress that marked her as a Choctaw princess, and it clattered down the steps, landing at the photographer's feet. He picked it up and handed it back, then loudly reminded the girls that this picture would be going in the tribal newspaper, *Bishinik,* and if they didn't straighten up he would just take the picture and they could all be embarrassed. The girl who'd lost her headdress planted it back on her head and crossed her arms under a long ruffle that fell over her shoulders like a shawl. She didn't look like she wanted to be a Choctaw princess today.

"Now that looks like Shasta," Jace commented. "She never was into all this stuff. Nana Jo made her do the princess contest, and Shasta couldn't have cared less. She's got a big pout on in every one of the pictures."

Outside, a little girl I recognized from Camp Reid turned to look into the building. Spotting us inside, she waved. The photographer about popped a cork.

"Guess we'd better get out of the way." Shaking a playful finger at the girls, Jace pulled the door closed. "Come on. We'll go out the other exit." Starting down the center hall, he gazed at a sepia photograph of an early tribal council on the wall to our right, and seemed to drift into his own thoughts. I'd begun to notice that about him—occasionally he turned quiet and contemplative, then he'd say something to start up the conversation again. He glanced at me as we wandered down the hall, and I wondered what he was thinking.

As usual, he asked me a question. "So, how did your morning go? Any luck?"

"Not much," I admitted. "I did get a copy of my birth records at the courthouse, but after that it was a dead end. I couldn't find my father's name or my grandparents' names in the phone book. I looked through high school annuals for the years around my father's graduation—no luck—and that was about it. The information from the courthouse says that my father was born here. I guess it's possible that his family moved and he grew up someplace else, but if he wasn't raised here and didn't have any family in the area, why would he have brought my mother here?" The last words ended with a wistfulness I couldn't conceal. This process of welling up with hope, only to run into a brick wall, felt like an endless series of crash landings.

"Genealogy isn't an exact science." It was the tone Jace had used when telling Autumn she was going to have a good time at her grandparents' house today—the tone that said he wasn't really sure himself, but felt obliged to offer a ray of hope. "Even the professionals don't usually get lucky enough to find lost relatives in a day. Give it some time. There are plenty of other sources—the Bureau of Indian Affairs in Muskogee, the archives in Oklahoma City. Granted, they're more useful for tracking down family members further back, but it's worth a try. You never know what you might dig up, given a little time."

I don't have time. My parents don't even know I'm here. "Maybe next trip." Would there be a next trip? How many times was I going to lie to James and Karen and take off for Oklahoma?

"Hang in there, kid. I've had students come up dry on their ancestor searches through several sources, then stumble onto something completely unexpected."

The word *kid* and being lumped in with his high school genealogists blanketed me with a heavy sense of disappointment. "I'm not one of your students." It sounded surprisingly petulant. Ever since I'd started this trip, my emotions had been like bullets fired into a room of mirrors and steel—ricocheting off one thing, crashing through another. There was no way to predict the trajectory from one minute to the next.

Jace's lips curved upward as he held the back door open for me. "I know that."

"I'm sorry." It wasn't like me to be so out of control. In fact, it wasn't like me to be out of control at all. One thing the Spencers loved about me in Ukraine was that nothing, from sick kids to hijacked supply shipments, rattled me. Since childhood, I'd known how to turn on the emotional numbness, how to be powerless in a world that went from peaceful to chaotic in an instant. When I'd needed to, I'd always been able to disconnect from what was going on around me. Why couldn't I do that now? Why was I so touchy, so close to the surface? "I didn't mean to snap at you. It's been a weird day." *Month, year . . .*

"It's all right." He was easygoing, as usual. I suspected that he knew the trick of turning up the mental static when necessary. It probably served him well, teaching school. He gave the impression that nothing got to him. "Tough morning, huh?"

"Yeah." As we wound through the festival grounds, passing tourists, musicians with instrument cases, and dancers dressed in powwow regalia, I related the story of the courthouse, of seeing my name in my father's handwriting, then sitting at the library, flipping through high school yearbooks, thinking that sooner or later I'd turn a page and there he would be. I would look, for the first time, into the eyes of the man who brought my mother to Oklahoma, who signed my birth records, then left both of us behind.

Jace reached across the space between us and rubbed my shoulder sympathetically. My skin tingled where he touched it. "Sounds like too much to handle on an empty stomach. How about some lunch?"

"That would be wonderful," I answered, and he veered off toward a booth where a group of women was serving up Indian fry bread covered with taco toppings. One of the servers knew Jace and slipped us a couple of tacos on the side, so we wouldn't have to wait in line. She asked how his kids were doing and gave me a curious look as we walked to a nearby picnic table to eat.

"The thing is, I don't know why, after all these years, I'm so tied in knots about finding my biological family," I admitted after sampling my taco. "I know I'm making a bigger issue of it than it is. It's not like I don't have a good life."

Straight, dark hair fell over his smooth cheek as he tipped his head and considered the comment. His gaze seemed to connect with parts of me that I didn't want anyone to see. "It's a big issue. Big enough that you drove all the way here from Kansas City without even a hotel reservation."

I blushed and looked down at my plate. "Not very smart, huh?"

"Some things you just have to strike off and do before you lose your nerve." I liked the way his lips curved upward when he knew I was partly joking and partly in need of reassurance.

Our gazes caught and held for a moment. "I guess so," I whispered, then we returned to the business of lunch. Jace asked about the youth music exchange program and my world travels. We talked about Europe and the orphans' home in Ukraine, which was in some ways similar to the Choctaw boarding school where he worked. The boarding school, which had been started in the eighteen hundreds as a Presbyterian mission, still dealt with the difficulties inherent in caring for kids in a group setting.

"Most of our kids aren't orphans," Jace pointed out, "but we do have a lot who've experienced some sort of family problems, or trouble in a regular school situation." Pointing with his fork, he turned the subject back to me. "So how did you go from touring Europe with the symphony to working at a mission in the former Soviet Union? Seems like quite a leap."

"It just sort of happened." As flaky as that sounded, I didn't have a better explanation. "My parents—my adopted parents—weren't too thrilled about it. They wanted me to come home and apply for Juilliard. There was a lot of pressure about the Juilliard thing, and I didn't know what I wanted to do. I guess maybe that's part of the reason I went to Ukraine—delay tactics." I'd never said that out loud to anyone.

"You don't seem like the type for delay tactics."

I wasn't sure how to take that, so I turned my attention to my plate. Nearby, a grandmother was trying to make it to a table while juggling two kids and three plates of food. I got up and helped her.

"See?" I said, when I sat back down. "Delay tactics."

Laughing, Jace pointed a finger at me as he finished the last of his taco and moved on to fry bread with honey. "You're not as innocent as you look."

"Don't tell anyone," I whispered, and he laughed again. I couldn't help laughing with him. His smile was infectious.

His dark eyes narrowed, taking me in, and suddenly it seemed as if there were no one else around—no noisy vendors, no crowd waiting for Indian tacos, no music floating from the amphitheater. "Judging from the concert you put on at camp last night, I think you should go for Juilliard. You're really good."

"Thanks." The praise was edifying, but behind it was the pressure that had come from all directions since I was thirteen, when James and Karen enrolled me at Harrington Academy. Everyone seemed to know where my life should be going but me.

Jace was about to say something when the motorcycle-riding stockbrokers from the tour group asked if they could use the other end of our table. They slid in, and Jace spent the rest of the meal answering questions about the museum tour, the festival, and various aspects of Choctaw history.

As soon as I'd finished my taco, we made our apologies and abandoned the table, then walked to Jace's truck and headed for Gibson Academy, where he taught junior and senior history.

"Are you sure you have time for this today?" I asked as we left the fairgrounds. "I feel like I'm taking you away from the homecoming festival and your kids." I couldn't help thinking about Willie and Autumn, and that they were missing all the fun. I could picture Autumn in a colorful Choctaw dress, dashing through the aisles, trying to win prizes at the carnival, laughing on the carousel.

"No, they're having a good time at Neenee's house. I checked on them before my last tour. Autumn started out timing how fast Willie could run across the yard, and then she built an obstacle course and tried to race him against the dog, but the dog ran off. By the time Autumn caught up with the dog, he was barking out by the fence. They found one of the baby goats with its leg caught in the wire, so now everyone's occupied with goat rescue and cleanup. Neenee's going to help her fix a stall and get the patient settled in the barn."

"That must be quite an adventure," I said as we drove under the brick archway that marked the entrance to Gibson Academy. The tree-lined drive wound lazily up the hill toward a complex of old brick buildings, which gave the impression of someplace well established and quiet, a Southern plantation or a museum. "Sounds like a busy morning." I leaned forward to take in the buildings as we came closer.

"I'm glad they're having a good time with their mom's folks," Jace admitted. "It's been tough for the kids to go there, especially Autumn. They have a lot of memories of their mom in that house, and then there are old pictures and belongings. It's just hard." He stopped the truck in front of the largest building, a three-story structure with enormous white columns and a grand set of stairs leading to a second-story entry. "This is the classroom hall. The library's on the third floor." As we stepped out, he pointed toward the rear buildings. I could hear kids playing basketball somewhere not far away. "The rec hall and dormitories are out back. Gibson was originally a residential school for Indian youth, but these days we're only about fifty percent residential. Some of the live-in students come from bad home situations. Some come from families who live too far away from the school to get them here every day. Some stay here during the week, and go home on weekends."

"It must be strange, living at school." I tried to imagine what it would be like to grow up in a place like this.

"It's a good place for the kids," Jace commented as we climbed the steps. "Our graduation percentage for foster children living at Gibson is much greater than for kids going to public school and dealing with the ups and downs of the foster care system. The kids here have a safe place to be. Something permanent until they're eighteen. They need the stability Gibson provides. It's hard for kids to move on after big upheavals in their lives." He glanced at me apologetically, as if he'd suddenly realized who he was talking to.

We climbed the remainder of the steps, and I stood on the landing, taking in the expansive front lawn as he fought with the old brass dead bolt.

"This thing has a mind of its own," he commented. The lock finally surrendered, and he opened the door. I stood looking up and down the silent hall in the dim glow from the doorways of sunlit classrooms. With its old wood floors, high ceilings, and arch-shaped windows at the ends of the hall, the place was reminiscent of Harrington Academy. For a moment I had the sense of being back in high school.

"The watch was a good idea, by the way," Jace said, distracting me from my thoughts. "It took Autumn's mind off the visit to Neenee's house, gave her something else to focus on. The first few minutes are always the hardest. When she walks in the door, she's hit with so many memories of her mom. Once she's busy with something, she has a good time there. It's just getting through those first few minutes." He opened the door to a stairway with light shining in from a tall window above. "In here."

"I was that way after Grandma Rose died," I said as we started up the stairs. "I'd wake up some mornings thinking of something I wanted to tell her. Sometimes I'd be up and putting on my shoes, and then it would hit me that she wasn't across the river anymore. It was like having her die all over again. For a while, it was hard going to her house because all the sounds and smells and sights were tied to her."

He nodded somberly as we walked up the stairs side by side. "I think that's how it is for Autumn. Willie's so young that he doesn't remember as much. It's easier for him to move on."

"It's good that they keep visiting their grandparents' house," I said. "Over time, you make new memories, and the place begins to seem complete the way it is now. If you don't move through that process, I think the place would stay suspended in time. Whenever you went there, it would be like going through the death again." I knew that was why I didn't dream very often about Grandma Rose or Mama now. Eventually, I'd had to let go so life could move on without the painful spasms of grief.

Jace caught my gaze as he opened the door to the third floor. We stood close together, our thoughts intertwined in a way that was powerful. *How long?* his eyes asked. *How long does it take?*

"She'll let go when she's ready," I said quietly, and he nodded as we walked into an enormous room with sloped ceilings and dormer windows all around. Library bookshelves had been set up at one end. At the other end, a maze of gray fabric office cubicles seemed out of keeping with the antique surroundings.

"In the old days, this was the grand ballroom," Jace explained. "Graduations and school plays and cotillions with the residential girls' school nearby were held here. These days, we're co-ed, and cotillions are out of style, so now it's a library and office space."

"That's kind of sad." I pictured the room filled with people in nineteenth-century costumes, dancing the waltz as moonlight streamed through the windows. "It's a beautiful room."

"Yes, it is." Jace surveyed the area with an obvious appreciation, then smiled apologetically. "The plan is to eventually turn this into a performance hall, once our new library building is ready, but for now we're making use of the space. The genealogy collection is over here." He ushered me toward the back, where an L-shaped row of shelves divided off one section of the library. "We've only been building the genealogy lab for a few years. When the kids finish their junior year history projects, they compile their information in one of these notebooks." He motioned to the shelf. "Then in their senior year, in technology class, they work on entering the various family names into a database and interfacing their information with research Web sites. Hopefully it opens doors for them a bit—helps them see there's a whole big world out there. It's not always easy for kids to make the jump from a protected schooling environment into the real world."

I winced inwardly, thinking that he could have been talking about me.

If the thought had occurred to him, it didn't show. He paused by the bookshelves. "Thanks for being so understanding with Autumn this morning."

"She's really sweet," I said.

He pulled a notebook off the shelf, leafed through it, then put it back again. "It's better that she wasn't at the festival all day. I don't know how she'd react to being there without her mom, especially during the princess pageant. Her mom made her a new Choctaw dress every year. . . ." His voice trailing off, he glanced over his shoulder at me. "I'm sorry to keep bringing it up. It's just on my mind today, I guess." He pulled down another book. "Looks like we don't have a research project specifically on the Clays, but try this one. When you have so many people drawing back to a small pool of ancestors, you find that a lot of the families are interrelated." Setting the book on a table next to me, he lowered an eyebrow. "Not too many branches on the family tree around here, if you know what I mean."

I went to work leafing through the first notebook, then several others, as Jace fished them off the shelves. I found plenty of Clays, but no sign of Nora or Audie. There were instances of women named Nora, but since I didn't know my grandmother's maiden name, it was impossible to discern whether she was one of those listed in the family trees. After sifting through dozens of notebooks, I finally let my head fall into my hands and sat rubbing my eyes. The day was starting to catch up with me.

"Take a break," Jace suggested as he scanned the computer database. "I'm about done here. Looks like we're probably not going to find anything. Guess none of your Clays have come through a genealogy project here."

"Guess not." I wanted to collapse on the table, go to sleep, and forget everything. If I sat there any longer, I probably would, so I got up and walked out of the library, feeling like I was crashing off another self-made mountain of hope.

What if the information from the courthouse was incorrect? What if Jamie was looking at the wrong file when she wrote my grandparents' names on my birth records?

The questions needled me as I wandered across the room and into the spill of window light near the edge of the cubicle maze. Bracing my hands on the windowsill, I stood looking down at the lawn.

The field below went blurry, and a sob pressed against my throat. Holding a hand over my mouth, I moved farther from the library, down the narrow aisle between the cubicles and the arched windows until I came to a doorway in the corner. I slipped through the partially opened door and entered a tiny corner room with ceilings sloping into dormers. A gauzy light crept through the windows and touched the keys of an old piano, the only piece of furniture in the room. Moving closer, I stood to one side and stroked a finger over the smooth, age-yellowed ivory. It felt welcoming beneath my hand, and in my mind a door opened. I sat down at the piano and slid my fingers onto the keys, closed my eyes, and stepped into the place where all the music was. Around me, the air filled with "La donna è mobile," then "Playera," then "Fugue in G Minor," and "Courante."

"Courante" faded into the soft, clear notes of a haunting tribal melody, the one Dillon had played at the campsite the night before. In my mind, I could both hear the flute and see the notes on an invisible sheet of music. On the piano, the song was as light and airy as the shadow of a bird flitting over new spring grass.

As the last notes died away, I became aware of someone else in the room. I opened my eyes, and Jace was standing beside the piano, leaning against the dusty wood in a spill of window light, watching me.

His eyes caught mine, his expression at once tender, sad, amazed. Slowly stroking his thumb and forefinger along his bottom lip, he pulled me closer with an invisible thread. I felt as if he were touching me, reaching somewhere deep inside me. I slid my hand toward him without realizing it. His fingers closed over mine, brought my hand into the sunlight. When he spoke, his voice was raw with emotion. "What in the world . . . ," he whispered, ". . . are you doing *here*?"

CHAPTER 18

" 'The Voices of a Thousand Leaves,' " Jace said as the melody faded to silence, the vibrations of the old piano dissipating into a hush. "The song you were playing. It's about a boy who's lost in a blizzard when his family is forced to make the westward journey on the Trail of Tears. For years, he wanders the world searching for the way home. Finally he finds a new people and joins their clan, but his spirit never stops yearning for the place where the leaves speak of his ancestors. When he grows old, winds from the east bring their voices to him. He sets off on a journey to see Nanih Waiya, the mother mound, one last time before he dies."

"You can hear the story in the music," I murmured, closing my eyes again and letting the music flow from my body into the keys. Notes, chords, hand positions whispered through my mind like the voices of the leaves, bringing me far into myself.

Opening my eyes, I looked up at Jace as the last notes died away. He had his arms folded atop the old piano, his chin resting there as if he were not only listening to the music but feeling it.

"It's a beautiful song," I said finally. "I've never heard it before—before last night when Dillon played it, I mean."

"I've never heard it that way." Jace nodded toward the piano keys. "Many of those old songs have never been written down in a formal arrangement. The words have been passed down orally, and the music travels from one flute player to the next."

"They should be written down," I said, thinking that if I spent some time here, I could do that. I could pick up a cheap cassette player, record the songs first, then write down the stories and arrange the music for piano. "Nothing so beautiful should ever be lost."

His eyes filled with layers of emotion, found mine. "No, it shouldn't." My fingers paused on the keys, and I felt the pull of his nearness, leaned closer to him, fell into an invisible connection. For an instant, nothing moved. My heart slowed, my breath shortening in anticipation of something to come. A soft pulse beat against his throat, and his lips parted slightly with a breath. My gaze fluttered there, then moved back to his eyes.

Stepping back, he broke the link between us.

I tucked my hands between my knees, blushed, and swiveled away from the keyboard. "Guess we should get back to work."

His focus turned to the doorway. "I finished looking through the database, but I didn't come up with anything. I do have another idea, though. I've had quite a few kids use land abstracts to trace their family histories. Land in this area was granted to members of the Choctaw tribe after removal in the 1830s. The abstracts for those properties read like family histories—all the marriages, divorces, children mentioned in last wills, and so forth. Depending on how many Clays originally received land grants in the area, and whether those grants have remained in the family, you might be able to trace forward from your family's earliest history here to the people you're trying to find. It's not a sure thing, but it is possible." He glanced at his watch, then out the window. "Of course, we couldn't work on it until after the weekend. It's four thirty, and all the offices will be closed after five."

The time surprised me. I glanced at my wrist, then remembered that my watch was with Autumn. "I've wasted your whole afternoon."

"It was anything but a waste." He stepped closer to the piano, braced an elbow against it and rested his cheek on his fist, then nodded toward the keys. "Play something else. Neenee won't be dropping the kids off at homecoming for a half hour yet."

I realized that my fingertip was slowly stroking back and forth over middle C. "I'd better not." Pulling my hand away, I stood up. My mind was filling with music again, and the compulsion to play was so strong that the keys seemed magnetic. How long had it been since I'd felt that way? "I'll make you late."

He looked down at me, a slight smile on his lips, his eyes so dark I couldn't see the centers. "I'm not worried."

"I get lost in it." I was already lost—lost in the music, the moment, him. In his nearness, in the sense that he understood so much about me that went unsaid. He knew what it was to be both tormented and compelled by the past, to have it ask questions you couldn't answer. I wondered if he was delaying our return to the festival because too many memories waited there for him.

His smile faded, became somber and earnest as he leaned closer and idly slid his fingers along the dusty ivory. "The best things in life are the things we get lost in."

I wanted him to kiss me. The realization was startlingly powerful. I could see him thinking about it, then he shifted away.

"Maybe one song," I said as I returned to the keys, my body alive with an excitement that had nothing to do with music. I could feel him watching me as I played, could hear the weight of his body changing the vibrations ever so slightly as he leaned against the piano. Bending over the keyboard, I abandoned myself to the moment, as melody after melody filled the room.

Finally, Jace touched my shoulder and told me it was time to leave. My throat was dry, testifying to the fact that I'd been singing or humming along with the music, providing an all-out performance in this dusty room.

"I told you," I said, embarrassed.

"You did."

I stood, then held my hands out and tiptoed backward, as if the piano were a ticking time bomb. "Okay, Dell, step away from the piano," I said.

He laughed, ushering me out of the room and closing the door. Together we headed downstairs, then drove back to the homecoming festival, talking about land abstracts and Choctaw history—harmless subjects that both of us could be comfortable with. By the time we reached the Reids' booth at the front corner of the closest craft pavilion, Autumn and Willie were already waiting. Shasta was babysitting them as well as her own little boy. Benjamin and Willie sat engrossed in playing trucks on a blanket, and Autumn moved around the booth, arranging silver jewelry and fringed leather items ranging from knife scabbards to hand-beaded cell phone holsters. When she saw us coming, she launched herself into Jace's arms. Wrapping around him, she sighed and laid her head on his shoulder.

"It's about time," Shasta complained. "I've had people coming by asking about your flutes all day, and you're not here." She motioned to a display of flutes on a table nearby. Carefully carved and inlaid with dark- and light-colored woods, turquoise, mother-of-pearl, and red coral, they were adorned with beadwork, the wood polished until it shone like glass. If Shasta was impressed with the workmanship, it didn't show. "You forgot to put prices on them this morning, so all I could do was sell your stupid CD and tell them you'd be back later. Now it's practically time to close up. The dances start in thirty minutes. They're already forming the circle on the capitol lawn."

I slipped around the table to look at Jace's picture on a CD next to the flutes. In the photo, his hair was long, and he was wearing a traditional ribbon shirt of bright cotton with appliqué work across the chest. He was younger, perhaps eighteen or twenty years old. With the long hair, he looked like his cousin Dillon but there was no mistaking Jace's eyes, or the thoughtful, somber line of his lips.

I turned to him with my mouth hanging open. "You have a CD?"

His knowledge of traditional Native American songs suddenly made perfect sense. Jace wasn't only a flute maker, he was a musician with an actual CD, bearing his photo. "You didn't tell me that."

"You didn't ask." His mouth twisted wryly.

I slipped past Shasta into the booth, grabbed one of the CDs, and read the back. "You said you were a history teacher."

He faced me from across the table, Autumn still clinging to him. "I am a history teacher."

" 'The Voices of a Thousand Leaves' is on here." Looking down at the flutes, I tried to imagine Jace playing that melody.

"I only keep the CDs here to use as flute demos." He snatched the case from my hand and set it on the table, facedown, so that his younger long-haired self was no longer staring up at us.

I reached for it again. "No. Wait. I want one. I want to buy one for my car."

He batted the CD out of reach, sliding it down the table like a beer glass on a bar top. Colliding with a box of porcelain baby dolls dressed in handmade Choctaw clothing, it ricocheted to the far corner, then teetered on the edge. "Sorry. That's the last one I've got."

Uncurling herself, Autumn leaned back to eye him quizzically, her arms still looped around his neck. Pointing toward the back of the booth, she shook her head. "Daddy, there's a whole—"

"It's an old recording. Not very good," Jace interrupted.

"I still want one," I pressed, spurred on by his obvious embarrassment. "I'll bet it's great."

"Nope," he assured me, bumping the table with his thigh, so that the CD fell off and disappeared into a pile of boxes and packing materials. "It's not."

"That wasn't nice." A giggle bubbled from my throat as I squatted down and crawled partway under the table, trying to spot the CD.

"Yeah, Dad," Autumn echoed. "We got a whole bun—"

"Ssshhh." Jace set her down and began digging through the pile of boxes and bubble wrap. "You really don't want that CD. It'd be elementary stuff for someone who plays like you do. It's old. It's been almost ten years since we recorded it. The recording's lousy." He was grinning, but there was a hidden chagrin behind the words, as in, *Please don't make me reveal my long-haired flute-playing self. I'm a history teacher now. A grown-up.*

"I want the CD."

"No, you don't." He found the case before I could, snatched it up, and sat grinning at me under the table. "Really. You don't."

I gave him the evil eye I'd learned from Karen. She used it on James when he felt the urge to add more guitars to the collection that had already taken over the game room and the guest room, or when we'd already stopped at twenty-five historical markers on a trip, and he was eyeing number twenty-six. "Give me that CD."

"Nope." Jace slipped it behind his back, then brought his hands out empty. "See. All gone."

I started laughing. "You're such a . . . a . . . ." With the kids nearby, my options were limited, so I finished with, ". . . turd. I played the piano for you."

"True. But you're really good."

"I bet you're really good too."

We hovered there in a stalemate, both crouched underneath the table, eyeing each other.

"I'll get it sooner or later," I vowed.

His teeth were straight and white against his dark skin. "We'll see."

Someone tapped my shoulder, and I turned to find Autumn squatted down behind me with a shoe box full of CDs. "Here," she offered. "We've got *tons* of these at home in the garage. There's boxes and boxes."

"And boxes," Willie echoed cheerfully from the corner. "Nana Jo puts her drink on one, so it won't make a ring on the table."

"Oh, look. Lots of CDs," I said, flipping through the stack of younger, long-haired Jaces, then selecting one and dangling it in the air between us.

He groaned under his breath. "You'll be sorry. I'm a lot better flute maker than flute player."

"Guess I can judge for myself," I said, and he grinned.

"You could just take my word for it."

"I'd rather discover the real you. Music doesn't lie."

"It's not—"

"For heaven's sake, you two," Shasta's voice came from somewhere overhead. "Cut that out. You've got a customer, Jace."

I climbed out from under the table and Jace stood up to talk to a middle-aged couple who thought a *genuine Indian flute* might make a good souvenir of their trip to the Choctaw Labor Day Festival.

"They're just beautiful," the woman commented, smoothing her hand along a gorgeous instrument of mahogany inlaid with a mother-of-pearl fish swimming in a tide of turquoise and lapis waters.

Jace guided her to an instrument made of lighter-colored wood instead. The dark ones, he pointed out, tended to gather dust too easily. Natural colors were better for display.

Shasta, who was pretending to be occupied with laying tablecloths over the merchandise in the booth, leaned over and whispered in my ear, "The dark one has a better sound. But they'll never play it."

"Oh," I said, watching Jace weave his magic with the flute-buying customers, just as he had with the tour group in the museum. Finally, the buyers settled on a blond flute carved with soaring birds and inlaid with lapis swirls, which Jace explained represented the invisible currents of air that brought the yearly migrations.

Shasta had finished closing up most of the booth by the time they were ready to pay. "Anything else?" she asked as she opened the cash box and slipped in their check. The woman glanced around the booth, but it was clear that everything was already covered, and Shasta was anxious for shopping time to be over.

"I guess not," the woman answered. "Is there more going on around here tonight? We're just so impressed with all of this. We never knew all of these Indian things were down here. We have just really enjoyed the day, and touring the museum, and seeing the people working in the traditional Indian huts across the street, and watching the Indian games over on the ball field, and all of the wonderful arts and crafts. It is a wonderful event. Just . . ." Holding her hands in the air to encompass all she'd seen, she finished with, "Wonderful."

Shasta handed her a box with the flute carefully packed inside, then flashed a huge smile that was anything but genuine. "Thank you. We're glad you've enjoyed *Choctaw* Labor Day. Tonight, there will be traditional *Native American* dances at the parade grounds. Anyone is welcome to bring a lawn chair and watch." She sounded like a flight attendant methodically repeating the litany of safety procedures. "Spectators are asked not to enter the circle without being invited, and not to take pictures of the dancers without asking."

Eyes widening, the woman popped her fingers over her lips, as in, *Oops. Already did that. Sorry.* "We didn't know. Jerry already took a few pictures of people in their Indian costumes today."

"The dancers prefer that you ask first." Shasta's tone held a forced pleasantness.

"The clothes are called regalia," Autumn chimed in, standing beside her aunt. "Costumes are what you wear at Halloween. All the stuff we wear at powwow has meanings. My mama made mine."

Jace shifted, as if he wanted to snatch his daughter out of the conversation before it could turn painful.

"That's sweet," the woman said, smiling down at Autumn. "I'll bet you look just lovely in it, too." She glanced from Autumn to Shasta and back, her eyes growing skeptical. "Is this your mother?"

Autumn giggled. "Huh-uh. This is my aunt Shasta. My mama died last year."

Jace caught his breath, frozen in place as the woman bent over the cash box, laying a hand on Autumn's shoulder and looking into her eyes. "My mama died when I was little, too. I sure missed her. I missed having her help me take a bath and comb my hair. Just silly little things, that's what I missed about her."

Autumn nodded earnestly. "Me too."

"But you know what I found out?" The woman tapped Autumn's folded hands with her fingertip, and Autumn pulled her shoulders upward. "I found out that my aunts and my grandma, and my best friend's mama knew how to comb hair, too, and they all loved to do that for me. Sometimes we'd even talk about my mama while they did it. Then later on I got a new stepmom, and you know what else?" Autumn shrugged again. "She loved to comb little girls' hair, too. Just about everybody in the world loves to comb a little girl's hair, I think, and I never knew that until after I lost my mama. After that, I started making sure to share my hair-combing time with lots of other ladies."

She smiled at Autumn, who smiled shyly back, and said, "You got pretty hair."

"So do you," the woman replied. "I'll look for you tonight in your lovely regalia. Maybe I can ask if it would be all right to take your picture." Tucking the flute box under her arm, she slipped her hand into her husband's, and the two of them walked away.

"Did Neenee bring my Choctaw clothes?" Autumn asked, hurrying to the back of the booth to search the area crowded with folded lawn chairs, coolers, jackets, quilts, duffel bags, and various Reid family personal items. "Where's my stuff Neenee brought?"

Shasta glanced at Jace and walked to the back of the booth. "We'll find it. If not, we'll run over to Neenee's house and get it."

"Here it is," Autumn said, pulling out a pink Gone to Grandma's suitcase. "Here's my stuff." She popped open the latches, and moved aside a pair of pajamas and a stuffed animal. "There's my Choctaw clothes. Neenee packed my Choctaw clothes, just like every year." She grabbed her things from the suitcase, then ran behind a quilt hanging in the corner. In a few minutes, she emerged, having traded her T-shirt and shorts for a traditional Choctaw dress made of red cotton, the tiers and apron adorned with intricate white trim and strip-quilted patchwork of yellow and turquoise. In her hand she carried ponytail holders with small leather discs beaded in a delicate pattern that matched her dress. She somberly crossed the tent and stood next to Shasta.

"Aunt Shasta, could you fix my hair?" Her voice was barely a whisper, and on their blanket, even Willie and Benjamin fell silent.

"Sure, honey. I'd love to help fix your hair." Shasta's hands trembled as she fished a hairbrush from her purse.

Autumn held the ponytail holders out to me in silent invitation. As I took them, she smiled and closed her eyes.

Resting a hand atop Autumn's head, Shasta bit her lip. Tears drew silky trails down her cheeks and left small, round circles of grief on her dress. After slipping the single pink hair band from Autumn's hair, she spread it out, then squeezed her eyes shut, shaking her head and handing me the brush. I took it and made a long, slow stroke through Autumn's hair, thinking of all the times I'd watched mother-daughter scenes on TV, around town, at Aunt Kate's house, and mourned the fact that I never had moments like this with my mother.

Swaying on her feet, Autumn leaned into the brush, lost in the moment, in memories. Her hair was thick and soft beneath my fingers as I slowly worked away the tangles until it fell loose and silky to her waist.

Shasta wiped her eyes, drawing a fortifying breath as I parted Autumn's hair, braided one side, and slipped in one of the beaded ponytail holders, glancing up at Shasta for approval. Nodding, she gathered the rest of Autumn's hair and began the second braid. I turned to look for Jace, but he was disappearing around the end of the building. His hands clenched behind his neck, he turned his face skyward like a marathon runner desperate for air.

I slipped away from Shasta and Autumn and followed him into the alley between the buildings. He was standing there, eyes closed, lips pulled back in a grimace of pain and withheld emotion.

"I'm sorry," I whispered.

He smoothed a hand over his face, then let his arm hang limp at his side. "I don't want her to hurt so much."

"I know," I said. "But little girls are more resilient than you think."

"I hope so." His voice cracked, then he exhaled sharply. "It's hard to see her suffer. I want to protect her. I'm supposed to be able to protect her."

"I know," I whispered again, then stepped closer and slipped my fingers over his. Covering them with his other hand, he pulled me near, his body curling over mine. I felt his grief, his exhaustion from trying to keep everything on an even keel.

"I'm sorry," he said again, and we stood there, leaning on each other. His heart beat slowly against my cheek, his breath touching my hair, his fingers clutching mine against his chest like he'd never let go.

Autumn called from inside the booth, and Jace broke away from the embrace, glancing around the alleyway like he'd suddenly realized where he was and what he was doing.

Willie bounded around the corner. "C'mon, Dad. Everybody's ready to go to the powwow."

Jace scooped him up. "All right, buddy," he said, clearly relieved to have the distraction. He didn't look at me as we returned to the booth, grabbed some lawn chairs, and started across the festival grounds with Shasta and the kids.

Ahead of us, Benjamin whined and pulled on Shasta's dress, wanting to be picked up. "Oh, baby boy," Shasta sighed. "Mom's already got about as much of a load as she can handle with little brother here." She patted her stomach, and Benjamin latched onto her arm, unconvinced.

"Here, I've got him." I jogged the few steps to catch up, then swung Benjamin up to my hip and fell into step beside Shasta. Benji snuggled under my chin, and I hugged him.

Shasta arched a brow, leaning close to me. "So . . . everything . . . go all right today?" Her tone said, *Come on, spill, girlfriend. I want the dish. What's going on between you and my brother?*

"Sure." The word sounded more innocent than it felt. "Why?"

Shasta tilted her chin like a bird of prey locking on to a mouse. "I saw the way you and Jace looked at each other. I saw you follow him out of the building."

I knew I was blushing, so I pretended to study a booth selling oil paintings by a Choctaw artist. "I just wanted to make sure he was okay."

"Mmm-hmm." Obviously, Shasta didn't believe me. "So, did you two have any luck today . . . with the family search, I mean?"

"Not much. We basically hit a dead end—for now, anyway. Jace has another idea, but it's going to take a lot of research, and . . ." *My parents are expecting me home at the first of the week.* "I doubt I'll have time, not this trip anyway."

Shasta pursed her lips. "I could help you with it. Maybe do some research while you're gone or something."

"Thanks." I glanced at her, and I was filled with an overwhelming sense of gratitude. "But I think you're going to be a little busy the next few months."

She butted me in the shoulder, knocking me sideways a few steps. "Then you'll just have to come back and do your own research, huh? You can stay at our place next time. Cody and I have a teeny house, but his folks keep their travel trailer parked out back. It's all hooked up and everything. You can stay out there."

"That's really nice. Thanks." I struggled to solidify the idea in my mind—me coming down from time to time to visit Shasta, seeing Jace again. As much I wanted it to, the picture wouldn't gel, and I knew why. I couldn't keep lying to James and Karen, and I couldn't tell them the truth. How could I possibly subject them to watching me return here, over and over, searching for a family other than the one they'd given me?

By the time we reached the parade grounds where the powwow dances were to take place, a huge circle of lawn chairs had already been formed, and near the east side, the only opening in the circle, a group of men in traditional Choctaw dress were positioning three huge ceremonial drums. Nana Jo and Shasta's mother had already reserved a Reid section near the announcer's tent, and they waved us over.

Benjamin slipped out of my arms and ran to his grandmother, who was helping Nana Jo sort through a box of quilts and smaller squares of fabric that looked like tablecloths with long fringes. Nana Jo hugged Benjamin, then let him help with spreading out the quilts. Glancing over her shoulder, she smiled at Shasta and me, and lifted her walking stick, motioning for Willie and Autumn to join her.

"Make yourself at home," Jace said, adding our lawn chairs to the Reid grouping. "I'll be right back." He strode off to catch someone passing by.

Shasta shifted our chairs to the front of the group, then sat down. "There. Now we'll be able to see." She motioned me to the spot next to her, and I slid in, self-conscious about having moved someone else's seats to the back.

Shasta gave the empty chairs a casual dismissal. "The rest of them will be up and down all night, dancing and helping with things. They won't mind." As she stretched her feet into the air, she curled and uncurled her toes inside her sandals. "Good thing I wasn't planning on dancing this year. My feet are killing me. I might make it through the grand entry, but that's about all." She paused to wave at Uncle Rube, who was seated with a group of drummers in the center of the circle. He'd balanced his oversized frame on a three-legged camp stool, so that he looked like a watermelon on an egg cup. He teetered precariously as he stretched to grab a long drumstick, the striking end of which was covered with a ball of tanned leather. Rearranging himself on the stool, he turned to explain something to Dillon, who stood next to him, apparently getting drum lessons.

Around the circle, spectators of all types were setting up lawn chairs and laying out quilts for children to sit on. Nearby, a contingent of basket-wielding Kiamichi Garden Club ladies were handing out free carnations with notes attached. In the field beyond the powwow circle, kids in brightly colored regalia ran with soccer balls, and a group of bare-chested teenaged boys played football, their traditional Choctaw shirts lying in a colorful pile on the grass. The laughter, the mix of voices, the drummers warming up, and strains of country music drifting from the amphitheater across the festival grounds made the event feel like a celebration.

From across the circle, the book-writing Harley riders waved, the husband holding up a new notepad with a handmade fringed leather cover. Waving back, I found myself thinking that James and Karen would enjoy this event, that I should bring them next year. On the heels of that thought, I realized how strange it would be, sitting here between them. They would seem as out of place as the stockbrokers on the other side of the circle.

Shasta waved something in front of my face. "He-ey. Hel-looo? Anyone in there?" She set a fringed square of cloth in my lap as I snapped back to the present. "We all have to have shawls to be in the grand entry. Here. You can wear the nice one."

"The . . . huh?" I muttered, unfolding the piece of cloth so that its long fringe fell over my legs. Embroidered with a floral design, it was a beautiful piece of work. "I'm not . . ."

Shasta leaned close. "Don't even try that with Nana Jo. Everyone dances the grand entry. Reid family rule. No exceptions. She even made me do it when I was thirteen and all my cheerleading friends from school showed up to watch the powwow. We were out behind the restrooms hanging out. Nana Jo tracked me down and dragged me off to the grand entry. I was so embarrassed, I could have died. No one else had to go do the grand entry, but that's just Nana Jo. She's superstitious about traditions."

"Oh," I muttered, fingering the cloth and thinking about finding some excuse to go to my car until the grand entry was over. *I need to go get my camera, I accidentally left my cell phone in the car*—something like that. I couldn't imagine getting out in that circle in front of all these people and trying to do some dance everyone thought I should know but didn't.

"Hey, Baby." Shasta's husband leaned over from behind and kissed her, and she drew back, surprised. He squatted next to her chair, then laid his head on her stomach. "How's my little muchacho?"

"Turning handsprings." Shasta rubbed her stomach, twisting away from me to face her husband. "Geez, Cody, put on your shirt." She slapped him away, and he stood up casually, pulling a brightly colored ribbon shirt from one shoulder and slipping it over his stocky frame. I realized he was one of the bare-chested football players I'd mistaken for a teenager, playing ball outside the circle. On the blanket next to Nana Jo, Benjamin heard his father's voice and popped to his feet, then rushed over and attached himself to Cody's leg.

Someone tapped me on the shoulder, and I turned to find BB from the garden club standing beside me with a basket of flowers. "Here you go, sugar." She smiled as she handed me a red carnation with a note attached. "How'd your day go? Any luck?" At my surprised expression, she added, "We ran into Jamie after lunch. She told us you had a little trouble with Lana at the courthouse. Did'ja find anything after you left?"

"Not really," I answered, checking self-consciously over my shoulder. Shasta and Cody were occupied with each other and Benjamin, and Nana Jo had Gwendolyn and the kids busy with quilts and shawls. Near the opening at the east end of the circle, dancers were lining up. "I couldn't find anyone with my father's or my grandparents' names listed in the phone book, or mentioned in the old high school annuals."

"Don't lose hope." She shifted her basket from one arm to the other and tapped the red carnation in my hand, then lifted a finger into the air. "You know, you should ask Cecil. She knows just about everyone in the county, I think—taught first grade for over thirty years, ran the Four-H summer camp program, and drove a school bus. If the family's ever had kids in school, or camp, or church, or Four-H around here, she'll know 'em." She tried to catch someone's attention across the circle, but around us the crowd was getting quiet, preparing for the dance, as an announcer mounted the platform on the other side of the circle. "Come by the garden club booth when you get a chance. We're right across the way selling meat pies and baked goods," BB added quickly. "We'll be there all evening and all day tomorrow, except for a little while in the morning, when we usually go over and see the art show before they start taking it down." She slipped her basket back onto her elbow, then quickly backed away and disappeared into the crowd of onlookers. I fingered the paper attached to the carnation, then turned it over and read:

COURTESY OF THE KIAMICHI GARDEN CLUB.

VOTE ELDON FLOWERS FOR CHIEF, CHOCTAW NATION.

I sat looking at the paper, thinking of how incredibly far I was from everything I knew and understood. There was an entire world hidden in these Kiamichi hills, yet I was tied to it in untold ways.

Beside me, Cody was helping Shasta out of the lawn chair, and the Reids were gathering to proceed to the head of the circle. Autumn ran over and grabbed my hand. "Hurry," she said, her eyes wide with excitement. "It's time."

"Oh, I don't think I should . . ."

Shasta snatched up my other hand, and together she and Autumn tried to pull me from my chair. "Come on." Shasta laughed as she stumbled, slightly off balance, then caught herself. "I'm not supposed to lift anything heavy."

"I don't know the . . . I mean I've never done . . ." I motioned toward the dance area, a lump forming in my throat. To the east, the Choctaw Nation Colorguard was preparing to move into the arena, carrying the United States flag, the Oklahoma flag, and the flags of the Choctaw and Chickasaw nations. The master of ceremonies began making announcements over the loudspeaker, introducing the arena director, the Head Man Dancer, the Head Woman Dancer, the Host Gourd Dancers, the men of the Southern Drum and the Center Drum, which included Uncle Rube, otherwise known as Bartholomew Tall Horse.

The drummers struck their drums, and it was obvious that we were about to miss the grand entry. "I don't know *how*," I protested, looking around at the huge crowd of spectators and thinking that the last, last, last thing I wanted to do was get out there in front of everyone.

Autumn frowned incredulously. "It's easy. I'll show you. C'mon." She jittered on her feet, her fingers still clutched around mine in an I'm-not-giving-up grip. "C'mon. Please?" Her face pleaded in a way that made it impossible to say no. The moment suddenly seemed significant. This was something she'd always done with her mother, and now she was willing to share it with me.

"Sure. Of course I will. I'd love to dance with you, but you'll have to show me the steps." My heart fluttered in my throat, and I silently prayed, *God, please don't let me make a fool of myself in front of all these people.*

"Get your shawl," Autumn whispered, and my fingers shook as I grabbed the fringed fabric from my chair.

Cody scooped up Benjamin, Autumn took Willie's hand, and the next thing I knew she and Willie were leading me behind the rest of the Reids as the master of ceremonies explained that the evening would begin with the grand entry, then a ceremony in honor of Choctaw military warriors, and finally an address by the current chief of the Choctaw Nation. Festivities would then continue with competitive dances of various types. Willie bounced up and down in place as we reached the end of the line and waited for our turn to enter the circle.

"Willie, stop it," Autumn scolded, grabbing his shirt and yanking him back. "This isn't anytime to be goofing around. Be respectful." With her face close to his, she scowled and pressed a finger to her lips. "Now, ssshhh. You're not a baby."

"I wanna go with Dad," Willie protested, looking up at me and pointing to where Jace was standing with a group of men, ready to enter the arena. At the sound of Willie's voice, he glanced back, seeming surprised, then pleased, to find his children with me, rather than Nana Jo or one of the aunts.

"You can't. You're too little. You're not a *man*," Autumn hissed, smiling at her dad through clenched teeth, the silent message being *Everything under control here, Dad. Don't worry.* "Let Dad alone now, and be good."

Willie was not to be dissuaded. "I wanna go with Dad," he whined, pulling against Autumn's hand. Ahead of us, Nana Jo glanced back, giving the outburst a scornful frown. In the arena, the opening ceremonies began and the crowd fell silent. Now was not the time for Willie to break into a full-scale fit, but Autumn had a death grip on his wrist, and the situation was about to turn ugly.

"Hey," I whispered, leaning close to Willie, "don't leave me, all right? I need someone to show me how to do this."

His eyes narrowed, the wheels turning inside his head. Decision time—*Throw a fit or go along quietly?* "Okie-dokie," he said finally, then tried to yank his arm away from Autumn again. "Leggo. I gotta help *her*."

"I have him," I said, and Autumn released her hold, huffing and pursing her lips.

Ahead of us, the line started to move and Nana Jo glanced back with a concern.

"You gotta put on your shawl," Willie whispered from the side of his mouth as we started forward. "With the stringy stuff hanging down." He motioned to some of the women ahead, who had covered their shoulders with beautiful, brightly decorated shawls. The long, silky fringe swayed in time with their movements as they proceeded into the circle.

I unfolded my shawl and slipped it around my shoulders, and Willie nodded his approval. My heart leapt into my throat as we reached the opening of the circle, and around me the members of the line became dancers, their feet taking up the beat of the drums, moving in a slow, swaying rhythm. Willie tapped my hand and demonstrated as we went in.

Down on the left foot, up on the right, down on the right foot, up on the left, I chanted in my head as we flowed into the circle, swept along like floating leaves in a river of color and movement, breath and sound. The chant in my head faded as the drummers began singing, filling the air with a lyrical melody of the Choctaw language. The sound spun deep inside me, the drums finding unison with my heartbeat, the song overtaking my thoughts, causing everything else to recede, until I was no longer nervous and afraid.

I was not one, but one of many, swept along on a tribal river that swelled from some hidden place deep in my soul.

CHAPTER 19

By the time the dance was over, I was exhausted, physically and emotionally. I stood swaying in place, trying to regain my bearings as the circle cleared.

"I thought you said you didn't know how," Autumn remarked, and I looked around for Willie. I'd been so lost in the dance I'd completely forgotten about Willie and Autumn.

"Willie's with Dad." Autumn pointed to Jace, who had just scooped up his son. Lana was beside him, leaning close to whisper something in Jace's ear. Holding a shawl in one arm and a clipboard in the other, she was clothed in a beautiful buckskin dress with long fringes and intricate beadwork, her braided hair adorned with beaded rosettes that matched the dress. She looked like an artist's creation, posed there, tall and svelte, beautiful and supremely confident.

A wave of embarrassment washed over me, catching me in a powerful undertow of self-consciousness as Jace started toward us. "You're quite a dancer," he said, smiling at me.

"I doubt that." I could feel Lana watching us, but I forced myself not to look. Instead, I focused on Jace. "But I did have wonderful teachers." I motioned to Willie and Autumn, and both of them grinned.

"You did great. Nobody would know you'd never been before," Shasta said, joining us. Wiping her forehead, she turned to head back to the lawn chairs. "That's enough for me. I'm pooped. I've got to sit down."

"Me, too," I agreed, anxious to put some distance between Lana and myself. Suddenly my legs were hollow and weak. Compared to Lana in her buckskin dress, I felt like an ugly duckling in the shadow of a swan. I wanted to melt into the crowd and disappear.

"Sounds good." Jace picked up Autumn, who, now that Jace was carrying Willie, had decided she needed Daddy time, too. He walked off the field, carrying one of them on each arm, and I followed in my shawl, thinking that we looked like one of the art show portraits of a migrating Choctaw family. I liked the way it felt, being part of the picture. When we reached the lawn chairs, Jace sat down beside me with the kids on his knees, and started explaining the upcoming series of competitive dances to me.

"Thanks for taking the kids through the grand entry," he said when his daughter wandered off to play go fish on a blanket with one of her cousins. "I figured Autumn would probably skip it this year." He watched his little girl twirl in a spill of bright cotton, then fall, laughing, to the blanket with her cousin. "I never thought she'd put on that dress. I told Neenee not to send it."

"Neenees always know best," I replied, and he smiled sideways at me.

"I guess they do." He rested his chin on his son's hair, and Willie snuggled in, yawning. "You tired, little man?" Jace asked, and Willie shook his head. "Didn't think so." Glancing at me, Jace winked.

Folding his hands under his chin, Willie sighed, his eyes drifting closed as the arena filled with military veterans preparing for a ceremony in honor of Choctaw warriors. Shasta and Cody left with Nana Jo and some of the other Reid women to sit by the arena entrance and help some of the Reid kids prepare to participate in upcoming competitive dances. Dillon wandered by carrying a paper plate with something delicious-smelling on it.

"Hey," he said, nodding at me in an interested-but-trying-to-remain-cool way that reminded me of high school.

"Hey," I replied, catching another whiff of whatever he had on his plate. My stomach responded with a bear growl, and both Dillon and Jace blinked at me, surprised. "That looks good," I admitted.

"Fried meat pie." He held it closer, and my mouth started watering. "The Kiamichi Garden Club's got 'em over there." He pointed toward the concession area on the other side of the circle, where various vendors were selling food from tents and portable trailers. "Want me to get you one?"

"No, that's all right." I stood up and squinted across the way, trying to spot the garden club ladies. "I need a drink, too. I'll just walk over there."

Dillon shrugged—"Cool"—then momentarily turned his attention to a group of teenagers passing by.

"Maybe we can play some music again back at camp," he offered, walking backward with his plate. "You can show me some more guitar licks."

"Sure. But I think I've shown you about everything I know. I'm not that good on guitar."

"Dang, I think you're good." Nodding to add emphasis, he gave a shy, flirtatious smile.

"You should hear her play the piano," Jace interjected. "She's good. Like Carnegie Hall good."

Dillon looked surprised. "Dang," he said again, then realized his friends were getting away. "Cool. Catch ya later, okay?"

"See you after a while," Jace answered.

With a shot-from-the-hip wave good-bye, Dillon jogged off, chasing after his friends.

I frowned at Jace, and he swiveled his hands, palms up. "What? You are good on the piano. It's not a secret, is it?"

"It's not . . ." I was about to say *It's not something that matters anymore,* but I knew Jace would probe into that answer, and it would open up a whole can of worms, so I finished with, ". . . something I usually just . . . bring up to people."

He studied me, his eyes reflecting an enormous orange moon climbing above the mountains to take flight in the deep blue twilight sky. "I can't imagine why not."

He probably couldn't, I knew. He couldn't imagine how the music lessons, and the performances, and the schooling and the expectations felt like a heavy coat—a thick layer of wool between me and the rest of the world, something that made me look much larger than I felt, a costume that hid the real me. Somewhere deep inside was the silent fearful girl from the paper-thin house on Mulberry Creek. She knew that one day, when things got bad enough, she'd build a boat and sail down the river to Oklahoma, to the beautiful place her mama remembered.

I couldn't, of course, tell Jace about that girl. I couldn't say that being here, where there were no music teachers, no symphonic directors, no adopted family filled with love and high expectations, I felt as if I could finally shed the costume and examine what was on the inside.

"Very funny, Mr. Secret CD," I joked. "Can I bring you anything from the concession stand?"

Jace gave a chagrined smile. Clearly, he didn't want to get into another conversation about his CD. "Whatever you're having."

"All righty, then." As I headed off, I caught Nana Jo watching us with that same wary, concerned expression she'd had in the café earlier—the one that preceded Shasta whispering in my ear, *He's too old for you, you know.*

I tried to put it out of my head as I worked my way around the fringes of the circle toward the concession area. I walked the long way around, so as to avoid Lana, who had settled into one of the chairs on the announcer's platform and was busily managing papers and her clipboard. By the time I reached the garden club's booth, the veterans had left the arena and lines at the concessions tables were growing longer. On the PA, the master of ceremonies announced that there would be a ten-minute break preceding the next event—a ceremony during which the current Choctaw princess would hand over her title to the incoming princess and bestow gifts to the chief and other dignitaries. Following that, the chief would deliver an official greeting and address to the crowd.

I waited as a group of dancers ordered meat pies, homemade cookies, and iced tea, and chitchatted with the garden club ladies. At the head of the table, Cecil, who was supposed to be taking orders and money, was doing more chatting than charging. The entire line seemed to be made up of Cecil's former students, or relatives of her former students, and each of them wanted to talk about everything that had happened since grade school. I gathered that she had been a very popular first-grade teacher—the type who made a difference in students' lives and was remembered, even twenty and thirty years later.

My stomach grumbled a complaint as Cecil began detailing her Hawaii retirement trip to a couple of former students in front of me. I considered moving to the booth next door, where the youth group from a Baptist church was selling hot dogs and canned sodas.

"Well, hi there." Nita, who was passing by with a restaurant-sized box of paper cups, spotted me as I stepped out of line. "You hungry?"

"Starved," I admitted, slapping a hand over my stomach.

"Cecil," Nita barked, tapping Cecil with the cups as she slipped behind the table. "Light a fire under your kettle, will you? We got starvin' people at the end of this line, and the princess ceremony'll be startin' up any minute."

Cecil glanced apologetically around her former students. "I didn't see you back there," she said as the students moved away, and I finally stepped up to the table. "I thought they were the last customers, or I wouldn't of stood there tellin' them all about Hawaii."

"Yes, you would of," Nita grumbled. "You tell everyone about Hawaii."

"That's all right." Slow service or not, I was glad to finally be at the front of the line. "I need two glasses of iced tea and two meat pies—well, make that three." It probably wouldn't hurt to get an extra, just in case Willie and Autumn hadn't eaten yet.

"Comin' up," Nita called.

Cecil began totaling my order, muttering and reading the amounts off the price list repeatedly. "Sorry," she said, after she became confused and had to start over. "Not the math whiz I once was. I used to do all this business in my head. Used to teach my students all kinds of good ways to memorize their math facts, and now I can't remember beans."

"That's what calculators are for," I joked, waiting for her to give me the total, then counting out exact change while the ladies started making my order. They ran out of tea halfway through pouring my cups, and I stood to the side while they fixed more. The people behind me wandered off to buy hot dogs next door.

Cecil took the opportunity to start up a conversation. "I'm sorry to hold you up. I just love the chance to see all my kids again. Once they've been through my classroom, they're mine, you know, just like my own family. Reckon I've got more kids and grandkids than anyone in the county."

Her mention of teaching school started the wheels turning in my mind. "Did you ever know a Thomas Clay? His parents were Nora and Audie Clay. I think he must have gone to school around here."

Drumming her fingers on the table, she repeated the name. "Thomas Clay . . . Thomas Clay . . ." I held my breath as her lips formed a silent O, her eyes widening in an expression of Eureka. "Well, now, let me think. . . ."

She adjusted her glasses and she scratched the loose skin beside her ear. My hopes hovered in thin air, like a cable car suspended by a fragile thread.

"Thomas Clay . . ." Squinting upward, she tapped a knuckle against her lips, then let out an exasperated sigh. "Now, isn't this pitiful? Time was, I could tell you all of my former students, where they lived, who their parents were, what year they started first grade." She rubbed her knotted brows in obvious frustration. "I know that name's familiar, but I can't quite place it. . . ." Finally, she shook her head in resignation. "My memory's just not what it used to be. I'm sorry. Sometimes I think I better have the doctor give me some of that Alzheimer's medicine my sister Lindy takes."

As she set my order on the table in front of us, Nita gave her a concerned look, then turned to me. "I put it all in a box, so you could carry it. There's mustard, catsup, straws, napkins, and silverware over there, so just help yourself."

"Thanks." I focused on the food to hide the fact that my emotions were in free fall again. I picked up the box and moved to the end of the table, wondering whether Jace liked mustard or catsup.

"Nita?" At the end of the counter, Cecil paused while arranging the money in the cash box. "Did you ever have a Thomas Clay in middle school? I'm just sure I should know that name."

"Hmmm," Nita mused, and my hopes crept upward again. "Well, I've had lots of Clays, Cecil. You know, I just never did keep track of all those kids like you do."

My emotions crested the hill and careened downward with a whoosh of air as I lingered over the condiments, afraid to hope, unwilling to give up and leave if there was any chance.

"There was a Tommy Clay in middle school for a while. He had an older brother in the ninth or tenth grade. Seems like those boys transferred over from Clayton School. Imagine they lived out there on Cataway Creek—remember, that year there was all those arguments about where the school district boundaries were and who was supposed to go to what school?"

Taking on a look of recognition, Cecil nodded. "Ohhhh, I do remember that now. That was the year Lane had to have all that surgery on his back, and I was gone so much."

"Ummm-hmm." Nita nodded, satisfied that their combined memories had pieced together the events.

"They didn't stay long." Nita chewed the side of her lip. "Something happened in that family—some kind of trouble—and they sent the kids off to Indian School, I think. I can't recall exactly. . . ."

Cecil shook her head, letting out a soft whistle of air between her teeth and bottom lip. "I just don't remember any of it, but that was a lost year for me. All I did was drive to the hospital down in Paris and then come home at night and try to keep my own kids fed, and washed, and homework done."

Nita nodded somberly. "We've all got times like that. Sometimes life gets away."

"Sometimes it does," Cecil agreed.

After folding a leftover order ticket neatly in half, Nita picked up a pencil and pointed the eraser at me. "You might try taking a drive out on Cataway Creek Road, where it winds way back in by the river, about fifteen miles off the highway or so." As she spoke, she drew the route on the back of the folded ticket. "It's a bit of a rough trip, but there's Clays that still live back in there. I drove the school bus on that route many a time over the years. I wouldn't swear to it, but seems like I might of even had Tommy and his brother on the bus that one year. Anyhow, the Clays I'm thinking of had a big ranch down by Cataway Creek, way back off the road. There was several families with houses on the place. The kids always got off at one relative's house or other. Nice folks. End of the school year, their grandma gave me a basket with home-baked bread and wild plum jam that was sure enough good." She turned the paper around and showed it to me. "You just go back toward Antlers and turn off on Cataway Creek Road, about eight miles before you get to town, then go another ten, maybe fifteen miles, until the road starts to follow Cataway Creek down through the holler. After the road moves away from the creek again, you'll see what's left of an old stacked stone fence, and then the driveway into their place. There's some mailboxes and old rock pillars there, as I recall."

"Thanks," I said, watching her draw the fence and the pillars, then trace the pencil along the curves by the creek. Cataway Creek, where the Clays had a ranch far off the road. Where Thomas Clay may have lived before something happened in the family. Some trouble.

I fixated on the note as she slid it into the box between the meat pies and the drinks. It was hard to believe one small scrap of paper might hold the keys to my past.

"There you go, darlin'," she said. "I wrote my number and Cecil's number down at the bottom, just in case you might ever need it."

"Thank you . . . thanks so much." My throat was raw, filled with a rush of hope that made the words tremble.

"Good luck," Cecil added as I turned and headed back through the crowd. "Hope you find what you're looking for."

In the arena, the chief of the Choctaw Nation was speaking, but I couldn't focus on the words. Instead, I watched the note twitter back and forth in my box, afraid that a sudden gust of wind might catch it and blow it away while I wasn't looking.

When I reached our chairs, Jace looked up, surprised. "I was starting to wonder if you'd been elected chief and dragged into the arena."

"Long line at the food tables," I answered, slipping into my chair and balancing the box on my knees. "It took a while." The words felt like they were coming from someone else, as if I were only watching the girl in the lawn chair. As I helped Jace balance both Willie and his supper, my mind was traveling far away, leaving behind the sound of the chief speaking, the music of a wooden flute playing in the distance, the sound of the family murmuring around me. I felt myself drifting away from all of it, following the pencil line on Nita's map—through the hollow, along Cataway Creek, past the stacked stone fence. Carefully folding the note, then tucking it in my pocket, I tried to imagine what was on the other end.

After we'd finished eating, Autumn wandered over and balanced on the arm of her father's chair, her shoulders sagging wearily.

"Long day, huh?" he asked, patting her softly on the back.

"Yeah," she whispered, yawning. "I'm tired."

"I know, baby girl," he said, and she frowned over her shoulder at him.

"I'm not a baby."

"I know."

Holding her arm close to her face, she squinted in the dim glow of the arena lights, checking the time on my Russian watch.

"You can keep that," I said, and she blinked in surprise.

"Really? From now on I can keep it?"

"From now on." I nodded, and Jace glanced at me. "You have fun with it, okay?" Grandma Rose always said that when someone had done a good turn for you, the best way to repay it was to do a good turn for someone else. The garden club ladies had definitely done a good turn for me.

"Awesome. Nobody in school's got one like this."

I chuckled. "No, I imagine not."

"Can you show me how to set it?"

"If I can remember."

Autumn scooted off Jace's chair arm, then slid into the seat beside me, and together we deciphered the workings of the watch as the chief's address continued in the arena. By the time it was over, we'd finished with the watch, and Autumn rested her head drowsily on my shoulder. In the arena, dancers wearing regalia adorned with long fringes were gathering for the Grass Dance, while the announcer told the legend of a young man who wanted to dance with the tribe but could not because he was born with a crippled foot. Praying for guidance, he went off into the prairie, and as he stood looking over the miles of swaying and swooping grass, he realized this could be his dance. The dancers in the arena, with their long strands of yarn and ribbon, represented the prairie grass.

As the dance began, Jace winked at me, and motioned to Autumn, who was drifting off to sleep. By the time the Grass Dance was over, she lay limp against my shoulder, her breaths slow and deep.

"Guess it's time to go," Jace whispered, leaning close to my ear.

"Guess so," I agreed, though in a way I didn't want to leave. It felt good, sitting there with him, listening to the drums, the high-pitched songs of the drummers, the swish of fabric and fringe, the movement of the dancers, the Reids coming and going as various family members packed up and called it a night. I liked the way it felt, having Autumn's small body curled against mine, hearing Willie's soft snores. The moment was settled and complete.

I glanced over at Shasta, who was sitting on a blanket with her family. Cody's arm was curled around her swollen stomach and Benjamin's head rested on her knee. *She has this all the time,* I thought. *She has this feeling every day, forever.* I understood, in a soul-deep way, why she was in such a hurry to form a family of her own.

Beside me, Jace stood up with Willie in his arms, walked over to say something to Gwendolyn, then came back and roused Autumn. Yawning and sighing, she climbed to her feet.

"I'll get the chairs," I offered, folding two of them and putting them under my arms. Even though I didn't want to, I glanced toward the announcer's stand. Lana was busy laughing and talking with the group of drummers seated below the platform. Backing into the shadows, I waited for Jace as he grabbed the third chair and a bag full of quilts, and carried them opposite Willie.

"We can drop these at the booth for Nana Jo," he said. "She rode over with Bubba and Dillon. No telling what time they'll finally get out of here."

Autumn slipped her fingers into mine, and Jace glanced sideways, watching our intertwined hands for a long moment. "You can stay if you want to see the rest of it. I don't want to take you away."

Was he trying to get rid of me? The thought was surprisingly painful. "No. I'd just as soon go . . . if it's okay with you, I mean."

His lips twisted to one side as we started walking. "Of course it's okay."

When we reached the booth, he put the lawn chairs and quilts inside, then quickly tucked his flutes into a small box filled with foam peanuts, and handed the box to Autumn.

Balancing it under one arm, Autumn slipped her free hand into mine again. "Can I ride back with Dell?"

"I guess you'd better ask Dell." Jace pulled a tarp across the booth opening as Autumn turned to me expectantly.

"Sure you can," I told her, thinking that it would be nice to have company on the drive out to the campground. "My car's kind of a mess after this morning, though."

She smiled at me. "I like messy cars."

"Good, then you're the perfect copilot for me," I said, patting my purse. "I even have a new CD we can listen to. It's by some guy with long hair and a brooding frown."

Autumn giggled, and Jace groaned under his breath. On his shoulder, Willie stirred, then snorted irritably at the noise before settling down again as we walked through the darkened fairgrounds.

"I'm parked in that lot." I pointed toward the parking area behind the softball fields, which was slowly starting to empty out. Jace's car was in a smaller, personnel lot closer in.

"I'll walk you over," he offered, and I didn't tell him not to. I liked strolling along with him, looking at the stars and listening to the drums in the distance.

Autumn gave me the box of flutes and took his hand, stretching between us like a bridge. When we reached my car, she hugged her

dad good-bye, then climbed into my passenger seat, moving the envelope from the courthouse out of the way.

"I'll be right behind you two," Jace promised, then closed Autumn's door and strode off with Willie hanging on his shoulder like
a life-sized rag doll.

On the drive back to the campground, Autumn recalled the
morning's skunk incident and theorized about whether or not the
skunk had vacated the motor home's dryer vent. I plugged in Jace's
CD and "The Voices of a Thousand Leaves" filled the car like the
earthy smoke of a campfire. It was easy to see where Dillon had
learned to play the flute. Jace played beautifully, and in his music
there was a deeper dimension, a soulfulness that spoke of the story
behind the music.

"I hope those people in the motor home left." Moonlight painted
the soft curve of Autumn's cheek, casting a blue-black glow over her
hair as she spoke. "They're not very nice."

"No, they're really not."

"They don't like us because we're Indian. Because Nana Jo makes
us talk Choctaw and stuff." With a frustrated sigh, she turned to me
for confirmation. "I don't like to talk Choctaw. None of my friends
at school talk Choctaw."

Her frankness surprised me, and I paused to think before I answered. "It's not always the best thing to be just like everyone else."
Grandma Rose had told me that once. "If God wanted us all to be the
same, He would have made us that way."

Twisting her arms together, Autumn threaded her hands between
her legs. "You don't talk Choctaw."

"I never had the chance to learn. But I'd like to, one day. It's
important to know your history."

"Nana Jo says that." On the stereo, the music changed to a lively,
high-pitched melody that sounded like birdsong. "I could teach you
some Choctaw."

"I'd like that." Dimly, I had the thought that I was making commitments I couldn't keep. I wasn't going to be here long enough to learn Choctaw. "Maybe not this trip, but one of these days."

"How long are you gonna stay?"

"I'm not sure. Another day or so, probably. I've been away from home a long time, and I need to get back and spend some time with my mom and dad, and my nieces and nephew."

Autumn frowned at me, momentarily considering what I'd said. "I could come to your house and teach you some Choctaw."

I took her hand and squeezed it. "I live a long ways from here, sweetheart."

"My dad could drive me. He doesn't have anything to do on the weekends. We could even bring Willie."

I was beginning to sense an agenda. "We'll see."

Autumn huffed quietly at the answer, knowing, as all kids do, that things *we'll see* about usually don't happen. Gazing out the window, she fell silent, and I listened to the music. When the song was over, she turned back to me. "I wish God gave me a different color hair. My cousin's got red hair. I like it. And she's got blue eyes."

"You have beautiful hair." In the rearview mirror, Jace's lights disappeared momentarily as we rounded a curve. I wondered if he'd ever had this conversation with his daughter. "And you have beautiful brown eyes. I wish I had eyes like that."

She threw her hands into the air, then let them slap to her knees. "You do have eyes like that."

"Oh, that's true," I agreed, and she giggled, then fell momentarily silent.

"My cousin's pretty." She watched the car lights reappear in the side mirror, then glanced at me. "You're pretty."

"Thanks," I answered, and she snuggled back in the seat, leaning close to the window to look out at the moon.

"I think you're even prettier than Aunt Shasta."

"Thanks," I said again. "But your aunt Shasta's really beautiful."

"I'm glad you came to camp out with us."

"Me, too."

The conversation ran out. By the time we reached the campground, Autumn had almost drifted off to sleep. As we parked and exited the car, she didn't even notice that the motor home was gone, the campsite now empty.

Jace carried Willie to the tent, and Autumn stumbled along behind. I found myself lingering outside my car, wondering if he would come back for the box of flutes. I was glad when he did.

"Out cold," he reported.

"It's been a long, crazy day."

"Yes, it has," he agreed, but in spite of the day, neither of us seemed to want to leave.

For some reason, I felt the need to tell him about the garden club ladies and the map.

"I'm going to go there in the morning," I finished, putting Nita's scrap of paper back in my pocket. "To see if I can find . . . I don't know . . . a mailbox with their names on it, or someone I can ask about them." Saying it out loud made it sound unlikely and ridiculous. I felt obliged to apologize for the plan. "I know it's a long shot. Do you think I'm nuts?"

He considered the question, and for a moment I was afraid he'd say yes, and I'd be hurt because he didn't understand the emotional roller coaster I was riding. "I think you shouldn't go alone. This isn't Kansas City. The Kiamichi is a different kind of place. Some of the folks who live way up in the hills don't like strangers coming around. For one thing, drug business goes on in some of those out-of-the-way places. More than a few hunters and sheriff's deputies have gotten into trouble stumbling onto someone's marijuana patch or meth lab."

"I won't be tromping around the woods." I wondered if he was trying to discourage me because he thought my plan was unrealistic.

"You still shouldn't go alone." I felt as if I were talking to my father. "I'll drop the kids at Neenee's and go with you."

I instantly felt guilty. This was supposed to be his family weekend. "I don't want to take up your day again."

"It's all right."

"But it's . . ." Somewhere in the back of my mind was the picture of the highway patrolman telling me not to be caught driving around his territory again with my expired license. Nita's map would take me right back to the same area.

"Would you mind driving?" I asked, thoroughly chagrined. "I got stopped for speeding on the way back from the courthouse today and my license is expired. If the same guy stops me again, I'm in trouble."

His head dropped forward into the shadow of one of the tents next door. I realized he was laughing under his breath.

"Did you tell him you were having a really tough day?"

"I cried like a baby."

"Did he give you a ticket?"

"No. I think he felt sorry for me."

Jace laughed again.

"Stop that." I swatted at him, and he ducked away.

"Stop what?"

"You're laughing at me."

"I'm not laughing at you." He caught my hand in midair. "I'm just laughing." His voice was soft and intimate, his face only inches away.

"I like the way you laugh," I whispered, and my body came alive.

Stepping back, he let go of my hand and cleared his throat, frowning at the bedding stacked in the back floorboard under Benjamin's child seat. "Are you sure you're all right in there?"

"I'm fine. It's pretty comfortable, actually. I've still got Shasta's baby seat, though. I hope she doesn't need it tonight."

"Gwendolyn and Nana Jo both have baby seats in their cars," he said, opening the door and unstrapping the seat. "Let me get this out of the way for you. After two kids, I'm an expert with these things."

"I guess you would be." I stood awkwardly by the door, reminded again that he had life experiences to which I couldn't relate. "My aunt Kate got to the point where she just kept a baby booster in every car, because it's so much trouble to move them."

He pulled the seat out and braced it under his arm. "Between the ones Shasta has bought and the ones Deanne passed down from our kids, Shasta's got about ten of these things. But she might need this one in the morning, if she can keep Cody away from the fishing hole long enough to go to the festival. I'll put it in her tent." Turning away, he started toward the Reid campsite.

"Your flutes are still in here," I called after him, and he nodded. "We enjoyed the CD, by the way," I added, and he waved over his shoulder, shaking his head. I took the flute box from the car, then carried it to the Reid picnic table and waited for him to come out of Shasta's tent. In the center of camp, the fire glowed softly, and the lanterns had been lit, but the place was empty. I pulled one of the flutes out of the box and sat admiring it. In the soft light, the wood was the warm color of rich earth, and the tiny mother-of-pearl swirls seemed to take on an inner life. Remembering the music of the night before, I was momentarily tempted to play. I'd studied flute for a while at Harrington, but not on an instrument like this.

"Try it out," Jace urged as he crossed the circle of firelight. "That's a good flute."

Running my finger along the fluid lines of glistening shell, I contemplated the hours of patient effort and artistry that went into creating the instrument. "I wouldn't know how to play it."

"My guess is that you could play just about anything." He leaned against the table beside me, so that we stood shoulder to shoulder. "Give it a whistle."

I held the flute out to him instead, then looked up and met his challenge with one of my own. "Show me how."

The lantern glow flickered against his dark eyes. "I don't play anymore."

"My guess is that you could play just about anything."

Taking the flute from my hands, he laughed under his breath, then wagged the instrument at me.

"Play something from the CD," I urged. "It's really good—the CD, I mean. You should play more often."

Shrugging off the compliment, he moved his fingers into position on the flute, then raised it and squinted down the plane as if he were checking to see if it was warped. "Well, you know, kids, house, job, yard to mow. Life gets in the way and you give up some of the things you wanted to do when you were twenty." He made it sound simple, but the hooded look in his eyes said that it wasn't. "Not all of us have what it takes to go to Juilliard."

"There's nothing so great about Juilliard." Right now, Juilliard seemed a million miles away. I didn't want to be there. I wanted to be here, with him.

"Yes, there is." Glancing sideways at me, he winked, then wet his lips and brought the flute to his mouth. His chest lifted, and a long, plaintive note trembled into the night, then rose slowly to a haunting song that was both beautiful and sad. Closing my eyes, I let the music swirl around me, envelop me, carry me into a warm pool of emotion and light.

As the melody faded into a final note, I opened my eyes. Jace set the flute on the table and reached into the box, sifted through the foam peanuts, and pulled out a smaller flute adorned with doves in flight. "Your turn."

"I can't," I protested, but he was already sliding the instrument into my hands. I lifted it to my lips, blew in, and produced a weak, wavering note, then offered the flute back to him, laughing. "That was awful."

He pushed it toward me. "Not so bad for a first try, but you're holding it wrong." Slipping his arms around me, he moved my fingers into place, slid the flute into position near my chin. "Like this."

My body was flooded with heat and electricity, so that I barely felt my lungs fill with air, or my lips pushing a clear, smooth note into the mouthpiece. I could only feel his skin next to my skin, his heartbeat steady and low against my shoulders, his breath soft against the back of my neck.

"Better." His words were little more than a whisper. His fingers closed mine over the polished wood. "Keep that one. It deserves to belong to someone with a musical soul."

"I can't take it. It's—"

"Ssshhh." The whisper caressed my cheek as I turned in his arms. "You'll do it justice," he said against my mouth, then his lips met mine and everything else fell away.

I knew I'd been waiting for this to happen since we met.

Then, as quickly as it began, the kiss was over. He pulled away, squeezing my fingers once before letting go.

"Good night, Dell," he said, then disappeared into the darkness.

CHAPTER 20

I awoke in the morning thinking of that kiss, remembering the way it felt—natural and wonderful. In the past, anything so intimate would have seemed awkward and uncomfortable. Even after years with James and Karen, even after years of dating Barry, every time he hugged me, I thought of Mama holding me so tight I couldn't breathe, or Uncle Bobby brushing by, touching me in a way that didn't feel right, then looking around to see if Granny was watching.

Cold fish, he'd say when I pulled back. *You don't learn to act a little more friendly, ain't nobody ever gonna like you, with that stringy hair and nigger skin. You better start bein' a little nicer, girl. . . .*

But Jace's kiss burned all of that away.

As I was reliving the moment, Autumn appeared at my car window with a hairbrush and a story about her hair being too tangled to brush because she'd fallen asleep in braids last night. After I combed it out and rebraided it, she ran back to camp to ask Nana Jo if she could walk with me to the restroom. As the two of us headed up the road, she chattered about her house outside of town and the new baby goat she was bringing home, and the dog who was about to have puppies, but only one litter, because after that they were getting the dog fixed. She wanted to know what fixed meant, and how the dog would be fixed.

She shadowed me through breakfast and made sure we sat with Jace and Willie. By the time Lana emerged from her camper, we were all settled in together, with four lawn chairs and an ice chest for a makeshift table. As Lana passed by, Autumn suggested that we should go fishing this morning—just the four of us—before heading off to the Labor Day festival. Whether the timing was intentional or not, I couldn't say, but Lana stopped on her way to the camp kitchen, gave me a narrow look, and laid a hand atop Autumn's head.

"You two were going to come do the bounce house on the capitol lawn this morning—remember, we talked about that the other night?" Lana's words came in a forced singsong, as if she were trying to redirect an errant toddler. She smiled down at Autumn. "I'll be working there all day, and this morning, before everyone else gets there, you two can have it all to yourselves. That'll be a blast, won't it? Maybe we can even get Dad in there to have a little fun, what do you think?" She flashed a flirtatious smile at Jace.

Willie clapped his hands together in anticipation, swiveling back and forth between Lana and Jace. Autumn tipped her head toward her father, seeming momentarily tempted by the prospect of his joining them in wild bouncing abandon.

Jace gave Autumn a parental look, and Lana took advantage of the opportunity to shoot a visual death ray in my direction. No doubt she was hoping to vaporize me where I sat, sweep away the dust, and plant herself in my chair.

"Good morning, Lana. You look really tired," I said, and smiled pleasantly, just to annoy her. It wasn't like me to be that way with people. Back in high school, when the snotty girls picked on me, I usually just took it and went on about my business. Barry constantly told me not to be such a wimp, said I didn't have to put up with that kind of stuff. All of a sudden, Lana was bringing out the mean girl in me. It felt strange, but in some way liberating.

Lana flexed her hands at her sides. "No, I'm fine. How'd you do last night, sweetie? Sorry, I can't remember your name."

"Dell." *Funny, I would think you'd remember that from my expired driver's license at the courthouse.*

"Oh, that's right." She crinkled her nose in a patronizing smile, then turned her attention back to the kids. "So, you guys ready for some fun this morning? I know you didn't get to do much at the festival yesterday because your dad got there so *late*." Her lips pursed in a reproachful pout, and she batted her lashes at Jace.

Clearing his throat, he stood up and tossed his juice can toward the trash, breaking the invisible undercurrent of female territoriality. "You two are going to Neenee's for a little while this morning," he informed Autumn and Willie. "Aunt Shasta said she'd drop you off on her way through town. "We'll have to do the bounce house this afternoon. Sounds like Aunt Lana will be there a while. Autumn, you've got a baby goat to take care of at Neenee's, remember, and I need to help Dell with a little errand this morning."

Eyes widening, Lana stiffened, her bottom lip hanging slack a moment before she reeled it up. She stood blinking at Jace as he gathered the paper plates and proceeded to the trash can. I took advantage of the opportunity to slip out of my seat and head to my car for my things. Jace, I had a feeling, had just put the ruby slippers on my feet and now the wicked witch would be after me. If he was aware of that fact, it didn't show. He was whistling as he pulled the full bag out of the trash can and tied it shut.

From nearby, Nana Jo took it all in with a concerned frown, then leaned over and whispered something to Gwendolyn, who shrugged with both hands in the air. They were still whispering back and forth when I returned with my purse. Jace seemed oblivious to the undercurrents as he packed his kids into Shasta's vehicle, then waited for me by his truck. Lana was standing near Uncle Rube, trying to slay me with her eyes, and even Uncle Rube seemed unhappy about Jace and me leaving together.

"Is she legal?" I heard him whisper to Dillon as I passed by. I knew he meant *of legal age.*

"Hardly," Lana muttered.

"She's in college," Dillon defended, and Uncle Rube shrugged skeptically.

Only Shasta seemed to be supportive of Jace and me spending more time together. She waved cheerfully as I climbed into Jace's truck.

"We could take my car," I said, feeling guilty for having caused such a commotion. Jace would undoubtedly hear about it later from Lana, and probably from his mother and grandmother as well.

"Cars are for city folks." Jace playfully patted the dashboard of the truck. "Some of those roads up in the hills are four-wheel-drive only."

By the time we'd reached Cataway Creek Road and traveled a few miles off the highway, I could see what he meant. The road was little more than two tire tracks, scattered with gravel and pitted with potholes and deep channels carved by streams of water running down the mountains. Silence settled in as we drove, and I felt the matter of last night's kiss hanging between us like a sheet of lead.

"Thanks for coming with me," I said finally.

"Didn't want you to get into any trouble." His lips twisted wryly.

In spite of the smile, his parental tone made me defensive. "I can take care of myself, you know."

He nodded, as if he could read what I was thinking. "It just doesn't seem like something a person ought to do alone—possibly meeting your birth family for the first time." He followed the words with a meaningful look in my direction. "It's a pretty big deal."

I instantly felt guilty and turned my attention out the window as we wound into a valley where the path ran along one side of a wide stream with a rocky bottom. I recognized it from Nita's map. We'd reached Cataway Creek. It wouldn't be long now. In a few more miles the road would separate from the waterway again and we would come to the remnants of a stacked-stone fence. Beyond the fence, there'd be an entrance with rock pillars, a driveway leading back toward the river, and along the driveway several houses where the school bus had dropped the Clay boys after school.

I tried to picture my father, or anyone who'd been so seriously involved with my mother, happily trotting off the school bus, giving the driver baskets of homemade bread and jam at the end of the year. The men who spent time with my mother were rowdy and loud. They arrived in beat-up pickup trucks, riding old motorcycles, or driving junky cars that stunk of cigarettes and weed. They had long hair, and emaciated bodies, and greasy ball caps with beer logos. They were like the man with the long, dark hair who took her away and never brought her back.

The only decent man she ever dated was Angelo's daddy. He wanted Mama to stay clean, straighten up, take care of her kids, keep a job. When she wouldn't, he took Angelo away. I hoped my father was someone like that, and that there was a good reason he hadn't come for me.

In a few more minutes, I might find the answers.

Was I ready?

If not for Jace, solid and steady and calm in the driver's seat, I would have panicked and turned around. "I'm glad you came," I said, and then focused out the window. "I didn't tell my folks I was coming. I couldn't."

"You don't think they'd understand?"

The question put a lump in my throat. Ahead, the road was diverging from the creek. We would be there soon. "I was afraid to find out. I was afraid that if they knew, they'd be disappointed and hurt, that they'd stop loving me."

His hand slipped over mine, warm and strong, his fingers tightening. "I can't imagine anybody not loving you."

I looked at him, and his eyes were curved upward in a smile that pushed away all the fear in me. "Thanks." My throat tightened with emotion and for just an instant we were frozen that way, looking at each other. The vehicle seemed to stand still.

Then he turned back to the road, pointed ahead. "There's the stone fence."

Suddenly I couldn't breathe. Pressing a hand to my chest, I rubbed hard, trying to take in air that had turned solid.

Jace slowed down, turned the truck into the driveway next to a bank of mailboxes. The closest one was decorated with a painting of an eagle in flight. *C. Clay,* the nameplate said. I stared into the bird's eye, trying to imagine the person who'd painted it.

My heart pounded against my ribs. "I can't breathe," I whispered, rubbing my chest harder.

Jace asked as the truck passed the culvert, "Do you want to go back? Maybe look up a phone number and call?"

"I tried . . . at the library." Closing my eyes, I attempted to calm myself, to take deep breaths the way my vocal music teacher had taught me to do when I got the jitters before a performance. "There were lots of Clays, but no listing for Thomas Clay, or Audie and Nora."

"Hmmm . . . ," Jace murmured, and I heard him picking up Nita's map. "There's no telling whose name might be on the phone listing. Folks around here are kind of clannish. They tend to figure that if they want you to call, they'll tell you the number."

I nodded, a lump pulsing in my throat as we came to a small brick house with a weathered split-rail fence. The driveway was empty and the windows dark.

"Doesn't look like anybody's there," Jace observed, and my spirits flagged. It was nine thirty on a Saturday morning. Not the best time to catch people at home.

Jace motioned to the road ahead, as if he'd sensed my thoughts. "Judging from the mailboxes by the entrance, there are several houses down here. Let's go on and see what we find."

I nodded again, my stomach constricting as if someone had tied a slipknot around my waist and was pulling the rope. What if we did find someone? What would I say? How would they react? What if this was another dead end?

What if my family was here? Would they know who I was? Would they be glad I'd finally come home?

What if my father wasn't dead, as CPS had assumed? What if he was here? Would he be like the father I'd dreamed about—a sad man who'd missed me all along, who thought of me every year on my birthday?

Hope crept upward inside me, welling from the little-girl center until it enveloped my senses.

Jace slowed the car at another house, a white clapboard structure older than the first one. A car was in the carport, but the windows were dark. "Want me to stop?" he asked.

I squinted at the small wooden sign hanging on one of the porch posts. CALVIN AND NAOMI, it read.

"Let's go on," I whispered, my throat raspy. I tried to keep calm as we drifted past another house on the right, then one on the left, where two teenaged girls were sitting on the tailgate of a pickup. Jace stopped next to them, and I rolled down the window as, curious, they watched us.

"I'm looking for Thomas Clay," I said. They frowned, shrugging at each other, so I added, "Or Audie and Nora Clay?"

They exchanged perplexed glances again, as if deciding whether to talk to us or not; then the nearer girl swiveled and pointed down the driveway. "Everyone's down by the river. Just go on this road until it ends."

I thanked the girls and we continued on, the driveway slowly disintegrating into a pair of muddy ruts with a grassy hump between. I was glad we'd brought Jace's truck instead of my car, but at the same time I felt guilty for dragging him into what seemed to be nothing but pine forest so thick that even underbrush couldn't penetrate it. As we drove, the truck lurched over loose rocks and exposed roots, the tires spinning through patches of deep pea gravel and sinking almost hopelessly into mud puddles. It was hard to believe anyone could live back here.

An overhanging branch scratched along the side of the truck, and I winced. "I'm sorry. I didn't know the road would be . . . like this." The fact was, I didn't know anything about where I was headed. I was trekking off into the middle of nowhere based on sketchy information. James and Karen would have a fit. They'd say that even if these people did turn out to be my birth family, I shouldn't just show up on their doorstep. I had no way of knowing what kind of people they were—what I was getting into. My mother had been an addict. She hung around with people who used, and dealt, and manufactured drugs. The people who lived down this road could be as messed up as she was, or even worse.

What if I got Jace into some kind of trouble? What if something terrible happened? People who wanted visitors didn't have driveways like this one.

"Maybe we should go back." A gnawing apprehension nibbled in my gut.

"This is nothing." Jace assumed I was talking about the road. Leaning closer to the front window, he squinted upward as a canopy of leaves brushed the cab, then he winked and smiled in a way that said he'd drive me all the way to the state line, if necessary.

"It's hard to believe anyone lives down here," I muttered, scanning the roadside barrier of blackberry brambles and trumpet vines.

"Someone does." Tapping me on the arm, he pointed toward an old log house, nearly hidden in the trees about fifty yards off the road. "Or did. Who knows if that's in use anymore."

I studied the squatty structure with its sloping porch roof. Wavy, four-paned windows watched like curious eyes as the truck rattled past. Gazing out the back glass, I wondered if my father's ancestors had hewn those logs from the forest, perhaps during the first bitter winters after so many died along the trail westward. I tried to imagine what kind of fortitude it had taken to go on, to forge new lives in the wilderness.

"Looks like we're coming to something." Jace's voice pulled me from my thoughts, and I turned around. Ahead, the dense forest thinned, and the road passed through another gateway similar to the one on the main road. Tall native stone pillars supported a heavy, rough-hewn pine beam that was gray with age. A carving of an eagle adorned the center, and beside it the words *Ant chukoa Achukma hoke* had been chiseled into the wood.

"It's a greeting," Jace explained as we drove underneath. "It means *Come in. It is good.*"

On the fence, a rusted metal sign slapped strands of barbed wire as we rattled over the cattle guard. The paint had long since washed away, so that the letters were only visible as bleached shadows in the rust, like images in a photo negative. CLAY RANCH, REGISTERED ANGUS CATTLE. But the cattle grazing in the pasture beyond the gate were scrappy crossbreds, feeder steers like the ones the lease man sometimes kept at Grandma Rose's old farm—just there long enough to eat the grass, fatten up, and go to market.

The steers raised their heads and bellowed as we drove through the field and continued on toward the riverbank, where two brown stone houses stood in a pastoral setting, surrounded by thick green lawns and faded white board fences. Massive willows and cottonwoods grew near the water's edge, their dappled shade blanketing the yard and lapping against wraparound porches facing the river.

It was exactly the kind of place I'd imagined. In my dreams, my birth family was waiting in a peaceful, welcoming home like this one, just right for Sunday dinners and Fourth of July picnics with aunts, uncles, and cousins. After eating, the kids would skin off their Sunday clothes, slip into shorts or swimsuits, and go to the river to fish or swim. On holidays, the grass-and-gravel parking area along the fence would be filled with cars, the porches crowded with relatives talking, swapping stories, commenting on how much the children had grown, and theorizing about family resemblances.

"So this is Thomas's daughter," they would say, as we all sat together in the long evening shadows. "My word, but don't you take after your father?"

The porches need rocking chairs, I thought as we neared the houses. *There should be rocking chairs.* Now that we were closer, everything about the place seemed slightly off. The lawns were mowed, but no one had bothered to weed beneath the fences. Where the cows couldn't reach it, tall spires of grass and stray honeysuckle vines grew up, twining into the fence and making the farm seemed neglected. Around the houses, the flower beds had been allowed to go to seed and the stone planters sat bare. A crusty coating of dirt and last year's leaves had settled into the corners of the porches, testifying to the fact that no one sat there anymore.

A flash of movement beneath one of the yard trees caught my eye, and both Jace and I turned as a lanky red hound bounded from the overhanging willow branches and ran at the fence, barking while wagging its tail like a propeller.

"Looks like the welcoming committee's found us." Jace motioned toward the dog, his eyes narrowing as it wheeled around and disappeared beneath the tree again. "I think someone's sitting under there."

I craned to look out the front window as Jace piloted the truck past the yard gate and continued on toward the willow tree. The curtain of leaves shivered apart, revealing an old man in a lawn chair. Despite the barking dog, the man's gaze was fixed into the distance, and he seemed unaware of our presence. Beneath his chair, the ground was barren, as if he sat there often. The dog barked, then nuzzled his fingers, and he patted it absently as we pulled up to the fence.

The dog made another run at us, then returned to its master, who finally noticed our car. Quieting the hound with a commanding snap of his fingers, the old man slowly retrieved a straw cowboy hat from one knobby knee. His hand trembled as he smoothed his thick silver hair, dropped the hat into place, and tipped back the brim to observe us. His brows drew together over dark eyes and high cheek-bones, and his full lips held a stoic, determined line as he braced his hands on the chair arms and pushed to his feet, his body quaking with the effort. Stooped over so that his weathered face was almost invisible beneath the hat, he made his way toward us. Jace opened the driver's-side door, and I sat frozen with my hand on the door latch. A tangle of hope and fear twined around my throat, making speech seem almost impossible.

What if this man was my grandfather? What if he wasn't?

"I don't think I can . . ." My words were soft and pale.

Jace circled to the passenger side and opened my door. "Hang in there." His fingers slid over mine, solid, determined, strong enough to hold me suspended on the edge of the cliff. "You'll never know unless you ask."

Yielding to the pressure of his fingers, I stepped down, watched my feet disappear into the thick grass. The ground beneath felt spongy and uncertain, quicksand covered with a thin carpet of color.

The old man waited at the fence, his arms propped on the top rail, his face tipped upward—a hardy, weathered Choctaw face, like those of the war veterans at the powwow ceremony.

I couldn't speak. I could only look at him, search his face for something, anything familiar, any sign that after all these years of desperate want, I'd finally found someone with a blood connection to me.

Jace squeezed my fingers again. I felt it dimly as I followed him to the fence, one uncertain step and then the next.

"We're looking for Thomas Clay," I said as we stopped on our side of the fence, waiting while the old man struggled to form words, his head and shoulders quaking with the exertion.

"N-n-n-not here." His voice trembled into the space between us, the words slurred, quivering like a willow leaf in a breeze. "T-T-T-Tom-my p-passed ulll-last year."

A swirl of darkness slipped between the old man and me, and a sparkle of stars made everything seem far away. My head spun, and I thought I might faint, just sink into the grass and disappear.

Tommy passed last year. My father was dead. He'd been alive until a year ago. How had he died?

"I'm sorry." My reply was a reflex, an automatic condolence addressed to no one in particular.

The old man's eyes, dark circles clouded white around the edges, met mine. "H-h-he had-had a t-t-t-tough go."

"I'm sorry," I whispered again, sounding emotionless. I should have felt something, but I didn't. I was hanging in thin air with nothing touching me, the way I'd learned to when Mama took off with her boyfriends and left me standing at Granny's gate. If you practice it enough, you can learn to watch things happen and not feel at all. It had been a long time since I'd done that, since I'd felt the need to. Pulling my fingers from Jace's, I crossed my arms over myself, tight like a barricade.

Jace glanced over, surprised by the sudden swing from emotional to emotionless, from dependent to distant. He hadn't known I had that in me.

"Are you Audie?" I asked.

The man nodded, tipping his hat, his fingers bent, pale, trembling. "A-Audie Sen-ior. Audie Jun-jun-junior's out of t-t-town." His thick silver brows rose. "D-do I know-know you?" He wheeled a hand beside his head helplessly. "M-my mind th-these days . . ." The statement seemed to go unfinished, and he sighed wearily. "You ulll-look famil-ur to-to-to me."

"My father was Thomas Clay." A spark of emotion flared inside me, pressing moisture into my eyes. I wiped it impatiently. Now was no time to break down. I had to keep it together, to handle this the right way. "I never knew him, but it's on my birth certificate."

It was too much information all at once. Audie Senior blinked and focused on the fence, his hat brim hiding his face as he slowly shook his head, then squinted up at me again, clearly struggling to comprehend. I looked into his eyes, pleading, searching, wanting him to know me. I was hanging off the cliff again, and this frail old man was the only one who could catch me. If he turned me away, what would I do?

"You're T-Tommy's daugh-ter?"

A screen door slammed at the house and all of us jerked upright.

"Daddy, who's out there?" A woman, perhaps in her forties, her dark hair cut in a stylish bob, shaded her eyes as she descended the porch steps. She was wearing brightly printed hospital scrubs, but no shoes. She traversed the grass as if she went barefoot often, inclining her head to one side as she came closer. "May I help y'all?" Her voice was pleasant, with a musical lilt that sounded almost like laughter. Stopping next to the old man, she rubbed his shoulder tenderly. "You all right, Daddy? You look a little washed out. It's too hot for you to be sitting out today."

"N-nah, I'm f-f-fine. I'm fine." Audie Senior brushed off her concern, then motioned to me with a crumpled fist. "T-T-Tommy's ulll-little girl come by."

The woman's gaze cut quickly toward me, then back to Audie Senior, her brows drawing together so that a network of wrinkles formed. Slipping her arm over the old man's shoulders, she turned toward the house. "Mama's got lunch ready. Why don't you head on in? I'll be there in a minute."

"All urrr-right," he replied, allowing her to guide him away from the fence. For a moment, he seemed to forget we were there, then, pausing a few steps away, he glanced back over his shoulder. "N-nice to s-s-see . . . see you. Sorry my ummm-mind ain't so good."

Jace raised a hand in farewell. "Have a good lunch."

The old man's face lifted in a one-sided grin. "He d-d-does talk. I wond-wondered." Waving stiffly, he shuffled off across the lawn.

His daughter waited until he was out of earshot before she spoke. "I'm sorry. About six months ago, he came down with a bout of what has finally been diagnosed as Lyme disease. Now that the doctors know what they're treating, he's getting better, but it's really taken a toll. He gets confused about things." She paused to check his progress toward the house, then turned back to Jace and me. "Did you say you were a friend of Tommy's?"

I shook my head. "Thomas Clay was my father. His name is on my birth certificate." Her reaction wasn't what I'd expected. In fact, she barely reacted at all, just continued squinting at me, and chewing her lip. Words became a jumble in my head, a train rushing too fast. "I never knew him. I . . . I wanted to meet him . . . his family . . . mine, I mean. My family. My birth family."

Her brows drew together in an expression of painful regret. "Tommy died last year." Behind the words, there was confusion, an audible note of doubt. My stomach sank, acid gurgling up my throat. This wasn't how things were supposed to be. This wasn't how I was supposed to be received by my . . . my aunt? My grandmother? Who was she?

We hung suspended in silence, the woman pinching her bottom lip between her thumb and forefinger. The moment stretched endlessly, until it seemed that if I had to endure it any longer, I would explode. Every beat of my heart rattled my body.

Dimly, I heard Jace break the stalemate by saying, "This may be a bit much to absorb, out of the blue."

The woman shook her head. "It's not that . . ." Backing away from the fence, she smoothed the front of her scrubs uncomfortably. "It's just . . . well . . . I think you've got the wrong Thomas Clay. My nephew Tommy had a hunting accident when he was fifteen.

The bullet grazed his spine and caused a massive amount of internal bleeding. He suffered brain damage and permanent paralysis. It's . . . it's not possible that he could be anyone's father." The crashing of my hopes must have been obvious, because she reached across the fence, into the air between us, her eyes soft and sympathetic. "There are more Clays in this county than you can shake a stick at, though."

"But at the courthouse, they said my father's parents, the parents of my Thomas Clay, were Audie and Nora Clay." I sounded desperate, and I was. I'd let my expectations soar when I'd seen this place, met Audie Senior. Staring at the ground, I struggled to get my bearings, to regain composure as the grass blurred behind a thickening veil of tears.

The woman came closer, leaned across the fence, and ran a hand up and down my arm. "I'm sure it's just a mix-up in information at the courthouse. I'm sure you'll find the people you're looking for. I'm sorry I couldn't help you more. There's no one else in our family by the name Thomas."

I nodded because I couldn't speak, then covered my face with my hands and ran to the truck. All I knew was that I had to get away. I was careening toward a low point I'd never even been close to before, and I didn't want to be standing here, in front of strangers, when I hit bottom.

CHAPTER 21

❧

I didn't remember leaving the Clay Ranch, crossing under the gateway, or rattling down the barely visible lane to the county road. I was only vaguely aware of Jace driving, tires crunching on gravel, the sound growing louder as the truck sped away from my hastily spilled dreams. Now, like parts of a tightly packaged puzzle, the pieces wouldn't fit back in the box. I had no idea how to pull myself together.

My hands shook, fingernails digging in around my hairline as I sobbed on and on. Why, with everything I knew about Mama, about the kind of people she hung around with, couldn't I just let this go? Why couldn't my heart embrace the present and release the past? Why couldn't I banish that frightened, silent girl, who curled herself into a ball under Granny's porch steps, hiding out, waiting for someone to come for her, while the TV blared, and Granny argued with Uncle Bobby?

His voice boomed inside my head. "Why not? You don' wan' her." The words were a slur of sound, half finished, as his footfalls staggered toward the window. Three steps, four, five. "All she's . . . she's just someone to go pick up yer pills, and your grub, and refill yer oxygen tank. Sheriff said . . . he said if he seen her again on the highway with her bike, he's callin' in CPS."

Granny's voice was raspy and weak, so that I couldn't quite make out her answer.

". . . take 'er to Oklahoma with me." Uncle Bobby's reply came quickly, sounding matter-of-fact, as if the decision were already made. "Got me a job waitin' there, place to live. Better'n this dump. She can have her own room, real bed, not some stinkin' mattress on the floor, and . . ."

Granny answered before he was finished talking. A convulsion of coughs came on the heels of the words, then ragged breathing. Pretty soon she'd puff on her oxygen tank, take a couple Darvocet, and pass out.

I knew I needed to head for the river before Uncle Bobby came looking for me. He would never check down there. He was afraid to go to the river after dark, with the coyotes yipping and the hoot owls screeching in the trees.

"Like heck!" his voice roared. He stumbled backward and collided with the front door so hard I ducked, thinking he might fall through and land on top of me. "I ain't never touched 'er. I ain't interested in no jailbait, whinin' little baby brat." He sounded dangerously sober now, as if the anger had cleared his fog. "Heck, wasn't for that sourpuss way 'a hers and that nigger-lookin' skin, she'd probably already be makin' the rounds 'a town, just like her mama did. You oughta be lucky I'd take her. Ain't nobody ever gonna want some half-breed little butthead like her. . . ." The door latch flipped upward, and I skittered out from under the porch, bolted around the corner, and crouched in the shadow of the house, my hands trembling as I unhooked Rowdy from his chain. Twenty feet to the cedar break, and we'd both be safe. I'd curl up out in the woods with Rowdy and stay until Uncle Bobby either passed out or got in his truck and went to town.

Rowdy whimpered, and I pressed a hand to his muzzle. "Ssshhh."

Uncle Bobby staggered out the door, and I scooted to the back corner of the house. When the dog didn't come barking on the chain, Uncle Bobby would know where I was.

His boots moved across the porch, and I bolted through the moonlight toward the trees. I didn't know if he saw me or not.

"You hear that, you little butthead?" His voice echoed through the dark. "Yer lucky if anybody wants ya at all. Better think about that, whenever I come back. Ain't nobody ever gonna want some ugly, stupid, little brown girl like you. Your own mama didn't even like you enough to stick around. . . ."

Your mama didn't even like you enough to stick around. . . . The words echoed in my head, and I realized I was sitting in Jace's truck, rocking back and forth with my hands over my ears, trying to rid myself of that voice. Why couldn't I make it go away? After all these years, those memories still flared up like wildfires in tinder-dry grass.

Jace's hand touched my shoulder, pushed my hair out of the way. "We're back at the campground."

"I'm sorry." Air felt raw against my throat as I pulled the door latch, then mopped my eyes. "I'm sorry I fell apart."

"It's all right," he said softly. Climbing from the truck, he came around and opened my door, sliding his hand under my elbow as if he didn't trust me to stand on my own.

I rubbed my eyes until my vision cleared. "I'm sorry. I didn't think I would . . . I don't know . . . come unhinged like that." Emotions, for me, were usually a tight little ball, painstakingly compacted, and stuffed down where it wouldn't disturb anyone.

Jace touched the side of my face, tenderly, sympathetically, and I leaned into his strength. "You've just been through a big disappointment."

Staring out at the lake, I struggled to get my bearings. "I thought I was prepared."

"You had your hopes up pretty high."

"I knew it was a long shot."

His thumb caressed my cheek, whisked away the last of the tears. "It's all right."

"That woman must think I'm crazy." I could only imagine what I'd looked like, dashing blindly to the truck with my hands over my face.

"It's all right," he whispered again, his voice so tender it drew me upward, until I was looking at him, my gaze captured by his.

"*You* must think I'm crazy."

His lips parted, then he shook his head slightly. Whatever he'd been about to say was burned away by some deeper emotion. "I think you're too beautiful a girl, inside and out, to carry all those scars." His lips found mine, and I pressed myself into the embrace. The kiss was soft, salty, powerful enough to take away everything else. I abandoned myself to it. His arms slid around me, a warm, strong circle, pulling my body to his, pressing me near to him so that I felt his heartbeat against mine. I let my hands move up his arms, encompass his shoulders. Beneath my fingers, his skin was slightly damp, the muscles tightly corded. The fringes of his hair lifted in the breeze, brushed my fingers as I drew him closer until there was no distance between us, yet something inside me yearned to be closer still. *This is right. This is the only thing that's right.* I wanted him in a way I'd never wanted anyone. I felt as if I could let him see things I'd never let anyone see. My body was heady and light, my thoughts in a euphoric swirl. I wanted him to hold me and never let go.

He pulled away, his lips parting from mine, taking away the electric sensation, allowing reality an entrance. His gaze was still passionate, compelling. He blinked, looked at me again, put his hands on my shoulders and stepped back, breaking the bond between us. "Dell, I . . ." Pausing, he arrested whatever he was about to say, took another step back, and finished with, "I'd better go. I have to help take down the art show at the museum, and I promised the kids we'd go to the carnival with Shasta and Benji." He checked his watch, as if suddenly he had a million places to be rather than here alone with me. "They'd love to have you come along." There was that hint of warmth again, that flicker of desire that told me he wanted me to go with them.

My emotions ricocheted, and I smiled without even wanting to.

"That sounds good." In spite of the morning's emotional crash, I was suddenly looking forward to the afternoon. "I think I need to just sit here a few minutes, think about things. Then I'll be over."

He ran a thumb along the outline of his bottom lip. "Sure you're all right to drive?" His eyes caught mine for a flickering instant, and I was pulled in again before he took his keys from his pocket and turned his attention to them.

"I'm okay," I told him. "I'll be along in a little while."

"You're not planning to ditch me and drive off searching for more Clays on your own—nothing like that, right?"

I shook my head.

He pulled a business card from his shirt pocket and wrote something on it, then handed the card to me and tucked the pen back in his pocket. "Here's my cell number again. Call me when you get over to the festival, and we'll meet up. I'll buy you an Indian taco."

I nodded, vaguely reminded that I had less than twenty dollars in my pocket, and ready cash would soon become an issue again. I couldn't ask Shasta's friend at the variety store to cash another check. And it was already Saturday. James and Karen would be expecting me back in Kansas City tomorrow, but the Choctaw tribal offices and the courthouse here wouldn't be open again until Tuesday. If I could catch Jamie away from Lana, maybe I could get her to check the online records again, see if she might have confused my father with this other Thomas Clay, the young man who'd suffered a hunting accident as a teenager and couldn't possibly have fathered a child.

I rubbed my forehead, my mind starting to race again. Jace slipped his fingers into my hair, tipped my chin up so that he could catch my gaze. The noise in my head stopped. He had beautiful eyes. Dark, and liquid, and warm like a blanket. I wanted him to kiss me again and make everything else disappear.

"Promise me, no setting off on reconnaissance missions alone."

"I can take care of myself."

His mouth straightened into a stern line. Part of me wanted to argue with him, the way I would have if my parents tried to tell me what to do. *I'm twenty years old. I've been around the world. I've been taking care of myself as long as I can remember. I can handle it.*

"I don't have any more leads to follow," I admitted finally. "The courthouse and the Choctaw offices in Durant are closed for the weekend. Where would I go?"

He nodded, seeming satisfied that I wasn't planning to do something rash. "Hang in there, kid." He gave my shoulder one last squeeze, then climbed into his truck, waved out the back window, and disappeared.

I wished he wouldn't call me *kid.*

After he was gone, I sat on the picnic table, decompressing, thinking about everything that had happened since my arrival on Thursday. My birth family could be anywhere—the next town, the next county, the next state, the next campsite, and I wouldn't know it. I might find them tomorrow, or I might search for years and never find them. My father could be dead, or he could be living somewhere, maybe with a family, kids of his own and a normal life. He might be happy to see me, and he might not.

I might never learn the truth.

Sitting in the quiet campground with only the dull flapping of canvas and the faraway sounds of human activity somewhere near the water, I tried to contemplate the possibilities, then finally I surrendered to the final one. I might never discover the truth about my father and the circumstances of my birth. One way or another, I had to learn to live with that. *Life goes on after the corn fails,* Grandma Rose used to say. *You can sit by the field and cry about it, or you can harness the mule and plant something else.*

Giving Camp Reid one last look, I harnessed the mule and headed for town.

Halfway there, my cell phone, plugged into the cigarette lighter on the dash, picked up a tower somewhere across the mountains, and started to beep. I checked the screen. VOICEMAILS: 11.

Adrenaline rocketed through my body as I disconnected the cord, punched the button, and read the list. The messages had started around midnight last night, while I was asleep at the campground, the phone out of range of a cell tower. The log told a frightening story. Karen Cell 12:25 a.m., Karen Cell 12:57, Karen Cell 1:43, Karen Cell 3:15, Aunt Kate Home 5:35, Aunt Kate Cell 7:00, Barry 7:26. . . .

My family had been desperately trying to contact me since the middle of the night. Something was wrong.

I thought of James, still out flying somewhere, and a cold dread soured in my throat and oozed to my stomach. He wasn't in my cell log. What if something had happened to him? An accident? A crash? I hadn't seen a television in two days. There could have been an airline accident, and I wouldn't even know.

Oh, God, I whispered, the phone shaking in my hand, my fingers suddenly too stiff, too clumsy to operate the controls. *Oh, God, please, God, no.* . . . Pushing the redial for Karen's number, I pressed the phone to my ear, but the call wouldn't go through. There was only static as the highway wound into a valley.

Holding the phone so that I could see the tower indicator, I pressed the gas, sending the car careening over hills and zipping around corners. As I crested the last hill and drove into town, the tower indicator shot upward, and I started trying to dial Karen's cell number, but my fingers wouldn't cooperate. I ended up dialing into my voice mail instead.

"Press seven to hear the first message," the electronic operator said, her pleasant greeting out of keeping with my frantic state of mind.

My thumb trembled on the seven, then I listened as Karen's recording came on.

"Hi, honey. I'm trying to get in touch with you, but I guess you have your phone off." There was a pause, a shudder of breath that said, *Where are you? I need you to pick up the phone. Now.* She finished with, "It's a little after midnight. Give me a call when you get this message. I'll be"—her voice choked out momentarily, then came back—"on my cell." The words were coated with an eerie layer of forced control, like a blast blanket over a bomb about to detonate. I'd never heard my mom sound like that. Just before she hung up, a car horn blared in the background; then a siren echoed through the phone.

The call-waiting beeped as I was closing the voice mail, and I answered, my body flushed, and my head pounding.

Karen was on the other end. "Oh, honey, thank God," she breathed, her voice thin and hoarse. "Where are you? Everyone's been trying to reach you since last night. I tried to look up Barry's number, but it wasn't listed. I tried his mother, and she was out of town. Then this morning, Barry called and left a message for you at the house, and it was obvious you weren't with him. I was scared to death. I finally called Mrs—"

"Mom, what's going on?" I cut her off before she could ask again where I was.

She took a long, slow breath. I knew that sound. She always did that when she was about to deliver bad news, when she was trying to decide how much to tell me.

"Mom, what's happening?" The pounding in my head was growing louder. In my hand, the phone felt like a hot coal. "What's wrong?" Tears quivered in my voice, and the overload of emotions from the morning came rushing back.

As usual, Karen sought first to protect me. "Calm down, honey. If you're driving, I want you to go ahead and pull over."

"Mom, tell me," I pleaded, turning into a Handi Stop and putting the car in park. "I'm pulled over."

Another deep breath. She blew out like a woman trying to calm the pain during labor. "James is in the hospital. Everything's all right now, but he'll be here for a few days."

"What happened?" A hundred possibilities rushed through my mind.

"Calm down, sweetheart. It's all right."

"You didn't sound all right on the voice mail." My emotions overflowed, and the words ended in a sob. This day, this trip, was suddenly too much. "Why is Dad in the hospital?"

She paused, carefully gathering her thoughts the way she always did. The wait was agonizing. "There was a fire at the house last night. James came home from the airport and found it. He didn't know I wasn't home, and he was afraid you were there, and he wasn't sure if the cats were inside or outside, so he took in some smoke, looking for everybody. By the time the fire department got there, he was experiencing chest pains."

The picture of James in the hospital squeezed around my throat like a fist. *It's my fault. It's my fault. If I'd been there, I could have made him get out. If I'd been honest about where I was and how long I'd be gone, he would have known not to look for me in the house.* "Is he okay?" I was sobbing now. I'd caused this. I'd caused it by leaving, by sneaking away, by acting as if a birth family I'd never met mattered more than the one that had taken me in, loved me and raised me. *I'm sorry, I'm sorry, I'm sorry.*

"He will be." The words were gentle, meant to wrap around and protect me. As always, Karen was trying to make things easier. I didn't deserve it. "They found a blockage in his heart that didn't show up on his last flight physical. They've checked to make sure his lungs are clear, and they've scheduled an angioplasty for the morning. A few days of rest and he'll be fine."

"They're doing heart surgery on Dad tomorrow?" I felt sick, weak. Memories flashed through my mind—James taking me fishing, teaching me to play the guitar, letting me tag along when he was scheduled for a long layover. Now he needed me, and I was miles away, searching for some stranger who hadn't even cared enough to stick around.

Please, God, please don't take my dad away. I love my dad. I need him. I don't care if I ever find my real father. I want the father I have.

"Honey, it's all right," Karen soothed. I realized I was sobbing into the phone, babbling, "I'm sorry, I'm sorry," over and over.

"Sweetheart, calm down," Karen said softly. "It's just orthoscopic surgery, like Grandpa Sommerfield had, remember? This kind of problem runs in the family. James will just have to keep on top of it from now on. Being young and healthy doesn't absolve you from plaque in the arteries, apparently." She waited as I tried to get myself under control.

"Can I talk to him?"

"He's sedated right now."

I started crying again.

Karen went on, probably afraid that if she ended the conversation I'd drive off in hysterics and have a wreck. "The fire department got the fire out, but there's quite a bit of smoke and water damage. Looks like an electrical problem in the downstairs bathroom vent fan started it. The bad news is, between the smoke and the water, most of the things in your room are damaged. The good news is Dad's fine, the cats are fine, and we'll be getting new carpet, and remodeling your bathroom, bedroom, and the kitchen." I knew she was trying to lighten up, to move into our family's usual disaster-recovery pattern. Whenever things got dire, whenever there was a crisis or an argument, someone eventually made a joke to soften the blow.

But I didn't feel like laughing. I felt nervous, and sick, and guilty, as if the phone were a high-voltage socket and my emotions were zipping around on the current. "I don't care about the stuff in my room. I just care about Dad. I'm coming home." I checked the clock on the dash. Almost noon. By supper time, I could be back in Kansas City. "Mom, I'm really sorry."

"None of this was your fault, Dell." She seemed confused by the apology. "It was an electrical fire and too much high-fat food. Your dad's going to have to give up Barbeque Barn and Cheesy Charlie's meatball sandwiches, that's all. Cheesy Charlie may have a tough time making it without our standard monthly contribution, but think of all the money we'll save."

She expected me to laugh, but I couldn't. A new wave of tears pressed my eyes, and I sniffled into the phone. "I shouldn't have left."

"Honey, you did *not* cause this. It was *not* your fault." Concern deepened in her voice. "The fire started in your bathroom ceiling and traveled to the wall between your bathroom and bedroom. It's a good thing you weren't home. You could have been sleeping in there."

If I'd been home, I might have seen the fire sooner, stopped James from taking such a risk. "I just wish I'd been there to help. I'm sorry you were worried about me, on top of everything else."

There was a gap in the conversation, and I could tell the joking was over. "Dell." All hints of laughter were gone. This was the serious tone, the firm-but-caring Mom tone. "I finally got in touch with Mrs. Bradford a little while ago, since she was the last one who'd seen you before you left town. She said she'd given you some information about the Choctaw Nation offices, and she thought maybe you were in Oklahoma looking for your birth records."

Everything inside me slowly sank. She knew the truth. "I didn't find anything," I said, as if that somehow mitigated what I'd done.

"But, honey"—she was in pain; I could hear it in her voice, and I knew I'd caused it—"why would you do that without saying anything?"

Why, indeed? Because I was a coward. Because I couldn't tell anyone that part of me was still waiting for Mama to come home and tell me she loved me, after all. "I didn't want to hurt anyone. I knew you and James didn't want me looking."

"Dell, we would have understood," she said. "When you were younger, your dad and I were always concerned about your father resurfacing, or his relatives finding out about you and trying to gain custody. You hear some awful stories about children being taken away from adoptive families after they've been together for years, and we couldn't take that risk. We felt it was best to leave the situation alone, but we always knew that there might come a day when you'd want to look for your biological relatives."

"I don't want you two to think I don't . . ." A ragged breath trembled from my throat, ended in a sob. "That you're not my mom and dad."

Karen sniffled on the other end of the phone. "Honey, James and I just want you to be happy. We know there are things in your past you're still dealing with. It doesn't change the fact that we love you."

"I don't deserve it." That was the heart of the matter, the essence of everything, even after all these years. In the back of my mind, there was still the question, *If my own mama didn't want me, how could anyone else? Ever.*

"Of course you do, Dell." Karen's voice held the soft reassurance of a mother's love. "You've had so much trauma in your past, and you've never let it stop you. You know, Grandma Rose used to say it's not how you fall down that matters, it's how you get back up. Every time I remember her saying that, I think of you. You deserve every good thing that comes your way. You're the strongest person I know."

I laughed and cried at the same time. How could she possibly mean that? "*You're* the strongest person I know."

"Dell, everyone has doubts on the inside," she whispered, and I could picture her face as she said the words. I wished I could hug her through the phone. "Finding yourself is just part of growing up."

"It's hard."

"I know," she replied softly. "Your dad and I don't mean to push you about Juilliard and all the rest of it. We want you to find your own way, and whatever you decide will be okay with us, I promise. Our love for you isn't conditional on anything, all right?"

"All right."

"Coming home?"

"I'm coming home." Checking the clock, I switched the car into gear. "I should make it by supper time, or a little later."

"Do me a favor," Karen said before she hung up. "Take a little while to dry your eyes and settle down before you get on the highway. Get a little lunch or something. Don't hurry. We'll be waiting for you when you get here."

"Okay." I pulled down the rearview mirror, then took a discarded napkin and started wiping my eyes. "I love you, Mom."

"I love you, too."

CHAPTER 22

❧

Pulling onto the road again, I thought about Jace and Shasta. Shasta had retrieved her quilt and pillows from the back of my car sometime after I'd left the campground, but I couldn't leave without telling her and Jace good-bye and that I'd be back again after the crisis was over back home.

Drifting by one of Shasta's murals, a warrior on horseback gazing at an eagle fly overhead, I felt a sense of loss. The warrior was so real, he seemed to watch me pass. His face, the strong chin, the full lips and pensive frown reminded me of Jace. I wondered if Shasta had used her brother as the model, or if I was only seeing what I wanted to see. In my mind, I was already writing a script in which Jace looked at me the way the warrior was looking at the eagle, as if it held him with a gravitational pull he couldn't understand, as if he wanted to bring it closer, even though the idea was impractical.

This doesn't make sense, part of me was saying. *You barely know him. He has kids, a family, a life.*

He's too old for you, Nana Jo added.

Despite the voices of reason, I remembered the way he looked at me just before he kissed me, the way I felt when his arms slipped around me, strong and firm, drawing me in until his lips met mine and a hush fell over everything. In that moment, time stood still and there was nothing else in the world. My heart beat with his, as if we were one person, not two.

It was like nothing I'd ever experienced, like something from a movie or a fairy tale. When Jace took me in his arms, I could pour myself into him, and it was wonderful. The only other thing that swept me away like that was my music. Now music and Jace were intertwined, two passages to the innermost part of my soul.

What if he was the only person I'd ever feel that with?

But how could I possibly explain this—him, this place—to my parents? This was as far from home, from what James and Karen wanted for me, as the other side of the moon. They would never understand and neither would Jace's family. Nana Jo, Gwendolyn, the aunts, even Uncle Rube had all made their opinions clear.

Is she legal? Uncle Rube's question repeated in my head as I came to a stop behind a line of traffic waiting to enter the festival parking. A teenaged girl with an orange flag smiled and waved as she directed customers into the parking area, where a stocky man in a Choctaw Labor Day Festival T-shirt efficiently guided cars into parking spaces.

Somewhere in the distance, the powwow drum hushed as my car came to a halt, and I sat with my hand on the keys, the final beats ringing in my ears. I looked at my cell phone on the passenger seat next to the card with Jace's number on it.

Maybe I should just get on the road, call him after it's too late to turn back, and let the decision be made by default. By then, I would be focused on home, on James in the hospital and Karen trying to salvage things from our house. Life would be filled with the usual static, like white noise preventing me from hearing anything else.

Is this where I'm supposed to be? There was a peace here, a connection to this place, to Jace and Shasta, Autumn and Willie, to an unexplored part of my heritage. There was a sense of membership here that went beyond the questions about my father and the circumstances of my birth. If I never found the answers to those questions, I would still belong to this place, to the tribe.

I turned off the ignition and waited while the family next to me unloaded baby strollers and wagons from their van, then I gathered my courage, stepped out of my car, and hurried across the parking lot. For once in my life, I was going to find the backbone to tell someone how I felt.

I was halfway to the festival grounds before I realized I'd left my cell phone and Jace's number in the car, so I headed toward the Reid booth, hoping either Shasta or Jace would be there.

Shasta was just handing the cash box over to her mother and buckling Benjamin into a stroller when I turned the corner. "Hey!" she said, smiling. "We're going to watch Cody play softball for a while before we go to the carnival. Want to go with us?" Glancing over her shoulder at Gwendolyn, she waved in a quick, curt way that told me they'd probably been fighting again. "We'll be back later, Mama."

Occupied with arranging some silver jewelry, Gwendolyn nodded without looking up.

Shasta snorted as she gave the stroller a push, and we started toward the ball fields. "Mama's mad because Cody's playing softball, and I asked her if Benji could stay with her while I watch. She thinks Cody ought to be keeping Benji this morning, and I should sit at that stupid booth all day, helping her. Then, when I pack up Benji to take him along, she's all over my case, thinking I'm going to let him wander off at the ball field, and someone's going to steal him or something. I swear, she's never happy. The only thing that would make her happy is if I didn't have kids at all."

Looking down at Benjamin in the stroller, she pressed her lips together and swallowed hard, her face filling with painful emotion. "I just don't . . ." Her voice cracked, and she squeezed her eyes shut momentarily, then shook her head and turned back to her son, who was swinging his legs in the stroller while playing with the toy from a McDonald's Happy Meal. "I don't understand how she can look at him and think he shouldn't be here. He's so amazing. Every time he comes running to me with one of his books, or when I watch him in his bed at night, I can't imagine my life without him, you know? I don't want some baby I might have ten years from now, or even five years from now after I graduate from college or something. I want my Benji. I want my baby boy, just the way he is. If I'd waited, I wouldn't have *him*. Mama just thinks it's the end of the world that I didn't go to college." She glanced sideways, waiting for me to say something, and I stood trapped in a tug-of-war of emotions. On one end of the rope there was Juilliard, my parents, and all the markers of success they wanted for me. On the other end there was Benjamin, with his sparkling eyes and his wide baby-toothed smile, holding up his toy and gazing at his mother with unqualified adoration and love.

"Just because you have a family doesn't mean you can't go to college," I said finally. I knew I was talking to myself as much as to Shasta. *Juilliard will take years,* I thought as Shasta leaned over Benjamin and babbled something while he giggled and reached for her. *Do I really want to wait that long? Do I have to? Who makes the rules, or do we only invent them ourselves?*

"I know." Shasta sighed wistfully, rubbing her swollen stomach. "One of these days." Pausing to pilot the stroller across a drainage grate, she changed the subject. "I didn't even ask about you, how did things go this morning? Last night after we came in, Jace told me about the map to the Clay place. Did you find anything?" Her face opened in hopes of an *Oprah*-worthy story of my reunion with my father's family.

"Dead end," I admitted. "There had been a Thomas Clay living there, and his parents had the right names, but he had a hunting accident when he was young, so there's no way he could be my father. The information from the courthouse computer must be wrong."

She grimaced with genuine sympathy. "I saw Jace helping take down the art show a while ago, and I thought it was awfully soon for y'all to be back—unless you hadn't found anything, I mean. He was busy, so I didn't get to ask him about it." She slipped an arm around my shoulders. "I'm sorry. But at least you're narrowing down the possibilities, and I can ask Jamie to look some more on the computer.

Eventually, you're bound to find the right people. In the meantime, you've got us, and we'll just keep trying, right?" Tightening her grip, she pulled me close, so that we staggered along behind the stroller like partners in a three-legged race.

"Thanks." Leave it to Shasta to find the bright side. Her optimism was as beautiful as she was.

Her lips spread into a wide, white smile. "Boy, you should have seen Lana after you two left. She was hotter than a biscuit on the griddle, I'll tell you. She's been hollering at kids in the bounce house all morning long, and as soon as Jace got here, she grabbed Autumn and Willie. I'm sure they're sick of her *and* the bounce house by now. You better get up there and rescue them. It's the big red-and-blue blow-up castle-looking thingy on the lawn, right by the capitol building."

A heavy sense of disappointment settled over me because I wouldn't be able to spirit Autumn and Willie away from Lana. In fact, after I was gone, Autumn, Willie, and Jace would be all hers. She could step in, play pseudo-mom to the kids, keep working on Jace. The idea was sickening. Was there really a chance that he would fall for someone like Lana?

"I can't," I admitted, even though the reality stung. "I have to go back home to Kansas City, at least for a little while. My mom—my adopted mom—called, and my dad's in the hospital. They're doing an angioplasty tomorrow, and I need to be there. I didn't want to leave without saying good-bye to you and . . ." A flush burned hot into my cheeks. "And to Jace. You've both done so much for me since I've been here. Not everybody would do that for someone they barely know."

Shasta glanced sideways, and I wondered if she could tell that my need to see Jace went so much deeper than just saying thank you. "I feel like I've known you forever."

"Me, too."

She stopped walking as the stroller wheels became mired in a patch of gravel. I picked up the front while she lifted the handle, and we carried Benjamin to the paved sidewalk.

Pausing to catch her breath, Shasta dumped gravel out of her flip-flops while leaning on the stroller handle. "Jace is probably somewhere around the capitol building, helping move the art around. They're putting all the winners downstairs in the main hall this year, sort of like a court of honor, then the other people can go ahead and take their paintings back and put them up for sale, if they have vendor booths here on-site." She slipped her footwear back on and tugged her maternity T-shirt over her stomach, then regarded me with a meaningful look. "Jace wouldn't want you to leave without saying good-bye." I blushed again, and she pressed her lips into a trembling, downward line. "I don't want you to leave at all, but I hope your dad's surgery goes all right."

"It will. He's in good shape, except for too much fatty food in his arteries. Thanks for everything you did for me," I said. She held out her arms, and we hugged across the stroller. "I'm going to miss it here."

Scoffing, she pulled away. "You're coming back."

"I want to."

"You'd better. Cody and I are in the book under C. W. Williams. Call me when you're coming, and I'll get the travel trailer ready for you to stay in . . . unless I'm at the hospital having a baby. But if I am, you can come anyway."

I laughed, and we hugged again, then said good-bye. I watched her walk away, pushing the stroller, her long hair swinging back and forth across her hips. When she'd rounded the corner, I started toward the capitol building, threading through the crowds of shoppers perusing arts and crafts and buying fair food. Vendors greeted me as I passed.

"Good morning, sister," an old Choctaw woman said as I rounded the aisle. She was perched on a bar stool, weaving a bracelet from brightly colored string. Her hands moved deftly as she spoke.

"Do you know if they're still taking down the art show?" I asked, standing on my toes to see across the park to the capitol building.

"I think so." She squinted up and down the aisle. "I saw a man pass by with a painting a few minutes ago." Her fingers moved skillfully over the thread, creating a woven geometric pattern.

"Thanks," I said, and hurried on toward the council house, where I found Willie and Autumn playing tag in the bushes by the front entrance. Bolting from his hiding place with his sister hot on his heels, Willie launched himself at me, capturing me in a leg lock. "Safe, safe, safe!" he hollered as I staggered toward a flower bed, then caught myself against an oak tree. "Safe!"

Autumn tagged him anyway. "Are not. Base is the front door, dummy."

"Is not!" Sticking out his tongue, Willie tightened his grip.

"Now, is that nice?" I frowned at him and then at Autumn. "What would your dad say if he saw you two calling names and making ugly faces at each other?"

Autumn twisted her lips to one side and crossed her arms over her chest, and Willie shrugged both shoulders, then slid down my legs and ended up sitting on my feet. "We wanna go on the rides." His face brightened hopefully, as in, *Maybe you could take us there.* "Dad has to do the awt show."

"Arrr-rt show." Stressing the *r*, Autumn checked her new Russian watch. "They have to take the paintings down and get them ready for the people to take back to their booths, but they were supposed to be done three and a half minutes ago."

"There he is!" Willie pointed toward the building, unwinding himself from my legs and popping to his feet as Jace came out the door. "Hey, Dad!"

Jace held up a hand, smiling at me as he crossed the distance between us. He seemed surprised to find me there with his kids.

"Where's Lana?" he asked Autumn. "You two were supposed to be with her at the bounce house."

Autumn rolled her eyes, jutting her hips to one side in a maneuver that reminded me of Shasta. "Somebody stuffed a T-shirt in the air thing, and it made a pop, and the bounce house fell down. Lana's mad. She told us to get out of the way so the guy could fix it."

Taking a step back, Jace looked toward the deflated castle, where Lana was bent over the compressor with a workman, her tie-dye camisole top affording a nice view, even from here. Laughing and talking as the plastic castle slowly reinflated, Lana seemed completely unaware that Jace's kids had wandered away. "Oh . . . ," he muttered, "Okay. Well, it looks like Dell's here just in time to go grab a snack and head for the carnival with us."

"Cool!" Autumn cheered, but I barely heard her. Jace's smile was making my body tingle. I wanted to spend the afternoon with him and the kids.

"I . . ." I was conscious of everyone watching me expectantly. "I can't. I'm sorry. I have to go home."

Jace's grin faded. "Is something wrong?" Sizing up the answer from my expression, he turned to the kids. "Tell you what, guys. Why don't you try the obstacle course over there for a minute? Stay where I can see you and let us talk all right? Then we'll head to the carnival."

"Okay." Sighing glumly, Autumn gave me a quick hug. "See you later."

"Bye, sweetheart," I answered, clinging lightly to one of her braids as she pulled back. I wanted to help take away the lost look in her eyes, to fill the void she felt, being at the festival without her mother for the first time. Unwillingly, I pictured Lana slipping into that role.

After studying me for a moment, Autumn took Willie's hand

and dragged him toward the obstacle course. "Come on, Willie. The adults need to talk."

Jace waited until they were out of earshot, then leaned against the tree. "Is everything all right?" He seemed blindsided and confused, worried.

"Yes." Down the hill, Autumn stopped at the edge of the course, released Willie onto the monkey bars, then sat down on a bench, looking back toward us. "No . . . I have to head back to Kansas. My dad—my adopted dad—is in the hospital, and he's having an angioplasty tomorrow."

Jace's bewilderment changed to sympathy. "I'm sorry. Is there anything I can do? Are you okay to drive?"

His concern only increased my desire to stay. "I'm fine. I just need to be there for the surgery." There were a million things I wanted to say, but I couldn't put any of them into words.

Jace seemed to be at a loss as well, as if he were also trying to decide what should happen next. What did we do now? Continue to share polite niceties? Say good-bye? Swap addresses? Exchange phone numbers? Make promises, or part ways, never to cross paths again?

The idea was starkly painful.

He looked down at the grass, his arms folded over his chest, his mouth a thin, determined line. "Be careful, all right?" he said softly. "I'm sorry you didn't find what you were looking for. Your birth family, I mean."

I did find something. Pressing a hand to my lips, I tried to form my thoughts into words. If I let this moment slip away, I would regret it forever. I felt something with him, a connection I couldn't explain and didn't want to lose. "Jace, I'll be back. I want . . ."

Lifting a hand, he silenced me, then just stood there, staring into the grass as the breeze teased dark strands of hair over his forehead. I wanted to reach up and gently sweep the hair back into place. "Don't come back, Dell."

I drew away, stung, wondering at his meaning.

He traced the outline of my chin with the backs of his fingers, and electricity raced through my body. "Come back to research your family if you want to, but don't come back for me."

All at once, I understood. He was cutting me loose. He wanted this to be good-bye, forever. "Jace, I feel . . ." Never in my life had I tried to explain such powerful emotions, such a deep longing. "There's something here . . . with you. I feel it. I know you feel it, too."

"You don't belong here, Dell." He swept a hand toward the capitol building, the festival, the mountains. "This place is a stop on the path for you, a scenic turnout on the road to finding yourself. Go home. Go to Juilliard. Travel the globe and fill it with music. Don't be in such a hurry to write all the answers in your book and settle down to a regular life. Once you do that, there's no going back." On the lawn, Willie squealed, and Jace glanced sideways, checking on the kids. "You should be out discovering the world, trying on different lives to see what fits." Willie squealed again, and Jace took a step away, squinting toward the obstacle course.

I caught his hand, pulling him back. "This fits. We fit."

He wouldn't look at me, but remained focused into the distance, his lips in a melancholy smile. I wanted to take that sadness from his mouth.

"*This fits,*" I said again.

"You only get one chance to be young." He shook his head at something happening on the lawn.

I was never young, I thought, following his line of sight to where Willie was standing atop the monkey bars with his hands in the air like the king of the world. By the bench, Autumn had one fist on her hip and was motioning for him to get down. I recognized myself in that stance. I was always the miniature grown-up, worried, afraid, my thoughts taken up with adult problems. I was never the king of the world, standing triumphant atop the monkey bars.

Jace turned to me, studying me so intensely that I felt it.

"I don't want Juilliard." Tears pressed into my eyes and I wiped them away impatiently. "Everyone wants it for me, but I don't want it. I love music. I love the way I feel when I play music—like I can forget everything, sail away from it and be someone new." *The way I feel when I'm with you.* "But I don't want a life of always having to perform. The symphony in Europe was exciting at first. It was fun being away from home, seeing something new each day, experiencing the world on my own, playing music. But after a while, it was so much traveling, so many people, so much noise, so many expectations. People were trying to make me into something I'm not. That was why I didn't come home and try for Juilliard last year. I don't want that life. I want . . . quiet. I want a normal life."

He sighed softly, and his tone was empathic when he spoke. "You don't know what you want, Dell. What you want is going to change so much over the next few years. I can tell you that because I've been where you are. We're at different points in life."

"I don't care about that." I felt the familiar sting of rejection, a fresh desperation in the part of me that had always believed no one would ever really want me.

"Dell," he said softly, his hand sliding into my hair and turning my face so that finally our eyes met. Leaning into his fingers, I felt the painful tug of hope, of need and desire. I wanted him to say, *Come back. Come back when you've taken care of things at home, and I'll be here.* "I'm sorry I started something with you. It was the wrong thing to do. You need to be out in the world discovering life and what you want from it. You don't need a man who's ten years older, tied to a small town in the middle of nowhere, with two kids to raise and no time for anything else." His thumb brushed away a tear, and he stood for a long moment looking into my face, as if, in spite of everything he'd said, he still felt the connection between us and was as confused by it as I was. "Two years ago you could have been one of my students."

My hopes crashed painfully, a small, tight ball bearing the razor-sharp edges of reality. "I'm *not* one of your students." I tried to pull away, but his fingers tightened slightly, forcing me to look at him.

"I know you're not." His eyes were dark, tormented mirrors of everything I felt. "I know you're not, but the facts still are what they are. Dell, you're incredible. You're beautiful, you're talented, you have an amazing way with people. When you look at someone, your heart's in your eyes." He smoothed a strand of hair from my cheek, tucked it behind my ear. In the distance, the drum had started, and I could feel us falling into the dance. "They're beautiful eyes," he whispered against my lips, then kissed me, and I felt it in every part of my body. My senses swirled as he pulled back, and I caught the tree behind me, waited a moment to look at him. "Good-bye, Dell. I wish things were different," he said, then turned and walked away, his shoulders stiff, as if he were willing himself not to look back.

Below on the lawn, Autumn watched as her dad approached the play area. When he stopped to talk to her, she swiveled toward me. I wondered what he was saying, if he was explaining things to her, and how he would. There was so much more than she could understand, more than I could understand, myself.

Her gaze remained fixed on me, as if she were willing me to come down the hill and step back into their incomplete picture.

I could love her, I thought. *I could love her the way I loved Angelo when he was a baby. I could be the one to comb her hair and listen to her secret thoughts. I could settle down, like Shasta, have the future planned out. No more uncertainty. No more questions, only the love of a family, my own family.*

The yearning was too painful to bear.

"Well, that was all very dramatic." Lana's voice sliced through the fog, and I turned to find her stepping out from behind the corner of the building. Crossing her arms under her breasts, she inclined her head to one side in a false show of sympathy. "You poor little thing. I tried to warn you."

"Leave me alone, Lana." The idea of her listening to my conversation with Jace was both humiliating and sickening.

Her lips curved downward in a pretend pout as she paused to adjust the strap on her halter top. "Now, don't take it personally, sweetie. I know your feelings must be hurt, but it's okay. You're not the first. All the girls get high school crushes on Mr. Reid. He's so good about setting you kids straight without breaking your little hearts. You know, young girls make the mistake of thinking a man's interested when really he's just trying to be helpful. Jace understands that y'all just don't know any better. It's okay, hon. Don't be embarrassed."

Anger flared inside me, hot and bitter, filling my mouth with venom. "You know what, Lana. I'm not embarrassed—why should I be? I'm not the one hiding around the corner eavesdropping on people. What's between Jace and me is just that—between Jace and me. What would really be embarrassing is if I were thirty-something and so desperate I couldn't tell when a man *wasn't* interested." Without waiting for an answer, I hurried into the building, pushed the door closed behind me, and stood with my back to the cool wood. The corridor was empty except for paintings and framed photographs waiting to be returned to their owners. Here and there, brightly colored award ribbons had been attached to various works.

Silent faces watched me from portraits of famous chiefs and nameless powwow dancers as I started down the hallway toward the back door, where I could exit without having to see Jace and Autumn again, without having to watch Lana gloat as I walked away. From the back of the building, I could walk up the road to the parking area, avoiding the crowds of happy tourists, the soulful flute music in the craft booths, the Reids' display, the memory of Jace and me laughing and joking about his CD, of Autumn asking me to comb her hair.

I could get in my car, and drive away, and pretend I'd never come.

But deep inside I knew there would always be questions left un-answered, desires unfulfilled. If life had taught me anything it was that unanswered questions, unsatisfied yearnings didn't wither away over time, dry up, turn to dust, and disappear like last year's leaves. Instead, they remained rooted like the trees themselves, growing each season until they cast a long shadow over everything.

For me, there would always be shadows here.

I glanced over my shoulder momentarily as the front door opened. For an instant, I imagined that the figure silhouetted against the bright sunlight was Jace coming back to say that good-bye wasn't good-bye after all. But the man in the doorway was only a mainte-nance worker with a pull cart. Parking it in the hall, he began care-fully loading paintings between sheets of cardboard.

I turned to go, but something stopped me. A flash of color. Blue eyes. A face. A smile. A small painting in a frame of rough-hewn lum-ber, resting on an easel between two larger works in intricate frames.

My heart stopped in my throat.

I knew that image from my memories, from the past, from my dreams. From a hundred feet away, amid a thousand other paintings, I would have recognized it.

CHAPTER 23

I stood mesmerized, staring into the eyes of my mother—paint on canvas, yet so real it seemed that any minute she would speak. She was sitting by a river, the water diamond-tipped and clear, the artist's brushstrokes so fluid I could hear the current moving. Her body was loosely wrapped in a Navajo blanket in shades of blue, her shoulders bare, knees curled against her chest. Long strands of auburn hair fell over her shoulders, catching the sunlight. She'd rested her head on her knees, glanced sideways at the painter. Wildflowers blanketed the ground around her, yet the first fall leaves were drifting by on the water. Her smile was wistful, as if she knew that summer was waning and winter pressing in.

"Mama." The word echoed into the silent hall, and maintenance man stopped to look at me.

"Ma'am?" After slipping a framed photo collage onto his cart, he took a few steps closer.

"This painting." I searched for a signature at the bottom near the frame, but there was none. "Who painted it? Where did it come from?" The artist must have known my mother long ago. In the image, she was young, just a teenager. Her skin was supple and smooth in the soft light, not dry and leathery, hanging over her bones the way I remembered. Her face was full and slightly blushed, rather than hollow and gaunt like the face of a refugee who'd seen too much and been hungry too long.

Compared to the girl in the picture, the Mama I knew was just a shadow. But still, this was her. I'd been haunted by her too long not to know.

The maintenance man crossed the hall, scooped up a blue ribbon that had fallen on the floor, and tucked it in the corner of the frame. "It's an award winner," he commented cheerfully, picking up the painting and reading something on the back. As the canvas moved, the water seemed to flow, as blue as Mama's eyes. "First place, portrait in traditional media. Entry form here calls it *Jesse in Blue.*"

"Jesse." My mother's name trembled upward from somewhere deep inside me. "Who . . . ?" Pressing my fingers to my lips, I tried to regain my senses. The building, the maintenance man, the other paintings, the rhythmic beating of the drum seemed far away. The moment felt dreamlike, airy and surreal, as if in an instant I would awaken and find myself back home in my room. "Who painted it? Who's the artist?"

The man squinted at the entry form. "T. Clay, booth 103, aisle D. It don't say if this one's for sale or—" He stopped in midsentence as I turned and ran for the door.

"Thank you!" I called back, then burst from the building and flew down the hill, my heart pounding. The park was nearly empty. Over the loud speaker, the master of ceremonies was announcing that a special presentation and Gourd Dance, honoring veterans, would begin in five minutes. Merchants were asked to close their booths during the ceremony out of respect. Dancers, veterans, active-duty soldiers, and spectators should proceed to the capitol lawn. In the vendor area, vendors were shutting down their booths as tourists made last-minute purchases and headed toward the dance circle. The woman weaving the bracelets had just finished taking money from a mother with twin toddlers in tow.

"The ceremony is about to start," she said as I slid to a stop, looking up and down the aisle. "It's that way."

"I know," I panted. "But I'm looking for booth 103, aisle D. Can you tell me where that is?"

"Well, let's see." She reached into a tote bag and pulled out a photocopied map of the grounds. Tracing a finger along the aisles, she muttered, "D . . . 103 D." The moment seemed to stretch on forever as vendors around us closed up and headed for the capitol lawn. What if the vendor at booth 103 D was closing up, too? How long would I have to wait for someone to return?

"That'd be all the way on the far side." The woman folded up her map and tucked it back into her tote bag, then pointed. "Right side of the building, about two-thirds of the way down. Look for the little metal plates on the posts." She pointed toward the doorway of her own booth. "Those tell the booth numbers."

"Thank you!" I spun around and hurried away.

"Good luck!" she called after me.

I waved over my shoulder, then rounded the corner, alternately running and threading my way through groups of spectators headed in the opposite direction.

By the time I'd reached the other end of the pavilion, the crowd had all but vanished, the booths were closed, and the last of the vendors were disappearing around the far corner. Skidding to a halt, I caught my breath. A silent plea repeated in my head over and over. *Please let this be the moment I finally find the truth. Please . . .*

My legs felt slow and sluggish as I started forward, reading the signs on the booths: 101, 102, 103. . . .

One step, two steps, three . . .

Around me, the world fell into an eerie hush, as if the breeze, the tablecloths, the heavy woven blankets on display, the rows of triangular flags overhead, even the powwow drum were breathless with anticipation.

Please . . . please . . .

My heart hammered against my chest, my hopes fluttering uncertainly, like a kite struggling to take flight in a fickle breeze.

Please . . .

There was a gate across booth 103 D. The plastic mesh had been stretched loosely and tied to the post with a single leather thong.

Moving closer, I saw paintings inside—images of warriors on horseback, powwow dancers, Native American women dipping water from a stream, a little boy investigating the wonders of a tiny blue jay feather, his chubby finger running gently along the edge, a hawk taking flight, Black Angus cattle grazing in a pasture. I recognized the houses in the background. That scene had greeted Jace and me as we'd driven through the entranceway at the Clay Ranch.

My pulse sped up again. Had the woman at the ranch been lying when she said Thomas Clay couldn't possibly be my father? Why would she invent something so terrible as a hunting accident if it wasn't true? *Tommy's little girl come by,* Audie Senior had said, as if it made perfect sense. If their Thomas was my father, why would that woman, his aunt, deny it and send us away?

Standing at the booth entrance, I stared at a painting of young powwow dancers preparing to perform as their mothers fussed over them, attaching headdresses, fastening necklaces, braiding hair, painting faces and putting on the finishing touches. The eyes drew me in. They were lifelike, shimmering with the light of individual souls, like my mother's eyes in *Jesse in Blue.*

Next to the painting of the powwow dancers, another small portrait hung unobtrusively. Nearly hidden among larger works of art, it pulled me in, and I stood once again captivated by the face of my mother. Her slim body was draped in a thin white sundress. Morning light shone through the fabric, outlining her breasts, her waist, her legs as she sat on the low-hanging branch of an oak tree, her back resting against the trunk, one leg propped up and the other dangling, her slim foot touching the grass. In her arms, she cradled a sleeping baby, just newborn, with dark, fuzzy hair and smooth skin the color of milky tea.

Her face was filled with love. In all my life, I couldn't remember my mother looking at me that way, with tender eyes, the way she gazed at my baby brother in the weeks after he was born, when she was trying to stay clean. Sometimes she sat with Angelo, her face filled with love and wonder, as if he were the most beautiful thing in the world. As much as I loved Angelo, I hated that look in her eyes because she never had that look for me. She never seemed to see me at all. But the baby in the portrait, the one she was watching with adoration and rapture, wasn't Angelo.

"That's me," I whispered.

"Pardon?" A voice from somewhere inside the booth startled me, and I jerked my hand away from the plastic mesh gate. Catching my breath, I slowly leaned inward to see around the front table, which was stacked with tall cardboard boxes holding prints for sale. A man sat perched on a stool in the corner, his back toward me, his attention fixed on a nearly blank canvas. He was roughing in the shape of a face in broad, sienna strokes. He was tall and thin, his hair jet-black with the faintest hints of gray, falling in waves around the collar of a button-up Hawaiian shirt that hung loose and wrinkled over faded jeans with holes in the knees.

"In the painting . . . that's me. That's my mama." A pulse pounded in my ears. I wanted to throw open the gate, run inside, grab him and make him look at me, shake him and say, *Are you my father? Did you know my mother?* If I confronted him, would he tell me the truth?

He nodded without turning around. "Some of the source photos came from last year's festival." His reply was pleasant but disinterested, as if chatting with customers wasn't his forte and he wished I would leave. "Booths are closed during the ceremony today, though. Sorry. New rule. They've always got some new rule around here." Sticking the paintbrush between his teeth, he grabbed a tube of white paint and squeezed some onto his palette, then picked up the brush again. "I'll be open the rest of the day. My partner handles sales. She'll be here after the ceremony." He went back to work, holding a photograph next to the canvas.

"Did you paint this?" I asked, and he glanced halfway over his shoulder.

"All of the paintings are my work. The weavings are my partner's." Something about him was familiar, but I couldn't place it. "Like I said, some of the source photos came from the festival last year, so if you see someone you know, that's probably why." His brush touched the canvas again, slid over the curved outline of a child's eye. When he was finished, those eyes would hold the soul of the child in the photo, a young Choctaw boy in a baseball uniform, his face still bearing the paint of a dancer.

Look at me, I thought. *Do you know me? Do you know who I am?* "Are you Thomas Clay?"

He lifted the brush from the canvas and set it in the tray without finishing the stroke. Laying his palette aside, he took a breath, and slowly turned around. I felt his eyes settle first on me, then follow my gaze to the painting of my mother. Neither of us moved.

"Are you Thomas Clay?" I asked again, but I couldn't look at him. I couldn't let him see that everything in me was hanging on this moment.

"I'm not," he said. "Tommy was my brother. He passed away."

The desperate, frightened girl inside me wanted to turn and run. *Maybe I shouldn't go any further. Maybe I should let the picture of Mama be enough—proof that, at one time, she wasn't too messed up to love me.*

Gathering my resolve, I faced him. I knew him even before his eyes, dark and deep like midnight, met mine. The passage of years had changed his face, his hair, even his voice, but his eyes were the same. He was the one who started coming around Granny's house when Angelo was a baby—the one who brought the stuff that messed Mama up and made Angelo's daddy break up with her. The one who took Mama away to Kansas City and never brought her back.

"Are you my father?" The question sounded surprisingly calm. Inside, I didn't know what to feel.

He shifted uncertainly, stood up, then sat on the corner of the stool again, wringing his hands in his lap. "Hello, Dell," he said finally, and my emotions, fully prepared for another crash, went limp. I stumbled back against the pole, and the thin leather thong snapped behind me, letting the gate fall open. Perversely, I reached out and caught it, not ready to surrender the safety of a barricade between us. Silence choked the air around me, and I clutched the plastic mesh, struggling to sort through the storm swell of questions.

"Let it go," he said softly, motioning to the gate. "It's all right."

I shook my head, not comprehending. "Why does my birth certificate say Thomas Clay if he's not my father?"

"It's a long story."

"I need to know," I whispered. Finally, after all these years, I'd found someone who could answer the questions that had burned so long inside me. "Please. I need to know." *Where was I born? Was I ever wanted? Why did Mama go away and leave me behind? Why did you? Didn't either of you love me at all?* "Nobody ever told me . . . anything. I need to know where I came from. I need to know about my mama." I had to learn the secrets of this man, who took my mama away, yet all these years later tried to capture her soul in paint on canvas.

Closing his eyes momentarily, he turned toward the image of her. "I did love your mother, Dell. I know it might not seem like it, but I did. The first time I saw Jesse, she was sitting on the curb in some hick town in Missouri. I was headed to Nashville to crash at a friend's place for a while. Jesse thumbed a ride, and I swear I'd never seen anything like her. She had a face like an angel, and my God, those eyes. Jesse's eyes were like a piece of morning sky. She didn't want to go home because she had trouble with her old man, and I didn't want to party alone."

Shaking his head, he laughed under his breath, smiling at her portrait, or the memory. "We took off together and partied all the way to Nashville. She talked about her old man, and I gave her some stuff to make her forget." His smile faded, and, combing a hand through his hair, he looked at the floor, like he couldn't face her picture anymore. "Sometimes I wonder how things would've been different if I'd left her on the curb that day. If I hadn't gotten her started on the stuff. If I hadn't been so fried myself. But that's the thing about hash and ice—you really don't care. You just want to party on. I played the clubs in Nashville, did some studio work, even sold a little art when I could keep it together long enough."

He took a rag off the table and wiped paint from his hands, then sat thinking, folding and unfolding the stained square of fabric. "After a while, it just got easier to deal than to work, so I started selling— hash, mostly. I could come home here, pick up a shipment, take it back to Nashville, and make some pretty good change. Weed's like penny candy in Nashville. Jesse didn't like it that I was dealing. She wanted me to keep on with the music. She'd sing in the clubs with me sometimes. That girl had a voice, but she'd never sing by herself, just harmony. She didn't like being up in front of people, having people look at her, but she was sure I could make it big with my songs. Jesse had a way of believing in you that could make you believe it your-self." Pausing, he took in the portrait of Mama and me, his attention still turned to the past. "She believed you'd be something special." He looked up and studied me for a long time. "Guess she was right. You look like her. You can drop the gate, Dell. It's all right."

I let the plastic mesh slip from my fingers, and it swished down-ward. He was wrong about me. I didn't take after her. I took after him—his dark eyes, his smile, his hair. He was a striking figure when my mother knew him—tall and wild with long hair and coal black, brooding eyes that scared me when he came around the house. Now he looked weary and worn, old in a way that had more to do with mileage than years. "Did she want me?" *Did anyone ever want me?*

Laughing softly, he turned back to her picture, as if there were a private joke between them. "When she found out she was pregnant, she asked me to stop dealing. I told her I'd think about it, just to get her off my back, but I wasn't going to change anything—just keep it a little quieter around her. Then we came home one day and the cops were at the house, with a couple of my buddies already in the car. Jesse and I didn't pull up to the curb—we just kept on driving. Ended up back here."

He gave the girl in the portrait a rueful look. "I always wondered if it was Jesse who called the cops in the first place. She wanted you to have a regular life, and she thought if we left Nashville, got away from all the hash and the ice, and the party crowd, we could do it. Trouble is, it's not the hash and the ice that's the problem. The problem is the thing inside you that makes you need the stuff in the first place. You can drive as far and as fast as you want, change houses, change scenery, but the thing inside is right there every time you stop. It eats you up until all you want to do is get high so you can't feel it. The stuff gets you numb. Jesse and I both needed it way too much. She stayed clean a while after we came back here, but like I said, Jesse needed the stuff way too much."

Squeezing his eyes shut in a grimace of pain, he unclasped and reclasped his hands, his fingers trembling. "The thing is, Dell, I loved Jesse. I loved you, but I wasn't any good for you or her. I was on a one-way path to hell, and I wasn't man enough to take that trip alone. I was twenty-one when I got six years in the federal pen for dealing. Jesse took you and went home to her mama's. She didn't have much choice. I hadn't seen my family in years. I never even told Jesse they lived right outside of Antlers. I should have told her that, but I didn't want them to know I was in the pen. When I took off after high school, my daddy said that was where I'd end up, and I didn't want to give him the satisfaction of knowing he was right."

You should have told them. You should have told them about me.

I tried to imagine how my life might have been different if he had, if Mama hadn't been forced to go back to Granny's, where she and Granny fought day and night, and Mama spent her time with any guy who could afford beer and meth.

"Why does my birth certificate have your brother's name on it?" I gripped the pole behind me, trying to keep my balance, to stay on a small raft of objectivity in an uncertain lake of emotions. I wanted the answers, all of them, no matter how painful.

He rested his elbows on his knees, then twisted his hands together, watching his fingers. "I just figured . . . I thought you deserved better than me. Tommy wasn't ever going to have kids, and it seemed like this was one thing I could do for him. I gave you Tommy Dell's middle name for your name, and when I was standing there with that nurse, filling out the papers for the birth certificate, I used Tommy's name. At the rate I was going, I didn't figure I'd live past twenty-five. I wanted you to have someone better than me. Tommy was a good boy—a clown, you know. Even when he was little, he'd hide in the feed bin and stuff like that so he could pop out and scare people."

"I went to the ranch," I said quietly. "I know about Tommy. I know about his accident."

His head sagged forward, his face a mask of pain. "Tommy didn't have an accident. I shot him. It was my bullet that put him in that wheelchair, that took away his mind." The muscles in his jaw tightened and he swallowed hard, shaking his head back and forth. "I didn't look close enough, and I shot my little brother while he was coming across the corn field to call me in for supper. People can say it was an accident, but it was my finger that pulled the trigger. My single, stupid, careless minute. I never could quite get hashed out enough to forget that. Even when I was so high I couldn't stand up, I could still see him fall down in the corn. I'd give anything to go back and change that one thing." He opened his eyes and pointed to a painting, a rider streaking across the prairie bareback on a white horse, arms outstretched, taking in the sky. "That's Tommy. He was a good kid. He was funny, you know. He liked to make people laugh. I couldn't stand to see him sitting there in that chair, drooling on himself."

I stared at the painting, tried to imagine that beautiful young man locked inside the prison of his own body. "Is that why you never went home?"

"There were a lot of reasons."

"Have you ever been back?" Looking around now, at his artwork, at the boxes of numbered prints on the table, at the collection of framed magazine and book covers hanging beneath a sign that read ART AND PHOTOGRAPHY BY TERENCE CLAY, it was hard to imagine that his family wouldn't welcome him home.

"Too much water under the bridge," he said. "The thing I learned in rehab, when I finally got so low there wasn't anyplace else to run, was that you can't change the past. I wish I would have done different things with my life. I wish I'd been a better man for your mama. I shouldn't have gone back for her after I got out of prison. If I'd left her alone, she might've married your little brother's daddy and lived a normal life. He seemed like a pretty decent guy. But, man, Jesse and I had a connection, and even though I wasn't good for her, I couldn't leave her be. I'm sorry, Dell."

Standing there watching him, I felt a change inside myself, a hard place beginning to soften. Since the day he took my mama away from me for good, I'd hated this man. In my mind, I could still see him laughing as he looped his arm around her neck and staggered out the yard gate with her for the last time. She'd packed her stuff and thrown it in the back of his truck. She wanted to take me along, but he said no. He said I'd be better off where I was. Now I knew why he hesitated at the gate that day, turned back and looked at me with some emotion I couldn't understand.

"You didn't kill Mama. She killed herself." I'd never admitted it, even in the privacy of my own soul. Mama left because she wanted to. She died because life was too hard for her and she was tired of hanging on. "Before she met Angelo's daddy, some guy dumped her, and she downed a bottle of Darvocet. When I found her, she just kept saying leave it be, leave her alone. She was mad when I called the ambulance." It was a memory I hadn't revisited in years. One I'd tried to lock away.

His head fell forward and he let out a long, slow breath. "Jesse had things inside her she couldn't fix."

"I know," I said softly.

He swiveled in his seat, then opened a small drawer under his paint tray and pulled out a flat cardboard box. The silver foil covering was dull with age, the printed candy canes having long since lost their color. "This was supposed to be for you." He held it out between us. "I'm sorry it took me so long to deliver it. Guess I couldn't let it go."

I stretched my hand out close to his and took the box. *For Dell,* it said on top, *From Mama.* A powerful wave of emotion knocked me back, and I sank against the table, the box shaking in my hands. All these years I'd wondered if my mother ever thought of me after she left for Kansas City. Now here was something concrete, something she'd left behind with my name on it. I opened the lid and tucked it under the box, then carefully touched the contents—a small gold ring I could remember her wearing, a silver heart on a leather thong, stiff with age, and beneath that a torn piece of an envelope with pictures tucked inside.

I pulled out the pictures, drank in an image of my mama holding me as a newborn, her cheek nuzzled against my head. Beneath it were three photos of her in the white sundress, cradling me in her arms, lifting me high into the air and smiling, watching me tenderly as she tickled the side of my face with a dandelion. The photos must have been taken the same day as the one used for the painting. The final image was a Polaroid of Angelo and me. He was just a baby and I was seven. Staring deep into the picture, I tried to guess how old he was, five months, maybe six. I couldn't remember the photo being taken. After Angelo left, the pictures of him disappeared and no one would say what had happened to them. When Mama died, the pictures of her were gone, too. Granny told me I wasn't to ask about it.

Now here they were, my mother and my baby brother, tiny images in my hands.

"Thank you." The words choked in my throat. There was no way to explain what the pictures meant. My mother kept them with her. Even as confused and desperate as she was, she took the time to leave them for me. Underneath the last picture was a yellowed slip of paper with Angelo's full name, his father's name, and the words *in Tulsa, Oklahoma, maybe.*

Tucking the mementos back in the envelope, I struggled to comprehend the fact that the contents of one small box could mean so much.

"You should have them all." My father held out another picture, one he'd taken from his wallet, the one he'd reproduced in the painting of Mama and me.

I touched it, then handed it back, trying to grasp the meaning of his having carried it with him for so long. "You keep it," I said. "The box is enough. It means . . . everything."

He tucked the picture back in his wallet, then crossed the booth quickly, and pulled the painting of Mama and me off the wall. "It's for you, if you'll take it. I wish . . ." The words were weary, uncertain, unfinished. His fingers gripped the sides of the frame, tightening, then loosening, then tightening again. He had the hands of a musician, my hands. His voice was raspy, like an old man's. It was hard to imagine that he'd ever been a singer. "I spent a lot of years hitting rock bottom and crawling my way back up. I never had anything to give you that was worth having. I wish I had more."

I wish I had more. Was he trying to tell me this was it? This painting, this box containing what remained of my mother was all he had to share?

Did I have a right to ask for more?

I closed the box, then took the painting, balanced it on my hip and held both things.

My father returned to his stool, and I stood uncertain, feeling the pressure of awkward silence between us. There seemed to be nothing left to say.

"Thank you." *Don't you want to know about me at all, even now?*

"I'm sorry it's not more."

Was that his way of saying good-bye forever?

I started toward the exit. He didn't stop me. In the distance, the drums had gone silent and the aisles were beginning to fill with vendors opening booths and tourists returning to their shopping. Soon we would be surrounded by all the familiar noise, pushed aside by it.

Stopping in the doorway, I was aware of the crowd slowly building, like a trickle of water predicting an oncoming flood. "I saw the painting of my mama in the art show at the capitol building." I hovered there, on the edge of the cement, ready to step off, but unwilling to.

"I dream about her sometimes," he said.

"Me, too." Over time the details of her face and voice had faded away. Until I saw the painting in the art show, she was an unclear memory, an out-of-focus photograph that hurt my eyes.

"She's always by the river, and she's smiling." His words held the faintest hint of joy. The first I'd heard in his voice. "I think she's in a better place."

I turned around, then rested my cheek against the cool metal pole, its rusty surface gritty against my skin. "I think she is, too." I smiled, and he smiled back. I'd wondered what it would be like to see him smile—not the haunted kind of smile from the past, but a real one. He had a nice face when he smiled.

The conversation ran out again. At the front table, a woman had stopped to leaf through the prints, and he glanced over the boxes at her.

"I guess I should go," I said, pushing off the pole and standing square on my feet again.

His gaze caught mine. For a long moment, he stared at me as if he were trying to look beyond, to capture my soul, my essence, the way he might in one of his paintings. "Are you all right? I mean, is everything good for you? Your life?"

Something inside me soared more than it should have at the simple inquiry. "Yeah, I am all right." For the first time in my life, I knew it was true. The part of me that had always been empty, that had always needed answers, was filled, not necessarily with joy, but with an understanding of where I'd come from, and that was enough.

"Good." He nodded slowly, a mist forming around the dark centers of his eyes. "I always wanted you to be all right."

"I play music," I offered, feeling a rush of empathy that was unexpected yet powerful. "I spent a year touring Europe with a youth symphony. I guess I got the music from you."

Throwing his head back, he laughed, smile lines fanning from the corners of his eyes. "I was never good enough to tour Europe. Best I ever did was write a few songs, pick a little on some studio tracks for Johnny Cash and Waylon Jennings."

"That's pretty cool." I wondered what he could have done if he hadn't spent his life weighed down with guilt and drugs. "I have an adopted family in Kansas—up around Kansas City."

"They're good to you?"

"Yeah, they are." Glancing down at the portrait of my mama, I wondered what Karen and James would think, what they would say if I told them I wanted to invite this stranger, my father, into our lives. "They want me to go to Juilliard, but we'll see."

He whistled a note of admiration, and I felt like I could float away on it. I'd always dreamed that my father, whoever he was, would be pleased with what I'd become. "Listen to your family, darlin'."

It seemed a strange comment, considering that he'd abandoned both the family he was born into and the one he'd created. I wasn't sure how to respond.

"Let me know how that turns out," he went on. "Juilliard, I mean." He reached across the table and grabbed a business card, then extended it between his fingers. "If you want to."

I could feel myself smiling, filled with an awesome joy that outshone whatever questions might arise in the future. I took the card and tucked it inside the box. "I will. Thanks."

At the front table, the shopper had selected two prints and a calendar of Native American artwork. She was growing impatient to pay for them. My father moved toward the cash box.

"Bye," I said. "Thanks for everything. Thanks for saving the pictures of Mama for me."

"You're welcome. Don't feel like you have to leave." He reached for a mailing tube, then turned to take the woman's prints from her.

"I need to. My dad's in the hospital." He frowned over his shoulder, and I added, "He's having an angioplasty in the morning. I need to be there."

He nodded absently while rolling the prints and carefully sliding them into the tube. "Family's important."

I stopped halfway out the door again. "Your grandfather sits in the yard and stares at the gate," I blurted. "It's just sand underneath his chair, like he's been looking for someone for a long time." I didn't wait for an answer, or stop to think about whether it was the right thing to say, or check his reaction. I stepped off the cement, and hurried away with a faith that the rest would work out.

Back in my car, I sat for a minute, catching my breath, gazing at the pictures of Mama holding me, our brief moment of joy frozen in time. I felt it settle all around me as I touched the silver heart and slid the ring onto my finger. It wasn't much to leave behind, not what a mother might dream of giving to her daughter, but it was what she had. Part of growing up is learning that people can't give what they don't have. The rest you have to find in yourself.

There was a newness in me as I started the car and flute music began to play on the stereo. Smiling, I switched into gear and headed home, leaving behind the capitol grounds, the artists, the dancers, and Jace, at least for the moment. The card with his phone number was on the seat with my mother's box and my father's phone number. There was so much left to discover here. The roots of my family tree were here. The branches stretched far and wide, as far back as the history of a people who walked a thousand miles in the winter cold with the bones and the soil sewn into their clothing, forward to my family in Kansas City, and beyond to places I couldn't see yet. The breeze whispered with voices I was just beginning to hear. The voices of a thousand leaves.

FALAMAT ISHLA CHI-KI, the exit sign said as I left, COME BACK AGAIN.

A
Thousand
Voices

Lisa Wingate

This Conversation Guide is intended to enrich the
individual reading experience, as well as encourage us
to explore these topics together—because books,
and life, are meant for sharing.

A CONVERSATION WITH LISA WINGATE

Q. Why did you choose to end the Tending Roses series with A Thousand Voices*?*

A. When I was writing *Tending Roses* six years ago, I never imagined the story as part of a series. After the book was finished, I found myself occasionally thinking about the characters and wondering how their lives might progress in the future. When the book was published, readers began sending letters, asking what happened to the characters after the story ended. Because I never know what will happen in a story until it's written, the only way to answer those questions was to write another novel. In the Tending Roses series, each story generated another story, resulting in *Good Hope Road, The Language of Sycamores,* and *Drenched in Light.* As the series progressed, Dell was slowly growing up, discovering the world outside her tiny house on Mulberry Creek, learning to leave behind the memories of her mother's drug addiction and neglect, and to accept the love of a new family. Dell was, in many ways, the catalyst for change in Grandma Rose's family, and in turn she was changed by Grandma Rose's family. It seemed only fitting that the series end when Dell had found her way to adulthood and become the woman Grandma Rose believed she could be.

Q. Even though they did not like one another initially, Grandma Rose and Dell share a deep spiritual connection that continues, even after Grandma Rose's death. Can you explain this connection?

A. Dell's childhood is a parallel to the childhood of my grandmother, whose stories inspired the creation of Grandma Rose in *Tending Roses*. Like many who survived the Depression, my grandmother didn't often talk about the difficulties she faced during childhood. She "married up," as folks used to call it, and felt she'd risen above a childhood stigmatized by poverty, alcoholism, and family mental illness. She was critical, as is Grandma Rose, of others who couldn't pull themselves up by their bootstraps and find success in life. During the opening chapters of *Tending Roses,* Grandma Rose is content to habitually bypass Dell and her family. As is often true in life, the things we are most critical of in other people are the things we like least about ourselves. As Grandma Rose becomes involved with Dell in *Tending Roses,* she is forced to confront her own past and is reminded of how it feels to be a child living in a hopeless situation. Like a growing number of children today, Dell is a victim of parental drug addiction and neglect. In opening herself to Dell, in becoming determined to change Dell's existence for the better, Grandma Rose finds a purpose for the last months of her life. In spending time with Grandma Rose, Dell finds security, acceptance, a kindred spirit, and the love she has always yearned for. After Grandma Rose's death, that special love becomes the gossamer bridge between earth and heaven. Love, not being a physical thing, is not bound by physical constraints, nor does it die when the body dies.

CONVERSATION GUIDE

Q. Your novels have frequently been chosen by book clubs and discussion groups. What do you think makes them so popular with groups of women who read together?

A. I can think of no greater gift to be shared among women who love and care for one another than the gift of story. As women, we often isolate ourselves in our problems, keeping concerns tucked down so as not to bother or embarrass anyone. It's easy to take in others' lives from the outside and become convinced that everyone else has things figured out, that others' lives are perfect, that we couldn't possibly reveal the imperfect parts of ourselves. In fiction, characters are free to be imperfect, to struggle, to fail and try again. In living through the characters' struggles, in discussing them among friends, we're free to also share parts of ourselves. My grandmother used to say that a burden shared is a burden halved.

Q. When you are speaking to audiences and communicating with readers and booksellers about your writing, what comments most deeply affect you?

A. All of them. I love hearing from readers who have enjoyed journeying through a story with me and found the books meaningful in their own lives. I hope others are inspired to share their own stories, both real and fictional, with friends, family, and the rest of the world. Each of us is a product of an individual set of experiences, a completely unique work of art. Only when we understand one another's stories can we really understand one another.

CONVERSATION GUIDE

Q. A Thousand Voices is your eighth published novel. What are you working on next?

A. A new novel, of course. When it's finished, I'll undoubtedly begin to wonder what the characters are doing with their lives now that the book is over, which will generate another story, and another, and another. Readers sometimes ask if I ever worry that I'll run out of ideas, but in truth, it's exactly the reverse—I worry that I'll never be able to write all of the stories I'd like to write. Everywhere I go, I find little slices of life, tiny windows into the hearts and lives of amazing, wonderful, interesting people. So often, those slices of life become the seeds of a story. The process of wondering what's behind the window, of attempting to mentally step into another person's shoes, is the soil that germinates the seed. Some seeds grow faster than others, but it's always fun to tend the garden and see what will develop.

Q. What is your ultimate dream, as a writer and as a person?

A. To make a difference to someone, somewhere, in any little way I can.

QUESTIONS
FOR DISCUSSION

1. Why, after years of living in a happy, supportive home, is Dell still haunted by her past? Why does she risk opening old wounds in order to search for the truth about her biological mother and father?

2. What do you think James and Karen would have said if Dell had, at the outset, been honest about her desire to find her biological family? Is it natural for adoptive parents to feel hurt or threatened by such desires?

3. As young adults, both Dell and Shasta have made choices in opposition to the desires of their parents. To what degree should parents, grandparents, or guardians attempt to control grown children? Should young adults be allowed to make mistakes and suffer the consequences? How have you dealt with this issue in your own family?

4. While in Tuskahoma, Dell experiences both rejection and acceptance due to her Choctaw heritage and physical appearance. Have you had similar experiences in your own life? Have you ever been accepted or rejected based on your appearance or your identification as part of a specific group? How did this make you feel?

5. In advising Jace about Autumn's grief, Dell says that, for years after Grandma Rose's death, she felt Grandma Rose nearby, protecting and guiding her. Is this imagination? Reality? Have you ever felt as if a lost loved one were helping or guiding you?

6. At twenty, Dell and Shasta have taken very different paths, yet the two young women look at each other's lives with longing. Can you identify with the longings Dell and Shasta experience? Have you had difficulty choosing among, or planning the timing of, education, career, and family in your own life?

7. Even before discovering connections to her own biological family, Dell begins to feel grounded in the roots of her Choctaw heritage. What elements of your own family history make you feel grounded?

8. Jace and Dell experience a strong connection and an undeniable attraction to each other, yet Jace chooses not to pursue the relationship due to their age difference. Is his choice the right one? Should age difference matter in relationships? Why or why not?

9. As Dell leaves the Choctaw council house grounds to return to Kansas City, the future seems to be opening before her, filled with new choices and possibilities. What do you think she will choose? What will she do next? Will she return to Tuskahoma or move on to Juilliard?